# OTHER BOOKS BY KATE L. MARY

**The Broken World Series:**
*Broken World*
*Shattered World*
*Mad World*
*Lost World*
*New World*
*Forgotten World*
*Silent World*
*Broken Stories*

**The Twisted Series:**
*Twisted World*
*Twisted Mind*
*Twisted Memori*

*The Blood Will L*

*Collision*

*When We Were Human*

*Alone: A Zombie Novel*

**The Moonchild Series:**
*Moonchild*
*Liberation*

**The College of Charleston Series:**
*The List*
*No Regrets*
*Moving On*
*Letting Go*

**Zombie Apocalypse Love Story Novellas:**
*More than Survival*
*Fighting to Forget*
*Playing the Odds*
*Key to Survival*

**Anthologies:**
*Prep For Doom*
*Gone with the Dead*

TWISTED Book Three

# TWISTED
# FATE

A Broken World Novel

# KATE L. MARY

# CHAPTER ONE
## Meg

The room was deathly still as my family stood in stunned silence, staring at Angus like he was an apparition. Standing in this long forgotten building, surrounded by dusty chairs and cobwebs, I found myself wondering if it could be true, because this most definitely didn't *feel* real. It couldn't be. Two decades had passed since Mom and Dad and everyone else had arrived in New Atlanta, and my uncle, Angus James, had been alive the entire time. He'd been a prisoner in the CDC, used like his life meant nothing, like he was nothing. I just couldn't believe it.

And now the same people who'd held him captive for all those years had my dad.

There was a part of me that wanted to cover my ears so I could protect myself from hearing everything Angus had been through. I knew my Dad was probably going through some of the same things at this very moment, and thinking about it hurt too much. But I also knew that I *had* to listen. We were on the run, had fled Jackson and his father through a secret tunnel in Dragon's Lair, and before we could do anything else, make any other plans or even think about trying to free my dad, we had to find out what we were up against. We needed to hear what was going on in the CDC for real. I wasn't dumb enough to think it was going to be easy to listen to, but it was necessary, and it would help us plan our next move.

Wherever we were, we were outside the city wall, and even though this place was attached to Dragon's Lair, it didn't look like it had been used in years. The windows had been boarded up, allowing only slivers of moonlight in through the cracks, and along one wall sat a cot similar to the ones that had been in the back room of the bar, as well as a table and a handful of rickety chairs. The few candles scattered around cast a soft glow across the dark room, highlighting the emotions flickering across the faces of my family. More chairs and tables that looked like they hadn't been used in decades were lined up along the wall, just waiting for us to claim them. My uncle Al stood closest, and when he grabbed a couple and moved them toward the table it seemed to snap the rest of us out of it. Slowly, as if waking up from a dream, everyone began to move.

Dragon and Helen stayed a good distance away as we settled into chairs, probably because they already knew what was going on—my Uncle Angus had been staying with them for a while it seemed—while the rest of us gathered around the dusty old table. Charlie took the chair her father had set down, and I slid into the one next to her while Al and Lila took places across from us. Parvarti sat just far enough away that she was on the outskirts of our little group. Her expression was calm, too calm considering what we were going through.

We hadn't really been there for her, I suddenly realized. Joshua had died, leaving Parv alone, and we hadn't been there to help her through it. I'd been too swept up in what was going on with Mom and Dad to really think about how much my aunt was hurting, leaving her to deal with it all on her own. Even though it wasn't my fault and my reasons for being distracted were glaringly legitimate, I couldn't help feeling bad. I needed to make it up to my aunt.

Mom slipped into the chair next to Angus, sitting so close that it looked like she was holding onto him for dear life. When he set his hand on the table, she reached out to take it. It seemed like she needed to hold onto him just so she could make sure he was real, and it made sense. I mean, after twenty years you kind of gave up hope of ever seeing somebody again, and having Angus sitting at the table right now had to feel like a dream.

The old chair wobbled under my weight and every breath I took in filled my lungs with dust, but the minor discomfort was overshadowed by the heaviness in my gut. I had so many questions about what was going on, but I didn't savor the thought of having them answered the way I should. Dad's life hung in the balance, and we'd already lost him once. Now, after finding out for sure that he was alive, I was terrified that something would go wrong and he'd slip away again.

Plus, I had someone else to worry about now. Donaghy. The CDC had him, had dragged him out of Dragon's Lair only a few hours ago. They could do whatever they wanted to him. Jackson could do *anything*, and his hatred for Donaghy went further and deeper than even I understood. I couldn't help feeling responsible for how things had turned out. My family had always hated Jackson, but I refused to listen to them. If I'd heeded their warnings, if I hadn't dragged Donaghy into this, things might have been different. If something happened to him now, it would be my fault.

How this man, a convict and a fighter, had come to mean so much to me in so little time didn't make sense. We'd only met a week ago, had barely gotten the chance to know each other, but I felt like I'd known him much longer, and the ache in my stomach told me that I cared about his safety almost as much as I cared about Dad's.

Silence covered the room and grew heavy, stretching out until I could barely stand it, but I couldn't bring myself to be the first one to talk. Angus's hand looked stiff under mom's, but I could detect a slight tremor in it too, and I could tell that he was having a difficult time working up to what he had to tell us. The memories of the last twenty years must have been awful for him to carry around.

"Have you been in the CDC this entire time?" Mom finally asked, watching him closely as if she was keeping an eye out for cracks. She kept her hand on his like she was hoping it would give him strength. Or maybe the other way around.

"Yeah." The word came out sounding like it hurt him, and when he winced it seemed to confirm that it did. "Sometimes, it feels like it all went by in the blink of an eye, but other times it feels like three lifetimes. Twenty years is a long time, and they weren't easy years. They was hard years. So hard that there was moments when I was pretty sure death woulda been better then livin' even one more day in there."

Glitter, the pink haired waitress that had only recently come into my life, was sitting on the other side of him, and she scooted her chair closer when his voice shook. He looked her way and his expression softened. He was the one who reached out and took her hand with his free one, but she seemed to welcome it. Almost as if she needed to make sure he was there just as much as he needed to be close to her.

Glitter was Angus's daughter. I still couldn't believe it. It made no sense. He'd been locked in the CDC for the last twenty years. How had this happened? I could only think of one way, but the idea was so sick it made me shudder. The scars that ran up the inside of her arms, the ones that I had attributed to drug use when we'd first met, seemed to confirm my suspicions, especially when Angus moved and I saw the same scars in the crooks of his arms. The two of them looked like walking pincushions, and I had a sick feeling that was exactly what they were. Exactly what my uncle had been for the past twenty years.

"What did they do to you?" Lila asked, drawing my attention away from the scars dotting my uncle's arms.

"Lots of things." He cleared his throat and glanced over his shoulder at Dragon and Helen. "You got a drink or a cigarette?" He shook his head and looked down, and when he spoke next it seemed like he was talking to himself. Like he hadn't yet gotten used to the fact that there were other people around to talk to. "Need somethin' else to focus on. Twenty years. That's a hell of a lot of memories."

"Angus," Mom said, squeezing his hand. "It's okay. We're with you now."

"Here." Helen held a cigarette out to him.

Angus returned Mom's gesture before pulling his hand out from under hers. When he took the cigarette from Helen, he was blinking, almost like he was fighting back tears. His hand shook as he slipped it between his lips, and he closed his eyes when Helen lit it, inhaling slowly as if he needed to focus on the act so he didn't lose his mind.

"It all hurts," he said, the smoke coming out with the words and his eyes still closed. "Every single memory."

When he opened his eyes, his gaze narrowed in on Mom's hand, still resting on the table. How must it look to him? Not the same as he remembered, that was for sure. At the moment her hand looked bony and frail, and the Vivian he'd known hadn't been a weak person. I'd heard the stories about how they'd come to be here, and I knew my mother had been strong once. She was the one who'd kept on going even after she should have given up. The one who had pushed everyone in those early days. That person had slipped away over the last three weeks though, ever since they took Dad, and it had seemed like that old Vivian was on the verge of disappearing altogether. It was the drugs they'd given her, logically I knew that, but even now that she was off them she didn't seem like her old self. It was like a part of her had gotten lost when Dad disappeared.

"Can you tell us what's going on in there?" Parvarti asked when the silence had once again stretched out for too long. "There are a lot of holes that need to be filled."

"I'm sure for you too," Mom said, reaching out to him but stopping with her hand halfway to his. "So much has happened."

"Yeah." Angus's hand shook again, and he clenched it into a fist like he didn't want us to see it. "The beginnin' is blurry, but I remember comin' through Atlanta and seein' the wall. Tryin' to get here. I remember bein' bit over and over, and pieces of them takin' us to the CDC. It was bright and there was people everywhere, but none of it's clear. There's a big hole after that."

"It's okay," Lila said, her voice soft and soothing in a way that reminded me of how she'd spoken to me when I was a small child. "Just take your time. Tell us what you can."

"I will." Angus stuck the cigarette between his lips and inhaled again, slowly this time, closing his eyes and savoring it.

I held my breath and waited, but before he could say a thing a bang echoed through the room. We all jumped, but Angus barely moved. When he opened his eyes though, his gaze went to the front door. At one time it had had a window in the center of it, but it had long ago been covered with a board that now seemed less

5

secure than it should be considering what lurked just on the other side. Around me, everyone reacted, whether it was pulling their guns like Al and Parv or getting to their feet like Mom. I stood too, my hand already moving to my bag where the gun I'd gotten on the black market was stuffed. I hadn't told anyone about it, although I wasn't sure why, and its existence suddenly made me feel more secure about my current situation.

"It's okay." Dragon's deep voice boomed through the room as he headed to the door.

I watched from where I was standing, not sure what was happening but certain that we could trust Dragon. He stopped in front of the door, which led to the outside, to the world beyond the wall that was infested with zombies and yet was — ironically — a lot safer than the one I'd grown up in. Still, I tensed when he pulled it open.

A gust of muggy air blew in, bringing with it two men. I recognized them right away. Al and Lila's son, Luke, and Jim, the man I'd met for the first time only a few days earlier in Dragon's bar. Back when I'd still thought my Uncle Angus had died twenty years ago and when I was certain my dad had joined him. Before I learned who Jackson really was and before I'd realized what Donaghy could mean to me. So much had changed since that day.

"Jim?" At my side, Mom's body relaxed when she realized that she recognized the man who'd just stepped into the room.

Less than a second later, Aunt Lila was on her feet and moving toward her son. "Luke!"

That was when everyone began talking at once. Luke's mom hugged him while his dad asked him questions, Mom talked to Jim, the dragon slayer I had just met but who she apparently had some sort of history with, Angus and Parv exchanged words that got lost in the chatter. The sounds bounced off the walls, mixing together until I couldn't make out even a single syllable. There was a frantic air to it all, but relief was mixed in as well. Relief that there seemed to be a plan, relief that some of the people we'd thought we'd lost weren't really gone at all, relief that we were outside the city walls. That at least some of us were safe.

After a couple minutes, Dragon lifted his hands and called out, "Let's calm down. We have some things that need to be done." Then he turned to face Jim. "Is everything ready?"

"Yeah," the man said, looking past Dragon to the door he and Luke had just come through. The one that led to the outside world. "The coast is clear and the city's pretty quiet. If we're going to head out, we should do it now."

"Where are we going?" Charlie asked.

She was staring at the door like the idea of going out into a zombie-infested city scared the shit out of her. I understood. I wasn't exactly thrilled by the idea of taking a second trip out there when my first one had been so dangerous, but I also knew we couldn't go back into New Atlanta. At least not right now. We weren't prepared. Al and Parv had guns since they were enforcers, as did Luke and Jim because they lived outside the walls, but other than those four, I was the only one armed with anything other than a knife. Regular citizens weren't permitted to carry guns inside the walls of New Atlanta, a law passed by Star years ago that now made perfect sense to me.

"There's an unsanctioned settlement not too far from here." Luke crossed the room and put his arm around his sister's shoulders as if he could see the fear in her eyes as plainly as I could. "It's going to be okay. We have a plan."

"You've known about this?" Al asked his son, his gaze going from Luke to Angus.

Luke nodded slowly. He gave Charlie's shoulder a squeeze before turning to face his dad. "Some of it, not all. I learned a lot more about what's been happening over the last week."

Mom turned to face Jim. She didn't say anything, but the silent questions in her eyes were blatant enough that she didn't have to. She was begging for answers. Begging to be let in on all the secrets that had been kept from her for all these years. At this point, she had no idea how many there were, but I had a feeling she'd learn it all soon enough.

"After I left the city, I started to learn more and more about what was going on," Jim said, his voice soothing, as if he was trying to warn her that the truth might sting. "There were things we couldn't talk about inside the walls. Things I couldn't tell anyone."

"Still can't." Dragon moved to the door, waving for everyone to follow him. "Not until you get further away from Star and the CDC. It's not going to take long for them to come looking for you.

When Jackson's men find Meg missing, they will no doubt come to the bar. We're on the outside right now and no one knows about the tunnel in the basement, but it would still be better if you weren't anywhere near the city when they show up."

"I'm not leaving." Mom didn't move from her spot. "Not when Axl is alive and trapped in the CDC. No."

"We have to." Luke abandoned his sister's side and crossed to my mom. "It's too dangerous. If Jackson gets his hands on you, it will be the end of everything."

"They ain't gonna kill Axl." Even though my uncle's words were meant to soothe, Mom still jerked away from him as if he'd slapped her. The next words came out softer, and laced with nostalgia and compassion. "Trust me, Blondie. You gotta trust me."

Mom swallowed as she slowly nodded, but I could tell it was hard for her. She and Dad had a love that had withstood death and grief and even the end of the world, and I couldn't imagine what it was doing to her to even think about walking away from him right now. It hurt me, so it had to be killing her.

The knowledge that Dad wasn't alone in there only added to my pain. Jackson had Donaghy, too. He wasn't immune the way my father was, so there was no guarantee that he would be safe for even one more hour, let alone the days it would take to plan a way to get him out.

Everyone started moving toward the door, Mom included, but I suddenly found that I was the one who couldn't make my legs work.

"What about Donaghy?" I whispered, afraid to voice my concerns when I wasn't sure if I wanted to know the answer. "What will they do to him?"

Helen and Angus exchanged a look I didn't like, and then the woman crossed the distance between us and took my hand.

"Honey," she said in a gravelly whisper. "He's going to be okay. We have a plan, and the sooner we get out of here, the sooner we can put it into motion. Every second counts right now. We can't hesitate."

I didn't believe her, but I nodded anyway because I knew there was nothing I could do on my own. My first instinct was to push Helen away and run back to the CDC, maybe even try to reason with Jackson. There was still a part of me that was clinging to the Jackson Star I'd thought I'd known for all these years, the one who was reasonable and caring. But the logical part of me knew that man didn't really exist. He had been all for show, a caricature of a person. The real Jackson wouldn't negotiate with me. The real Jackson wanted to trap and control me, to bend me to his will.

"Okay." I nodded twice, which was more for me than for Helen this time. I looked at the weathered woman in front of me and then at Dragon, and it suddenly occurred to me that they hadn't headed for the door. "What about you? Are you staying?"

"We have to keep up appearances," Dragon said.

Helen gave my hand a squeeze. "If I don't show up at work, Star will know I'm involved. As it is, I'll be questioned the second I set foot in the CDC."

"You'll be okay?" Fear gripped me at the idea of Helen getting taken by Star, but I was ashamed to admit even to myself that more of it had to do with the idea of losing our inside person than concern for her.

"There's nothing concrete to tie us to anything right now other than Helen's position at the CDC. She's been there a long time and has gained Star's trust, but if we leave now it will be a huge red flag," Dragon said. "And you need someone on the inside if our plan is going to work."

"We'll be okay," Helen assured me.

I turned to look at Glitter, who was currently clinging to her father. "What about Glitter?"

"I'm going," she said, holding onto my uncle tighter.

"We ain't gonna risk her gettin' sent back," Angus growled.

This time when the group headed for the door, both Mom and I moved. I gave my boss and Helen one last look before stepping forward so I was standing next to Mom. She slipped her hand into mine and gave it a squeeze, and I suddenly felt like the woman I'd grown up with was back. The woman who had survived an abusive childhood and the virus that had wiped out most of the population, who had weathered the early days of the apocalypse with a strength that had made her stand out. Vivian Thomas—Vivian James now—was back.

"I know I've missed a lot," she whispered to me, "and I don't know what's going on with you and this guy, but I'm here for you. I'll always be here for you."

I returned the gesture when she squeezed my hand again, hating how bony her fingers felt in my grip but loving the strength her support gave me.

Jim paused when we reached the door so he could glance back over his shoulder. The expression in his eyes as he looked everyone over seemed to shine in the shadows of the room. It was a mixture of anguish and pain; as if being with this group reminded him of something he'd lost. Under the lines from sun exposure and age, and the scars that seemed to tell a story of how wrong his life had gone, lingered the remnants of another man, and I couldn't help wondering who he'd once been and how he'd come to be this person, this zombie slayer who lived on the outskirts of civilization. Who was battered and scarred, yet carried so much pain right beneath the surface.

"Is everyone armed?" Jim asked.

Around me, heads bobbed and weapons were pulled from sheaths and hidden pockets. I pulled out my own knife, leaving my gun tucked safely in the bottom of my bag. It was a good thing to have, but it would have to be a serious situation for me to use it. Guns would only draw more zombies, and possibly give us away if someone was searching for us right now. Which I was certain they were.

Charlie alone was unarmed, and when Luke rolled his eyes and pulled a knife out for her, I found it difficult not to smile.

"You should know better," he said, holding the weapon out to his sister.

Charlie ripped it out of his hand and her face scrunched up so much that it reminded me of when we were kids, and I was suddenly certain that she was going to stick her tongue out at him. Instead, she looked away. The room was so dark that I couldn't be positive, but it looked like her cheeks were red.

"I didn't know what was happening when I was ripped out of my bed at the ass crack of dawn," she said, trying to cling to her sassy attitude but failing miserably when her voice shook. "The last thing I ever thought I'd be doing is going outside the wall."

"In the apocalypse, you always have to assume you're going outside the wall," Luke replied, which only made his sister swallow.

Lila put her hand on her daughter's arm and whispered something while Luke turned back to face Jim. The older man's hand was resting on the doorknob. Luke nodded and Jim turned the knob, and then the door was pulled open and we followed the two zombie slayers into the outside world.

The city was black and felt as endless as a nightmare you couldn't escape, while the silence surrounding us seemed to defy reason. The trees that had long ago taken over the city swayed noiselessly above our heads, as if they didn't dare make a sound, and our footsteps were just as defiant to the laws of nature. There was no crunch of gravel when I took a step, no shuffling of feet from the people surrounding me. No creak or thump or thud. There was nothing but noiseless progress as we moved away from the building we'd just left, packed together in a tight clump of bodies.

The humidity in the air was less responsible for gluing my shirt to my back than the close proximity of my friends and family was. I found myself somewhere in the middle of the group, making the moist Georgia air feel even more oppressive than usual. Glitter walked on one side of me and Charlie was pressed up against the other while the people in our group who had more experience with the dead surrounded us like a protective cocoon. Mom, Angus, Parv, Al, and Lila had all traveled the country together during the early days of the outbreak. They'd struggled and fought and made their way here to safety—or at least that's what they'd thought. Jim and Luke were zombie slayers, so they were prepared. The most I'd done was go to the shooting range with Mom and Dad so I could learn to fire a gun, which now felt horribly insignificant. That was how I felt too, insignificant and useless. Why wasn't I more prepared for the world I'd grown up in? Why had my life up until the last few weeks been so cushy and sheltered?

The darkness made it nearly impossible to read the expressions of those around me, but I could tell by the stiff movements of my family and friends that they were on edge. Just as Jim had promised though, the city was clear. The road in front

11

of us, while littered with debris and overrun with weeds and plants that had sprung up during the years of neglect, was empty. I inhaled slowly, pulling as much of the muggy Georgia air into my lungs as I could, but it was clear and fresh. Wherever the zombies that ruled this city took cover at night, it wasn't anywhere close to where we found ourselves now.

"How far?" I heard Mom whisper.

She glanced back and the dim light from the moon made her eyes shine in the darkness. I knew the tremor in her voice had nothing to do with her own safety. No, her thoughts were of me. She'd lost two daughters already, one way back at the beginning of the apocalypse, and another not that long ago. Right now I was in danger. Out in the open in a city that was crawling with the dead, unable to defend myself the way I should have been. I had no doubt that my mom was cursing herself for how she'd failed me. She and Dad had embraced the idea that I would never have to face something like this, that the wall surrounding our city would be enough to keep me from experiencing the horrors they had once gone through.

"Our rendezvous point is two streets over," Jim replied.

"Exactly who are we meeting?" Parv asked with a slight edge in her voice.

It couldn't have been suspicion. No, she knew Jim. It had to be something else. Nerves, dread, or maybe even a tinge of hopelessness seeping through.

"We—" A moan echoed through the air, cutting Jim off.

Mom's steps faltered and I found myself slamming into her back, while to her right Al walked faster. All around me the others did the same, some people slowing down while others seemed to be grabbing for the person next to them as they moved faster. The tight clump we'd been traveling in broke up, creating craters between us that felt insurmountable when yet another moan cut through the air. Charlie whimpered and grabbed for my arm. I let her hold it even though her nails felt like they were cutting into me. I slipped my other hand into my bag and fingered the gun hidden there. My gaze was on Jim though, waiting for his cue. He was the zombie slayer. He knew what he was doing.

"Everyone just needs to stay calm," he said.

He reached behind him and pulled a shotgun off his back even though he already had an eight-inch knife out and ready. Luke didn't pull his own gun, but he looked as ready to pounce as Jim did.

A third moan rang out and Jim turned to the left. It was hard to see anything in the thick darkness that surrounded us, but he acted like he knew where the sound was coming from.

"Let's move," he said, his voice a low hiss. "Before they find us."

This time when we started walking, our footsteps seemed louder than a crack of thunder. Every step felt like it was pounding through the city, echoing off the buildings and calling out to every zombie within a mile. There were nearly a dozen of us, and the pounding of our feet against the street was deafening in the silence of the city.

Our pace was brisk, not quite a run but faster than a walk. We slowed when we reached the end of the street, but only long enough for Jim to look around the corner. The coast was clear though, and then he was moving again and we were following, sticking so close to one another that it felt like we were a single person. Down the dark street, then cutting through an alley before emerging on yet another desolate stretch of old Atlanta roadway. This time we were met by the low rumble of an engine, and the sound of it in the midst of the starkly silent city was enough to make my heart beat harder. I could just make out the silhouette of a large truck in the darkness, and Jim was already heading that way when its headlights flashed once.

When we got closer, the driver's side door was shoved open and someone jumped out. "You're late," a husky yet feminine voice growled.

"I'm right on time," Jim replied with no malice in his voice.

The woman snorted but didn't contradict him. "We have to go."

Luke's voice broke through the darkness. "Everyone get in the back."

There was no argument from us. The moans of the dead had increased, and even though none of them sounded particularly close, I wasn't willing to wait around and find out how long it would take them to locate us. Especially with the hum of the truck's engine calling out like a Siren's song.

I tried to get a good look at the driver when I passed her, but all I could make out was a surprisingly small shape that was nearly swallowed up by the black night. Luke followed the rest of us to the back of the truck while Jim stopped next to the driver. They spoke in low words that I couldn't make out, but the throaty tone of her voice seemed to defy her desire to whisper.

The truck was an old military vehicle that had benches lining each side in the back and a canvas cover — now patched and ripped and filled with holes. I climbed in behind Charlie, who clung to me when we took a seat. Mom was on my other side, but beyond that I couldn't tell who was who. It took less than a minute for all of us to climb aboard and take our seats, and what seemed like only a second later the truck lurched forward.

The drive was bumpy, the vehicle moving much faster than it should have considering the damaged streets in front of us. We bounced on our benches when the tires rolled over obstacles in the road, and Charlie's hand tightened on mine, but no one spoke. Partly because it was too loud in the back of the truck to even attempt a conversation, but also because none of us knew what to say at this point. We only had a vague idea of what was going on, and speculating not only felt pointless, but terrifying as well. Every time I allowed my mind to wander to Jackson and the CDC, I imagined the horrors that could be happening right now. The experiments being performed on Dad — who I now knew was immune — the virus they could be injecting Donaghy with, turning him into the same kind of creature they'd transformed my Uncle Joshua into. It made me sick, so it was better not to think about it right now. Better to instead focus on the people around me who were safe, and the knowledge that we had people with us who were informed and prepared. Who had a plan. That's what I told myself at least.

# CHAPTER TWO

## Donaghy

H ow many hours had gone by since Jackson and those asshole guards of his dragged me out of Dragon's Lair? A few hours at the most, although it felt like longer. Still, I'd been in this damn cell long enough to know that morning was right around the corner, and when Jackson showed up outside my cell it seemed to confirm my suspicion. The little shit stopped in the hallway right outside my room. He barely glanced my way, but he looked over long enough to give me a great view of the smug expression on his face. The sight of it made me clench my hands into fists and jump to my feet. Even after my short time in New Atlanta, I'd been around him long enough to know what that look meant. He had a bomb to drop. One I wasn't going to like.

In the cell across from me, Axl didn't move. But he did stare at Jackson like he was imagining what the asshole would look like with his stomach slashed open and his guts pouring out onto the floor. I had to admit, the image gave me a warm fuzzy feeling, but at this point I knew I would never have the chance to make it happen. Being stuck in a cell in the CDC put me at a pretty big disadvantage.

Jackson stood in front of Axl's cell and stared at the older man through the glass, and the smile on his face made him look even more sick and twisted than he ever had before. A shiver ran down my spine, repeating itself when Jackson stepped forward and pushed the button on the wall outside Axl's cell. My own intercom was off and the prick's back was to me, making it impossible to tell if he was talking, but somehow I knew he hadn't uttered a word. He was staring at Meg's dad the way a cat stares at a mouse, cool and calculating and eager to pounce.

It took less than a minute for Axl's mouth to move and I was able to read his lips just well enough to know that he was asking about his family. About Meg and her mom, Axl's wife, probably everyone else he loved too. Jackson turned his face just enough that it was partly visible when his smile stretched wider. He said something I couldn't make out, but then paused and turned to face me. His smile as he crossed the hall was the coldest thing I'd ever seen, and then he pushed a button and the intercom crackled to life.

"As I was saying—" Jackson's voice filled my room. "—Meg and the rest of your family are on the way."

I growled and Axl's gaze snapped to me. There were dozens of questions swimming in his gray eyes as he looked me over, but he didn't say anything. Didn't ask who I was or why this news seemed to hurt me, which it did. It made me feel like a knife had been plunged into my heart.

Instead, Axl turned his gaze back on Jackson and said, "Don't hurt her." His words had no hope.

"There's no reason for you to be concerned," Jackson sneered. "I don't intend to keep you in suspense. You'll be able to witness the entire thing. Right here." He stepped closer to Axl while shooting me a look, like he wanted to make sure he had my undivided attention. "You'll be able to watch as I take her. I'll let you hear her cries. Your family, her mother, will all be right there—" He motioned to the hall behind him. "—watching. I know how close your family is, and I wouldn't want any of you to miss the show."

I clenched my hands tighter, wishing I had the strength to punch a hole in the window in front of me. Wanting to shatter it and jump through so I could wrap my hands around Jackson's throat and squeeze the life out of him.

Across from me, Axl's Adam's apple bobbed, but he wasn't the one who yelled. It was me. Curses ripped their way out of me as I slammed my fists against the glass, a useless action that I knew would only wear me out, but one that I couldn't control.

"You son of a bitch!" I growled, my voice coming out sounding feral and crazy. "Don't you touch her! I will rip you to pieces!"

Jackson only grinned. "You aren't exactly in the position to make threats."

I continued to bang my fists against the glass, but in the cell across from me, Axl looked broken. He was still solid and broad despite his age, but right now his body was slumped, making him look suddenly old. The lines on his face deepened as if to illustrate the stress and violence and hard times he'd witnessed during his forty plus years on this Earth. There were dark circles under his eyes, and the lights above him emphasized the gray hairs dotting his head. He looked like he was on the verge of withering away, and I had a strange sense that if he had to witness the things Jackson was describing, he just might.

Before the little prick could say another word, the door behind him opened. I pushed myself closer to the glass, holding my breath, but the guards that stepped through were alone. There were no crying prisoners, no frightened and tear-filled eyes. Nothing but a group of guards who couldn't even meet Jackson Star's gaze.

"Where is she?" he growled, stopping the men in their tracks.

"The family was gone," the man at the front of the pack said. He glanced up as if wanting to verify that Jackson wasn't charging him before once again focusing on the floor. "We checked with the surveillance team. They left in the middle of the night, but there's no mention of where they went and we haven't been able to locate them anywhere."

Jackson, who was usually controlled to the point where he seemed almost mechanical, shook with fury. He looked on the verge of exploding, and he seemed to lose himself to the rage. He had always been a creepy guy, but the transformation he went through was something I'd never seen before. It was like a wild beast was breaking out of him and taking over, changing him into a creature even more terrifying than the zombies, more evil than the devil himself.

He had the door to Axl's cell open before I could even register what was happening, and then he was inside. I pressed my hands flat against the window in front of me, watching in horror and feeling utterly helpless as Jackson's fist slammed into the other man's face. Blood sprayed from Axl's nose, painting the white room in dots of red. The enraged man struck again and this time Meg's father fought back, getting in a few good punches, but Jackson didn't seem to feel a thing. It was like he wasn't in his body, like Axl's knuckles hadn't made contact with his eye. He didn't stumble back, didn't blink, didn't even grimace.

Before long, Axl was unable to fight back. The older man was on the floor before the guards were able to react, and even I found that it took too long for me to muster up the shouts that had been trying to force their way out of me. I slammed my hands against the glass and yelled for the guards to do something even as they rushed to Axl's aid. They were shouting too, a few of them running to drag Jackson off the prisoner while two others fled the hall, probably for help. Everyone was yelling. Me, the guards, Jackson, who sounded more animal than man. Everyone except Axl.

Eventually, they managed to drag Jackson from the cell, but not before he got in a couple good shots with the guards. He thrashed and fought so hard that despite his height disadvantage, it took several men to subdue him. They had him face down in the hall outside my cell, but I was too focused on trying to get a look at Axl to pay attention to the furious man in front of me.

People poured into the hall. Doctors and nurses who rushed to Axl's aid, Jackson's father, who looked only slightly less furious than his son. They shouted questions and yelled orders, and the atmosphere was so chaotic that I found it impossible to grasp even a single thing that was happening. I just knew that someone needed to help Axl. Someone had to save him before he died, because Meg had lost enough.

Jackson was covered in blood. So much that it left streaks behind on the white floor. His knuckles were cut and bruised, but it was the splatters of red on his face and neck that had my attention. It wasn't his blood and there was so much of it. Too much.

One of the doctors produced a syringe and something was injected into Jackson's neck, making his entire body jerk. His struggles had lessened already, and after the injection, his body began to relax even more. He blinked and his eyes seemed to grow heavy, and then, finally, his body went slack.

That was about the same time that someone yelled, "We're losing him!"

My attention was pulled to the other cell. The doctors were working furiously to repair the damage Jackson had inflicted on Axl. A gurney was brought in and his body was loaded onto it, giving me my first really good look at Meg's dad as they rushed by. His arm flopped over the edge as the doctors pushed the gurney down the hall, and his face was a swollen and bloody mess. A head injury was likely with as much damage as there was, and I found myself saying a prayer that he'd pull through. It couldn't end like this.

It wasn't until he'd disappeared out the door that another thought occurred to me. Maybe we'd all be better off if he died.

I hated to even think it, but it was something I had to consider. Axl had definitely been brought here because he was immune to the original virus, and whatever the CDC was doing couldn't be good. I'd met Star and I knew he was slimier than a slug, but Jackson was even worse. Whatever was going on here, it wouldn't turn out well for humanity, and for some reason they needed Axl James to achieve it. Maybe everyone in New Atlanta, maybe even this whole damned world, would be better off if Axl died today and the Stars were never able to achieve their goal. It would no doubt be the end for me if Axl did die today, but I couldn't help thinking that if it saved the world from whatever Star had up his sleeve, it might be worth it.

Two guards dragged Jackson out only a few minutes after Axl, and then I was left alone, staring at the blood streaked across the floor. Unsure of what I wanted to happen. Unsure of what my future held.

Hours passed with me pacing the room before I finally gave into my exhaustion and plopped down on the bed. I'd been waiting, hoping to get some news about Axl, but I knew that was idiotic. Not only was no one thinking about coming back to tell me how Meg's father was doing, but if he was as injured as he looked, he wouldn't be coming back this way any time soon.

# CHAPTER THREE
## Meg

The drive seemed to take forever even though Jim said the unsanctioned settlement wasn't far. It was impossible to tell how long we drove, though. More than thirty minutes but less than an hour after climbing into the back of the truck, we finally slowed. I leaned forward so I could look out the back, but the landscape was impossible to identify with the darkness surrounding us and how overgrown everything was. It all looked the same. Trees on top of trees on top of trees, with an occasional rundown building peeking through the foliage, the civilization that had once existed here had been swallowed up, and it now seemed like that whole world had been nothing but a fairy tale.

We all lurched toward the front when the truck came to a stop. Voices managed to make their way to us, and Charlie's hand was still gripping my arm, my skin now sweaty under her grasp, but I barely noticed it because I was straining to hear what was being said. It was impossible, though. Between the distance, the canvas that separated us from whoever was talking, and the hum of the engine, I couldn't make out a single word.

"Where are we?" I asked, searching the darkness for Luke.

I couldn't make out his face, but I knew it was him when he leaned forward. With his thick clothes—which he wore despite the heat so he could protect himself from the claws and jaws of the dead—and the bundle of weapons strapped to him, he seemed larger than the rest of us.

"An unsanctioned town," was his only response.

"You already told us that," Parv piped in before I could. "Where?"

"A place that existed before the virus. It's been expanded since then, but it's secure."

"A town?" Mom asked.

"Yeah. Something like that."

No one spoke, as if we were all trying to figure out what that meant, and then it was too late because the truck had started moving again, tossing us around. The sound of the engine and the crunch of the tires made it impossible to ask the questions we were all most certainly entertaining, let alone have a conversation.

I stared out the back and gradually the darkness gave way to the soft glow of what could only be firelight. It flickered and bounced off the gate that shut behind us, highlighting the people guarding the wall and illuminating more of the world as we continued driving. The street was lined with buildings that had probably once been stores or restaurants, and the wall we'd just passed through cut across the road, blocking it so no one could get in or out without being seen, while the buildings formed the rest of the barrier.

"Wait." My uncle Al got to his feet but stayed low. He made his way to the back of the truck, shaking his head, and stared out at the street as we drove slowly through town. "I recognize this place."

"How?" Lila asked. "You never came to Georgia before the virus and we've been in New Atlanta since we got here. How could you recognize this?"

Al turned to face his wife. "Because this is Woodbury." No one said a word, so he shook his head again. "From *The Walking Dead*."

I had no clue what he was talking about, but everyone who had been alive before the virus reacted in different ways. Mom and Angus turned to look out the back and Parv shook her head.

My aunt Lila snorted. "Twenty years and you still haven't let that show go."

"Maybe I would have if it didn't feel like I'd been sucked into it," Al responded.

"What are you talking about?" Charlie asked.

"It was a television show." Al turned his back on the street just as the truck rolled to a stop. "About zombies. This was a town in one of the seasons." He turned to look at his son. "Right?"

"That's what I heard." Luke nodded and got to his feet. "It's also why people took refuge here when the zombies first popped up. Because there was already a walled community. Come on, I'll show you."

He climbed out of the back and the rest of us followed. I was fourth, right behind Mom, and when I made it out I turned my back to the gate we'd just come through so I could get a look at what Luke was talking about. That's when I saw it, the wall in front of us. Steel and reinforced with beams, it surrounded a pretty good size group of houses. You could tell which part of the wall was original and where it had been expanded to include more of the town, and from the looks of it, the little community that had been built for a television show had come in very handy when zombies suddenly became reality and not just fiction.

"I can't believe it," Al said from behind me.

"So this is where they filmed the show?" Charlie asked.

Luke nodded as he passed us, heading to the front of the truck where Jim stood with the woman who had picked us up. "It is."

I followed, as did the rest of our group, and for the first time I was able to get a good look at her. Her husky voice had made her sound like someone much more mature, but in the light of the fire I discovered that she wasn't much older than me. Twenty-five, maybe a year or two older, but not much. She was small, fit but thin, maybe only five inches over five feet, and strikingly pretty. Even without a stitch of makeup her porcelain skin was flawless. Her long, blonde hair was twisted into dreads and pulled back into a ponytail, and she wore army green cargo pants that had seen better days—hell, better years was more like it—and a threadbare black tank top that clung to her curvy frame. Her arms were covered in tattoos, flowers and animals entwined by vines that snaked up and curled around her neck and chest. The ink was dark against her flesh, but hidden between the lines were scars that told stories about the hardships she'd endured living in this unsanctioned town in the midst of a zombie apocalypse.

She and Jim stood close to one another in a way that indicated they shared some kind of intimacy, but at the same time he held himself slightly back. Like there was a barrier between them that he couldn't quite get over. They both turned when we stopped in front of them, but for a moment nothing was said. I had a million questions, a million thoughts and ideas and concerns, but I held back because I knew all of it would be answered in time.

"Welcome to Senoia," the woman said after a moment of silence. "I'm Jada. I know who most of you are just from hearing about you." Her gaze moved across us, stopping longer on Angus than anyone, before saying, "I'm sure you have a lot of questions, and we'll get to all of them, but first I'd like for you to follow me."

We did as we were told, maintaining our silence as we followed the small woman down the street toward the steel wall that used to serve as the set for a television show. I didn't have much more than a minor understanding of all that—mostly gleaned from my research about my biological mother, Hadley Lucas—and seeing how elaborate the set had been made it even more confusing. I'd watched movies with Jackson, seen how the world used to go to great lengths to create realities very different from the one they existed in, but seeing it in person, being able to reach out and touch the now rusted steel walls and support posts, was a totally different sensation. These things were real. They had built a fake walled city out of real materials, around real houses to combat an apocalypse that had been fiction at the time. How few worries that old world must have had.

We followed Jim and Jada through the town, but it took until we were a good distance from the fire to realize that the sky was gradually growing lighter. The tops of trees, as well as the wall that kept the dead out, blocked the horizon from view, but if I looked hard enough I could discern a faint glow in the distance that told me a new day was on its way.

Jada led us to a house that had probably been beautiful when it was new, but now reminded me of an old man who had lived on the edge of shantytown for as long I could remember. Gnarled from age just like he was, the porch was slightly crooked and the siding, which had once been white, was now only a little lighter than the old man's weathered skin. The house wasn't alone in its age or disrepair since all the homes we'd passed on our way through the town had been in the same state, but there was something about this house in particular, which was larger than the others on the street and I imagined had once been more grand, that stood out.

The porch protested when we piled onto it, as did the hinges when Jada pulled the door open without knocking. Inside, the house was well kept and clean, but lacked the care that I imagined the people who'd built it would have shown. There was no clutter, but a layer of dust covered everything and one of the rooms we passed on our way in was stuffed full of boxes. They were piled on top of one another, nearly reaching the ceiling and filling most of the space, leaving only narrow walkways that ran through them, as if they were islands separated by rivers of flowing water.

No one spoke as we followed Jada and Jim, but I wasn't sure what our silence was a result of. The long night in which none of us had gotten any rest, the shock of finding out that Angus was alive and that Dad was being kept in the CDC, or the uncertainty of what was to come. For me it was a combination of all those things, as well as the sinking feeling in my gut that told me we weren't done being surprised by what was happening in New Atlanta.

The scent of cooking meat hung heavy in the air. As we progressed further into the depths of the house, the smell was joined by the sizzling sound of something being fried. My stomach rumbled, reminding me that I hadn't eaten in a while, but I wasn't sure if I would be able to choke anything down even if it was offered to me.

"Jada?" a female voice called.

"We're here," she responded.

She looked back over her shoulder at us, her expression filled with uncertainty. It was as if she saw us as soft, which I guess we were compared to her and the other people in this town, and she wasn't quite sure what we could bring to this mission. If, in fact, this was a mission, which I still wasn't sure of. She shook her head before turning away, and seconds later we were crossing the threshold of the kitchen.

The sizzling grew louder, and I was now able to see a short, plump woman standing in front of a gas cooktop where several cast iron skillets had been set up. In them bacon sizzled, and next to it a plate was already piled high with the salty meat. My stomach growled again, but my eyes were already moving around the room, studying my surroundings so I could take in everything as fast as possible like I suspected this was a trap.

It could have been. Not set up by Jackson, but by these people who had plans to use Angus for their own agenda. After what we'd just learned about the CDC, I wasn't in a very trusting mood, and I was suddenly grateful that I had a gun buried deep inside my bag. I slipped my hand in and the feel of the cold steel against my skin was comforting, especially when a man stepped out of the doorway to my left and I was overcome by the sudden feeling of being surrounded.

"You're back," the man said.

His footsteps thundered through the room in a way that I hadn't expected, and based on the reactions of those around me, neither had anyone else. Jim was in my way, blocking my view of the man, but when I stepped a little to the right I was able to see that both of his legs were prosthetics from what appeared to be the thigh down.

"Afghanistan," the man said as if answering the silent questions each of us were entertaining. "Lost 'em when I was twenty, so I barely notice it anymore. Or at least I wouldn't if the gears didn't get so banged up."

"Sit down," Jada snapped, but the words were laced with affection.

The man, who was probably in his late fifties, took a seat at the table in the center of the room, making a face that was more annoyance than pain while Jada grabbed a can off a shelf. She knelt in front of him and applied some kind of oil to a couple gears at the ankles and knees of each prosthetic, nodding when they rotated without squeaking.

"Thank you, love," the man said, and Jada smiled.

I watched them, trying to get a sense of who they were to each other. They looked nothing alike because the man was clearly at least part Hispanic and Jada's hair was white blonde, too light to have any of the same blood running through her veins as this man.

Earlier I'd gotten the sense that she was with Jim, but even that didn't seem to fit in my head because he had to be at least twenty years older than she was.

I was still in the middle of trying to figure the puzzle out when the woman at the stove turned to face us and smiled, showing off gaping holes where her teeth used to be and a face that was covered in scars. The right side wasn't bad, the marred skin had healed and left only a handful of deep lines in her cheek, and everything was where it was supposed to be, but the left side of her face wasn't even recognizable as human. Her eye was gone, scarred over by deep lines and so sunken that it was clear the eye was no longer in its socket, and her ear was missing completely. The worst part though, was the gaping hole next to her mouth that gave us a perfect view of her teeth and gums.

Her good eye sparkled, the blue of her iris standing out against the pink skin of her face, and her expression was nothing but welcoming when she looked us over. When she turned to look at the man, it was clear that they were in fact a couple.

Jada turned to face us after she'd set the can of oil back on the shelf. "This is Bonnie and Max."

The two nodded and I waited for Jada to introduce us, but she didn't.

"Help me," Bonnie said, motioning to the counter.

Jada did as requested; carrying the plate of bacon to the table while Bonnie went back to cooking. The sizzling seemed loud compared to the silence of those gathered here. There were more than a dozen people crowded into the room and yet not one of us said a word. Jim leaned against the wall with his arms crossed, staring at the back of Jada's head while at the table Max seemed to be adjusting one of his legs. Glitter was leaning on her father like they had spent their entire lives together as the rest of us shuffled around, waiting for something, anything, to happen, and Jada brought plate after plate to the table. Not only was there bacon, but there were scrambled eggs as well, fluffy and yellow and piled high on a platter. Two stacks of toast sat next to that, and at its side was a plate of butter, a luxury I'd rarely had in my life and one that made my mouth water and my stomach growl even louder than ever.

It wasn't until Jada had brought the last plate of food over that she turned to face us. "We'll talk while we eat."

"Or perhaps after," Bonnie said. She stood behind Jada, wiping her hands on her shirt and shaking her head, and once again I felt as if I was about to receive bad news.

Clearly I wasn't alone in that thought, because no one moved. Jada frowned, but before she could say anything Mom stepped forward.

"We appreciate the food, but I think we'd all like to know what's going on. You can start with who you are and why we're here."

Max sighed and waved to the table. "Let's sit down, then."

We did, moving into the kitchen where extra chairs had been squeezed around the table. There weren't enough for all of us, but Jim, Jada, and Bonnie all stayed standing. Luke, too, didn't sit, but he also didn't keep his distance. As if he found himself trapped between the two groups and unsure of where exactly he belonged anymore. I couldn't say that I didn't agree with the feeling. He and I had been close growing up, spending most of our free time together as children, but things had changed over the last few years as I'd found him missing from my life more and more. Charlie and I had grown closer, which I never would have thought possible considering what a pain in the ass she'd been when we were little. I'd thought Luke had a girlfriend or something, but now that I saw him, looking like a zombie slayer instead of an apartment kid in New Atlanta, I had to wonder if there wasn't more to it. Clearly he knew things about the city that we didn't, but I wasn't sure how.

"You're here for safekeeping," Max began once we'd all settled in. "That's the best way I can put it."

His gaze was pulled from Mom's when Jim cleared his throat, and everyone turned his way. He was frowning and Jada was looking up at him, nodding. There was an expression on her face that made my gut clench and I found myself reaching for Mom without thinking. She startled when I closed my hand over hers, but didn't look away from Jim, and I knew that she could feel it too. This was it. This was the moment I'd been dreading.

"We didn't want to tell you this until after you were out of the city safely. This is going to be a shock. I'm sorry." Jim looked down for a second, swallowing like he couldn't get the words out, and then dragged his gaze away from the floor until he was looking Mom in the eye. "It's Margot."

Mom's fingers dug into mine, and her back stiffened. "Margot?" she whispered.

Jim didn't blink before saying, "She's alive. In the CDC."

The words had no meaning because all I could picture was my little sister's smiling face as the memory of her laugh filled my head, making it impossible to focus on anything else. Not even when Mom's hand went slack in mine and her body dropped to the floor. The room swirled around me as everyone moved at once. Words and cries were thrown around and I blinked, but I couldn't comprehend what was happening.

Margot wasn't alive. She couldn't be.

But Jim had said she was, and he seemed to know a lot more about what was going on than we did.

She was in the CDC.

But why? Margot wasn't immune. She couldn't have been.

Only, I knew she could. Angus was, and so was Dad, so it made sense that Margot could have inherited whatever it was in their blood that protected them from the zombie virus. The CDC would have known it too. It would have been easy for them to get a blood sample when Margot was born, and they had already proven that they wouldn't tell us. But how had they gotten her? How had they saved her that day the zombies flooded the city? Had they staged the breach just so they could steal my little sister, who had only been nine years old at the time, and lock her away in the CDC just like they had with Angus? No. That was crazy. That was impossible.

Only it wasn't and I knew it.

# CHAPTER FOUR
## Meg

Luke knelt in front of me. "Meg."

"Did you know?" I whispered, thinking about the way he'd acted that night I saw him at the bar, as if he knew all the dark secrets the CDC was hiding from us. "Did you know about my dad? About Margot?"

He looked away. "I found out a few weeks ago."

I sucked in a deep breath, holding the air in my lungs until I felt like they would burst. When I let it out, I found myself lashing out at Luke, my hand flying through the air and making contact with his cheek. The slap of flesh against flesh cut through the chatter in the room and everyone froze. All eyes were on me, my half-conscious mom forgotten as everyone in the room focused on the red handprint that had sprung up on my cousin's cheek.

My face grew hot, not from embarrassment but from anger, and I was suddenly afraid that I would lash out at Luke again or at someone else even. At Jim, who had clearly known all along that my dad was alive, at Glitter who was in on this too. At Angus who had saved me more than once but had also kept secrets from me. At Al and Parv who'd known for years that Dad was immune.

I needed air.

I pushed away from the table and stood, leaving everyone behind. The rooms I'd passed through only a few minutes earlier flew by in a blur. When I pushed the front door open and burst outside, I was met with early morning light that nearly blinded me. I sucked in a deep breath, but the air was thick with humidity and muggy and not the least bit refreshing. If anything, it made my insides tighter. Made it harder to breathe. I leaned against the porch rail and took slow breaths in through my mouth, blowing them out through my nose, but I couldn't calm down.

Margot was alive. I knew it had to be true, but accepting it was a different story altogether. I had been there, I'd witnessed what had happened that day and I could remember it all with perfect clarity. Now though, facing this truth and knowing what I did about Jackson and his father, I couldn't help feeling like the vivid memories from that day were nothing but a lie that had been carefully planned out and spoon fed to me by someone who knew I'd swallow them without a second thought.

The last day I saw Margot had been the first day of my friendship with Jackson. I'd always known who he was of course, because not only was he the son of the Regulator of New Atlanta, but he was also charismatic. Even at the age of eleven I hadn't been able to ignore the magnetic pull he'd had on me. We'd never spoken, but I remembered how he'd smiled at me that day as I stood outside the school. How it had made me feel hopeful and excited and had filled me with a buzz that seemed to energize my body.

How much time had passed before all of that changed? Ten minutes at the most, probably less. One second I'd been sharing a look with a boy and the next I'd been running with my mom and sister, fleeing the dead that had somehow managed to penetrate the safety of our walls. Mom had disappeared, and then Margot, and I had been left alone. People had run by, too panicked and worried about their own asses to even notice me.

Jackson had popped up out of nowhere and saved me. He'd comforted me, stayed with me, helped me when it was all over, and I had trusted him. To me it had seemed like he'd been sent from God, like his sole purpose had been to save me, and that feeling had stayed with me for years. More than that, it had grown stronger until I had been certain that Jackson Star was the only person I could depend on.

But it had all been a hoax. Margot wasn't dead, and it made the whole thing twice as devastating. After she'd disappeared, I'd given up while my parents had clung to hope. I'd been so certain that they were fools, but I had been the fool. I'd let Jackson trick me and manipulate me, had let the fact that he'd listened to me cry trick me into thinking he was something he wasn't.

I shouldn't have given up. I should have held onto Margot harder. Should never have let her go.

The door behind me opened and I stiffened. "What?" I snapped without turning to look at the person who had come out.

"You sure do remind me of your mama," Angus said.

I turned to face my uncle. His gray eyes took me in, and they were so similar to my dad's that I found myself wondering how I had never noticed it before. When he'd first approached me in the street and given me a note, at the bar when I'd been shocked by the appearance of Joshua's zombie corpse in the ring, in the street when my uncle had saved me from being attacked. All those moments and I'd somehow missed the obvious similarity he and my dad shared. Of course it made sense, because I hadn't been expecting that my supposedly long-dead uncle could ever pop up, but it probably wasn't really an excuse. Not when I had known something strange was going on.

"I hope that's a compliment," I said, because I had no idea how else to respond.

He stared past me, out over the town that was just now waking up for the day. "It is. I didn't like much of this world before all this went down, but after, when we was tryin' to learn how to live, I found that I appreciated a hell of a lot more than I had before. She was one of them things I woulda liked either way, though. Hollywood was a tough little thing from day one. Probably why she was able to survive what happened in Vegas."

"What happened in Vegas?" I asked, and then immediately found myself wondering if I really wanted to know. Right now, I wasn't sure I could take in anything new.

Angus lifted his eyebrows. "Guess your folks never told you 'bout all that."

"Do I want to hear this?"

"There probably ain't much 'bout that time that anybody would wanna hear, but I'll tell you if that's what you need."

"Why?" I asked.

"'Cause I know that right now you're feelin' like you been left in the dark a little too much, and you need to know it ain't 'cause we didn't think you couldn't handle it. It was to keep you safe. You and your mama and everybody else in there. Them people in the CDC would slit your throat to keep you quiet. That's who they are, and we didn't want nobody else to die."

"I guess that makes sense." The words should have come out grudgingly, but the truth was, it did make sense and I knew it. That didn't mean it didn't sting to learn so many horrible things at once.

"Is my sister okay?"

"I ain't seen her." Angus frowned and it seemed to darken his irises until they looked like clouds just before a storm set in. "She's immune though, so they ain't tryin' to kill her."

"But she could die?"

He pulled his gaze from the houses at my back and focused on me. "They all did. All of 'em but me."

I closed my eyes and let out a deep breath. I'd wanted the truth, but it hurt like a bitch. Dad, Margot, and Donaghy, all three of them were now in Jackson's clutches and I wasn't sure how we were going to get them back.

I opened my eyes and focused on my uncle. "Do you have a plan?"

"We do," he said, but he didn't sound thrilled about it.

Of course, at that moment I wasn't sure if I wanted to know why he rolled his eyes the way he did or what the tight-lipped expression he wore meant. I honestly didn't want to know anything else. Not what Angus had been through over the last twenty years, not what Donaghy or Margot or Dad were going through right now, and not what Jackson had in store for us. I just wanted to take some time, even if it was only an hour, to absorb the information I'd gotten before shoving anything new into my brain.

"I should check on Mom," I said, turning toward the house.

My uncle followed me back inside without a word, almost like he knew I couldn't handle any more information right now.

Mom was resting on the couch in the living room, her eyes closed and a cold compress on her head. I paused in the doorway and Angus stopped at my side, and together we stared at my mother in silence. She was still trembling and her face was pale, and even though I knew the shock of finding out her daughter was still alive and being held in the CDC had to be overwhelming, I couldn't help being disappointed. This wasn't who I wanted her to be. I wanted the mother who'd raised me back. I wanted her to pull herself together and get up, to show the fire and determination I knew she had inside her.

Her eyes opened and she gave me a weak, sad smile. "Come here," she said, holding her hand out.

I did, crossing the room while Angus stayed where he was. I sat down next to her, positioning myself on the edge of the couch. Her hand grasped mine and she squeezed, and something flickered in her brown eyes that gave me hope.

"We're going to get them back."

"How?" I found that I was the one teetering on the edge of losing hope, and I suddenly understood that the emotions swirling through my mother didn't make her weak. They made her human.

Her hand tightened on mine. "I don't know yet, but I do know that I won't rest until we've done it. Even more, I want to see Star pay for what he's done to our family." Her gaze moved past me, back to where Angus stood. "To all of us."

I swallowed when a lump of tears tried to force their way up my throat, but I found words impossible, so instead I just clung to my mom's hand and held her gaze, letting the fire and strength swimming in her eyes sink into me.

"Get some food," she said, loosening her grasp on my hand. "We need to stay strong."

Most of my family was still in the kitchen, Luke included. I ignored him and instead focused on the plate of food that was waiting for me. It was cold, but my stomach was begging to be filled and I found that I couldn't really taste anything anyway. I chewed the eggs, now rubbery from sitting on the counter, ignoring my cousin who was imploring me with his eyes to forgive him. Deep down I knew he wasn't the one to blame here. It was Jackson's father and whoever else was in the CDC doing his bidding, not Luke. Not Jim. Not any of my family members who had kept secrets from me.

Around the table my family did the same, their movements as they ate almost robotic. The silence was heavier than it had ever been before, worse than after Dad had disappeared, thicker than when Joshua died. This silence was weighed down not just with pain, but with questions and uncertainty.

Jada stood on the other side of the room, leaning against the wall with her arms crossed. She stared at me like she was trying to figure something out, and the look was just hostile enough to have the hair on the back of my neck standing on end.

"Can I do something for you?" I finally snapped.

When she shook her head, her blonde dreads swished across her shoulders. "No."

But she didn't stop staring at me, her blue eyes locked on mine like she was caught in a trance. This girl, whoever she was, was impossibly beautiful, but something about her was also threatening. The way she carried herself, the way she barely blinked, the intelligent expression in her eyes.

She didn't look away until Jim came into kitchen, and when she turned her gaze on him, everything about her softened.

"You ready?" she asked.

Jim nodded, barely looking at her. "Yeah."

If his indifference hurt her, Jada didn't show it. She pushed herself off the counter, the same air of self-confidence radiating off her that had before he'd come into the room, and headed to the front of the house. Luke followed, not looking my way.

Jim cleared his throat. "We have some things to discuss."

"No shit," Al muttered.

Jim headed after Jada and Luke, his only response being, "Follow me."

We did, mainly because no one knew what to say. We followed them out of the house and down the street, through the walled city and past old houses. The sun was up now, as were the people, and they turned to watch us as we passed. We stood out because most of the people here looked like Jada, covered in tattoos and piercings, hair cut short or twisted into dreads so it was easier to maintain. My own dark hair was loose and hung down my back, occasionally getting caught on the wind and whipping across my face. I felt unexpectedly plain in the midst of these people who had turned their bodies into works of art, who had missing arms and eyes and legs, who limped or sported scars that were highlighted by lines of tattoos rather than hidden away.

These people were survivors, and in comparison I felt like a silly child who'd lived her life sheltered from reality. No wonder Jada stared at me the way she did.

We reached a house at the end of the street and were led inside to discover that it had never been completed. Some of the drywall had been put up, but in other places the beams and electrical work were totally exposed. The floor was nothing more than planks of wood and there were no cabinets in the kitchen, although the plumbing told us where the sink was supposed to be.

From there, Jim led us to a closed door, and when it was opened a set of stairs that descended into darkness were revealed. We followed him down in a tight line, but the sharp scent of death hung so heavy in the suffocating space that I had to cover my nose before I'd made to the halfway point. The basement came into view, revealing prison cells lined up along both sides, each of them containing a zombie. There was an underlying smell of disinfectant, bleach and even vinegar, and I could tell they'd done their best to keep the space clean, but with these creatures locked in such close quarters and slowly decaying, it would be impossible to ever clean the space up completely.

The sight of us sent the dead into a frenzy, filling the room with a mixture of moans and growls and snarls. Most reached through the bars as if trying to get us, but a few only watched. The calculating expression in their eyes was one most of my family had probably never seen before, but I had. I saw a zombie just like this only a few nights earlier when Jackson sent a zombie to Dragon's Lair for Donaghy to fight.

It was the first time we'd ever seen a hybrid, and remembering it sent a shiver down my spine. That zombie had been so different from anything we'd ever experienced before, and Donaghy had struggled to win the fight. The creature's hairless skin had almost been translucent under the fluorescent lights of the bar, his gaze cold and calculating and his movements quick like lightning. The moment when Donaghy realized the creature wasn't quite dead, but that his heart was still beating away in his chest, was tattooed on my mind.

I was right behind Mom when she skittered to a halt. "Why?"

She was blocking the way for anyone else to come down, but I doubted anyone was going to complain. Everyone looked as disgusted as she did at the scene in front of us, as disgusted as I felt. It made me think of my uncle Joshua and how he'd popped up in Dragon's after being gone for weeks, how he had probably been locked up just like these creatures were. They were a threat, they would rip us to shreds if we let them, but they had still once been people and I felt like they deserved more respect than this.

Jada and Jim, who had led the way down, turned to face us. They didn't seem the least bit fazed by the close proximity of the zombies.

"These are the different strains," Jada said simply. "Each of these zombies represents what we thought was a different mutation of the virus, but what we now know was just a manipulation by the CDC."

I found myself moving at her words, pushing gently past Mom so I could travel deeper into the basement. The creatures closest to me were old, decayed so much that bone could be seen beneath rotten skin. They reeked of death and a few even had maggots crawling through their putrefying flesh. Beyond that though, there were different ones. Zombies who were faster, who snapped at me through the bars, and then the ones who looked like they were studying me, searching for a weakness, and then finally, in the last cell, a hairless creature.

"How did you get them?" I asked, turning to face Jada.

"Jim." She nodded to the zombie slayer at her side. "All except the last one, that is."

Jada crossed the room so she was at my side, but she wasn't alone. Most of the group had now moved deeper into the basement so they could get a look at this thing, this hybrid zombie that was caught somewhere between man and monster.

"This one we created on our own." When I spun to face her, she lifted her hands. "I know, it's sick, but we had to know what we were dealing with. Helen got us the virus and we used it on a criminal. A rapist."

Jada held my gaze as if waiting to defend her actions a second time, and all I could think about was that night on the street when I was attacked after leaving the bar. How if Angus hadn't shown up I would have been in trouble.

"Okay," I said, because it was.

"What have you learned about it?" Parv asked.

She was standing dangerously close to the bars with her hand on her knife, and I couldn't help thinking that she was teasing the thing, testing him to see what he would do if he thought he could get her. His eyes, milky but alert at the same time, moved to the weapon on her hip and he tilted his head. He didn't move. It was as if he knew what she was doing too.

"Technically he's alive, because his heart is still beating," Jada said. "But he isn't susceptible to everything that humans are. He doesn't sleep; he doesn't need to eat. He will stand still for hours on end, but strike faster than anything I've ever seen if given a chance." She looked around as if to make sure we were all listening. "We've sent rodents into the cell to see what he does."

"He's the ultimate killing machine," Jim said, his voice sounding loud in the confines of the basement. The expression on her face was somber. "That's what Star is doing. He's trying to create an army of dead. Not like the zombies that are out there right now and not like this one, he can still be killed the same way a human can, but something in between. Something that is dead, that can't be destroyed without taking out the brain, but who will follow orders unquestioningly. He wants an army of followers who will help him control the world for the rest of his life."

"He can't do that," Lila said. "Can he?"

My aunt looked around, her eyes wide and a terror in them I'd never seen before. I understood. Star's current level of control was scary enough, but the idea of him having an army at his disposal, of knowing how dark and twisted Jackson's mind was and how he would one day take his father's place, was a horror I never could have imagined.

"He's very close," Jada responded.

The group fell silent, but it was broken when Angus swore and turned away. He stalked up the stairs and Glitter was right behind him, hurrying to comfort her father. I wasn't sure what was bugging him though, the idea of the army of the dead, the memories of what he'd gone through for the sake of creating that army, or the idea that his brother was now going through the same thing. There were too many options to choose from.

"Let's get out of here," Charlie muttered, following the others.

They filed up the stairs, but I stayed where I was, staring at the creature. He was thin, not the type of person Star would have chosen to infect with the virus, but I doubted that made the creature in front of me any less lethal. I thought of the hybrid zombie that had been sent to Dragon's Lair, the muscles the creature had had, indicating he had been a fit man in life. Was this what the future had in store for Donaghy? Was this what Jackson had planned?

The basement emptied out until it was just Jada, Jim, and me. I turned to face the others, stepping further from the cell now that my back was to this calculating creature.

"Tell me you have a plan and that we'll be able to get everyone out of the CDC soon."

"Everything takes time," Jim said.

I turned my gaze on Jada, who seemed to know so much for someone who had never lived in New Atlanta. "Is this what will happen to Donaghy?"

She nodded, but shook her head a second later. "Yes, but probably not yet. This strain isn't what they want, so I don't think they'll inject him until they've altered it. They'll want to test a new strain on him."

I blew out a deep breath. "How long will that take?"

"It's impossible to say. It could take days, or maybe even weeks."

"Or less," I muttered.

"Or less," Jada agreed.

# CHAPTER FIVE
## Meg

We went upstairs to join the others and found them gathered in the backyard, practically circled around Angus. He'd been locked away for the past twenty years but he'd also been in the CDC, and for the first time it occurred to me that he might know something that would help us get Dad out.

The adults were gathered closely around him while Charlie and Luke hung back a little. I wanted to know what was going on, but like my cousins I felt like I should keep my distance. Right now the conversation probably had a lot more to do with filling in the gaps of the last twenty years than with our present worries, although those were at the forefront of everyone's minds as well. Only Glitter dared get close to the adults, but mostly so she could be by her father.

It was odd, still thinking of them as the adults when I knew I was an adult now myself, but that was what they were. My mom, as well as my aunts Parv and Lila, and my two uncles, Al and Angus. They had been the adults in my life for as long as I could remember, even Angus who hadn't been physically present.

These people, my aunts and uncles and mom, were gathered under a large live oak tree, the shade of the branches blocking out the hot Georgia sun but doing nothing to keep the humidity at bay. Parv and Angus smoked, sitting next to each other in a comfortable way that made it seem as if twenty years hadn't been lost. Across from them sat Mom, Al, and Lila. They looked up when Jim came over to join them and Mom patted him on the leg. The gesture was so familiar that it sent a shock through me, and I had to remind myself that they had a history I couldn't possibly understand. They'd been out there on the road, fighting to survive. Whatever had happened to drive Jim outside the walls of the city, it didn't change what they'd been through. Nothing ever would.

I didn't know if I'd want to hear everything they had to say, but I couldn't make myself turn and go back into the house. Instead, I took a place next to Charlie, who barely glanced my way. She was too intent on listening, seemingly holding her breath as she waited for the truth to spill out of my uncle.

Once Angus started talking it seemed to go on forever. He told stories about living inside the CDC, about the tests they'd performed on him and the viruses he'd been injected with. I listened as Angus told my family about the original strain and how it had been released by Star; how he and his team had been behind every single mutation the virus had gone through. He talked about the other immune people who'd been brought in, each of them put through the same torturous treatment he'd endured over the last twenty years, but how none of them had survived it. His voice nearly broke when he talked about watching the progression of victims being brought in alive and fighting, and then wheeled out days or weeks or months later in body bags.

No one interrupted him, but it wasn't long before I noticed a change in Parvarti. I could see the stiffening of her shoulders and how she shifted her body away from Angus as he talked about Glitter's mother, a woman named Jane who he spoke about with a mixture of sadness and bitterness that made no sense to me. His voice was pained and angry when he told everyone about having a daughter he knew about but could do nothing to save. He talked about hating the girl's mother, the doctor who had at one time been Star's most trusted scientist, but how he had longed for her at the same time. Not just for the human contact, but for her. He'd fallen in love with her, the woman who had helped torture him and Glitter, who had done unspeakable things not just to us, but to the entire human race.

It wasn't until he'd finished speaking that Parv broke the silence that had settled over everyone. "You can't be serious about loving that woman."

Angus nodded, but the way his shoulders slumped said that admitting it didn't bring him any joy. "She was evil. I know what she did and I felt the pain of it more than anybody else, but she did right in the end. Jane saved Glitter, and she saved me even though she was long gone. I suspect she's in hell, and she probably deserves it, but I still love her." He shook his head. "For better or worse and all that bullshit."

Parv's deep intake of breath following his statement was so loud it felt like a crack of thunder. "She destroyed me."

I leaned forward at the same time that my uncle did.

"How's that?" he asked.

"Joshua was her apprentice and he trusted her. He believed her when she told him there was a new vaccine. Something they were giving pregnant woman so babies would stop dying after birth." Parv's voice was so strained that it didn't sound a thing like her. She turned her gaze on Angus and stared at him, and the rays of sunshine that broke through the trees reflected off the tears shimmering in her eyes. "We trusted her and it almost killed me. It did kill our baby."

Baby. I remembered the conversation I'd had with Parvarti only a few days ago, after Joshua's zombie had been brought into Dragon's Lair. I'd retrieved his wedding ring and taken it to my aunt while she was working the wall, knowing she would want it back and that she needed to know the truth of what had happened to her husband. She'd told me about how they'd fallen in love, slowly and with so much hesitation that it had taken two years for them to admit it to one another. She'd mentioned wanting to have a family, but she'd said it had never happened for her. Now I was about to find out why.

"What'd she do?" Angus asked, his voice as strained as Parv's was.

Silence followed, and after a few moments it was Mom who spoke up. "The baby tried to rip it's way out of her. It was—" Her voice broke and she had to pause so she could swallow. "It had turned in the womb. There was so much damage that Parv almost bled to death. They had to do a hysterectomy to save her."

43

"That woman stole our family from us." Parv's voice was low and fierce.

Angus's shoulders slumped. He looked resigned and maybe a little tortured when he said, "She's in hell."

"I hope she suffered when she died," Parv spit at him.

He nodded slowly as he took a long pull on his cigarette, the end of it flaring bright and red as if imitating the fiery pits of hell. When he blew the smoke out he said, "She did, and so did I. So did all of us."

# CHAPTER SIX
## Donaghy

Axl wasn't brought back to his cell the next day, but Jackson didn't come back either. Part of me thought that was a good thing, but another part knew it would only be matter of time. He'd lost his shit, but Jackson was the boss's son and as long as Axl recovered, all would be forgiven. Maybe even if he didn't.

Only, I had no clue which result I was rooting for.

My day started too early, with the lights in the cell bursting to life and waking me from a fitful sleep where Jackson Star cut my sister's throat over and over again. I was drenched in sweat, as was the bed under me, and breathing so hard anyone passing by might think I was having a heart attack. It felt like I was. It felt like my insides were on the verge of exploding, and all I could do to hold myself together was press my hand against my chest and pray that God would make this all end soon—one way or another.

The image of Jackson Star's sick smile stuck with me more than the image of what my sister had looked like the last time I'd seen her or how hopeful Meg had been when she'd learned that her dad was alive, because I knew what fate was in store for me. I had a one-way ticket to zombieville with Jackson in the driver's seat. That's why I was here. That sick asshole was going to inject me with something and then watch me turn. What he'd do with me after that I didn't have a damn clue, but I had no doubt that if he did manage to find Meg and her family and drag them here, my zombie self would somehow be involved in their torture.

I was honored with breakfast in bed, which included a bowl of slimy oatmeal and a huge-ass vial of blood being drawn. Two guards held me down while I thrashed, one sticking his knee in my back so hard that I felt like my spine was about to break in half. It hurt like hell, but I used all the strength left inside me, refusing to let these pricks off easy. Before they left, I got a kick to my already sore ribs that left me breathless and curled up on the floor of my cell.

Lunch came a few hours later, this time with no blood draw, but that was about it. I was locked in a cell with nothing to do but replay every bad thing I'd done in my life that might have landed me in this shitty situation, but for the life of me I couldn't come up with a single thing that would have deserved this kind of karma. Nothing. Sure I'd been an asshole from time to time, but for the most part I'd minded my own business and worked hard to keep my sister safe. A lot of good that had done her.

My shitty sandwich—something that I thought was supposed to be egg salad—had only been gone for about an hour when the door in the hallway finally opened. I stood, half expecting to see Jackson, but instead caught sight of the head asshole himself. Garrett Star, the big shot Regulator of New Atlanta. He barely looked my way when he passed me, too engrossed in a conversation with the man at his side. I watched as they headed down the hall, pausing outside several cells to discuss something.

From where I was I could see straight into Axl's cell, which was currently empty, but I also had a glimpse of the one to the right of that. Just on the other side of the glass stood the guy I'd met only a few days earlier in Dragon's Lair, the man from Meg's crew. I couldn't for the life of me remember his name, and at this point he was nearly hairless, the sprinkling of black hair that had still clung to his chest when I'd been brought in seemed to have vanished overnight. His skin had lost most of its color and was taking on the same translucent look the hybrid zombie I'd fought had. I remembered how it had felt under my grip, soft and thin, as if it would rip if I grabbed him too tightly.

Whatever Star was doing here, he was utterly engrossed in the cell next to me. It was the one that held the teenage girl I'd seen when I was dragged in. Her brown eyes had been sad and swimming with pain, her barely covered body strapped down while tubes ran from her veins to the IV bags that dripped only God knew what into her bloodstream. I had a pretty good idea who she was, but it was an idea I couldn't bring myself to entertain just yet because it was just too dark, too twisted. Even for this place.

Star and the man stood outside the cell talking for a few minutes before he finally nodded and turned to go, leaving the other scientist to do his bidding. Thinking about what it might be gave me the chills, and I found myself wrapping my arms around my body like they would protect me from the cool air whooshing through the vents in my room. The head asshole glanced at me when he walked by, but it was a passing look, one that told me he hadn't given me a second thought since I was brought in.

I wasn't sure if his indifference to me was good or bad. I knew I was here because Jackson had a beef with me, and I doubted the plans he had for me would do anything less than give me nightmares. What would his father do with me if Jackson wasn't allowed to return to his position? Would I be forgotten and simply left to rot, or would I still find myself injected with whatever strain of this virus they were currently working on?

The scientist outside the girl's room went in and I waited with my breath held to find out what was going on, but he was out again in no time and the girl wasn't with him, so I had no way of knowing.

Being behind the window made me feel like a lab rat, and it cut me off from everything in a way I'd never experienced before. I'd been in prison, in the DC colony, but it hadn't been like this. That place was a hellhole, a city of scum who lived in filth and behaved like they were animals, not human beings. Here everything was pristine and white and sterile, but there were no sounds other than the ones I made. I could lie on my bed with my eyes closed, holding my breath, and discover what utter silence actually sounded like. It was shocking in its intensity. The way it seemed to cover me, coating my body and making me heavy. I'd been here for less than a day, but already the lack of sound and human interaction threatened to drive me mad.

I tried to distract myself by thinking about Patty, but that just made me ache. She was dead and it was my fault for getting wrapped up in all this, for not taking care of her the way I should have. So instead I thought about Meg and tried to allow the knowledge that she was at least safe calm me. No matter what happened to me, no matter what kind of horrible death I was facing, Meg was at least someplace where Jackson couldn't find her. She was with her family and hopefully working on a plan to rescue us, but even if she didn't make it in time, even if I died before she managed to get here, she would be okay. That was enough for the time being. It had to be.

# CHAPTER SEVEN
## Meg

The day of revelations seemed never-ending. Angus would share stories about things he'd seen through the window of his cell or been told by Jane, Glitter's mother, and my family would fill him in on little details about the last twenty years. Mom wept when she learned that Dad was immune and had hidden it from her, but no matter how many times she asked the others why he'd felt he had to do it, no one had a good answer. It was entirely possible that there wasn't one, but either way, he was the only one who could answer any real questions about his motivations.

Jada stayed with us in the backyard but remained separate from the group. She acted like she was waiting for something, and even though we were all anxious to learn how we were going to get into the CDC, no one asked any questions. Probably the only thing that could have distracted us from the impatience of being filled in on the plan was learning what the last twenty years had been like for Angus. And his stories seemed to be endless.

It was late afternoon by the time Bonnie poked her head out the backdoor. The gnarled side of her face was turned in our direction and she had to twist her head so she could see us out of her remaining eye. "They're here."

Jada, who sat on the grass at my side, nodded. "Thanks. We'll be right there."

"Who's here?" I asked, voicing the question I was certain was on everyone else's mind as well.

"Hopefully our allies. We'll have to see." The blonde woman barely glanced my way as she hauled herself to her feet, her gaze too focused on Angus. "Are you ready for this?"

My uncle grunted as he dragged himself up off the ground. He had a cigarette between his lips and a scowl on his face, but he nodded to Jada. When he looked the rest of us over, sucking the toxins from the cigarette into his lungs in the process, his expression was unreadable.

He plucked the cigarette out of his mouth and blew the smoke out. "This ain't gonna make much sense at first," he began to no one in particular, "but you just gotta trust me. We got a plan."

Jim had crossed the lawn to join Jada and together they started walking, but they didn't go into the house. They went around it, heading to the front yard instead. Charlie and I walked side by side with the rest of the group, and when she caught my eye I shrugged at the silent questions in hers.

On her other side stood Luke. He glanced my way, but I still couldn't look him in the eye. I felt betrayed. Of everyone here, I felt like he'd lied to me the most. Why I wasn't sure, but I couldn't shake the feeling that he'd found out something major and had kept it from me for no reason. At least no good reason.

We rounded the house and I stopped dead in my tracks at the sight in front of me. Of everyone I'd expected to find waiting for us, these people would have been on the bottom of my list, and I could tell by the confused expressions on my family's faces that they were feeling the same way.

The people in front of us wore robes constructed of thick, red material that made me sweat just looking at them. They didn't open in the front like normal robes, in fact they were unlike any robe I had ever seen before. The neckline was wide, open to below the chest and giving us all a glimpse of the bronze pendants they wore around their necks. A swath of excess material at the back of the robe formed a hood, and the sleeves were long and fitted, the hem going all the way to the ground and so heavy that it barely moved in the wind.

While most of the people standing in front of us had their hoods down, allowing us to see their faces, the woman leading the pack had hers pulled forward so much that it shadowed her face, making it nearly impossible to discern her features. Not that I needed to see her to know who she was. Everyone in New Atlanta knew the High Priestess of The Church, my family especially.

For some reason she had a fairly large group of followers with her, but even more baffling than her entourage were the two zombies standing at the back of the group. The creatures' arms had been cut off and they had collars around their necks, as well as square metal cages fitted over their heads that were made of thick steel bars that crisscrossed on every side and had been welded together, making it impossible for them to bite anyone

"Priestess," Jada said, stepping out in front of the rest of us.

The High Priestess lowered her hood dramatically when she stepped forward, either so she could look us over or so we could get a good look at her. It wasn't the first time I'd seen her, but her appearance was no less shocking now than it had been every other time. Her blonde hair was pale enough that it looked almost silver, especially in the sun, and her eyebrows and lashes were the same shade, giving her eyes a hairless look that brought a lizard to mind. Or the freaky hybrid zombie Donaghy had fought only a few nights ago. The High Priestess had strikingly pale blue eyes, so light that they seemed nearly as colorless as her hair, and her skin was the purest ivory I'd ever seen. It gave off the impression that she'd never set foot outside in her life, and I found myself holding my breath, waiting to see if she would burst into flames now that she was exposed to the sun's rays. She did not.

"I am here at your request," she said, nodding to Jada but not giving away if she was curious, annoyed, or thrilled about being summoned here.

"Yes." Jada glanced back at us before saying, "We have someone with us that you might be interested in meeting."

The High Priestess's nearly invisible eyebrows lifted, but she didn't smile. "I highly doubt that anyone who chooses to degrade their bodies in the way that you have—" She looked pointedly at Jada's tattooed neck. "—would be of any interest to me. I am a prophet, sent here by God to pave the way for the Savior. I am pure. I do not mix with the likes of you."

To her credit, Jada didn't even blink at the insult. She did, however, turn and nod to Angus.

My uncle, who was still smoking, walked forward with a swagger in his step that should have looked out of place on a man who'd just been released after nearly twenty years of captivity, but instead fit every story I'd ever heard about him perfectly. When he stopped in front of the High Priestess he had a smirk on his face that brought to mind how many times I'd heard my mom or dad mention what an asshole he could be. He hadn't shaved today, and the growth on his face made him look scraggily and worn next to the woman in front of him. Despite the fact that I despised her and everything she stood for, I couldn't help thinking that standing next to him, she did look pure.

The High Priestess looked him over and for the first time a small smile formed on her lips. "This man?" She shook her head. "I have no interest in this man."

Angus sucked in a mouthful of smoke, holding it in his lungs longer than necessary and then purposefully blowing it in her face. The High Priestess frowned and two of her followers stepped forward. They were tall men who looked silly in their red robes, their muscles making it seem like they were playing a child's game when they should be out guarding the city.

"See here," Angus said, his smirk growing, "that's where you're wrong."

The High Priestess must have seen something in his expression that interested her, because she lifted her hand to stop her men from moving forward. "Go on."

My uncle grinned as he took another drag on his cigarette, seeming to draw the moment out as if was a game. When he finally spoke again, smoke came out with the words. "I'm Angus James, and from what I hear, you've been waitin' for me to come back."

Silence followed his revelation as everyone from The Church tried to absorb this information and my family waited with baited breath to find out what was going to happen.

Angus alone seemed unaffected by the moment. He simply smoked and stared at the woman in front of him like he was trying to size her up, or possibly trying to figure out just how insane she was. He inhaled slowly, pulling smoke into his lungs, and then drew it out even more dramatically when he exhaled. He scratched his arm, pulling his sleeve up to reveal the tattoos on his bicep, faded from time and age, and grinned like he knew the woman in front of him was going to be disappointed.

"You are not," the High Priestess finally said.

Her gaze moved past Angus to the rest of us, and when she took in the group behind him, doubt flickered in her translucent eyes. She knew us, had stalked us for years. She'd stood outside our building holding up signs that told everyone how special the James family was, how they had holy blood and that Axl would one day take his place at his brother's side. She was fully aware that standing in front of her were some of the few people in the settlement who actually knew what Angus James had looked like.

My uncle stuck the cigarette between his lips so he could pull his shirt over his head. When he tossed it aside, no one was watching to see where it landed. We were all too focused on his chest and arms.

He was more muscular than I'd expected considering his years in a cell, but it shouldn't have been a surprise. He'd already told us that he'd spent a lot of time exercising, even after he'd given up hope of escape, just in case he ever managed to get his hands on Star. But it wasn't his muscles that drew our attention; it was the scars that dotted his arms and chest. There were dozens of them. Crescent in shape, they were jagged the way only teeth marks could be. Some were dark and stood out against his pale skin while others were small and shiny and red, and others were so faded from time that we wouldn't have been able to see them if it weren't for the sun shining down on us now, but there was no mistaking what they were. Human teeth left very distinct marks behind.

"Like I said—" The cigarette between my uncle's lips bobbed when he spoke. "—I'm Angus fuckin' James."

One of the followers stepped forward. "Mother."

Sabine was several years older than me, but our school had been small thanks to the decimated human race and even if she hadn't treated me like I was something special, I would have known who she was. Everyone did. Not only was she the daughter of the High Priestess, but Sabine had been the first person to ever receive the vaccine after the CDC released it.

"This cannot be *him*," she said.

The way she spit out the last word made Angus laugh.

"Shit. I heard you was puttin' me on a pedestal, but I didn't believe it." My uncle waved to the people behind him. "Shoulda talked to somebody who knew me. If you had, they woulda told you what an asshole I was."

The High Priestess sucked in a deep breath, seemingly trying to gather herself. "This is unexpected, but nothing we can't deal with."

She waved to the people at her back without looking over her shoulder just like my uncle had only a moment before. The followers at the front of the group moved aside, making room for two men who were standing at the back. The ones who were in charge of the zombies. They came forward, pulling the chained creatures with them, and as they moved the red robed followers began to chant.

"*They are dead, they will not live; they are shades, they will not arise; to that end you have visited them with destruction and wiped out all remembrance of them. They are dead, they will not live...*"

"Fuck," my uncle muttered under his breath as the chant went on and on.

The High Priestess kept her eyes on him as the zombies were pulled forward. She didn't join in the chant with her followers, whose voices had grown louder. They echoed through the settlement, bouncing off the surrounding houses until the words made even less sense than they had when they'd first started. It made the hair on my arms stand up.

When the men had pulled the zombies to the High Priestess's side, she raised her hand and the chanting died down. Her pale eyes were focused on Angus, her gaze intense and calculating, and even creepier than the chanting had been.

She once again raised her pale eyebrows at my uncle and said, "Kill them."

"You talkin' to me?" Angus asked, chuckling again.

"I am." She nodded to the zombies, who thrashed in their cages like they were desperate to get free. "If you are Angus James, then you should be able to kill them."

"Sure." Angus stepped forward and pulled out a knife. "Just take them bars off and I'll be done with it."

The High Priestess raised her hand as if the simple gesture should stop anyone from moving. "You will say the words and they will die."

Angus let out a loud, barking laugh. "You gotta be shittin' me. Look lady, you wanna put a statue of me in town and kneel in front of it, be my guest. But I'm gonna let you in on a little secret, I ain't a god. Hell, I'm 'bout as far from it as a person can be." He shoved the knife back into its sheath.

"So you cannot kill the zombies?" the woman asked.

Angus grinned. "Now, I didn't say that."

The High Priestess nodded, but her expression didn't change. "Go on."

"If you agree to help us, and if I can get into the CDC, I'll be able to take care of the dead once and for all."

"What?" Mom said from behind me.

Angus didn't look back, not when other people threw questions at him or when murmurs started moving through the crowd of fanatics in front of us. He kept his gaze on the High Priestess, waiting for her to give some indication that she'd finally accepted the truth of who he was.

"You know I'm him," Angus said when the woman still hadn't spoken. He waved to the scars on his body, then to the ones in the crook of his arms that matched Glitter's. "They've had me this whole time, up there in the CDC. They got my brother now and they're doin' stuff that will make the zombies you got here seem like kittens. We gotta save my brother, and then we gotta stop the CDC once and for all. And I know how."

"How?" the High Priestess finally asked.

"See, there was a woman. A woman who was evil, who is now burning in hell, probably waitin' for me to join her, but who did somethin' right in the end. She was a lot like me, which is probably why I loved her. I always was a good for nothin' too, but when push came to shove I chose to do right, and so did she." He sucked in a deep breath like he was trying to control his emotions, and when he spoke again his voice was loud but there was a slight waver to it as well. "Before she died, she told me there was a failsafe. A bacteria deep in the CDC that would eat away at the brains of the dead, killin' 'em once and for all. If I can get back into the CDC, I can get it."

The High Priestess's icy exterior cracked a little as Angus talked, and I could see the conflict in her eyes. I knew why she was hesitating. If she chose to accept what he said she'd be admitting that she'd been wrong. For years she'd been preaching that Angus James had died twenty years ago, but that one day he would be resurrected from the dead. She'd look like a liar. But she had to know that this plan, this bacteria that Angus had mentioned, was possibly the only way to bring about the rest of her prophecy: that Angus James would destroy the zombies once and for all.

We all seemed to be holding our breath, waiting for her to make a decision. Deep in my chest my heart thudded from the possibilities of what my uncle was saying. There was a way to stop the zombies, to wipe them out so we could return to the way things had been before. To stop Jackson and his father from destroying things even more than they already had. All of this could end.

So suddenly that it came with no warning, the High Priestess turned and faced her followers, lifting her arms above her head. "The prophecy will soon be fulfilled. Angus James is back, not from a literal death, but from a different kind. From the death of the soul. This man—" She waved to Angus without looking at him. "—has saved his soul by choosing what is good and pure. He will go back into the CDC, he will rip the walls down, and he will release a savage death on the zombies who have held us captive for more than twenty years." She spun back to face Angus, sweeping her arms forward in the process. "Behold, your savior."

Behind her, every one of her followers dropped their knees at the same time and bowed their heads as the chant once again began to rise up, this time quieter, making it easier to discern the words. And as they spoke a chill ran down my spine, because I realized that if we succeeded the words would end up being more prophetic than I ever could have guessed.

"...*you have visited them with destruction and wiped out all remembrance of them*..."

# CHAPTER EIGHT

## Meg

The group from The Church hadn't returned to New Atlanta, but our plans had been put on hold for the moment. It was prayer time.

Apparently, they prayed every evening at six o'clock on the dot, which meant that at the moment they were kneeling in the center of town while everyone else watched. The chant that rang through the air this time was different than it had been before, but I could neither make out the words nor make myself care what they were saying.

They'd brought a statue with them for the occasion, which my Uncle Angus was currently staring at with an amused expression on his face. It looked nothing like him, not that anyone from The Church seemed to care. The man depicted in stone was too broad in the shoulders, and his face was too serene. I'd only been around my uncle for a day, but the Angus I knew seemed to always be restless, seemed to always have a barely contained storm simmering in his eyes. He had a hard look about him, even when he and Parv sat side by side smoking, which was one of the few things that seemed to ease the storm raging inside him.

Jim sat with them now, a cigarette between his lips as the three of them talked quietly and stared out over the praying members of The Church. There was a similar expression on all three of their faces, something that got lost between grief and bitterness and incredulity.

Jada stood a good distance from Jim, her gaze alternating between him and the prayer vigil. She had a cigarette perched between two fingers on her right hand, her elbow hooked on her hip. Smoke rose from the smoldering stick, getting caught on the muggy breeze that swept between the houses and carried away. Jada didn't seem to notice that the cigarette had burned down to almost nothing, almost as if she'd forgotten she was holding the thing.

I went over to stand at her side, nodding to the group kneeling on the grass. "Is this the first time you've been around them?"

She startled, and then shook her head as she brought the cigarette to her lips. She inhaled before saying, "No." Smoke came out with the word and I batted it away. "I'm a registered zombie slayer, so I go into town every now and then."

I couldn't help looking her over, imagining her going out into the wild world and taking zombies down. She was only a little bigger than me, more muscular for sure, but no more than a few inches taller and still thin. Yet she exuded a toughness I would never be able to compete with.

"Aren't you scared?" I asked, thinking of the one time I'd been outside the wall and how terrified I'd been.

I'd made it back safely and had held my own, but I'd been scared shitless. And that was with a group to back me up and a good distance between the zombies and me. Jada, however, had probably had to get up close and personal with the dead on more than one occasion, and yet she continued to go out there. I didn't get it.

She lifted her eyebrows as she looked me over, and I felt like a child under her gaze. A sheltered, soft little girl, who had been coddled behind a wall, protected from the big, bad zombies.

"This is all I've ever known." She put the cigarette between her lips again and inhaled slowly, pulling the smoke into her lungs, but this time she was nice enough to turn her face away from me when she blew it out. "It's normal out here. We're pretty secure, but things happen. We have to scrounge for supplies we can't grow or make ourselves, which means leaving the safety of the walls." She paused and lifted her eyebrows. "You know what that's like?"

I shook my head. "No."

"I didn't think so," she said, but there was no malice in her voice. "Things happen and I don't like having to depend on others, so learning to defend myself made sense to me. So does going out there and killing the dead. I'm registered in the city, but only so I can get supplies for our town. I don't want a thing to do with New Atlanta otherwise."

It did make sense, and seeing it from her perspective made it sound a lot less scary than hiding behind these walls and hoping nothing bad ever happened. Hell, I'd lived inside the city my whole life, but even my parents had taught me to shoot a gun. It was a necessity these days, especially out here.

"That's how you met Jim?" I asked her. "In the city?"

"No. I met him after he left New Atlanta. He helped some of our people on the outside and came back with them. I was just a kid then, only seven." A smile curled up her lips. "I doubt I left much of an impression on him, but I'll never forget that day."

Jada's gaze moved to where the man in question was sitting, and when she looked at him, her expression said it all. She was in love with him. Big time.

"You're together, right?"

"He keeps my bed warm when he's in town," was her answer, although it was clear that it meant more than that to her. "Jim had a woman before, one he met after the virus. She's dead now, been dead for a long time, but he's still in love with her. He'll never stop loving her. Never stop missing her." Jada shrugged as if it was no big deal, but when pain flashed in her eyes, her expression once again gave her away.

"He's a lot older than you," I said instead of calling her out on her lie.

"Twenty years, not that it matters these days. An age gap like that probably meant something before, but now you take what you can get."

She was still staring at him, and I did the same, trying to see what she saw. He was tall and had shaggy hair that went down to his shoulders. It was a combination of dark blond and gray that matched his close-clipped beard. If he was twenty years older than

59

Jada that put him in his mid-forties, but his tanned and weathered skin made him look older than he was, or at least more worn. His blue eyes softened his features though, and they also told me that he had at one time been attractive. It was obvious that to Jada he still was.

"What happened to his woman?" I asked after a moment of silence.

Jada glanced my way out of the corner of her eye. "Star had her killed."

I sat up straighter. "Why?"

"She overheard something. Well, not overheard exactly. She was deaf, which is the only reason someone was stupid enough to spill top secret information in front of her. She could read lips though, and when Star found out what she'd overheard, he had her killed. Made it look like an accident, but by then Jim was already suspicious and he didn't buy it. That's when he left the city."

"I never heard any of this," I whispered, shaking my head. I felt like every time I turned around I learned something new and devastating that my family had been keeping from me. I hoped the surprises would end soon.

"They wanted to keep you safe," Jada said, and this time there was a little malice to the words.

Not for the first time, I found myself wondering how I looked through her eyes. They were the eyes of a hardened person. Someone who had lived outside the protective sanctuary of our new government, who'd killed zombies for a living and had the scars to prove it. There were so many peeking through the lines of her tattoos that it would have been impossible to count them all if I'd tried—not that I wanted to—but they branded her as a strong person. And her scars weren't anywhere close to being the most noticeable scars in this settlement.

"What about Bonnie?" I asked after a moment of silence in which Jada smoked and watched The Church going about their prayer time. "Is she your mother?"

Jada's eyebrows shot up. "Do we look alike?"

I flushed because I'd already made the observation that no, they did not look alike. But then I thought of my own Mom and how she had come about the job and my back straightened. "You don't have to share blood to be a mother. Especially these days."

Jada nodded, once again sucking chemicals into her lungs. The end of the cigarette flared red, burning more of the paper away and leaving ash in its wake. When she'd inhaled enough of it, she dropped it to the ground and stubbed it out with the toe of her boot.

She turned her face away from me and blew smoke into the air before saying, "That's true."

Her eyes were on me, their expression too penetrating and full of questions. I was as much of a mystery to her as she was to me.

"Max found me after the virus. My parents had died, along with most of the rest of world, and I was alone. I was three, so I don't remember much from before other than flashes here and there. This is the only way of life I've ever known." She looked over her shoulder to the house. "Bonnie came along a few years later. She'd been attacked by a starving dog and was barely alive. Somehow she'd fought the thing off, but not before he did a lot of damage. If a group from the settlement hadn't been out scavenging for supplies and found her, she would have died for sure. She healed, and she and Max got together. They're the only parents I remember."

"My parents died too," I told her.

The way she arched her eyebrows made it seem like she didn't believe me. "But you're a James."

"Not by blood," I said. "My father was killed a few days before I was born, on the way to New Atlanta, and my mom died shortly after I came into this world." I looked across the yard to the porch where Mom and Lila sat. "This is my family now. My mom, aunts and uncles, cousins." My gaze flicked to Luke when memories of our childhood played through my mind. "This is all I've ever known and it was good, at least when Star allowed it to be." I turned back to face Jada. "I know what I must seem like to you, coddled and weak, but the CDC has destroyed a life that should have been perfect, at least as perfect as it can be in this world, and I'm not going to let them get away with it. I may not be a seasoned zombie slayer like you, but I plan to help take the CDC out or die trying."

Jada pressed her lips into a pout that made her even more attractive, but this time when she looked me over, the expression in her gaze was different. There was a respect that hadn't been there before. "If you need some tips for defending yourself out there, let me know."

Looking at the tough woman in front of me, I couldn't imagine a better teacher, and as soon as I figured out what was going to happen next, I planned on taking her up on the offer.

I let out a deep breath, trying to blow out the anger my words had stirred inside me. It didn't work. "I'll do that."

Prayer time ended and we headed back into the house with the High Priestess, her daughter, and a couple other followers while the rest of their group sat patiently on the grass beside the statue of their fake god. We had to crowd into the living room, which had probably never been intended to hold this many people, but everyone was too anxious to get things settled to complain.

The High Priestess took a seat in a red overstuffed chair. It had a few patched holes on the arms and sat at the head of the room, almost as if it had been placed there specifically for her. Sabine stood at her side, her back as straight as her mother's and her eyes just as pale and intense, while the other members of The Church stood directly behind the two women.

The furniture in the room was worn, and there wasn't nearly enough to go around, meaning most of us were left standing. Angus took the couch across from the priestess with Mom and Al and Parv, and Jim stood at their side with his arms crossed. He was loaded down with weapons like he was planning on heading outside the walls, and I couldn't help wondering if he was always this armed or if he was anticipating trouble. I didn't think there'd been any. The Church, however creepy, was famously non-violent.

Max had settled on the other side of the couch, leaning against the wall like he was only there to observe, and Jada stood next to Jim. This time, however, it seemed less about her desire to be close to him. She seemed to be taking the lead, this small woman who was barely older than me, but something about the authority she carried on her shoulders made her seem older and wiser. Like she'd been around much longer than anyone else in the room.

When we'd all settled in, I found myself shoved at the back of the group with Charlie and, oddly enough, Glitter. It was the first time since I'd learned who she was that she had separated herself from her dad, and it occurred to me that she'd done the same thing outside when the High Priestess and her entourage had arrived. It made sense. The Church would never suspect that my uncle had a biological daughter, and whether or not these people offered to help, there was no way in hell he would want them to know she existed. She'd been through enough because of the James blood flowing through her veins.

I positioned my body so I was mostly blocking her from view, and Glitter shot me a grateful smile just as Angus cleared his throat.

"We ready to get on with this?"

The High Priestess lifted her eyebrows like she always seemed to do before talking, and then nodded. "How can we help your cause, Angus James?"

"We got a plan," he began, his gaze moving to Jada, "and we need it to happen in two days."

The High Priestess pressed her lips together for a moment before saying, "The day of our festival."

"That's right," Angus said, grinning.

The festival. God, how I hated the damn festival. Every year it got bigger and bigger as more people fell for the teachings of this ridiculous group, and every year it was a source of tension in my family. As a kid I'd wanted to join in, not realizing what it all meant and only seeing that people were out in the streets celebrating and having fun. Then I got older and learned what it was all about, and suddenly I understood why my parents didn't want to dance around in the streets and celebrate, why for them it was a painful reminder of what they'd lost. It celebrated the anniversary of the day Angus James died. Or at least the day we'd thought he died since we now knew none of that had been true. Somehow, in the midst of all this craziness, I'd managed to block it out, but it was coming up, and this year was a big one. Twenty years.

"What do you need?" the High Priestess asked again, drawing my focus back to what was happening now.

"First, we need you to have the biggest celebration you've ever had," Jada said.

Piercing blue eyes focused on her, but she didn't squirm under the gaze. I didn't know how. The woman's eyes made her look possessed. By what, I wasn't sure, but something evil. It was also glaringly obvious that the High Priestess had no desire to deal with Jada. The younger woman was damaged goods in her eyes. Tainted. Soiled. Not only had she marked up her body, but she was also a zombie slayer, which was contrary to the teachings of The Church. In their eyes we should leave the zombies alone and wait faithfully for Angus James to wipe them out. Killing them only showed a lack of faith.

It was the biggest load of bullshit I'd ever heard.

"That will not be a problem." The High Priestess turned her gaze back to Angus. "What else?"

"That's it for now," he said, nodding. His mouth scrunched up, making it seem like there was more to it, but he didn't say anything else.

The High Priestess saw it too, I could tell, but she didn't ask him about it. "This is something you did not need to call me here for," she said instead. "This year will mark the twentieth anniversary of our Savior's death."

Angus only snorted in response to that.

"This is also to serve as a warning," Jada piped in, once again drawing the disapproving eyes her way. "We are going to need your followers to be armed that night."

Blue eyes narrowed on Jada, who couldn't possibly know what she was asking. The Church was against violence. They were all about faith and letting destiny happen. Guns were forbidden inside the walls of New Atlanta, but most people carried knives everywhere they went just in case. Nothing was certain anymore, and it was better to be prepared. The Church, however, had been preaching against this practice almost from the beginning. They said that faith was the best weapon against the dead. There was a part of me that had always wanted to see a zombie back the High

Priestess into a corner with nothing but faith to protect her. I doubted it would go the way she thought it would.

"Why do my followers need to be armed that night?" the priestess asked.

She tilted her head, her gaze focused on Angus as she waited for a response. I watched him too, but when he gave nothing away my gaze moved to Jada and then to Jim. The High Priestess wasn't the only one who didn't understand why they were requesting that the members of The Church be armed. I couldn't imagine a scenario where it would be necessary. The walls of New Atlanta were secure, so a breach was unlikely, and going up against the guards of the CDC—who had automatic weapons—would be a useless venture. Knives wouldn't get you very far against bullets.

"They need to be ready to defend themselves if necessary," Jada replied.

The High Priestess didn't nod, but instead asked, "What are your plans for that night? We will back Angus James, but only if we are not kept in the dark."

Jim and Jada exchanged a look and I found myself leaning forward, my breath held as I waited for them to let us all in on what was going to happen.

"We're goin' into the CDC," Angus said before anyone else could speak up. "But we need a distraction and the party you got planned ain't gonna be 'nough. We need somethin' that will force all them guards Star has out into the streets. It's the only way we'll make it through without gettin' ourselves caught. You and your people gotta be ready to defend yourselves when it happens."

His explanation seemed to satisfy her, because the High Priestess nodded once. "It will be so. Is that all you wished to discuss with me today?" When Jada and Jim nodded, the priestess got to her feet, her eyes on Angus. "I require your company on the way out."

I waited for my uncle to growl and tell her to go to hell, but instead he got up too. The expressions of surprise on the faces of everyone else in the room told me I wasn't the only one shocked by this, but it was the scowl on Jada's face that got most of my attention. She obviously had a good idea what my uncle wanted and she wasn't the least bit happy about it.

She started to follow them, but Jim put his hand on her arm and shook his head. "Let him."

Jada stayed where she was, but her frown deepened.

Glitter took a tiny step forward when her father headed for the door, but she was smart enough not to follow. Sabine walked only a few steps behind her mother, her head down like an obedient servant. I hadn't known the girl very well in school, only who her mother was, but the few interactions I'd had with her had always left me with a bad taste in my mouth. She was worse than her mom because she followed without a second thought, had probably never had a thought of her own in her life, and would never consider that this whole thing might just be insane.

When they'd disappeared out the front door, Glitter let out a deep breath.

"Are you okay?" I asked.

My gaze went to the crooks of her arms and I realized I hadn't given much thought to what she had been put through. It was understandable, the twenty years my uncle had spent locked up kind of overshadowed the years Glitter had been a prisoner, as well as the fact that my sister and dad were still in the CDC's clutches, but the girl at my side had gone through more than I could ever imagine. She'd been created so the CDC could use her. That had been her only purpose. In there, she hadn't even been a person. Test Subject 06, that's what Angus had said they'd called her. It made my stomach twist. That's how sick it was.

"I'm fine." She wrapped her arms around her chest and stared at the door her father had just disappeared through before turning her gray eyes on me. "I'm sorry."

"For what?" I asked, even though only a few hours earlier I'd been as angry at her as I was at Luke.

"I wanted to tell you about Jackson that first day we met, when you came to the bar with him. I wanted to warn you what he was really like, but I couldn't. It would have put us all in danger." Her gaze dropped to the ground. "I wanted to tell you."

"I wouldn't have listened," I said, and I found my hand resting on her arm. "People tried to warn me about him before, my family had always hated him, but I didn't want to hear it. He had me fooled." *I was a fool*, I'd wanted to say, but I bit the words back.

Glitter tore her gaze from the floor. "I still feel bad."

"Don't," I said. "Some secrets need to be kept..."

My gaze moved across the room to Luke when I realized that didn't just go for Glitter. My cousin had lied to me, yes, but he'd had a reason, one that wasn't much different from the one the girl at my side had.

# CHAPTER NINE
## Meg

Mom was on Angus the second he was back from talking to the High Priestess. "What did she want?"

I was a little surprised she hadn't noticed that my uncle had indicated to the priestess that he'd wanted to talk, but it seemed like she assumed the conversation had been all this crazy woman's idea.

"Nothin' to worry 'bout, Blondie," my uncle replied. "Just chattin'."

"About what?" Jada asked, her voice so loud that everyone in the room turned to look at her.

Angus held her gaze, his lips pressed together like he was trying to decide what to say. "'Bout The Church. 'Bout what they believe and what they want from me now that I'm here."

Parv leveled her gaze on my uncle. "You're not seriously considering helping them?"

"Never said that." He pushed past everyone so he could cross the room to Glitter. Once he was back at her side, she looked more relaxed. "Was just curious is all."

He was lying. I barely knew my uncle, but even I could tell he wasn't being honest with us. Even crazier was the fact that he wasn't even trying to hide it. It was like he wanted everyone to know that there was more to the story that he wasn't willing to share just yet. It had something to do with The Church and his supposedly divine state, I was sure of it, only I couldn't figure out *why* Angus would want to align himself with them.

"Are we sure this is something we want to get ourselves involved in?" Al said, pulling everyone's attention away from my uncle.

"What do you mean?" Mom asked.

"I mean," Al replied, speaking slowly as if he was trying to figure out how to spell it all out, "Have we considered how this could turn out? I mean, most of the people in New Atlanta already believe that crazy woman is preaching the truth. If we involve The Church in our plans, if it gets out that Angus is actually alive, what do you think will happen?"

Mom and Lila exchanged a look, one that said they got where my uncle was coming from. I did too, and he was right. I hadn't considered it until now, but this whole thing could turn out very badly.

"He's right," Parv said. "This is insane."

"We shouldn't have brought them into this," Mom agreed.

"Can we still get out of it?" Lila looked around the room. "Separate ourselves from them somehow?"

Angus stiffened. "We ain't backin' out. It's the only way."

"Why?" I asked, speaking up for the first time. "Why is it the only way?"

"We need them," Jada said. "We need the numbers and the distraction."

"We could have had that *without* calling them here," Al argued. "I mean, I know I'm not in your little club at the moment and I have no clue what you've been cooking up over the last few weeks, but you knew the festival was happening and that the city was already going to be distracted, so why bother even talking to that crazy woman?"

"Because we needed her to be ready," Jada said calmly.

She and Jim stared at Al with unwavering, unblinking eyes.

"Ready for what?" Parv asked.

Jada let out a sigh and turned toward the door. "Follow me."

We did as we were told, following her into what had once been a dining room but now looked more like a planning area. The chairs had been pulled away from the table and were lined up against the wall in case they were needed, and several different maps and diagrams were stuck to the walls with pushpins. A rough drawing of the wall surrounding New Atlanta, complete with notes and circled areas and even a few red X's in certain places. A map of Georgia, one of all of Atlanta, old and new, and another drawing that had to be the layout of the back halls of the CDC, as well as others like it that I was sure were other floors and areas inside the building. They had it all.

Jada pulled the diagram of the wall surrounding New Atlanta down and spread it out on the table, motioning for all of us to gather around. I leaned forward, trying to get a look so I could identify the areas that had been circled. One was the gate, and next to it some notes had been written about the guard shifts as well as where the spotlights were. Another circled area had to be the wall right outside Dragon's Lair, but the third was a place that I knew as well. A place I knew better than anyone else in this room. It was the section of the wall that I used to climb so I could look out over old Atlanta.

"We plan to go in during the festival," Jada began once we'd all gathered around the map. "We'll go back in the way we came, through the tunnel leading to Dragon's. We'll be able to wait in the basement until it's time to make our move. "

"How will we know when it's time to make our move?" Parv asked, and I could tell by the way she had her eyes narrowed on the younger woman that she already had a good idea what was coming.

For my part, I was stumped. The only thing I could think was that they were going to cause some kind of scene—an altercation or something—at the festival. Maybe a riot. That might motivate Star to pull his guards out of the CDC, although even that was doubtful. There was really only one thing I could think of that would be big enough to need more gun power, and that was a breach.

My eyes snapped to Jada, who was staring at Parv calmly as if this whole thing were no big deal. When I looked at Jim though, the expression on his face was slightly more torn. There was pain in his eyes, but determination too.

Jada looked away from my aunt and tapped the place on the map that I'd already recognized. "This is where we will blow the wall. For some reason, this small section wasn't cemented up like the rest of it was, so it will be easier to create a hole in it."

"I think it was because of me," I found myself saying as I stared at the map, thinking about all the hours I'd sat in that very place. "Jackson and I used to sit up there. I loved looking out over the old city, imagining what the world had been like. When they started sealing up the wall I was upset that I wouldn't be able to climb it anymore. Jackson never confirmed that he had anything to do with it, but when that section got missed, he didn't seem too surprised."

"Well, it will help us," Jada said, her gaze still on the map.

The realization of what was coming had my stomach in knots, and had me wishing that Jackson hadn't done that for me. That this section hadn't been missed. That it had been cemented up at the same time that rest of the wall had.

"We couldn't get our hands on a lot of explosives," Jada continued, "but since this section isn't packed with cement, what we have should be strong enough to blow a hole in it."

"Then what?" Mom asked, looking back and forth between Jada and Jim. It was obvious by the expression on her face that she had come to the same conclusion I had, but that she was hoping she was wrong.

"Zombies," Jim said simply.

Silence stretched out across the room.

There had only ever been one breach in the history of New Atlanta, and it was the same one that had claimed Margot, as well as a dozen or so other people. Of course, we now knew that my sister hadn't died after all, but that didn't make the devastation of that day any less intense. We'd mourned for her, cried, we'd had a funeral even though we'd never recovered her body. If we let zombies into the city other people would go through the same thing. People would die. People would lose their children, their parents, their loved ones.

"We can't." Lila was the first to break the silence. "People will die."

"Maybe," Jim said, "but it's for the greater good."

"Greater good?" Mom shook her head and the expression on her face said that she thought he might have gone insane. "No. You can't really think that."

Jim's blue eyes captured hers. "I do."

"And if Amira were still here? If you'd had the family you wanted and they were in the streets when the zombies broke through, would you feel the same way?"

Jim's entire body stiffened as he glared at Mom across the table. "She isn't here, so there's no use talking about it."

"You know just as well as I do what the devastation of losing someone you love is like," Mom said through clenched teeth. "How can you, of all people, be okay with this?"

"Because I know who took her from me and I will do *whatever it takes* to make sure they get what they deserve," Jim said, his voice quivering with barely restrained fury. "If we don't do this, who the hell knows how many more people will die."

They stared at each other for a moment before Jim shoved away from the table and stomped out of the room.

Jada watched him go, the look on her face a mixture of jealousy and concern.

She didn't let it distract her for long, though. Only a couple seconds later she had turned back to the map and was once again focused on the plan. "We'll already have the zombies rounded up by that point. Max is going to lead a group into Atlanta to gather them. When the wall is blown open he'll release them, and then one of our men will take off through the hole so we're sure the dead head into the city. The blast will of course lead more zombies to the wall, but we want to make sure a big group gets in there as soon as possible."

The tension grew as Jada went over the plan in more detail, but no one argued. Mom was right, but so was Jim. People were going to die, but we needed to distract the CDC so we could get in. It was the only way to get the failsafe Jane had told Angus about all those years ago, and getting it had to be our priority.

"You're leading this thing?" Al asked Max, who was present in the room but still standing off to the side like he was only a spectator.

Max nodded. "Sure am."

Al's gaze moved to Max's prosthetic legs. "What if things get out of control? Will you be able to run?"

"I'll be about as effective as anyone else would be I suspect," Max replied, his expression staying the same as if he was neither offended nor surprised by my uncle's concerns. "Truth be told, I've had these things for so long that I barely remember what it was like to have real legs. Know what I mean?"

When Max stared pointedly at Al's missing limb, my uncle frowned, but then let out a low laugh. "Yeah, I guess that's true. Sometimes I wonder if I'd be as effective at my job if I still had both arms. I mean, putting my sword prosthetic on has to make me look pretty intimidating."

Charlie rolled her eyes at her father. "Yeah, Dad, everyone is just terrified of an enforcer who can't stop smiling and joking around."

A little laugh moved through the room that seemed to lessen the tension. It wasn't a lot, but it was enough that when Jada cleared her throat and continued, she didn't get any glares.

"Once the zombies are inside there will be panic. Every available enforcer will be sent to take care of them, which will give us the opening we need." She pushed the map aside and turned so she could grab another one off the wall, this one of the CDC. "Helen's contact will meet us at this door—" Jada tapped her finger on the map. " —at ten o'clock on the dot. We can't be late. Can't miss him. This will be our only chance to get in. There are cameras everywhere, and after this Star will know that he has a spy working amongst his most trusted guards."

"Who is this guard?" Mom asked, eyeing Jada doubtfully. "Who did you find to betray Star?"

"Helen found him," Jada replied. "Years ago, back when she first got Glitter out."

All eyes turned to the girl with the pink hair, who shifted closer to her father.

"He helped get me out too," Angus said.

"Apparently this man had a family when Star released the virus. A wife and newborn twin sons." When Jada pressed her lips together, she looked like she was on the verge of spitting. "He's not the forgiving type, and when he found out that Star released the virus, he was more than happy to double cross the man."

"Who could blame him?" Lila muttered.

"Exactly," Jada replied.

"What do we do once we're inside?" Parv asked, moving us back on track. "What then?"

"Helen will be with us, as will the guard. They both know the halls inside and out, and they will be able to get us where we need to go." Jada ran her finger along the map, tracing a hall. "This is the observation wing where they keep all the test subjects. Axl, Margot, and Donaghy will all be there."

Mom let out a deep breath like she was trying to hold it together, her eyes on the hall Jada had indicated. I looked at it too, thinking about how small the little squares seemed and how suffocating it must be in there.

"Then the failsafe?" Al asked.

"We gotta get somethin' outta my old cell first." Angus leaned forward and tapped one of the little squares. "A code Jane left behind. I tried to memorize it, but I think the drugs and stuff they gave me messed up my memory. I'd have it locked away one day, and then forget it completely the next." He shook his head. "It's a damn good thing I wrote it down."

"How does this thing work exactly?" Parv said, looking up to meet his gaze. "What are we supposed to do with it?"

"Let it loose," Angus said simply. "Jane said that all we'd hafta do is break the vial on the streets and it would work."

"But how?" I asked him.

"Don't know exactly. I ain't a doctor and I can only tell you what Jane told me. That it would eat away at the zombies' brains but leave people alone. That's it."

"It seems too simple," Mom said.

"They're already dead, though." Lila looked around. "I mean, they aren't alive, so who's to say it would take something major to stop them? Maybe that's the point. All this time people have been looking for a big, complicated solution to the problem that they totally overlooked the small things."

More questions were thrown around, but it only took a minute for me to realize there were a lot more questions than there were answers. Angus was going by the word of a woman no one had trusted—except for him—and one everyone else seemed to despise even all these years after her death.

Jada finally raised her hand, putting a stop to the conversation. "We can go around and around about this all night, but it would be pointless. At least until we can talk to Helen. She has more information about how this thing works than we do."

"She knew about it?" Parv asked.

Other than earlier when Angus revealed his love for the woman I could only think of as a mad scientist, my aunt had remained as unemotional as a statue throughout our planning. She'd always been reserved, but this ran much deeper, and it didn't take a genius to realize it had a lot to do with Joshua and the baby they'd never had.

"Helen has worked deep within the CDC since the very beginning," Jada replied.

Parv looked toward my uncle. "She was there, working on the same wing where you were held for all those years?" If the accusations in her tone weren't enough, the look in her eyes when she moved her gaze to Glitter said it all. "She didn't just stand by and watch it all happen, did she? She helped."

Silence stretched over us. I didn't know Helen that well, but the woman I'd gotten to know over the last few days didn't seem like the type who would be okay with the things the CDC was doing, but she had to have been. She'd been there. She'd stood at Dr. Helton's side and participated in experiments. She'd watched Angus suffer, knew Glitter was there and that she was suffering too. She'd known about Margot and Dad the first time I'd met her.

Angus nodded, but his expression didn't change. Parv held his gaze, waiting patiently for him to answer. He took his time though, lighting a cigarette as he and my aunt looked at each other, inhaling slowly before he spoke.

"There was a time when I woulda thought somethin' like this was black and white," he said, smoke coming out with his words. "But that ain't how it is and what happened inside them walls is as gray as it can get. Helen was there. She was one of the first people I saw when I woke up twenty years ago, but she wasn't the one behind all this and she was as much of a victim as I was." His gaze moved to Glitter. "She raised my girl. Did a damn good job, too. When they took Glitter from her, it just 'bout killed Helen. She only came back 'cause she knew she couldn't leave Glitter behind. From then on, everything she did was aimed at helpin' us get free. Even when Jane got our daughter out and I was left behind, Helen stayed. She knew 'bout Margot and I know that's gonna be a tough thing for you to forgive, but you gotta. She didn't tell you 'cause it wasn't the right time."

A sniff drew my gaze away from Angus and I found Mom's face streaked with tears. "I don't know when everyone decided I was too weak to handle all these secrets."

"That ain't it," Angus said, his voice softer. "It was too dangerous. That's all."

Mom just shook her head. "It wasn't any more dangerous for me to know that Axl was immune than it was for anyone else, but for some reason I'm the one who was left in the dark."

Angus crossed the distance between himself and mom, and pulled her in for a hug. The cigarette was still between his lips when he said, "I don't know why Axl didn't tell you, but I know he must've had a damn good reason. He loved you from the first day you met. I knew it back then and I know it ain't changed, even if it's been twenty years since I've seen him. If he didn't tell you it was 'cause he wanted to protect you."

# CHAPTER TEN
## Donaghy

t was early. What time I didn't know since there wasn't a damn clock anywhere, but early enough that the lights hadn't been on longer than thirty minutes. I was still lying in bed, my arm thrown over my face to block out the blinding lights, but even with my eyes closed the beams seemed brighter than the goddamn sun. Or it could have been my mood that made them seem that way. I'd been in this cell for maybe thirty-six hours and already I was depressed. I wanted to turn the lights off and burrow under the scratchy blanket covering my bed, to pull it up over my head and block everything out. But like everything else in this world, I had no fucking control over the lights.

My door clicked and a whoosh of air rushed in from the hall when it was pushed open, letting in the scent of death and bleach. I moved my arm just enough to uncover one eye, cracking it so my retinas weren't scorched by the lights. I let out a low curse that ended up sounding more like a snarl when Jackson's cocky face came into view.

"What the fuck are you doing here?" I growled, not moving.

When he grinned down at me, the overhead lights highlighted the bruise on the right side of his face and the cut on his lip. Other than that he didn't seem at all affected by what had happened the last time he was here, and I couldn't help picturing the battered face of Axl James when they'd wheeled him away.

I pushed myself up to a sitting position before the prick in front of me could utter a word. "Is he alive?"

Jackson's eyebrows jumped up. "Axl?"

"You know exactly who I'm talking about."

I pushed myself to my feet, hoping to intimidate the little man in front of me, but he didn't take a step back. Two guards walked into the room behind him, and even though I hated to admit it, their presence sure as fuck intimidated me.

"He's alive. Head injury. It should heal, but he's being monitored."

Jackson shrugged like it was no big deal. Before I had a chance to respond he nodded and the guards were moving forward. These men were with him for a reason, and whatever that reason was, I knew it had to do with me.

I took a step back, but there was nowhere for me to go. The bed was behind me, and when I moved all it did was cause me to topple down onto the mattress. Before I had a chance to get back to my feet the guards were on me. They held me down, overpowering me even though I fought as hard as I could. My bruised side throbbed with every move I made, but there was no way I could get free. An arm was shoved against my neck, choking me just enough to send a jolt of panic through me, but not enough to stop me from breathing.

"Meg's disappearance has put a wrench in my plans." Jackson walked forward until he was standing over me. "I was furious at first, but I've had time to think it over and I believe I've come up with an alternative." He pulled a syringe from his pocket. "It won't be quite as gratifying as what I'd had planned, but I'm a flexible person."

He moved closer, his gaze holding mine as he pulled the cap off the needle. I growled and squirmed and pushed against the men holding me down, but they only held me tighter. Jackson smiled. He put his hand on my cheek and pressed my face harder against the mattress, and every muscle in my body strained as panic set in. The poke of the needle against my neck made me jerk, and then I felt it, the slight burn of something entering my blood. It moved down my neck to my chest, spreading out faster than I thought possible. I sucked in a breath as the burn moved through me, wanting to scream in frustration, to rip away from these men and beat the shit out of Jackson.

But when he finally stepped back and the guards let me go, all I could do was sink to the floor. The burn had faded, but it didn't matter. I knew what he'd done and I knew what was going to happen, and I had a feeling that no matter how painful the ache in my chest was right now, it would be nothing compared to what I was in for.

"You have time," Jackson said, drawing my gaze to him. He waved the now empty syringe in front of me, still smiling. "It's an old strain. The first mutation. Remember that one? Remember how slowly it worked, how people would turn before their hearts had stopped beating?"

His words made my own heart pound faster because I had a very good idea where this was going.

"So?" I muttered, trying to sound tough even though I felt on the verge of crumpling.

"So, we are going to let you go." His lips twitched like he was holding in a laugh.

"You want me to lead you to her?" I shook my head and didn't bother holding back a laugh. "I don't know where she is you asshole. I was here when they took off, remember?"

"I never thought you'd lead me to her." Jackson shrugged. "But I have no doubt in my mind that she'll find out what you're going through. It may draw her out, or it may not. Either way, Meg will hear about every second of pain you go through."

He snapped his fingers and the guards were back. It was like a reverse of when I'd been brought here, only instead of being dragged in I was dragged out. Out of my cell, down the hall, passing the other victims trapped here until I was pulled outside. The sun was brighter than the lights had been, making it impossible to see, but I could hear the truck's engine as clear as day.

I fought, but there was no real point. What could I do? Run back into the CDC? No. That would be insane and it wouldn't get me anywhere. The best thing I could do was let them take me back to Dragon's and pray that there was a cure stashed in the bar. Pray that he and Helen knew where Meg was and that everything turned out all right.

Once I was in the back of the truck it took off down the road. The guards sat next to me, glaring like I was scum or already a zombie, but as far as I knew Jackson had stayed behind. Which was fine with me. If I never saw that little asshole's face again it would be too soon.

It was a short ride, and when we pulled up in front of Dragon's I was dragged out and practically tossed onto the ground. My already bruised body hit the pavement, causing the air to whoosh from my lungs, and my head didn't fare much better. A throb started at my left temple from where it had made contact with the ground, sending an ache through my skull.

The truck sped away, doing a U-turn in the middle of the street and leaving me lying on the ground. I stared up, blinking to make the dragon above the door come into view. From this vantage point it looked bright and gaudy, especially compared to the awful condition of the rest of the businesses around me.

It took me a few minutes for me to pull myself together, but once I had I dragged myself to my feet. The door was locked, which was no surprise since it was early, so I banged on it until my hand throbbed. The thump of my fist against the door bounced off the surrounding buildings and echoed down the empty street, but no one answered.

Hopefully Dragon and Helen hadn't run too. If they had, I was royally fucked.

I waited nearly a minute after knocking the first time, and when no one answered I pounded my fist against the door again. This time it was yanked open so fast that it nearly scared the shit out of me and I found myself taking a step back.

"What—" Dragon's words died on his lips when he saw me.

His eyes darted past me, and then he grabbed my arm and yanked me inside. I stumbled forward, nearly tripping over my own two feet, and the door was slammed behind me. The bar was quiet and dimly lit. The stench of death hung in the air, but it wasn't quite strong enough to mask the other smells: alcohol, sweat, and mildew.

"How did you get here?" Dragon said when he had the door securely locked.

He looked me over, frowning at the way I held my side or maybe the sweat beaded on my forehead. Hell, for all I knew he could see the puncture mark on my neck where Jackson had stuck me or some other sign that I was infected.

"Jackson had me dumped here." I paused and took a deep breath, finding the words nearly impossible to get out. "He injected me."

Dragon's eyes widened. "With the virus?"

I snorted but it nearly got caught in my throat on the way out. "Of course. What the hell else would he inject me with?"

Dragon's Adam's apple bobbed, but I wasn't sure if he was trying to rein in his anger or if he was scared out of his mind at the thought that I could be injected with a strain he knew nothing about.

"How long ago?" he asked.

"Fifteen minutes, probably less."

Dragon headed for the bar, calling over his shoulder, "We have the vaccine."

"It won't matter," I replied, stopping him in his tracks.

He turned to face me almost hesitantly. Like he knew what I was going to say but wasn't sure if he wanted to hear it. "Why not?"

"It's the first mutation."

The revelation was met with silence.

Jackson hadn't needed to tell me anything about that particular strain for me to remember it. The first mutation had had a pretty big impact on the remaining population for a few reasons. For starters it had been the first time the virus had presented differently, but also because it was the first time those infected with the virus weren't predictable. Before this strain we'd known what to expect, how long we had until the infected person turned and the pattern the virus would take. But this strain had changed everything and people died because of it. And not just the infected. People waited too long to put a blade through their loved ones brains, thinking they had time. Only this strain of the virus had caused them to become violent while their hearts were still beating, meaning they would attack before they'd actually died. It caught us off guard. Caused a lot of casualties.

But that had been eighteen years ago now, and the virus had changed so many times since then that we barely saw that strain anymore. The vaccines distributed by the CDC had changed with the mutations too, and I doubted that anyone who had a stockpile of meds would still have the vaccine from that particular mutation in their possession. Dragon included.

I felt like dropping to the floor. My side throbbed and I was fairly certain I had a couple bruised ribs, but worse than the pain in my side was the ache that was currently moving through my veins. I could actually feel the virus making its way through me, working its twisted magic and slowly turning me into a monster. Would I know I was turning before it happened or would it be a surprise? Would I be aware of the hunger growing inside me or would I snap in the blink of an eye?

"Get up," Dragon's voice boomed through the bar. "We're going."

I dragged myself to my feet even though I didn't really see the point. "Where?"

God, how could a person have so little hope left inside them and still manage to stay on their feet? Just going by the dejected tone of my voice, you'd think I was curled up in a ball on the floor.

Dragon charged toward the back of the bar and headed down the stinking hall that led to the bathroom and the basement. I followed, dragging my feet as I thought about the night I'd met Meg. All I'd wanted was to get cleaned up after the fight, but I'd stumbled upon her in the bathroom. A man had been in the middle of attacking her, and if I hadn't stepped through that door when I did, the asshole would have had his way with her, but I'd gotten there in the nick of time.

The smells from the bathroom were rank and offensive. They should've turned my stomach, but instead they reminded me of how Meg had looked that day. Innocent and scared, and utterly beautiful and perfect. Of course, I didn't register how pretty she was in that moment because all I'd been able to think about was Patty. My sister who'd been violated in the same way, who'd suffered more than anyone should have to. I'd seen red and had attacked, ripping the asshole off Meg and killing him before I'd even registered what I was doing.

Dragon passed the bathroom and headed down to the basement. I was dragging my feet but I did my best to keep up with him. I wasn't sure if my hesitation was from the hopelessness I was feeling or the virus working its way through me, though.

I'd only been in the basement one other time, back when I'd helped Glitter and Meg bring more booze up, and just like the first time I was struck by how pristine it was compared to upstairs. Dragon headed for the door I'd noticed the first time I was down here, pausing to type a code into the keypad beside it. The lock clicked and he pulled the door open, revealing an apartment unlike anything I'd ever seen. Other than the Regulator's house, there was nothing nice anymore. Most people lived in homes or apartments that wore two decades of age and neglect on them. Not this place, though. It was like the apocalypse hadn't touched the apartment. Like we'd walked through a portal to another period where people had time to clean and where furniture could be purchased brand new.

"What the hell?" I muttered, stumbling over the threshold behind Dragon.

He didn't look over his shoulder when he said, "I like things clean."

That was an understatement.

He waved to the kitchen table and I took that as my cue to sit down. Or more like fall down, my ass barely hitting the chair. I felt like I was watching everything happen around me, not living it, and I had to be imagining the chill creeping through me because there was no way this virus worked that fast. It couldn't have been longer than thirty minutes since I'd been injected, and I knew this thing would take a good two days to change me completely. That was what I'd always heard, anyway. As long as the vaccine was given within forty-eight hours, the infected person usually survived.

The question was: would we be able to find a vaccine in that time?

I swallowed and found that my throat felt as dry as a desert. When was the last time I'd had something to drink? I couldn't remember, so I got up and stumbled to the sink. When I turned the faucet on, water poured out and I shoved my face under it. It was lukewarm but somehow felt hot against my skin, and even though I sucked a bunch down, my mouth still felt like it had been stuffed full of cotton.

"We need to leave."

I turned at the sound of a scratchy voice and found Dragon and Helen standing behind me, but for a moment I couldn't figure out why. There was a hissing sound and when I looked back the other way I found the water running in the sink. Did I turn that on? I swallowed, but I had no saliva, so I leaned down and sucked up water from the faucet. It was lukewarm but somehow —

"Donaghy." Dragon's voice made me stand up straight. "We need to leave."

"Where?" I asked.

"To Meg," Helen said, holding her hand out to me like she thought I was a small child and I needed a helping hand.

Maybe I was. I felt like it. I felt like I didn't really know what the hell was going on. But I did know that I wanted to go see Meg, so I took Helen's hand and walked when she pulled me forward.

Dragon headed back out into the basement before opening another door, and when we stepped from the spotless room into the tunnel, I felt certain that I was dreaming. Cobwebs brushed my face and got caught on my hair. They clung to my arms and things — bugs or rodents, I wasn't sure which — scurried through the darkness. The tunnel seemed to go on forever, and then we were climbing or flying, up and up and up, finally stepping into a room that looked as if it had been the center of the apocalypse.

Helen still had my hand and I followed obediently, unsure of where we were going but aware of every single thing happening in my body. The tingle of the virus moving through my veins, the burn that continued to throb at the injection site, the goose bumps that popped up on my skin as the chills moving through me grew more intense, the burning need for water that made my mouth feel like it was on fire.

We were outside in minutes, and then moving down the street. The stench of death was all around me and I braced myself for the zombies that I knew would soon be charging. I imagined that I was in the ring, that two of the creatures were chained up on the other side, fighting to get free. When I looked at them, their faces transformed, becoming other people. Meg, her face unchanged but resting on the shoulders of a decaying body that hung with loose and rotting flesh. Patty, snarling as she snapped her teeth and reached for me with black fingers.

I tried to jerk away, but Helen kept her hand wrapped tightly around mine. Then we were at a vehicle that looked like it hadn't been used in a dozen years and she was urging me to climb in. Her shove was firm but gentle at the same time, and I did as I was told, finding myself wedged in between Helen and Dragon. When the engine roared to life it made me jump.

"Where are we going?" I asked, suddenly imagining that they were taking me back to DC, back to the prison colony I'd worked so hard to get away from.

"To Meg." Helen patted my knee. "Sleep if you can. It will take us almost an hour in this piece of shit."

I nodded and leaned my head back. My brain felt like it was swimming and I was shivering and drenched in sweat at the same time. My teeth chattered and my joints ached. Images that made me want to scream ripped through my mind but sleep refused to come, and even though I had a difficult time clinging to reality, I did my best to hold onto one thought: I was going to be able to say goodbye to Meg.

# CHAPTER ELEVEN
## Meg

Jada was a badass. That was all I could think as she pulled a leather jacket on. The rays of the Georgia sun were sweltering as they beat down on her from above, but she didn't even blink.

Jim was at her side, and even though most of the time he seemed more like a spectator in everything happening around him, at this moment he didn't. He came alive as they prepared to leave the walls of Senoia. Not because he was excited or in any way pumped to go out and kill some zombies, though. No, it was subtler than that, but I noticed it. Noticed the way he watched Jada pull on her leather gloves, how he zipped her jacket up further as if wanting to cover every inch of her flesh. How he counted the weapons she had strapped to her body, eyeing each one like he needed to be sure it was sufficient. He may have held back when it came to committing to her, but he cared. I could see it in his eyes and body language.

I was watching them, sitting on the front steps of the house we'd crashed in last night and holding a weak cup of coffee, when Luke slid onto the step at my side. I stiffened and he let out a deep sigh that reminded me of our childhood, the way he used to get exasperated and roll his eyes at me.

"You going to be mad at me forever?" he asked.

I sipped the coffee and kept my eyes straight ahead. "I don't know. No." When I glanced his way out of the corner of my eye, keeping my face forward in hopes that he wouldn't notice me looking at him, he was staring right at me. "You should have told me."

He nodded but said, "Maybe. Maybe it wasn't my secret to tell, though. Maybe I had to think about the big picture."

"Maybe," I relented.

"But maybe I'd be pissed too if our situations were reversed."

When he put his hand on mine, which was resting on the steps between us, I didn't pull away. Instead, I leaned my head against his shoulder and exhaled. Luke hadn't been around much lately, but I wished he had. I could have used the support. With everything going on — Dad going missing, Joshua dying, Mom nearly losing her mind — I'd felt so alone. Charlie was the feel good person, the one I turned to when I wanted to have a good time and drink my troubles away, but Luke was the one who actually listened to my problems.

I kept my head on his shoulder as I scanned the town, watching the people who lived here go about their day, seeing my family blend in. Mom and Angus were sitting under a tree talking, and the sight of him still gave me a jolt.

"Twenty years," I whispered and Luke shifted until I was forced to lift my head and look up at him. "Did you know about Angus?"

He gave a little shrug. "I found out the day before you did. I'd met him, but no one told me who he was. I think they were afraid I'd spill the beans earlier." Luke let out a hard little laugh. "Maybe I would have. That's a pretty big revelation."

"No shit," I muttered, and then asked, "Are you living here now?"

Luke nodded, but I didn't miss the flush that spread across his cheeks. "I have a place to crash when I come in. A bed, really."

I tilted my head so I could study him. He looked so much like Charlie that they could pass for twins even though he was a year older than her. They both had their mother's good looks and their father's almond shaped eyes, as well as his dimples. Luke's dark hair was longer now that he was living in the wild, but it suited him. Made him look tougher.

90

We'd grown up as cousins, Luke and I, but I wasn't blind and even if all the girls our age hadn't had a thing for him, I would have noticed that he was attractive. Whoever had stolen his heart, she was lucky.

"Good for you," I said.

"Don't tell Mom, she'll want to meet her and I'm not ready for that." Red spread across his cheeks yet again, and when he laughed I knew he was trying to distract me so I wouldn't notice that the thought of his family meeting his girlfriend embarrassed him. "It's not serious and out here people don't really worry about getting married or even defining their relationships. Anyway, Jim and I don't always make it back to town, so we end up crashing in old buildings a lot."

A shiver shot through me. "That sounds terrifying."

"It can get scary, but I like knowing how to handle myself, like understanding what's out there and what I have to do to stay alive."

The idea of living without a wall to keep me safe scared me, terrified me actually, but he had a point. Hadn't I just been thinking about how capable Jada was compared to me? Didn't it make sense in this world to know how to handle yourself, especially faced with zombies?

"I get that," I said, and then frowned when a thought occurred to me. "Is that why you left? You were doing the apprenticeship with your dad one day, and then the next thing I knew you were running off to be a zombie slayer. What happened?"

He tore his gaze from mine and I could tell he was hiding something. "It was nothing."

"Luke," I said, grabbing his chin and forcing him to look at me. "What happened?"

"I heard a rumor when I was at work."

Even though I now knew those rumors about Dad had been true, the thought that Luke had heard one still made my heart skip a beat. "About my dad?"

He nodded, and then shook his head. "And about Colton."

The mention of my dead boyfriend's name made everything freeze. Rumors about Dad and Angus were normal, but this was something I hadn't expected.

"What was it?" I whispered.

"The day after your dad went missing, I heard these guys talking about it. About how there was no reason he should have been outside, but how stuff like that always seemed to happen when someone got in Jackson Star's way. So I asked them who else had gotten in his way."

Jackson. I should have known, but until now it had never occurred to me that he would have had something to do with my boyfriend's untimely death. "What did he do?"

"From what I hear, when Colton went outside the wall alone it was on Jackson's orders. We both know he never came back from that trip."

The truth felt like a sledgehammer hitting me in the stomach. It made sense, so much sense that I felt like an idiot for not seeing it before. Those months that I was with Colton were the only time since Margot's disappearance when my relationship with Jackson had suffered. Even back then I'd known that he was jealous, but I'd convinced myself he'd get over it, and then he didn't have to because Colton was gone.

"Did Jackson kill Colton or did he have someone else do it?" I whispered, afraid to hear the answer but needing to know.

"I don't know for sure. There were rumors, but these guys gossiped more than women. It might not have been true."

I looked up into my cousin's eyes, blinking back tears. "Tell me."

"Someone swears that Jackson drove through the gates only a hour before Colton went out."

All the things he'd done to me already and yet I was still surprised by his cruelty, by how sick and twisted his mind really was. If I ever came face to face with him again, I would kill him. I wouldn't give him the chance to take me out, and I wouldn't let him have the upper hand. I would rip my gun out and pull the trigger without hesitation.

The only problem with that was obvious: I wasn't a fighter. I wasn't like Luke or Jim or Jada. I was soft and coddled and would be totally useless in a fight.

But Jada had offered to help me out.

I glanced over to where she and Jim stood. They were still getting ready, but it wouldn't be long before they headed out. If there was ever a time to learn or people to learn from, this was the time and these were the right people.

I swiped my hands across my cheeks to get rid of the tears and got to my feet. "I want to go out."

"Out there?" Luke asked in disbelief. "Now?"

"Yes." I nodded to the other zombie slayers. "Jim and Jada are getting ready to go, so I'll have plenty of capable people to watch my back."

Luke got up almost reluctantly, shaking his head. "I don't know, Megan."

The expression on his face told me he was going to take a lot of convincing, so I turned my back on him and instead headed over to where Jim and Jada stood. They were all decked out in leather, but they hadn't yet headed for the gate.

"Hey," I said as I jogged up. "I was wondering if I could go out with you. If you could show me a few things."

Jada's thin eyebrows pulled together as she looked me over. "You want to go out?"

"I do." I turned my gaze on Jim. "What do you say?"

He'd known both sets of my parents, the biological ones and the ones who'd raised me. I'd heard enough stories about the beginning to know that all four of them were strong and capable, so if anyone would be willing to take me out there, it would be the man who knew how much strength and endurance ran in my family.

The older zombie slayer didn't blink as he looked me over. He pulled on a pair of gloves, his blue eyes focused on my face alone. Not on my thin frame or small stature, not on my impossibly unmarred skin. Just my face.

He nodded once before turning to Jada. "You got extra leather?"

She blinked and then shook her head, but she didn't argue the way I expected her to. "Yeah."

"Good," he said, "and we have to get her a gun."

"I have one," I said. Things had been so crazy that I'd forgotten all about the gun I'd bought on the black market. "In my bag."

Jim blinked and Luke shook his head.

"How do you have a gun?" he asked.

"Black market. When things with Jackson got bad, I thought I should be prepared."

"Your folks raised you right," Jim said with a nod.

Jada let out a little laugh and waved for me to follow her. "Come on."

WE WERE ABOUT THE SAME SIZE, WHICH MADE ME FEEL more secure about my decision to go out, even if she did have a huge advantage over me in the muscle department.

"You're not going to tell me I'm too soft to do this?" I asked as I pulled the leather pants on.

"I trust Jim and he thinks you can do it." She tossed me a leather jacket once the pants were on and headed for the door, saying over her shoulder, "Just know that if you're responsible for either one of us getting our faces eaten off you'll regret it." She glanced back. "And I'm not talking about having to live with it on your conscience."

I let out a little snort as I pulled the jacket on and followed her out.

Luke was also suited up and waiting with Jim when we got back outside. Within minutes I was on the way to the gate, so loaded down with knives and guns that I felt twenty pounds heavier.

"Aren't you going to ask if I can shoot?" I asked Jim as I twisted my long hair into a knot on top of my head so it was out of the way.

He shook his head, not even looking over at me. "Don't have to. Axl and Vivian James raised you. There's no way in hell they let you go through life without learning how to shoot a gun."

"I was seven the first time they took me to the shooting range."

For the first time since we met, Jada actually looked impressed when she glanced my way. "Seven?"

"My parents wanted to make sure I knew how to handle myself. Just in case."

She nodded in approval.

After the praise from both Jim and Jada, I was feeling pretty good about my decision to go out. At least until the gates opened in front of us.

Inside the gates, the city of Senoia was neat and tidy, even if it was a little rundown, but that ended at the wall. Outside the streets were littered with branches and debris from the trees, the pavement was cracked thanks to years of neglect, and weeds had sprouted through the holes. It was clear the people in the settlement had done their best to keep all major obstacles off the street, but that didn't mean the surrounding area didn't look abandoned and worn. The houses, much like the ones close to New Atlanta, had been stripped of everything useful, and what was left were little more than shells. The same had been done to the vehicles that lined the streets. They were on blocks, their tires gone, the hoods open, most if not all of their engines missing. What was left of them were rusted piles of metal. Weeds that towered over my head, and in some cases even trees, grew up through the now empty engine compartments and even some of the interiors. Animals had made homes in a few, old bundles of twigs or grass a sign that the car was now inhabited by creatures who weren't meant to live in metal shells.

I studied it all as we walked, so intent on taking it in that I nearly jumped out of my skin when the gate slammed behind me.

Luke chuckled, not looking the least bit repentant when I shot him a glare. "Starting to second guess yourself?"

He spoke too loud, at least in my opinion, but no one else seemed the least bit concerned by the way his voice carried down the street and bounced off the trees and remnants of buildings.

"No," I said in a tone that was much more defensive than I'd wanted it to be. "It just surprised me. I was too focused on—" I waved to the buildings, at a loss for how to describe them.

Jim glanced back at me but said nothing.

Jada, however, wasn't as reserved. "It's the same thing you can see on every street in every city all over the country. Nothing too exciting."

"To you maybe," I said. "But I've spent my entire life inside New Atlanta. I've never seen another street or another town until yesterday."

Jada's steps slowed, but the look she gave me wasn't judgmental or accusatory. "I never considered that." She shook her head. "I can't imagine staying in one place your whole life. Being out here can be risky, but it's better than being stuck behind a wall. At least this way you get to experience life."

I nodded because she had a point, but I also knew that my parents had made the decision to stay in New Atlanta because they'd thought it was what was best for us. They'd been on the road, had struggled to get where they'd thought we'd be safe, and to them that wall hadn't signified a prison, but a source of hope. Too bad it hadn't turned out that way.

A moan broke through the air, cutting our conversation short.

"Heads up," Jim said, pulling his knife free from the sheath on his hip.

Luke did the same, freeing the knife that was strapped to his chest while Jada mimicked the movement. I did too, and it didn't escape my notice that I was the only one whose hands were trembling.

"Were you scared?" I whispered to Luke as we continued down the road in a close group. "The first time you came out, I mean."

Luke let out a small laugh. "Shitless."

"How long did it take you to get over it?"

"Only a couple nights."

"More like a couple months," Jim piped in.

Luke flipped his middle finger up, managing to cling to his knife in the process. "You know I was a natural."

Jada rolled her eyes.

A zombie stumbled from between a couple old buildings right then and all conversation stopped. Not just that, but so did the three zombie slayers I was with. The zombie caught wind of us and changed courses, heading our way, and my heart beat faster. I waited for Jada or Jim or even Luke to get the thing, but none of them moved. Instead they all stared at me.

"What?"

Jada nodded toward the zombie. "You wanted to learn."

I swallowed and tried my best not to look like I was on the verge of peeing my pants, but it wasn't easy. This was nothing, or so I told myself. I'd been out before, had faced a horde with my crew when we'd gone out to patch the wall. Plus, I'd been around some pretty nasty zombies in Dragon's Lair. Sure they had all either been in cages or fighting Donaghy, but it still counted. At least in my book.

My fingers tightened on my knife as I stepped forward. The air I filled my lungs with was thick with moisture and the scent of decay. I sucked a mouthful in anyway and kept moving, focusing on the creature in front of me.

He was pretty old. His gray skin was ripped and saggy. The black blood I'd come to know so well dripped from the cuts, as well as every visible orifice. He had little left in the way clothes, not that he needed them, and his arms and legs were so rotten that I was pretty sure I could actually see bone in a few places.

He was a walking skeleton. With teeth, but even so, I couldn't imagine how this bony thing would ever be able to overpower someone. Not even a thin apartment girl who'd spent her entire life inside the walls of New Atlanta.

I took a deep breath and moved.

The zombie was less than five feet away from me, which didn't give me much time to consider how I wanted to do this. In fact, I was still trying to come up with a plan when the thing lunged. I let out a little squeak as I dodged out of the way and the zombie stumbled past.

Behind me there was movement and I heard Jim say, "She can handle it." But I didn't turn to see what was going on. I was too focused on the dead man in front of me.

I gripped the knife tighter and took a deep breath. I needed to get behind the thing. It would be a hell of a lot easier to get the blade into its brain if I didn't have to worry as much about his teeth and nails—assuming he still had some on his fingers, which was unlikely with how decayed he was.

This time when he charged, I ducked and twisted so I was behind him. Before he could register that he'd passed me yet again, I popped up and grabbed what was left of the collar of his shirt. He growled when I jerked him back, and even though the sound made my heart thump harder, I didn't ease my grip or hesitate to lift my knife and slam it into his skull.

The blade sank in, but the impact of metal hitting bone was more jarring than I would have thought. Still, it did the trick, and in seconds the zombie had gone slack and dropped to the ground.

I was out of breath, but feeling good. The thing was down and it hadn't been nearly as scary as I'd expected it to be. Of course, if I'd been facing a horde I'm sure I would be feeling differently, but that didn't mean I wasn't going to allow myself the satisfaction of knowing I'd been able to take the thing out.

When the others came over, Luke slapped me on the back. "Good work."

"Thanks," I said, beaming.

Jim nodded to the body as he knelt next to it. "You're not done yet."

It took a few seconds for me to figure out what he meant, and then I remembered that I was expected to collect the zombie's ears. It was how the zombie slayers verified that they were actually doing their job, and in New Atlanta the decaying ears of a zombie could actually be traded in for credits.

"It's all yours," I said, wrinkling my nose and backing away.

Luke gave me a little shove. "You're not getting off that easy. It's part of the gig."

"You want to be a zombie slayer, right?" Jada said, a teasing tone in her voice.

"Not really." I looked around, waiting for them to give in and cut the ears off themselves, but no one moved. "You seriously want me to do this?"

Jim grabbed my arm and pulled me down so I was kneeling next to him. "It's not a big deal. The guy's already dead."

Since I didn't think I was going to be able to get out of it, I grabbed one of the ears and slowly started to saw it off with my knife. The skin that covered the cartilage was soft and gooey, coated in both dirt and zombie blood. Not only that, but being this close to the body made my stomach twist thanks to both the smell and the view. I may have spent my life surrounded by zombies, but that didn't mean I was used to the stink of death.

It only took a few seconds to get the ear free, and when I did I held it out to Jim. "Take it."

He did, chuckling to himself as he slipped it into a pouch he wore on his hip. He was still laughing as he flipped the body over so he could get the other ear, and I jerked back when he expertly cut it off with one swipe of his blade.

"That's how you do it," Luke said, grinning.

"She did about as well as you did the first time," Jim said, standing.

I stood too, turning just in time to see Luke give Jim the finger for the second time since we'd left the settlement.

"Come on," Jada said.

She rolled her eyes at the two men just before turning away, but there was a small smile on her lips too.

Luke hurried after her but Jim stayed at my side while I retrieved my knife from the zombie's skull. It slid out with a squish that made me cringe, and I took a moment to wipe the blade on some weeds before tucking it away.

When Jim and I started walking we were a good five feet behind the other two, but he didn't hurry to catch up. Instead, he lit a cigarette and walked at my side.

"So you knew my parents?" I asked, taking the opportunity to ask the question that had been nagging at me since I'd learned this man had come into New Atlanta with the rest of my family. "Jon and Hadley, I mean."

Jim didn't turn his head my way, but his eyes did dart toward me. "I did. Although I knew your mom as Ginny."

"Ginny?" I shook my head because I had never heard anyone refer to her by that name. "Why?"

He pressed his lips together as if trying to decide what to tell me before saying, "I think she just needed a fresh start."

The statement reminded me of what Angus had said to me about Vegas, about how strong my mom had been to be able to get through it. Something bad must have happened to her there, but whatever it was, my parents had never mentioned it to me.

"Doesn't matter." Jim shook his head as he took a drag off his cigarette. "I knew your dad better. Jon and I worked together in Colorado, helping clean the dead out of the city. I didn't trust many people back then, but he was one of the few that I would have trusted to watch my back."

"Is that why you left Colorado with him?"

"Partly. Ginny was determined to get to the CDC because she was expecting you and the babies out there were dying. Jon wanted me along to help keep her safe, so that's what I did. Then he died along the way and so did she, and I felt like my promise extended to you. So I did what I needed to do to keep you safe."

My steps faltered. "What did you do?"

"You don't know?" Jim slowed too, his cigarette forgotten halfway to his mouth.

"No."

He made a sound, but I couldn't figure out if it was a laugh or a grunt of annoyance, and then took a long drag and started walking faster. I hurried to keep up, ready to badger him until he answered me, but it wasn't necessary, because he started talking like he'd intended to tell me all along.

"We were trapped in a house, surrounded by zombies, so I ran out the back and led them away so everyone else could make a run for it. I got to Atlanta weeks after everyone else."

I'd never heard this before, but I had no clue why no one had ever mentioned it. It couldn't have been a secret, like whatever had happened to my mom in Vegas obviously was, but for some reason no one had ever mentioned Jim's name or what he'd done for them. What he'd done to save my life.

"Thank you," I said, throwing my arms around him so suddenly that I caught him totally off guard. "I had no idea."

He didn't hug me back, and when I pulled away he looked more than a little uncomfortable, but he nodded and mumbled a quiet, "You're welcome." We walked for a few seconds in silence before his eyes darted my way and he said, "It worked out. That's how I met Amira…" The sadness in his voice left little doubt in my mind who Amira had been.

"Jada told me that you'd had a woman before, but that she died shortly before you left New Atlanta."

Jim dropped his cigarette to the street and ground it out violently with the toe of his boot. "Star had her killed."

"I'm sorry." I swallowed, thinking about what Luke had just told me. "I had a boyfriend who died a few years ago."

"I know. Colton." His eyes darted toward me again and then quickly away.

"You knew him?" I couldn't figure out how, except that maybe they'd met when Jim came into the city to get credits or supplies. Colton had worked the wall with my dad, which was how we'd met to begin with.

"Met him a couple times." I didn't miss the way he wouldn't look me in the eye.

"You know."

Jim pressed his lips together but didn't respond.

"You don't need to pretend. Luke told me that Jackson had him killed." I hesitated, unsure of how he was going to react but feeling compelled to say what I was thinking. Life was too short. "It's why I brought him up. It hurt when he died, still hurts, but that doesn't mean there isn't a chance to have something good again."

This time Jim didn't look my way. He looked toward Jada. "I know she didn't put you up to this. It isn't her style."

"She didn't. I just thought I'd bring it up. Since we're being honest with one another."

To my shock, he let out a little laugh. I didn't know him well, but I never would have thought butting into his love life would have gone over so well.

Then he said, "You sure do remind me of your mom," and I knew why he was laughing.

"I've been hearing that a lot lately," I replied.

"I bet you have." Then he turned his body so he could look right at me, his gaze sweeping over my face like he was trying to take all of me in. "But you have a lot of your dad in you too."

Tears pricked at the back of my eyes, but I didn't know why. These were people I'd never known, and even though I'd always dreamed of meeting them and wondered what they'd really been like, I already had parents. Good parents.

Still, if Jon and Hadley hadn't died, so much would have been different. And when I thought about it, about how they'd been killed on the way here when they could have stayed in Colorado and been safe, I realized for the first time that Star was to blame for their death too. If they'd refused to come here, if they had run off with Angus instead of bringing him to Atlanta, things would have been different for all of us.

Then again, if that had happened, we never would have found out about the failsafe. Maybe all of this, every horrible, awful thing Angus and the rest of my family had been through, was fate.

# CHAPTER TWELVE
## Meg

W e only stayed out for about an hour, long enough to take a few more zombies down and for me to get a couple pointers from Jada about how to use my height to my advantage. Target practice would be next, although we could do that inside the gate and it wasn't necessarily something I needed help on. I was a good shot. I wasn't sure if any of it would help me if I had to go up against Jackson, but at least now I felt a little more capable than I had before.

"Was it as bad as you thought it would be?" Luke asked as we crossed the street and headed for the gate.

"No." I hadn't given it much thought until now, but thinking back on it, my time outside the wall hadn't been anything like I'd expected. "I think I built it up to be scarier than it needed to be."

"Don't drop your guard based on what went on out there today," Jim said. "Sure, most days are like this one, an occasional zombie that isn't very difficult to wrangle, but there are still hordes. You can get into trouble fast out there if you aren't paying attention."

"I'll keep that in mind," I said even though I had no real intention of ever doing what these three did. Not to mention the fact that if we were successful in our mission, the people at my side may very soon be out of a job.

We were less than ten feet from the gate when the sound of an engine made me turn. An old faded green truck that was so rusty it didn't look like it should be able to drive was coming down the road fast. The sun was shining on the windshield, making it impossible to get a look at the driver, but the expression on Jim's face told me he knew who it was, and when Jada started jogging toward the gate, it reinforced that impression. Seconds later, Jim took off after her.

"Why do you think they're here?" she called as she and they ran side by side.

"No good reason," he replied. "They weren't supposed to be here until tomorrow."

The truck sped by us, but it was moving too fast for me to get a look inside. The gate was already open for us, giving the truck an opportunity to drive right in. Jim and Jada obviously knew who it was, which meant that the gate guards probably did as well, so no one bothered to stop them.

The truck screeched to a stop at the end of the road and within seconds it was surrounded by people who had hurried out to see if they could help. Jada had started running full speed, as had Jim, and when Luke picked up the pace I followed his lead. I didn't know what I was running toward, but I knew the others wouldn't be running if this was nothing.

"What is it?" I yelled as I ran alongside Luke.

He shook his head but I barely saw it because my gaze was trained on the vehicle in the distance. Someone climbed out of the passenger's side, but the door prevented me from getting a good look at them. Then the driver stepped out and the dark skin of the man forced my legs to move faster. It was Dragon. It had to be. A sense of foreboding came over me, but I didn't know why until he dragged a barely conscious man out of the cab, and then I knew.

"Donaghy," I gasped.

Jim reached Dragon and together they worked to help Donaghy across the lawn toward the houses. Every single person who had been outside when they'd pulled up seemed to have frozen in place, and people stood watching as the group made their way across the settlement. The closer I got to them, the heavier my body began to feel and the harder it got to catch my breath. I could now tell that Donaghy was conscious, but he was shaking for some reason and barely able to lift his legs. What had happened? He didn't look hurt other than a couple bruises, but his skin seemed impossibly pale. I tried to tell myself I was only comparing him to the men on either side of him, Dragon who had skin the color of chocolate and Jim who spent his days out in the Georgia sun, but I knew that wasn't it, and the reason behind Donaghy's lack of color terrified me.

Jackson. Another shudder shook my body as I ran up behind them.

"What happened?" I called, barely recognizing my own voice thanks to the tremor in it.

"Angus!" Dragon's voice bellowed through the settlement.

Helen left the men and ran to my side as if she knew I was going to need comfort. "It's going to be okay. There's time."

I shook my head as my steps faltered, trying to move away from her outstretched hands. "No. No."

Helen reached for me, but I ignored her and watched as Donaghy was pulled up the steps. I snapped out of it and ran after them, as did a handful of other people I couldn't identify at the moment. I had tunnel vision and all I could focus on was Donaghy, on taking in every inch of him, trying to determine where he was hurt, hoping to convince myself that it wasn't true.

They laid him out on the couch and I dropped to my knees at his side. "Donaghy," I whispered, grasping his hand.

"Meg."

His voice sounded strained, as if he was in so much pain that he found it difficult to talk. His hand was clammy in mine, his skin as hot as a skillet that had been sitting on the stove. The heat radiating off his body made me sweat twice as much as the leather clinging to my body had.

"It's going to be okay," I told him even though I had no clue if it was. "You're here now."

"I wanted to tell you goodbye. Jackson came to the bar and dragged me out, but I wanted to be able to say goodbye." Donaghy's blue eyes filled with tears, and when he blinked they spilled down his cheeks. "I didn't get to say goodbye to Patty."

"Shhh." I leaned forward so I could press my lips against his. They were dry and hot, and I could only imagine that this was what it would have felt like to kiss the parched ground of a desert. "It's going to be okay."

"We're going to try to give him a blood transfusion." Helen's scratchy voice broke through my thoughts and I turned to find her standing in front of my uncle. "It's all we can do right now."

"Don't you have a vaccine?" I looked around, taking in the faces standing in this room. "You had some at the bar. I know you did. I saw it. Why didn't you give it to him? Why didn't you bring it?"

Helen didn't look my way. She was too focused on Angus, on sliding a needle into his vein.

I tore my gaze from her and focused on Dragon. "Tell me what's happening."

"It's an old strain. It won't respond to the vaccines I had."

"You need to tie me up," Donaghy said. My gaze snapped back to him, only he wasn't looking at me. He was looking up at Dragon. "Please."

"What's he saying?" I asked.

Dragon's eyes were focused on Donaghy when he said, "It's the first mutated virus, which means he'll turn before he's dead. We have forty-eight hours to get the vaccine into him. That's it."

"Except we don't have a vaccine for that strain." Realization dawned on me. "And even if we manage to get it in time, he could still attack us before he gets better."

Dragon nodded solemnly.

"You need to give me space," Helen said, nudging me aside.

The command was forceful, yet soft at the same time, and I found myself scooting away. Donaghy's hand slipped from mine, and the loss felt permanent. His features were twisted in pain, and every move he made seemed to make it worse. My own body ached, but it was a pain that started deep inside me. It was so intense I was afraid I would implode.

Mom, who I hadn't even known was in the room, knelt at my side and placed her hands on my shoulders. "It's going to be okay."

I nodded even though I didn't believe her. But that was what we did, wasn't it? Cling to hope that didn't really exist. It was the only way to get through the twisted world we lived in. I was sure things had been different at one time, but not anymore. Now we had nothing but empty promises and the certainty that things could always get worse.

"What are you doing?" I asked.

Helen inserted a needle into Donaghy's arm. "We're hoping the antibodies in Angus's blood will slow the virus down. He's a universal donor, so they tried it in the CDC in the early days, transfusing his blood straight into the infected." She loosened the tourniquet on my uncle's arm and turned to face me. "It's a long shot, but worth a try. If it doesn't work, we haven't lost anything."

I watched the dark red liquid fill the tube and slide into Donaghy's vein. It was magic blood, blood that had kept Angus alive through the initial outbreak, and then after being bitten over and over again. It was strong blood, able to fight off a virus that was designed to destroy a person. If anything could save Donaghy, this was it.

"Did it work in the CDC?" Mom asked.

Helen gave a shake of her head that was noncommittal. "Sometimes it slowed down the progression, sometimes it didn't."

I swallowed. "When will we know?"

"If it's going to slow things down, we'll know within the hour." Helen got to her feet, still looking at me. "It's not a cure. That's buried deep in the CDC."

"We can get it when we get Dad and Margot out," I said.

Helen's gaze held mine. "If he lasts that long."

Mom's fingers tightened on my shoulders and I winced even though her grip wasn't hard enough to hurt me.

After she finished with the transfusion, Helen stood to leave, and I wiggled my way out of Mom's grasp so I could once again be at Donaghy's side. When I slipped my hand back into his, his skin felt fiery against mine.

"Don't you need to be in New Atlanta?" Mom asked Helen as the nurse cleaned up.

"I was already questioned about Meg's whereabouts. Then put on leave. I don't think Star believes I have anything to do with it, but Jackson was suspicious. He was probably hoping that I'd run for it when they put me on leave and lead him straight to Meg."

"Will your code still work when we get in there?" someone else asked, Parv I thought.

"I have a code that will," Helen assured her.

People drifted out of the room while Donaghy did the same, drifting in and out of sleep, delirious most of the time and burning with fever. My family wandered in from time to time, probably trying to keep an eye on him just in case, but everyone pretty much left me alone.

Mom sat on the other side of the room watching me, and I could see the questions in her eyes but I wasn't ready to talk about everything she'd missed out on while she'd been out of her mind. Not yet. Maybe not ever if things went south.

Eventually Aunt Lila drifted in, bringing Mom a cup of coffee and taking a seat next to her. I listened as they talked about how different this strain had been from the first one. How the original didn't cause a fever, but had instead cooled the person to where they'd barely felt alive. How the infected had lapsed into a lethargic state before improving, giving their loved ones hope that they might beat it. Then their hearts would suddenly stop beating and they'd change.

I was focused on Donaghy, watching the way his face twitched from whatever nightmares he was living through during his fever-coated sleep, but I couldn't tune them out completely no matter how hard I tried. I knew who they were talking about. Mom's first child, Emily, who she'd had at the age of sixteen but given up for adoption. Emily had been the reason my parents met.

After the virus spread, Mom left Kentucky where she'd been living and had headed west, back toward California to check on the daughter she hadn't seen in four years. Dad and Angus had picked her up when her car broke down, and by that point the virus was already so bad that there was little hope left in the world. I'd heard all about it so many times that a part of me felt like I'd actually lived through those early days of confusion and horror, but there was another part of me that couldn't imagine a world where no zombies existed. How would it feel to walk down the streets of a city that wasn't surrounded by a wall? To have no fear that the virus would mutate yet again and turn your neighbor into a monster? It seemed impossible, but if what Angus had told us was true, it wasn't. It was a very real and very tangible possibility, one we could make happen very soon if we were successful.

"If he doesn't get better soon," Al was saying, "we'll have to tie him down. This strain was unpredictable. There was very little warning."

I looked over my shoulder, back to where he stood with Lila, Mom, and Parv. I hadn't even realized he or Parv had come in, but everyone was nodding at his words. I wanted to argue, but I knew I couldn't. They were right. We should have forty-eight hours, but there were no guarantees. Not with this strain. Some people had turned as early as ten hours after being bitten, becoming a living monster who craved flesh and living that way for twelve hours or more before their hearts had finally stopped beating. Until the heart stopped it was still possible to bring them back with the vaccine, but that didn't mean they wouldn't attack. It didn't mean they couldn't kill the people they loved and never even know what they were doing.

I leaned closer to Donaghy and pressed my lips against his ear. "Get better. Please. Just hang in there for a little longer and we'll be able to get the vaccine."

He groaned in his sleep and shifted, but didn't open his eyes.

The change that happened was so gradual that I didn't notice it right away, and then I thought for sure I was imagining things. First Donaghy's skin felt cooler against mine, and then his breathing eased and became less labored, as did his expression. He wasn't shifting around as much as he had. Then, as if by some miracle, he opened his eyes and looked right at me.

"Meg."

"You're awake." I moved so I was sitting on the edge of the couch next to him, perched so close that our bodies were right up against each other. His skin was cooler, no longer burning with fever. I pressed my hand to his forehead and a half-laugh half-sob broke out of me. "Your fever's gone. How are you feeling?"

He swallowed. "Better. Did we get the vaccine?"

He didn't remember. His fever must have been on the verge of frying his brain if he wasn't able to remember the transfusion he'd gotten.

"My uncle Angus gave you blood. It helped slow the virus."

"Angus?" Donaghy shook his head like he wasn't sure what was happening or he thought he might still be hallucinating. "He's dead."

"He's alive. The gray man from Dragon's Lair. It was Angus. He's been in the CDC this whole time. A prisoner."

Donaghy still looked confused, but the comment seemed to jog some memory because he tried to sit up. He winced like his body hurt and I could tell the virus was still working its way through him. He wasn't out of danger yet.

I pressed my hands against his shoulders and eased him back down. "Take it easy."

"Your Dad. I saw him." Donaghy did as I said, but his hand tightened on mine. "In the CDC. Jackson—"

He broke off like he wasn't sure what to say, but I knew by the look on his face that something had happened, and it made my heart stutter and almost stop.

"What? What did Jackson do?" How many times had I asked that question over the last week?

"He sent the guards to find you, and when they came back empty-handed Jackson lost his shit. He went into your dad's cell and beat him. The guards had to drag him out, and then they rushed Axl away." Donaghy paused to swallow again. "Before he injected me with the virus, Jackson told me your dad had a head injury. I don't know how bad it is."

Ice flooded my veins. No. This couldn't be happening. We were so close. Less than two days and we would be able to get him out. What if he didn't make it? What if Jackson killed him just to get back at me? What if he killed Margot?

"Did you see my sister?" I asked, trying to swallow my panic down. "Margot? Did you see her?"

Realization dawned on Donaghy's face, mixed with disgust. "The girl. I saw a girl, a teenager. She was strapped down and hooked up to IVs. That was Margot?"

I nodded because the ache inside me made it impossible to talk. Nine years she'd been gone. Was that what she'd had to endure the entire time? Was that what Glitter had gone through? I looked over my shoulder, searching for the pink haired girl who I'd recently learned was my cousin, but she was nowhere in sight.

110

Maybe it was better that way. Maybe I didn't want to know what had gone on in there.

"I'm sorry," Donaghy whispered.

He pulled me down and wrapped his arms around me, and I felt myself clinging to him like he was the only thing keeping me afloat. Having him back after being so worried should have been a happy thing, but it was tinged with fears that I couldn't even name. The knowledge that he might turn into a zombie, and the revelation that both my dad and sister were still in serious danger. I wasn't sure how I would survive the next forty-eight hours, but I knew they would be the longest of my life.

# CHAPTER THIRTEEN
## Donaghy

My body still ached, but it got better with each passing second. My mind was still fuzzy though, and I found it hard to grab onto what had been real and what had been a hallucination.

I was out of New Atlanta. That much I knew. I was in a town somewhere not too far from the walls of the city we had just fled. I was with Meg. Her family was here. Her Uncle Angus... Was he really alive? Could he be? It had been twenty years, but from what I knew of Jackson and the CDC, it was totally possible that Angus had been alive this whole time. Only, I still wasn't sure if I had dreamt that part. It didn't seem real, but a part of my brain told me it had to be, because how else would I be getting better? Helen had injected me with Angus's blood, which was the only reason I wasn't burning with fever and hallucinating that zombies were feasting on my body at this very moment. It was the only thing keeping me from turning.

When the infection had taken hold, my body had ached from head to toe, but now only a dull burn remained. The fever had disappeared, but I still felt worn out. It was impossible to keep my eyes open at times, and even though I didn't want to waste what could be some of the last hours of my life on sleep, it wasn't long before I had to give in.

Meg sat at my side, holding my hand like she was holding on for dear life. "Don't fight it," she said. "If you're exhausted, just go to sleep."

I tightened my grip on her hand, fighting to keep my eyes open. "I don't want to leave you."

"You're not going to." The tremor in her voice forced one of my eyes open, and I saw her swallow. "We are going to get the vaccine in time."

I wanted to believe her, but the never-ending ache in my body made it difficult.

She leaned down and pressed her lips against my forehead and whispered, "Sleep."

Even though I wanted to with every inch of my being, I found it impossible to fight the overwhelming exhaustion and finally gave in.

Hushed voices woke me an indiscernible amount of time later. I cracked one eye to find that I was in the same room I'd been in before, and still resting on the couch with a lumpy pillow under my head. It was so dark that at first I thought it was night, but then I shifted and saw a blanket covering the window. It was tacked against the walls with what looked like nails, and rays of sunlight peeked around the edges.

Whoever was talking, they were trying to keep their voices low. Something about the tone drew my attention, though. It was serious. Maybe even a little tortured.

"I can't bear thinking that he suffered, but I still need to know," said a woman whose voice I didn't recognize.

It felt wrong to eavesdrop, but I was still trying to figure out what was real and what wasn't, so I shifted my body, doing my best to be subtle about it so I didn't piss anybody off.

On the other side the room sat Helen and a woman I'd never met. She looked Indian, and had dark hair that was barely streaked in gray despite the worry lines creasing her forehead. Her eyes were dark and at the moment brimming with tears, but despite the emotion in them and the fact that she was small, something about her seemed tough.

"You can't unlearn some things," Helen whispered, her scratchy voice coming out louder than she probably intended.

"I know. But not knowing is a million times worse," the other woman said. "There's no peace, no closure. I can't shut my eyes at night without wondering what happened to him."

Helen let out a deep sigh, and then nodded. "Okay. If you think you can handle it."

"I have to."

"He was snooping around," Helen began, "his earlier suspicions had evaporated years ago. Maybe after Jane's death, or a short time later. It's impossible to know for sure. Star had him under surveillance, though. He had all of you under surveillance. After Axl disappeared, after he was brought to the CDC, Joshua started acting suspicious. I don't know exactly how Star found out because I'm only a nurse and my duties don't go much further than drawing blood and taking vitals, but I saw Joshua in the observation wing when I showed up to work that morning, locked in one of the rooms, and I knew. I knew it was over for him. I knew that he had pushed Star too far." I watched through cracked eyes as Helen reached over and covered the other woman's hand with one of her own. "I wanted to talk to him, I tried, but Star didn't give me a chance."

The Indian woman closed her eyes and let out a deep breath like she was bracing herself for what came next. "What happened?"

"Star injected Joshua with the most recent strain of the virus. It wasn't the first time he'd tested it, so he knew it would work fast. He chose that strain because he knew your husband would lose the ability to talk very quickly, giving the CDC an opportunity to spin their lies."

"It wasn't even four o'clock in the afternoon when they called and told me. He'd only been at work for seven hours, and yet he couldn't say a word when I went to tell him goodbye."

"I know," Helen said gently. "They did that on purpose. So you would buy the story they told you, or at least not have the opportunity to question it. If they allowed you to come to the CDC and say goodbye to your husband, it would draw suspicions away from them."

The other woman opened her eyes and focused on Helen. "When I went to see him, they told me that even though he couldn't talk, he could still understand me. Was that true?"

115

"It was," she said.

The other woman let out a deep sigh and closed her eyes. She looked like she was saying a prayer or gathering her strength, but it was impossible to know which one since I had no idea who she was, but something about this story was starting to sound familiar. Something about it had tickled a memory; only I couldn't quite grab hold of it yet.

"He looked so bad," the Indian woman whispered, her eyes still shut. "They had him on the bed, in a room like he was a regular patient. There were tubes running to his arms like they were trying to save him, but even then it made no sense because I knew there was nothing they could do. But he was also strapped down. He was tied to the bed like they were afraid he would attack anyone who came near. He tried to reach for me when I stopped at his side, but all he could do was lift his hand because his arm was tied down. I held his hand. His grip was strong, but his skin was like ice. It was gray, pale and lifeless-looking. His eyes were so wide, expressive even though I knew he couldn't talk or communicate, and I felt like he was trying to say *something* to me. The way he looked at me, the way he tried to sit up even though he was strapped down. And I just *knew*. I didn't need him to say the words because I knew just by looking at him that it had been no accident." She finally opened her eyes and met Helen's gaze. "I know where he ended up, I know about the fight and how he met his end, but that was two weeks later. Where was he for those two weeks? How long did it take him to turn? How long did he suffer?"

Suddenly, I knew who this woman was. She was Meg's aunt, the Judicial Officer of New Atlanta. Parvarti. I'd never met her before, never even laid eyes on her until now, but there was a reason this story sounded familiar. She and I had a connection she didn't even know about, because I was the person who had sent her husband to his final death.

When Jackson had the impossibly tall zombie sent into the ring, I'd thought it was a message for me, but it hadn't been. It had been for Meg. Still, I was the one who'd had to kill him. The one who'd retrieved his wedding ring before his body had been hauled away. Even though I knew, just like Parvarti did, that he had been beyond saving at that point, it didn't stop guilt from creeping up on me when I saw how devastating his death had been for this woman.

"I'm not going to lie," Helen said, "it was a brutal strain. I can't say with certainty how long he was consciously aware, but it took nearly two weeks for the virus to stop his heart."

Helen hesitated, and I could tell, just as I was sure the other woman could, that she was holding something back. I hadn't known the man, had never even met him when he was still a living person, but even I found myself holding my breath. Waiting to find out what horrors Helen had been witness to.

"He was in the observation wing that entire time," she finally said. "He had a bed in a temperature controlled room. I know it isn't much of a consolation, and I know it's hard to believe, but things could have been worse for him in the end."

She was lying. No, not lying, but sugarcoating the truth. Meg's aunt wasn't dumb and she no doubt knew the truth as well as I did, but she didn't call Helen out for lying.

"Thank you," she whispered instead.

I knew the woman sitting across the room had to be tough. She was small, but had risen in the ranks of enforcers to become the Judicial Officer of New Atlanta. She was a woman who'd seen pain, who had felt the ache of loss and come out stronger for it. But everyone had limits. No matter how strong a person was, they had a breaking point and this was obviously Parvarti's.

Helen patted her hand and nodded, "I've been wanting to tell you, I just had to wait for the right time."

Meg's aunt sniffed as she got to her feet. "I think I need to be alone."

"I understand." Parvarti left the room, but Helen was only quiet for a few seconds before saying, "I know you're awake."

I opened my eyes and found her heading my way. "I didn't want to bother you."

"I know." She knelt in front of me and put her hand on my forehead. "How do you feel?"

"Better." I sat up, forcing Helen to skitter back a little. "I'm not in as much pain."

"The fever's gone too." She got to her feet. "Meg went to get something to eat. She'll be back soon, I'm sure."

My stomach growled at the suggestion of food, which was a miracle considering how awful I'd felt earlier. I stood slowly, testing my limbs before heading into the other room. My legs had been shaky before, but they felt a hell of a lot steadier now.

"I might get something too."

"Even better," Helen said.

Meg wasn't the only one in the kitchen, but she was the only one who jumped to her feet when she saw me. "You're up! I shouldn't have left."

She hurried over to me, her face a mask of concern even though I was up and moving around.

"I'm okay, and you deserve to eat." I swallowed, hesitating before saying the next words because we still had a long road in front of us and I didn't want to get her hopes up. "I feel better."

Meg reached up to feel my cheeks just like Helen had, and the smile that spread across her face helped chase away some of my uncertainty. This was going to work out. I was going to be okay. Maybe if I said it to myself enough, I'd start to believe it.

# CHAPTER FOURTEEN
## Meg

The cigarette between Helen's lips bobbed when she talked, threatening to drop ash onto the map we were all leaning over, but no one seemed to care. "The most important thing will be getting the failsafe."

We were all crowded into the dining room at Bonnie and Max's house once again, fighting to get a look at the diagrams currently spread out on the table. Between Helen, Parv, Jim, Angus, and Jada, the air in the room had gone from stifling to toxic. A fog of smoke hung over us, thick like clouds right before a storm rolled in. Donaghy stood close to my side, and with each passing hour he seemed to be doing better and better, but I knew it was only temporary. Eventually, the virus would win out over the magic blood Helen had pumped into his body and the fever would return, but it seemed to have at least bought us some time. Which we desperately needed.

"But we're getting Margot and Axl first, right?" Mom pushed her blonde hair out of her face as she looked around, her eyes wide like she was terrified someone would argue with her.

"Yes," Jada said, answering for Helen.

"I hate to bring this up," Donaghy said, pausing to clear his throat when all eyes turned on him. "But when I left the CDC, Axl wasn't in his cell."

He glanced toward me and I gave his hand a squeeze. "I told them what you said."

He gave Mom a sympathetic frown. "I'm sorry."

She swallowed even as she reached out to pat his arm. "It's okay. We need to know."

Helen shook her head as she pushed the map across the table. "If he's not in his cell he'll be here, in the top secret medical wing." She tapped a room that was three halls away from the observation wing. "As long as he's stable though, Star won't keep him here long. It would mean moving the guards and changing the routine, which he hates." She glanced up and her blue eyes looked especially pale in the darkness of the room. "He's a man of habit."

"So we check the observation wing first?" Al asked.

"Stick with the plan," Jada agreed, looking around like she wanted to make sure everyone was listening. "If he isn't there, we'll get him on the way out. After the failsafe."

"After?" Mom shook her head and her brown eyes suddenly looked twice as large. "No. We need to get him to safety."

"We need to get the failsafe," Helen said softly.

Mom frowned, but before she could protest again, Angus reached out to her. "I'll get him. Don't you worry. Even if a few of us gotta stay behind, we'll get him out. Right?"

"Hell yeah," Al said. "Parv?"

Parv nodded, but her gaze was still focused on the layout of the CDC. "I won't leave until he's free."

It seemed like she'd only done two things since getting here: study the layout and smoke. It was like she was trying to memorize every nook and cranny even though we would have the map with us, and I found myself wondering if it had something to do with Joshua. If she was also staring at the drawings of the halls that were lined with cells and labs, wondering which one her husband had spent his final hours in.

"I gotta get the crossword puzzle I left behind." Angus practically pushed himself forward so he could tap his finger on a tiny square in that very same hall Parv was focused on, and I couldn't help staring at it, thinking about how small it was and how he'd spent nearly twenty years locked away in that little box.

"Crossword?" Lila asked, shoving a mass of dark hair that was streaked with gray out of her face.

Angus puckered his lips in a way that reminded me of Dad. "It's where I wrote down the code. I gotta have that book if we're gonna get to the failsafe Jane told me 'bout."

Parv's expression hardened at the mention of the woman's name. "Jane betrayed Star. What if he suspected that she told you the code? What if he changed it?"

"He didn't know nothin' 'bout us." Angus looked toward Helen for confirmation.

"Star assumed Jane's betrayal was all about her daughter. He had no idea she'd been sneaking around with Angus," she said. "It never would have occurred to him that she'd strayed that far from their plans."

"She did right in the end," Angus said firmly.

"Right," Parv muttered.

Jim ignored my aunt and said, "Once we have the code a small group will be in charge of getting Axl and Margot to safety."

Mom's head jerked up, her eyes focused on the zombie slayer. "I'm going with them."

"I thought you might want to." Jim nodded twice. "Once they're out, the rest of us can go for the failsafe."

"And the vaccine," I said.

I found my hand reaching for Donaghy's, holding it. His skin was clammy, but not hot. I knew the sweat was from the packed room and the Georgia humidity, which was impossible to escape this time of year, but I still found my hand sliding up his arm as if trying to reassure myself that he wasn't burning with fever once again. His muscles flexed under my palms and the memories of the last time we were together flipped through my mind. He'd just finished a fight and I'd gone to see him in the shower. I'd stripped down and joined him under the water, needing him and knowing that he needed me too. We'd resisted before for some reason that I now couldn't remember, but that day I'd found it impossible to hold back, and afterward I'd been glad we hadn't waited. I just hoped we'd have a chance to be together again before heading to Atlanta.

Helen's intensely blue eyes locked on mine, and she actually took the time to pull the cigarette out of her mouth so she could say, "The vaccine will be the last thing we worry about. I'm sorry, but this could be our only chance to get the failsafe and we can't risk it. Not after twenty years."

I started to protest, to point out that we could split up, but Donaghy stopped me by saying, "We get the failsafe first. No question."

Helen nodded once before turning back to the diagrams. This time she moved the top one aside, the one that featured the holding cells and secret labs, revealing a different map of a different floor.

"Biosafety Level four." She tapped her finger against the paper twice. "It used to be reserved for viruses like Ebola and Lassa, and they're still sitting in there, but Star also uses it to store the different strains of the virus he's created, as well as the vaccines that go along with them. The failsafe is there, too."

A hush fell over the room that I didn't understand completely, but instinctively knew had something to do with the other viruses Helen had named. I'd never heard of them, but I could tell by the somber expressions on the adults' faces that they had.

"Are these other viruses deadly?" I asked.

The cigarette was back in Helen's mouth when she nodded, and this time ash did drop to the map. It landed on top of the lab, right on Biosafety Level four. "The viruses in this lab were the deadliest ones known to man. At least they were until Star put his twisted plan into motion. Going in there is dangerous and you're going to need a lot of backup," she continued, "It's going to take some time to get in there."

We all listened as she explained the protocol. Putting on a positive-pressure, air-supplied body suit, how it would attach to a tube once inside the room that could feed it with oxygen pumped in from a separate source. How whoever went inside had to enter and exit through an air-locked room to ensure that nothing deadly could escape.

"Only two people should go in," Helen looked around at everyone standing in front of her. "I'll be one, but I'll want a second set of eyes while I'm in there."

"I'll go," Parv said as she reached up to push her dark hair back out of her face.

"Perfect."

Helen's expression said she thought it was a good choice, but there was something else there too. A look that said she was thinking about my aunt's dead husband. Donaghy told me what he'd overheard, and it felt like the reality of what had happened to Joshua was weighing on Helen.

She cleared her throat and turned her eyes back to the map. "While we're in there, we're going to need everyone else to stand guard. We can't be rushed or we could accidentally release something just as deadly as the original virus was."

A few people had slipped into the room while we talked. Two men from the town, only one of which I recognized. He was in his forties and so average looking that he would be entirely forgettable in this settlement of tattooed and pierced people if it wasn't for the fact that he was missing his left hand. The day before I'd heard this very man and Al swapping horror stories about the day they'd been bitten, and the terror of getting a limb unceremoniously amputated. Just thinking about it made me shiver, but for them it had been so long ago that the conversation had come across as almost mundane, if not a little humorous at times. Which was normal for Al.

The other man who'd come in was burly, also in his forties, and had a face full of brown wiry hair and arms covered in tattoos that were so faded that it was obvious they'd been there well before the virus had shown up.

The third person was a woman, and when she settled in next to Luke I stood on my tiptoes, trying to get a good look at her. She was only a year or two older than me, but like Jada was covered in tattoos and piercings. Her raven black hair had been shaved down to the scalp on the right side of her head, but on the left side it was about four inches long and sat flat against her head. As I watched, her blue eyes flitted up to Luke's face and she stood on her tiptoes, her hand resting on his arm as she said something to him. Her lips were so close to his ear that it almost looked like they were kissing. This had to be the woman he'd been seeing, and I wasn't the only one whose interest had been piqued by her sudden appearance. My aunt's gaze zeroed in on them as well.

"How many people do you need standing guard while you're in the room?" Mom asked.

"As many as we can get," Helen said.

123

She exchanged a look with Dragon, who wore an expression on his face I'd never seen before. A somber one. One that said this could be a suicide mission.

"Everyone needs to be prepared," Jim said, as if echoing my thoughts. "We have a solid plan, but this is the CDC. Not everyone is going to make it out of this alive, so the more people we have, the better off we'll be when one or two of us get taken out."

*Taken out.* He meant killed, but he acted like he couldn't quite say the words.

"Who's willing to go in with us?" Jada asked.

"I'm going," Al said.

"Me," Luke agreed.

"I'll be there," Mom said, "but I'll be leaving with Margot and Axl."

"You stay with them." The tone Helen used was the one she usually reserved for Glitter, and it made her scratchy voice sound soothing and almost grandmotherly. "They're going to need you."

Dragon said he was obviously going, as did Angus, who insisted we needed his knowledge of the CDC, which was insane considering he had rarely left his room over the last twenty years. Honestly, I was pretty sure he was just hoping to run into Star and get some payback, which no one could blame him for.

Aunt Lila tried to volunteer, but Al insisted she stay behind so Mom had some support when she came back with Dad and Margot, which made my aunt scowl even though she agreed. Charlie said nothing, but I wasn't sure if her unwillingness to volunteer had to do with being afraid or something else. Maybe she felt inadequate. I couldn't blame her. Even after my little training session outside the walls I felt pretty useless in comparison to Jada and the other people from this town. I knew I had good aim, but there was no way to deny that the zombie slayers were a hell of a lot more prepared for this than I was.

"Britt, Tony, and Kelly are going to be joining us too," Jada said, nodding to the three people from Senoia who'd just joined us.

I saw both Charlie and Aunt Lila's gaze move over the woman, Kelly, and I could tell by the way he shifted that Luke saw it too. He was going to get bombarded with questions. There was no escaping it now.

"We already have people driving around the outskirts of old Atlanta collecting zombies in a truck, right?" Jim asked, glancing toward Jada.

"Max headed out with a group a little bit ago," she replied. "They're taking care of getting the bomb set up too. If charges aren't set on that wall already, they will be soon. Tomorrow, once the sun has gone down and the festival is underway, they'll start luring even more zombies toward the wall."

"Good." Jim nodded as he spoke, almost like he was checking things off on a list.

"And that's pretty much all we can plan for now," Helen said. "My contact will meet us at ten and hopefully everything will go as expected."

My back stiffened. "What about the vaccine?"

As far as I was concerned, they'd left a very important part out: where the vaccine was.

"That will be in the same lab as the failsafe." Helen straightened, her gaze focused on me. "There won't be any syringes there, but we'll get one as soon as we can. On the way out we'll pass dozens of labs that have them. We're going to need to give the vaccine time to work its way through Donaghy's system before we can release the bacteria, though. An hour probably."

"Why?" I found myself asking.

"What happens if we don't wait long enough?" Mom piped in.

Helen frowned, hesitating before saying, "It will kill him too."

Ice coated my veins and next to me Donaghy seemed to turn to stone. I looked up at him. It seemed unbelievable that something so small could take out the man at my side. He was big and broad, and didn't just tower over me, but over most of the people in this room.

"But he's still alive," I managed to get out. "Will it really attack his brain even though his heart is still beating?"

"It isn't necessarily the brain that's being attacked," Helen said. "It's the virus living in the brain. The brain is just destroyed in the process. When they created the bacteria, there was no need to try and preserve the brain, so they didn't worry about it."

I trembled and found myself holding onto Donaghy for support. "Then we'll wait a couple hours. We need to be sure the vaccine has worked."

"Thanks." Donaghy squeezed my hand like he was trying to support me, but his tone was light and I knew he was trying to come across as unconcerned. It didn't hide the worry in his expression or ease the fear swirling through me. "I'd really like it if my brain didn't get eaten away."

I wasn't really in the joking mood, so I just nodded.

The meeting broke up, and while most people filed out of the room, Lila and Charlie hurried to Luke, ready to pounce just like I'd thought they would. My brain was swirling with plans and concerns for the safety of my family still stuck inside the CDC, as well as the bomb Helen had just dropped on us about how the failsafe could very well take Donaghy down too, but even I found myself moving toward my cousin. Despite everything else going on, I was curious about the woman Luke had been seeing.

"This is Kelly," he was saying as I stopped behind Lila and Charlie

Luke's brown eyes looked past his Mom and sister to me, and the pleading in them was almost comical.

"Nice to meet you, Kelly," my aunt said. "Are you a zombie slayer too?"

The woman laughed and went on to explain how she had no problem killing zombies, but that she had never set foot inside the walls of New Atlanta. Unlike Luke, she seemed totally at ease. Even under Charlie's piercing gaze.

"What's all this?" Al said in a booming voice as he came up to join the rest of his family.

"Luke has a girlfriend," Charlie said, earning her a glare from her brother.

"Kelly." She stuck her hand out to my Uncle Al, not even blinking when he offered her his stump instead of his hand. "I've heard a lot about all of you."

"Funny," Lila said, giving her son a look. "My son hasn't mentioned you once. It's like he's trying to keep secrets from me or something."

"Maybe he's embarrassed by us," Al said, grinning.

Luke rolled his eyes. "I wasn't until now."

"So you've lived *here* your whole life?" Charlie asked.

"I have," Kelly replied, still not the least bit upset by the people surrounding her.

I almost laughed, but also understood how Luke felt. Since Donaghy had reappeared Mom had been hovering around him the way a fly does a pile of trash. Not that I could do anything to save Luke from the interrogation he was about to get.

*Sorry*, I mouthed and gave him a sympathetic smile.

He rolled his eyes, but the more Kelly talked, the more relaxed he looked. She could hold her own, I had to say that much for her.

I left them to their grilling, turning to find Donaghy waiting for me. It seemed like an insane urge in the midst of everything else happening, but I couldn't wait to be alone with him. Maybe it was the knowledge that he could slip back into a fevered state at any moment, or the realization that even if we got our hands on the vaccine he might not make it. We had no real way of knowing how much time we would need to wait to make sure he was safe from the bacteria that would wipe out the zombies. Or if any amount of time would help him.

"Still feeling okay?" I asked him.

He nodded as he took my hand. "I'm okay. Tired, but nothing like before."

"Good," I said.

Darkness was closing in, so I pulled him through the house, heading for the stairs. The room I'd occupied the night before was small, but the bed was big enough for two and I felt almost like it was calling out to us.

I'd just started to ascend the stairs when Helen grabbed my forearm, her bony fingers surprisingly strong and her expression sharp. "What are you doing?"

Heat flamed across my cheeks before I could stop it. Donaghy was at my side, his feet at the bottom of the stairs that would lead us to privacy, and I had no doubt that Helen had guessed what was about to happen.

Before I could answer, her fingers tightened on my arm. "You know you can't, right?"

The heat that had warmed my cheeks turned to ice and seemed to melt down my body. "What?"

I knew what she was saying, but it hadn't occurred to me until now. It was a part of the infection I'd never considered: that the virus could be spread through sexual contact.

"The chance of transmitting it that way is slim, but it's still there." Helen's gaze moved to Donaghy. "Don't even kiss her. Don't risk it."

Her fingers were still digging into my arm, but I didn't even feel it anymore. I was too focused on Donaghy and the regret moving through me. We wouldn't even be able to have a real goodbye. Even if I was willing to risk it, which I wasn't, I knew he wouldn't put me in danger like that.

"I won't," he said, affirming what I already knew.

His words freed my arm from Helen's grip.

"I'm sorry," she said.

"Me too," Donaghy replied.

After that our trek up the stairs was somber. My legs felt heavy, but not as heavy as my heart. I shouldn't have felt this way. Donaghy had been injected with the zombie virus and I knew, had always known, what that meant. I must have allowed his remission and our plans to recover the vaccine to blind me to what was really going on, but Helen's warning had brought reality into sudden and horrifying focus.

We didn't say a word until we'd reached the room and the door was shut. Even then I found it difficult to know what to say. He did too apparently, because he wrapped me in his arms without uttering a word.

I rested my face against his chest and closed my eyes, focusing on how strong he felt right now instead of what could happen to him. I didn't want to think about how just a few hours ago he'd been burning with fever and writhing in agony. I didn't want to acknowledge that it could happen again very soon.

"When this is over," he finally said, his lips pressed against my head and his breath hot on my scalp. "I want to start a life. A real life."

*A real life.* It seemed intangible right now with so many things that could still go wrong, so many pitfalls that could swallow us up if we didn't do everything right. But I wanted to believe that we could make it happen, and that it would all play out the way we hoped it would. That we'd free Dad and Margot, that their time in the CDC, as well as my uncle's, wouldn't have damaged them too much. I wanted to be able to picture a future where we could be a family, where we could live in a zombie-free world. Happy. Hopeful. Free.

"I want that too," I said, my eyes still closed and my mind grasping for a picture of the life I wanted, working hard to conjure it up even though it felt impossibly out of reach at the moment.

"I know we just met—" He loosened his arms so I could lift my head and look him in the eye. "—but there are some things in this world that you just *know*. And I know that I want you."

I thought about Mom and Dad, and how they'd met. How fast they'd fallen in love. Donaghy was right. If it hadn't been for my parents I might not have trusted these feelings, but I'd witnessed what *real* love was my whole life, and while I wasn't ready to use that word, I knew that this man had the capacity to make it happen more than anyone else I'd ever known. Even more than Colton had.

"I want you too," I told Donaghy.

He held my gaze, his eyes telling me that he wanted to kiss me more than he'd ever wanted anything. I knew he wouldn't, but I found myself holding my breath anyway.

When he pressed his lips against my forehead, I closed my eyes and let the intimacy of the moment sweep over me. I'd never felt closer to a person than I did right now. Never felt like anyone held a part of me the way he did. It was exhilarating and terrifying at the same time. I loved it, loved being in his arms and being vulnerable to him, but it was also scary because I knew it could all come to an end very soon. I'd lost a boyfriend before, and I knew what it felt like to grieve for someone you'd thought was going to be a permanent fixture in your life. The thought of having to do that again, and with someone I felt such a strong connection with, nearly took my breath away.

"How are you feeling?" I asked.

The thought of losing him had brought back all my fears about the virus and if we'd have time to get him a vaccine, so I opened my eyes and pressed my right hand against his forehead. His skin was cool against mine, but I didn't trust myself, so I moved my hand down to his cheek.

"I'm fine," he said, covering my hand with his. "I can feel the virus working through me still, but it's less intense than it was."

My heart skipped a beat. "You can feel it?"

He moved my hand so it was on his chest, his resting on top of mine. His heart thumped against my palm, and even though I was pretty sure he was doing it to calm me down, it had the opposite effect. I could almost picture the virus spreading through him with every beat of his heart, taking over his body more and more until it would very soon consume him, turning him into something grotesque.

"I'm okay right now," he whispered.

I swallowed the tears that had lodged themselves in my throat. "Does it hurt?"

"Not right now."

Which meant it had, and it would again very soon.

# CHAPTER FIFTEEN
## Donaghy

It crept up on me slowly, the ache that had faded away after the blood transfusion. It wasn't as intense as it had been, but it was there, a burning in my bones, the sensation that my blood was heating up. Meg was asleep next me on the bed, her body pressed against mine. I wanted to reach out and stroke her head, but I didn't because I didn't want to wake her, so instead I just watched her sleep while I tried to decide what to do. If I told the others that the virus was winning, they might not let me go. Staying here meant I might not get the vaccine in time, but going could put them at risk. I could turn while we were out there and attack someone. Kill someone. I could destroy everything.

I needed to tell them.

I slipped out of bed quietly, leaving Meg to sleep. I'd fill her in on what was happening — people had kept enough secrets from her and I wasn't about to jump on that bandwagon — but I wanted to talk to the others first. To Dragon and Helen mainly, because I knew them better than everyone else and I knew they'd be straight with me.

The hall was dark, but light shone up the stairs from the first floor, telling me that someone was up. Whoever it was, I hoped they'd know where everyone had settled in for the night. The last thing I wanted to do was tiptoe through a dark house looking for Dragon, but I would if I had to.

It turned out that I didn't have to, though. He was up, along with Helen and a bunch of other people, including Meg's mom. They were gathered in the kitchen talking and didn't seem to notice me when I approached, too caught up in their conversation.

"So it's been there all along?" Mom asked.

Helen nodded, a cigarette between her lips as usual. She looked exhausted in the dim light of the kitchen, older too. She'd always looked like a woman who'd spent too many hours in the sun, but at the moment she had dark circles under her eyes as well, like she hadn't gotten enough sleep over the last few weeks.

Helen turned her head and blew the smoke behind her even though it didn't matter; the kitchen was full of it. "Star created it before this thing was ever released. At least that's what Jane told me."

"And you trusted her?" Parvarti asked.

Helen shrugged and nodded at the same time. "Yes, as much as it pains me to say it. Jane was as cold as stone when I met her, totally dedicated to her work, but somewhere along the way she changed, and the woman she was by the end..." She shrugged again. "I can't explain it, I just know what I saw."

"I don't believe it," Parvarti spit out. "People don't change."

"You changed," Angus pointed out. "I like to think I changed too, even if I can still be a pain in the ass."

Meg's mom put her hand on top of his. "Some things will never change."

"Doesn't matter," Parvarti replied. "I can't believe she changed enough to make me trust the things she told you."

"That's understandable," Helen said, and then looked at Angus. "But I know why she changed and I also know she hated herself a little bit for it. She fell in love."

All eyes were on Angus, who was staring at the table like he couldn't bring himself to meet anyone's gaze. His shoulders were slumped, and the expression on his face illustrated the pain all these memories had brought up.

"How does it work?" Lila asked, as if she wanted to change the subject.

"It attacks the virus living in the zombie's brain, destroying it and the brain in the process. Humans can be carriers, which will help spread it faster, but it doesn't affect them at all. At least that's what Jane told me." Helen shrugged for the third time. "Whether or not you choose to believe that is up to you."

Heat moved up my arm and I clenched my hand into a fist, shifting my feet in the process. The floor creaked under me, and everyone turned to look my way.

"Sorry," I mumbled. "I didn't mean to interrupt."

Helen frowned as she took me in. "You feeling okay?"

I shook my head. "I'm not."

She got to her feet, already motioning to the hall at my back. "Go to the living room and sit down. Let me look you over."

I did as I was told, hating the way my joints ached with each step. It was a hell of a lot more muted than it had been before, and I hoped to God it stayed that way, but I couldn't deny that the symptoms were returning.

When I'd taken a seat on the couch, Helen knelt in front of me. "It's coming back?"

"It just started, but I can feel it again. Not as strong, but still present."

Vivian and Angus had come into the room behind Helen, and Dragon too, but everyone else had stayed in the kitchen.

"This is normal," Helen said. "The symptoms should feel muted for a while still, but you have to let us know if it changes. If you feel like you're changing."

"How?" Vivian asked.

When I lifted my gaze to hers, I found her brown eyes filled with worry and I understood why. I'd been alone in a room with her daughter. I was putting her only truly safe family member in jeopardy just by being with her.

Helen let out a deep sigh. "I don't know specifically since I've never been infected, but this is what I've been told. You start to feel like you're slipping away. Like you're observing everything instead of participating. Then, as the virus takes over more of your brain, you start to feel an overwhelming hunger. It's different than a normal hunger though, more intense."

Vivian stepped forward. "He can't come to New Atlanta with us."

Behind her, Angus and Dragon listened silently, Meg's uncle still smoking while her former boss just stood and watched.

Helen stood and faced Vivian. "You know what that will mean, don't you? If he doesn't go he won't get the vaccine in time."

"If he does go he could attack someone," Vivian said firmly.

Angus scoffed. "Don't sound like you, Blondie. Wasn't you the one who was always running off to save somebody you didn't know?" He nodded at me. "You know this boy. Even more, your daughter's in love with him."

My shoulders stiffened at the words I'd found myself thinking dozens of times but had never managed to force out. Did everyone know how I felt? Did Meg?

"You gonna leave him here to die?" Angus narrowed his eyes on Meg's mom, and then shook his head. "You and me both know that ain't how this is goin' down, so don't pretend."

Vivian let her gaze drop to the floor, her expression torn. "I just want everyone I love to be okay."

"Then you gotta let him go. If you fight this, Meg'll never forgive you."

Vivian lifted her head so she was looking at me. "You tell us if something changes. Right away. Understand?"

"I won't put her in danger," I said. "Ever."

Vivian nodded, but it seemed to be for her own benefit more than mine. Then she turned and walked back into the kitchen, leaving me with Helen, Dragon, and Angus.

"You need me to put a bullet in your brain, you just say the word," Angus said. "It's been twenty years since I killed a man and I never planned on doin' it again except to take Star out, but I ain't gonna let nobody suffer neither. I seen too much of that in my life."

"I will," I assured him. "I promise."

"That's good 'nough for me," he said, and then headed back into the kitchen with Vivian.

"Right now the only thing you can do is sleep," Helen said. "I wish I had a miracle cure, but unfortunately, all of those are locked inside the CDC."

"We'll get it, though," Dragon said.

I stood. "I hope so."

Meg was still asleep when I made it back upstairs, so I crawled into bed next to her and tried to get some rest too. It was impossible, though. My mind was spinning in circles, my thoughts swirling around impossibly fast and going over everything that needed to happen and everything that could go wrong.

Axl might not be in his cell.

Jackson could be waiting with a trap.

Helen could be a CDC spy out to lure us inside.

Jane could have been lying about the failsafe.

We might not get the vaccine in time to save me.

I might kill Meg.

The failsafe could destroy my brain.

There were too many possibilities, which made it impossible to relax, and the longer I lay in bed, the more the ache inside me increased. It was still nothing like it had been before, and I wasn't delirious either, but it was there and it wasn't going to go away until we had the vaccine.

Dawn came, the sun rising outside and eventually penetrating the thin curtains that covered the window. In the early morning light I was able to stare at Meg, to memorize her face, her body, and the feel of her next to me. Then my brain moved on from all the horrors of the world to the miraculous few moments we'd spent together. On the cot in the back of Dragon's stinking bar, her body under mine as we kissed and explored one another. In the shower, both of us naked under the cold stream of water. I remembered how she'd felt in my grasp, how small she'd seemed when I'd lifted her, how close we'd been when she'd wrapped her legs around my waist. I wanted that again, to be close to her, to explore her body.

She woke slowly, shifting so she could stretch, and her eyes flew open when her hip brushed against me. "Good morning," she said, lifting her eyebrows. "Good dreams?"

"I didn't sleep," I said, scooting closer and pulling her small body against mine. "I couldn't, not when all I could think about was you."

"Don't torture yourself," she said. "You know we can't risk it, as much as I want to."

"There are other things we can do," I whispered.

I pressed my lips against her neck, and then moved them down to her chest. The tank top she wore was cut low and thin, making it easy to caress her skin through the fabric. I ran my tongue across her chest, right over the swell of her breasts that barely peaked out above the neckline of her shirt. She shivered under me and I moved my mouth lower, kissing the soft skin of her breasts through her tank top while pushing the hem up. Then my lips moved lower, down to her bare stomach before making my way back up, following her shirt as I pulled it higher. It was over her head in seconds, and then she was naked in front of me except a pair of black cotton panties. I cupped her breasts and ran my tongue between them. Her nipples were hard points, and when I flicked my thumbs across them, I was rewarded with a gasp of pleasure.

I looked up, meeting her gaze to find her watching me as I dragged my tongue across her breast to her nipple. She sucked her bottom lip into her mouth, sinking her teeth into it in anticipation. Waiting. Begging. I closed my mouth over her nipple and sucked it into my mouth, and she let out a low moan that went straight to my groin. She grasped my head between her hands as I teased her, her fingers threading through my hair and pulling me closer. The way she squirmed told me she was as excited as I was, so I took the hint and ran my fingers down her body and over her thigh, not stopping until I'd almost reached her knee. Then I moved them back up, this time over her inner thigh.

"Donaghy," she gasped out my name. "I want you. You won't infect me."

"It's not happening," I said. "But this is."

I pushed the fabric of her underwear aside so I could slide my finger into her. She gasped once, and then a second time when I closed my lips over her nipple again.

"Don't," she moaned. "Don't stop."

I didn't, but not because she begged me to keep going, but because I wanted to. I wanted to kiss and feel every inch of her, to make her beg for more. Not just now, but for the rest of our lives.

I moved my lips up her neck, wanting so badly to devour her lips but holding back as I teased her with my fingers. Every gasp, every moan she let out sent a jolt through me. I moved my hand faster, paying close attention to her body's cues, and it wasn't long before she was holding onto me while she gasped out her pleasure, her body quaking around my fingers.

My heart was racing by then, and from out of nowhere pain spread through me that I didn't understand. It was like lava in my veins, like a fire spreading through me. Meg was still coming down from her orgasm, but I was suddenly paralyzed by fear. I'd gotten swept up in my lust, had taken for granted that Angus's blood had bought me time, but the sudden pain coursing through my body brought everything into sharp and startling focus. I was risking too much, pushing my luck too much, and putting Meg in danger in the process.

She reached for my pants, but I pushed her hand back, my eyes still closed. "No."

"I want to," she whispered.

I wanted it, so much, but the ache in my body had gotten worse and I was finding it difficult to sit still. "I can't."

Meg pulled back and I finally opened my eyes to find her staring down at me. "Why? What's wrong?"

"It's back. The pain." I shook my head, afraid to say the words but even more afraid to stay here with her a moment longer.

"No," she said. She put her hands on my face so she could look me in the eye. "No. You have to hang on. We still have hours until we can get the vaccine."

The fire that had spread through began to subside, but I had to swallow before I could speak. "I'll be okay. It's—it's not as bad as it was. I can make it."

Tears filled her eyes and she pressed her face into the crook of my neck. "I just want all of us to get out of this safely."

"Me too," I said, clinging to her even as I told myself I needed to leave. "That's what I want too."

# CHAPTER SIXTEEN
## Meg

By the time Donaghy and I dragged ourselves downstairs, the house was a whirlwind of activity. We still had hours before we left for the safe house, but everyone who was going with us was busy getting ready for the trip, and even a handful of people who weren't. Extra leather had been brought in so we'd all be covered, as well as guns and knives. The dining room table was overflowing with the stuff.

Donaghy sat in the corner, away from everyone. He was in pain still, I could tell by the expression on his face even though he tried to downplay it, and he acted like he didn't trust himself to be around anyone. I sorted through the stuff on the table even though I still had the leather I'd borrowed from Jada and a gun, looking for anything else I might need, but I was keeping an eye on him at the same time, so I saw it when Helen knelt in front of him.

Their conversation was too low for me to hear over the hum of voices filling the room, but I watched as she took his vitals, checked his pulse, his temperature, even listened to his breathing with a stethoscope like this was a doctor's office. She nodded before standing, and even though it was impossible to know what they'd said to each other, I felt like it was an indication that everything was going to be okay. Or maybe I was trying to convince myself.

I stopped Helen before she left the room. "He's okay?"

"For now." She twisted the stethoscope in her hands, rolling it into a loop. "He knows the signs, but it could come on quickly, so you need keep an eye on him."

"What am I looking for?"

Helen pressed her lips together before saying, "If he's not acting like himself."

I swallowed when her meaning hit me. "You mean if he's staring at me like he's considering taking a bite out of me?"

She didn't even blink when she said, "Yes."

Fear gripped me, but I pushed it down and told myself we could do this. We had time. Angus's blood had given us time.

WE WERE ALL DECKED OUT IN LEATHER NOW. EVEN Donaghy, who seemed to be hanging on despite the pain. I'd expected some pushback about the idea of him coming, but no one said a word. Not that it mattered; I would have fought any decision to leave him behind. I wanted to be able to inject him with the vaccine the second I got my hands on it. The sooner he got it, the sooner we'd be able to release the brain-eating bacteria that would hopefully wipe out the zombies once and for all.

The mood was even more tense than it had been before. No one spoke, not even Jada and Jim who didn't look the least bit nervous but whose silence indicated that they were more on edge than they were letting on. As for the rest of us, we all seemed to find it impossible to hide the nerves buzzing through us. Mom was chewing on her bottom lip like crazy, and at her side my Uncle Angus seemed to find it impossible to stand still. Even Parv, who I'd always thought of as the least emotional person I'd ever met, was showing cracks in her normally calm exterior.

"Everyone know their jobs?" Jim asked as he hooked a knife to his belt.

Around the room, everyone nodded.

"Good." Jada reached back and pulled her dreads into a ponytail, reminding me that I needed to do the same thing with my own hair. "We're taking two vehicles, that way Vivian will be able to get Margot and Axl to safety when we get them out. For now, ride wherever you want to." She started to head to the door, but was stopped by Bonnie, who grabbed her hand on the way by. Jada's gaze held her adoptive mother's for a moment before she said, "Take a moment to say your goodbyes."

Lila reached out to Mom and gave her hand a squeeze.

"See you soon," my aunt whispered. Then she turned to Luke and pulled him into a hug. "Be careful out there."

"I will," he told her.

When he stepped back, Lila shook her head as she wiped at the tears in her eyes. Her gaze moved to Kelly, who was standing at Luke's side. "Watch out for him."

"I promise," Kelly replied.

Charlie hugged Luke next, and then did the same with her father. When she stepped away, there were tears in her eyes. She wrapped her arms around her chest like she was trying to keep herself together.

Lila and Al's hug was longer, and so intimate that it almost made me feel like I was intruding.

"Bring our son back in one piece," she said.

"He'll be fine."

Lila pulled back so she could look up at her husband. "And don't you leave me, understand? I'm not ready for that."

Al kissed her gently and whispered, "I plan on being old and gray by the time I leave this planet."

"I'm going to hold you to that," Lila said.

At the back of the group, I saw my Uncle Angus hug Glitter.

"I'm afraid I'll never see you again," she said as she pressed her face against his chest. "I want to go too."

"If you're there, I won't be able to focus. I'll be too worried 'bout what's happenin' to you." He closed his eyes like the thought of her getting captured physically hurt him. "Don't you worry 'bout me. I ain't gonna let them take me out now."

"You promise?" she said.

"I promise."

Her face was streaked with tears when she said goodbye to Dragon and then to Helen, the woman who had raised her since birth. The four of them stood together for a few minutes, talking quietly. They were an odd little family, one created by this crazy world we lived in, one forced together by Star and his sick plan to dominate the world, but they were a family and it was obvious that they loved each other.

A few other goodbyes were said, Britt and Tony both had family to see them off, and then we all headed out.

It was early evening and the sun was low, giving us a couple hours until it was full dark. The safe house was a few streets away from the wall, but close enough that our headlights could be spotted in the total darkness that had taken over old Atlanta, so we wanted to move in while it was still light out. It would take about an hour to get there from Senoia, and then we'd have to wait until after the sun had set completely to head to Dragon's where there would be even more waiting. We couldn't make our move until the city had converged on the square for the festival or we risked being spotted.

I sat in the back of the same truck I'd ridden in on the way to Senoia, this time feeling less in the dark but probably even more terrified than I had before. Beside me, Donaghy seemed to be made of stone. His body was tense from the pain coursing through him, and added to that was the worry that he might turn and hurt someone, which I was sure made it impossible for him to relax.

There was nothing I could do to help him other than hold his hand. Having him with me had been a comfort back when I'd been uncertain about where my dad was and if my mom would ever snap out of it, and I could only hope that the support of having me at his side was in some way a comfort to him.

The drive seemed to take no time at all, and when we rolled into old Atlanta, the sky had just begun to darken. We parked down the street from the safe house in a driveway so obscured by bushes and weeds that the branches scraped against the sides of the truck. When we stopped, the thick greenery made it impossible to see out onto the street.

We climbed out, careful to be quiet so we didn't draw too much attention from the dead that now ruled this city. The sound of the truck's engine had no doubt drawn some of them this way already, so before I'd even set foot on the ground I had my knife out, as did everyone else.

"Keep your eyes and ears open," Luke said.

He was the only zombie slayer with us at the moment since Jim had driven one truck and Jada the other, but we were quickly joined by the rest of our group. Once we were together again, we headed out, pushing past the branches that concealed us until we found the street. Like every other road in the old world, it was covered with debris and had weeds sprouting from the cracks.

I sniffed as we walked. Old Atlanta smelled like a totally different world than the city inside the walls, and it had nothing to do with the stench of death. Inside, the air was ripe with human misery. The stink of poverty, the smell of hopelessness, the odor of waste that coated the people who'd long ago given their lives over to drugs and booze. But out here the air was fresh as long as none of the dead were around, and the smells of nature called out to me as we walked, telling me that there was a better alternative to what New Atlanta had to offer.

It had been like this in Senoia, too. The settlement was thick with the smells of life—cooking meat and fires burning into the night—but had also had moments when nature was the most prevalent scent. The air there was fresh and clean, and not tainted by the hard life the people in New Atlanta knew. The inhabitants of the unsanctioned town may have worn scars on their skin that illustrated how brutal their existence could be, but the marks also branded them as free. Free to roam the world as they saw fit, free to leave the walls when duty called, free to take care of their families in the ways that they wanted to instead of the ways that were dictated to them by the government.

These were the thoughts going through my head when a breeze blew and we were suddenly engulfed by the scent of death. Jim and Jada, who were leading us through the city, didn't slow, but I noticed that the steps of those around me did falter a little. No one stopped, and since we were all already armed and ready there was no need for anyone to pull a weapon, but the eyes of everyone surrounding me began to sweep the area.

There was nothing for us to see but the shells of old houses and the rusted skeletons of cars. Weeds and other plants that had long ago grown out of control covered everything, making the world a sea of green. Anything could be hidden in their emerald depths. The dead or feral animals just waiting to attack, or even raiders who had taken cover in the middle of scavenging when they'd heard our approach.

The unknown had my heart racing, but despite that my opinion of this world hadn't changed. This was a life. Out here people were able to fight for themselves away from the confines of a corrupt government. This was a world that forced people to be strong or die, but one that was also ripe with possibilities.

"Just keep moving," Jada said, her husky voice barely over a whisper.

As usual, I was impressed by her ability to stay so calm and in control.

We reached the safe house without any trouble, although I did catch sight of a few figures shambling down the street in the swiftly fading light.

I could see into the house through the gaping holes that had once been windows. The main floor had been stripped bare, freed of everything useful years ago, and I had no doubt that the second floor was equally naked. I didn't get to find out though, because we didn't go inside but instead pushed past the overgrown bushes and made our way into the backyard. Once there Jim and Jada worked together to move a moldy, old mattress, revealing a cellar door.

The hinges screeched through the silence when the door was pulled open, revealing stairs that disappeared into a dark abyss. Jim walked down without hesitation, and seconds later a light flickered on, flooding the stairwell with light.

"In here," Jada said, waving for us to follow Jim as he continued into the basement.

We shuffled down in a mass, so close that the air was stifling despite the chill of the basement. Below us more lights flickered on as the sound of Jim's footsteps echoed through the room.

Jada had told us that the basement was only used in the most severe situations, like when someone got cornered and couldn't make it out of the city, and when we made it to the bottom of the stairs I could see why. It was a hole. Rugs had been spread out on the floor that were damp from years of moisture leaking into the space, and the walls were splotched with mold. Cobwebs and bugs had taken over every corner, and the only furniture was a handful of wooden chairs.

Since people who were about to reverse a two decade old apocalypse couldn't really complain about where they hid from

144

zombies, I settled onto the floor with Donaghy and tried not to think about the toxins we were breathing in. He was shivering, but his skin was only slightly warmer than usual, nothing like it had been before, and I found myself praying that the fever would hold off long enough for us to get into the CDC. If he was delirious, we'd have to leave him behind.

"Can we try doing a second blood transfusion?" I asked Helen when the nurse paused to feel Donaghy's head.

She shook her head. "It did nothing when they tried it. Sorry."

I believed her, but it gave me no comfort.

"Come here," I told Donaghy, patting my lap.

The big man laid his head on my legs like he was a small child, and I stroked his soft hair. The dark fibers tickled my palms and he let out a sigh, and I found myself wishing we'd had more time to be alone before leaving Senoia. Not that we could have done much more than we already had, but at least I would have been able to pretend that all this shit wasn't really happening. It was impossible now.

"You shouldn't have turned me down that day in your room," I whispered as I ran my fingers across his head, remembering the first time we'd kissed in the back room of Dragon's Lair.

His icy blue eyes, which had looked so cold and unemotional when we'd first met, now seemed to swim with feeling. "You know it's not because I didn't want you."

"I know." I leaned closer so I could press my lips to his cheek, right next to his mouth. "When all of this is over, you have to promise that we'll spend an entire day in bed."

I wanted him to nod or tease me or say something to lighten the mood surrounding us, but he didn't. Instead, he continued to stare up at me, his gaze intense as he studied me.

"You know I might not make it." I started to shake my head, to get angry, but he put his hand on my cheek and stopped me. "It's true, and I want to acknowledge that so I can say this. I'm glad I came here. Glad I met you. It's a hard thing to wrap my brain around when I know Patty is dead because of it, but it's true."

I could hear the confession in his words, written between the lines like a secret neither one of us wanted to spill. *I love you.* It seemed impossible considering we'd just met, but Mom and Dad had always told me that bonds formed faster when you were faced with certain doom. That was how it had been for them, for Al and Lila, for Jim and the woman he had been with before Jada, probably even Parv and whoever she'd lost all those years ago. When death was around every corner, you didn't have the luxury of second-guessing your feelings. You grabbed hold of them and embraced them and thanked God that something real and beautiful could exist when the rest of the world was nothing but shit.

I got it now, but I also got that neither Donaghy nor myself could say the words out loud. Not when we didn't know what might happen tomorrow.

"I'm glad too," I said instead, and then kissed his cheek again. "And when this is over, regardless of what happens inside New Atlanta, I want to settle in Senoia. I don't want to go back to being trapped behind a wall and having no choice about my life. I want to be able to live."

He nodded, and I could tell that he understood what I meant.

AFTER THE SUN HAD GONE DOWN, WE LEFT THE basement and headed through old Atlanta. My mind had been spinning two days ago when we'd fled the city, which meant that when we finally reached our destination, the building didn't look the least bit familiar. In the soft light of the moon I was able to make out the words on the sign, now faded and peeling with age, but still legible: *Randy's Carpet Emporium*. Whoever Randy had been twenty years ago, I seriously doubted that he would be any more likely to recognize this place today than I had been.

The inside was unchanged, just like the tunnel we went through to get back to Dragon's was. The basement, however, had not been untouched in our absence.

The place had been ransacked while we were gone, tables turned over and several bottles smashed on the floor, although most of the alcohol that had once lined the shelves was now conveniently missing. There was no doubt in anyone's mind what had happened. Jackson had sent his men here and when they'd

146

been unable to locate Donaghy, Dragon, or Helen, they'd gone to town on the place.

Dragon kicked at a large chunk of glass and it skittered across the floor, clinking when it hit the wall on the opposite side of the room. "Bastards."

Helen, who stood behind him, put her hands on his shoulders and patted them gently. "We'll get it all back and more."

Dragon just nodded.

"Looks like they tried to get into the tunnel but couldn't." Jim nodded to the keypad next to the door.

The wall was nicked up and a big chuck had been taken out of the wood molding, but the steel door was as pristine as ever.

"Here too," Angus muttered, nodding to the same marks surrounding the other door.

I'd only been in the basement twice. Once to get more booze to take upstairs, and a second time when we'd fled the city in the middle of the night. I only knew that Dragon's apartment was behind that door because Glitter had told me the first time I'd come down here. Of course, that didn't prepare me for what it looked like when he typed in the code and the door popped open.

"Holy shit," Al muttered as we walked through the now open doorway. "It's like going back in time."

It must have been, because I'd never seen a place this nice before, with the exception of Jackson's house, which was so grandiose it had always felt unreal to me. Only in a totally different way than this place did. Dragon's apartment felt cozy and comfortable. The way a family home should have felt.

"Get settled in," Dragon growled. "We have a couple hours yet."

We did as we were told, spreading out between the living and dining room while Dragon and Helen disappeared into what I could only assume was a bedroom. I was used to it because they'd done the same thing at the bar, always sneaking off to the office so they could be alone, and I also couldn't blame them. We were about to head into a situation that could be the end for any one of us, so it made sense that they'd want to be alone right now.

Conversation was sparse thanks to the tense atmosphere. It felt like all of us were counting down the minutes until we could head out. A heaviness had fallen over me that became more and more intense the closer the time came, but there was also a restless need to get the whole thing over with. To get into the CDC and see with my own eyes that my sister was there, that my dad was okay. To watch them leave and know that they were no longer in Star's grasp. That they were safe.

Then there was the knowledge that getting through the CDC was going to be tricky no matter how many distractions we created in the streets. I barely knew Jackson's father, but I knew that man was an obsessive workaholic. That he sometimes spent twelve or more hours a day in his office. That it hadn't been unusual for him to stay there for days at a time.

An indiscernible amount of time passed before Dragon and Helen reappeared and announced that it was time to leave. I noticed that Jim and Jada were already up, and that they looked as antsy as I felt.

Upstairs, the bar was just as trashed as the basement had been. Every piece of glass behind the counter had been shattered, and not a single drop of booze was left as far as I could tell. Tables had been turned over and chairs smashed. It didn't look like a single item in the room had been left in usable condition.

Dragon glowered as Helen patted his arm.

"It's okay," she whispered. "We knew this would happen."

He nodded, but didn't seem the least bit comforted.

We stepped out onto the street to find the city dark but not silent. The entertainment district wasn't completely deserted, but it wasn't as busy as it usually was this time of night. Music still floated from the open doors of a few buildings and two people who where clearly intoxicated argued in an alley, but otherwise it seemed that most of the population was off at the festival. It sounded that way, too. Music rang through the air, rising between the buildings and filling the sky with its pulsating rhythm. Cheers and chants joined the beat, making it nearly impossible to talk as we headed down the street.

We stuck to the shadows as we walked, pausing at the end of each street so we could make sure the coast was clear. We passed a handful of bums and addicts, but thanks to the recent flu a lot of the people who usually skulked in the shadows were now gone. I hated thinking like that, hated thanking a bug for killing people needlessly, but right now I had to. The fewer people we ran into, the better off we would be.

The closer we got to the CDC, the louder the festival became. My Uncle Angus was in front of me, and he seemed incapable of going more than a minute without shaking his head in disgust. It was probably a pretty big thing to wrap your brain around, people celebrating in the streets because you'd supposedly died twenty years ago. I couldn't even begin to imagine how he felt.

We stopped when we were still a block away from the CDC and hunkered down in a dark alley. Donaghy was at my side, and even though he hadn't complained once, I could feel his body trembling. It terrified me, thinking that he may not make it through the CDC, that he may be forced to flee with Margot and Dad. If that happened, I wouldn't be able to get him the vaccine right away. Depending on how long it took us to get out of the city, the injection could be delayed by hours. Did he have hours? The transfusion had helped, but I could tell that the virus was once again winning the war raging inside him.

I wrapped my hand around his. "Hang in there."

He only nodded.

The explosion was our cue to get ready. It rocked through the air, seeming to shake the buildings around us even though we were so far away that I was sure it was only my imagination. A fire blast followed only a few seconds later, lighting up the sky. Screams rose up from the festival but the music didn't stop. I wondered how the High Priestess would explain it. Would she say it was Angus knocking the walls of New Atlanta down? It would keep people calm, but if the crowds didn't flee they would end up as sitting ducks for the horde that would soon be heading their way.

It was only a matter of minutes before more screams broke through the air. Gunshots followed and we knew the zombies had found the partygoers. I cringed but tried to tell myself we'd had to do it. People were dying, but if we could get into the CDC, everyone who survived today would be saved.

"Let's go!" Jim hissed over the chaos that was spreading through the city.

We moved as a group. Donaghy and I were somewhere in the middle and I stuck close to him, knowing that he might need help if the virus suddenly took hold of him the way it had earlier. It took us less than five minutes to reach the door, but we were all panting when we stopped outside. Helen knocked twice while I looked from Donaghy to the people around me, and then the street at our backs, half-expecting to see someone or something chasing after us. There was no one though, and a second later the door was ripped open.

"It's clear," the man in front of us said, waving for us to come in. "Let's move."

I got a good enough look at him before he turned and ran to determine that he was in his late forties, with a bushy mustache and salt and pepper hair. That was the biggest impression he made, but it didn't really matter once we were inside and running down the bright, sterile halls of the CDC, because my focus switched from the man who had let us in to what we were about to face.

We'd only been in the building for two minutes tops when guards turned the corner in front of us. Shots rang out, echoing in my ears and head before I'd even had time to register that there was trouble. Jim was in the lead, with Jada and Angus running at his side, and I wasn't sure who had fired, but it didn't matter because the men blocking our way went down in a burst of red and then Jim was yelling for us to keep running.

When we reached the bodies we had to hop over their motionless forms to keep from tripping, and even though I did my best not to look them directly in the eye, I couldn't help myself. I knew their blank stares would haunt me forever.

The building was a maze, the halls twisting and turning, looking exactly the same no matter how many times we turned a corner. White walls, white floors, bright lights, and dark labs. I was in the middle, holding onto Donaghy's arm as I ran, and I was thankful that the others were leading the way. Before we'd left I'd spent time studying the map just like everyone else had, but never had I pictured every hall and room looking exactly the same. It all blurred together as we passed doorway after doorway until I couldn't keep track of how many turns we'd made or how long we'd been in the building.

Thank God Helen was with us.

By the time we finally reached the end of the line, I was having a difficult time catching my breath. The group screeched to a halt outside a closed door and Donaghy practically collapsed against the wall. His forehead was beaded with sweat, but he was shivering and his skin seemed three shades paler than it had when we'd left Dragon's apartment. I pressed my hands to his cheeks while in front of me Helen got to work on the keypad, punching in numbers so fast that the beeps blended together. His face was on fire.

"You okay?" I asked. "Are you going to make it?"

"I'm okay." He shook his head like he was trying to clear it and I couldn't help wondering if he was delirious yet. If he wasn't now, he would be soon.

"We're in!" Helen called.

The door was pulled open and we all rushed to get through the door at once. I was pushed through a few people ahead of Donaghy, but for the first time I didn't care because he wasn't my focus now.

The hallway that stretched out in front of us was as white and clean as the rest of the building had been, but the scent of death hung heavy in the air. Just like every other hall we'd run through, windows and doors lined each side in perfect rows, only these were all accompanied by a keypad.

I moved forward, pushing past Jada and Jim and stumbling deeper into the hall. The first window I came to looked into a room that was as white and sterile as a doctor's office. It held a bed and a couch, a table and a couple chairs, and even though it was empty of people, the sight of it made my heart pound faster.

Behind me someone gasped, and I spun around. The face in front of me was so familiar that I could have drawn it with my eyes closed. He was right on the other side of the glass, banged up and bruised, but alive and staring back at us with a shocked expression on his face.

"Dad," I stammered, stumbling forward just as Mom gasped, "Axl."

Helen was already typing in the code, the beeps echoing through the hall in tune with my pounding heart. Then the door to the cell clicked open, and the sound was so loud that it sounded like chains falling away.

Dad yanked the door open wider and stumbled into the hall, reaching out for Mom before doing the same with me. She didn't hug him so much as run her hands over his bare chest and up to his face, as if desperate to feel every inch of him. He put one arm around her shoulders, pulling her close while doing the same to me with his other arm, and the three of us stood like that for a few seconds, clinging to each other and to this moment.

When he pulled back, it was only enough that he was able to look us over. "Never thought I'd see you again," he whispered, his voice thick with emotion.

I took a moment to get a good look at him, taking stock of what Jackson had done in his rage. One of my dad's eyes was so swollen that it was sealed shut, but the other was alert and filled with tears of happiness. He had a cut on his lower lip, just above the scar on his chin, and the entire left side of his face was purple and swollen, but he was in one piece. He was alert and standing and obviously healthy enough that they'd sent him back to his cell. Thank God.

"Here!" Helen called from behind us, breaking through our reunion.

All three of us turned at the same time to find her standing outside another open door, waving for us to hurry.

"We need to move. Now!"

"Margot," Mom gasped.

She pulled away from Dad and hurried down the hall. I turned to follow, but just as I was about to step away, Dad leaned against the wall like standing was too much for him. He didn't fall to the floor, but he acted like he might if he wasn't careful, and I found myself reaching for him, holding him up the way I had with Donaghy as we'd rushed through the CDC only moments before.

"Are you okay?"

Dad nodded, but the wince of pain that passed over his damaged face told a different story. "I'll be alright. We're all gonna be okay now."

"Help your momma," Angus said from behind me. "I got him."

Dad looked up at the sound of his brother's voice, and the recognition that flickered in his gray eye was filled with both awe and pain. His mouth dropped open as he reached out, his hands grabbing at Angus's shirt like he was trying to find something to hold onto. Dad's lips moved, but no words came out, and he couldn't stop shaking his head.

"It's me," Angus said, taking my place at his brother's side. "You ain't seein' things."

"Angus," Dad finally managed to get out.

This time when he slumped forward, his head dropped to the side.

"What happened?" Mom asked, coming up behind us.

She had Margot, who was wrapped in a sheet and trembling. I hadn't seen my sister in nine years, but I'd recognize her anywhere. Her eyes, glassy and unfocused, were exact replicas of Mom's. Brown and soft and so beautiful it made me want to cry.

"Margot," I gasped just as my uncle said, "Passed out. It's probably the head injury. We gotta get him outta here."

My sister looked at me and blinked. She didn't seem to know what was happening or who any of us were, but she didn't fight Mom or protest. In fact, she didn't say anything. What had they done to her? It made me ache to think about it, and I found myself hoping that she was simply out of it from something they had her on. Once it had worked its way out of her system, she would remember us. She *had* to.

"You need to go. Now," Helen called.

Angus tried to haul his brother—my father—toward the door, but we all knew he couldn't leave. We needed him here with us because he was the one who knew about the failsafe and where the code was.

When Dragon stepped up beside him and took Axl's arm, Helen frowned. "He's going to need help," Dragon told her.

Helen pressed her lips together, but it only took a moment for her to nod. "Fine," she snapped, and then turned to the guard who had let us in. "Lead them back the way we came and make sure they get out of here safely."

The guard nodded and headed for the door.

Mom took one step after him before stopping and turning to face me. Her eyes swam with worry and pain and so many other emotions I couldn't name them all, but she looked more like herself. Like the strong woman who had raised me.

"Be careful." She had one arm around Margot and my sister was leaning on her like she couldn't stand, but Mom used the other one to give me a half hug.

I swallowed and pushed the images of my sister being tortured and writhing in pain from my mind. "I will."

Mom squeezed me so hard that it felt like my ribs would snap. "I love you, Megan."

"I love you," I replied.

I stepped back when she released me, but not before grabbing my sister's hand and giving it a squeeze. I didn't know what to say, so I said nothing and instead allowed Mom to pull her away.

Next to me Dragon and Helen were saying their own goodbyes, but when I stopped at my boss's side it was my unconscious father I was focused on.

"Hang in there, Daddy," I whispered as I kissed his temple. I hadn't called him Daddy in probably fifteen years, but at that moment I felt overwhelmed by the memories of my childhood. By the images of this man playing with me, tickling me, making me laugh.

"Be careful," Dragon said to Helen.

"I will," she replied.

The kiss she gave him was quick but full of feeling, and then he was off, supporting Dad as he followed the rest of my family down the hall and hopefully to safety.

# CHAPTER SEVENTEEN

## Meg

Before the others had even disappeared from view, Angus charged into the room we'd just freed Dad from. Through the window the rest of us watched in tense silence as he rummaged through an old bookshelf. It only took seconds for him to find what he needed, and when he came back into the hall he was holding a book of crossword puzzles. He frowned as he flipped through it; his gaze so focused on the book that he seemed to forget anyone else was around. He turned page after page until he was near the back of the book, and then he froze as if mesmerized by whatever was written there.

He snapped out of it fast though, and then he was heading back into the cell with his thumb stuck between the pages, muttering, "Need a pen."

"Angus," Jada called. "We need to hurry."

"I'm doin' what I can," he responded.

When he sat down at the table, the tattooed woman let out a huff and went into the room. I did too, feeling suddenly compelled to find out what was happening. He was flipping through the pages again, stopping every now and then so he could jot a number down on his arm. When I leaned forward and got a better look at the pages, I saw that most of the puzzles were filled in, but not with answers. With names. Axl. Vivian. Emily. Hadley. Jon.

Rambo. Megan. Jane. Baby. Father. Daughter. It looked like the ranting of a mad man, but to Angus there seemed to be a pattern.

"What are you looking for?" I asked when he jotted the number five down on his arm, and then flipped the page again. It was the seventh number, and he was still searching.

"See here—" He pointed to eight down where the word Jane had been filled in. "Every time I wrote her name it's a number in the code. I just gotta find 'em all."

"It's genius," I said, marveling at the way he was able to hide something so important in a book that looked like nothing but nonsense.

"I knew I wouldn't be able to remember it forever, so I hid it." Angus nodded twice and flipped to the last puzzle in the book. There the name Jane was written in three across.

He shut the book after he'd scribbled the final number on his arm, and then got to his feet, but he didn't leave it behind. Instead, he folded the book in half and shoved it in his back pocket. I couldn't believe he wanted to keep it. It must have held some horrible memories, years and years of sitting here as a prisoner, of living a hopeless and miserable existence. Why would he want to remember that?

"Let's go," he said as he headed for the door.

I found Donaghy in the hall, just past Dad's former cell. He was leaning against the wall, barely able to stand, but when I went to help him he waved me off.

"Look," he said, waving to the cell at his back.

I looked through the window, but the sight I was met with forced me to take a step back. Matt. He was a zombie now, a hybrid zombie who was pale and calculating and totally hairless, but I'd recognize the member of my crew anywhere. He'd gone missing after sitting down to talk to me about my dad's disappearance and I'd known something bad must have happened to him, but this?

"Oh my God," I whispered.

"I saw him when I was brought in." Donaghy pushed himself off the wall and stood. "Do you want to put him out of his misery?"

"We have to leave!" Jada called.

I did want to put him out of his misery. I wanted to open the door and shoot him and make sure he wasn't trapped inside the head of that creature, but not only was it a risk—the hybrid zombies were fast and calculating—I also knew there was no time.

"The bacteria will do it for me when we release it," I said, shaking my head. "We have to focus on that."

"Okay." Donaghy grabbed my hand and pulled me away from the cell, but I had a hard time tearing my gaze from the calculating eyes that followed us.

Everyone else in our group was already on their way down the hall when we hurried after them. We caught up in seconds, and then moved through the CDC in much the same way as we had before, this time with Helen and Parv taking the lead. Donaghy and I were somewhere in the middle of the group, each of us armed but safely tucked in among the others just in case we ran into trouble and he lacked the energy to fight. I couldn't help thinking of the rest of my family as I went, praying they'd made it out and were on their way to safety. Dragon was with them, which made me feel better, but I wouldn't be able to relax until we were all in Senoia and together once again.

We stayed in the main halls of the CDC until we reached a locked door. There we paused just long enough for Helen to type a code in, and then it was pulled open to reveal stairs that descended into near darkness.

We plunged into the black abyss, not saying a word. The stairwell was unlit except for the red lights that signaled each landing, and the glow from their crimson bulbs was almost foreboding, shining down on the stairs as they wound around and around, descending deeper and deeper into the belly of the CDC. We ran at a brisk pace that seemed to defy the seriousness of the situation rather than highlight it. Our footsteps echoed through the empty stairwell as we moved, making me jumpy with the knowledge that we were creating a lot of noise. Too much noise. By now, everyone had to know we were in the CDC and they were probably looking for us. Jackson, his father, all the sick bastards who worked day and night to mutate viruses in an attempt to take over the world. They had guards who lived and worked in this building, their sole purpose to protect the secrets held here.

We passed two doors before Helen stopped. The third was steel and yet another keypad was mounted on the wall at its side. The rest of us could barely hold still as we waited for Helen to type the number in once again. I held my breath, wondering when luck would run out and the code she had would no longer work. She couldn't have access to the entire CDC, could she? Even if she did, it was entirely possible that Jackson or his father would disable her code when they realized she was here.

"What if your code doesn't work?" I asked as Helen jammed her finger against the numbers mounted on the keypad.

"This isn't my code." She glanced over her shoulder, her gaze focused on Angus, not me. "Jane left me a note in case things went south. In it she told me about the failsafe, but she didn't tell me how to find it. She told me that Angus knew all the details and that if I wanted to save the world, I would have to rescue him from the CDC." She punched the enter button on the keypad and the door clicked open. "She also gave me Star's security code so I could access everything when the time came."

She turned back to face the open door, charging through like a woman on a mission, which was exactly what she was. The rest of us followed, bursting out of the stairwell and into the hall, and coming face-to-face with the door that lead into Biosafety Level four.

The hall we were standing in was just as white and sterile as every other one we'd passed, and it seemed to stretch on for what felt like forever on both sides. I had no idea where these halls went or if there was another stairwell that led to this level, but standing here made me feel like I was surrounded, especially with the door in front of us screaming at me to turn away.

It was plastered with warnings, all of them declaring that only authorized personal were allowed to enter and cautioning anyone who passed through that the room held certain death. The door had a small window in the center, allowing us a view of the inside. It looked like a locker room for the most part, with a few lockers on the wall and benches mounted in front of them. Only the bulky plastic suits destroyed the illusion. They were hanging on the wall, ready and waiting for some fool to step inside and put them on, and the very sight of them sent a shudder shooting through me.

Suddenly, I was very thankful that I wasn't the one who was about to step into this room.

"This is it," Helen said as she pressed her fingers against the numbers.

Angus stood at her side, his arm out so she could read the numbers written there, and with every beep I started to sweat even more. The door let out a hiss when it popped open and Angus took a step back, almost like he was afraid he'd catch some thing if he stood too close.

Helen didn't step through right away, but instead turned to face us. "Parv and I are going in. Everyone else, stay out here and make sure no one bothers us."

No one spoke, but like me everyone nodded in agreement. The tension was thick, the mood somewhere between grim and anxious. I'd only just met most of the people with me, but the others were my family. My uncle Al, Luke, and Parv. Donaghy. Losing any of these people would be devastating, and I knew that standing in this hall outside the door of Biosafety Level four, we were sitting ducks. If anyone came running out of that stairwell or down one of these halls, we would have nowhere to hide.

Helen took a deep breath and stepped through the door. Parv was behind her, just inches away from safety when the gunshot cut through the air and she went down in a burst of red and screams.

I ducked, as did everyone around me, trying to take cover from an unknown assailant. My aunt was on the floor, just outside the open door, and I twisted my body so it was around hers, blocking her as if I were a shield instead of a person who was just as vulnerable as she was. She was bleeding from her shoulder, her dark shirt already saturated with blood, and there was red dotted across her neck and face. Helen was already through the door, crouching down and staring back at us as if trying to decide what to do. I covered my aunt's shoulder with shaky hands, wanting to stop the bleeding, to make sure she got through this alive, while at my back a group of soldiers rushed toward us.

All around me the people in my group had their guns up. Luke and Jim and Jada fired, Angus too. Donaghy had his body draped over me just like I had done with my aunt, and the heat emanating from him was stifling. I focused on Parv though, trying to block out the soldiers rushing toward us and the fever raging

159

through Donaghy. Trying to help her even though my body was trembling.

Parv groaned and tried to push me away when I pressed my hands more firmly against her wound. "Megan, you need to go." She seemed to have super human strength when she shoved Donaghy and me off her. I lost my balance and nearly fell getting up, but that didn't stop her from giving me another push. "Help Helen."

I didn't want to leave her, didn't want to go in the room of death and be cut off from what was happening, but I knew she was right, and before I could think twice I found myself moving. Gunshots burst through the air around me, but in seconds I was falling through the door and Helen had slammed it shut, cutting us off from the chaos in the hall.

She grabbed my arm and pulled me to my feet, her hands on my shoulders as she looked into my eyes. "Focus, Meg. You hear me?"

I nodded, but I didn't know for sure if I *could* focus. The door was shut, but I could still hear the gunshots. Or maybe it was my imagination. Maybe they were echoing through my head, because I couldn't believe that the sounds would be able to penetrate the thick door Helen had just slammed shut. I looked down, and the sight of the blood on my hands made me shake. Trembles moved up my legs through my body, and I wanted to turn and run back out into the hall. I needed to help my aunt. Needed to help my friends.

But I also knew I was needed here.

"You have to calm down." Helen's gravelly voice penetrated my worries, bringing my thoughts into focus. "You can't go into this shaking and out of control. I need you, but if you can't handle it I can go in on my own."

I tried to turn so I could look out into the hall and find out if my family and friends were okay, but Helen grabbed my face between her hands and stopped me. She forced me to look at her, and something about the intense expression in her blue eyes helped some of my anxiety melt away.

"Focus. There is no one here but you and me. Got it? *No one.* Close your eyes, take a deep breath."

I did as I was told, breathing in slowly through my mouth and then letting it out through my nose before repeating the process. Trying to block out everything that had just happened in the hall. Trying to put my worries into a compartment where they would be safe until later.

"There's no one else here."

With my eyes closed, I could almost believe her. The lab was so secure that no noise was able to penetrate the door. The sound of gunfire had been in my head, and it finally began to fade. With it gone there was no other noise except Helen's breathing and the whoosh of the ventilation system as it pushed clean air into the room.

"Okay?" she whispered after a moment.

"Okay," I replied and opened my eyes. "I'm okay."

Helen nodded once. "Let's get suited up then."

I kept my back to the door and did as I was told, focusing on my breathing and Helen's calm voice. We stripped the leather from our bodies and put on scrubs, and then we pulled the suits on. Then the gloves, using tape to secure them to the sleeves so none of the possibly contaminated air inside the lab would be able to leak into the suit. We did the same with the booties we put on over our shoes, and with each new step I found my body relaxing even more. It was a long and tedious process, but I focused on each individual action instead of what I was about to do or what might be happening behind me, and it helped keep me calm.

Our hoods were the last things we put on, and once they were in position Helen pointed to the side of her head. It took a moment for me to figure out what she was trying to tell me, but through my gloves I was able to feel a tiny button on the side my hood. When I pushed it, a burst of static crackled in my ear.

"Can you hear me?" Helen's voice broke through the static.

"Yes." I swallowed when my voice shook.

Now that we were ready, the reality of what I was about to do started to sink in. Inside that lab there was more than just the zombie virus to worry about. On the other side of that thick steel door, dozens of deadly viruses sat just waiting to be released so they could wipe out even more of the population. One false move and I could die a horrible death. In a way, those viruses were even more of a threat then the zombie virus. The CDC had vaccines for that, but the others, the viruses that hadn't been created by Star, could very well be unstoppable if released.

"Okay." Helen's voice seemed to slam into my eardrum. "Just do as I say and everything will be okay."

I nodded, but since she had already turned and headed to the next door, she didn't see me.

My breath bounced off the window in my hood when I exhaled. It was hot and moist on my face, but I knew it was only temporary. Once we were in the lab we'd hook the suits up to one of the many oxygen tubes hanging from the ceiling, but before we had a chance to do that we would have to go through two sets of doors.

Helen got the first one open and I followed her through. This room was only big enough for a handful of people, four at the most. It housed the decontamination shower we'd have to go through when we came out, as well as a separate ventilation system to ensure that none of the air from inside the lab could leak out.

We stopped once we were in the small room and closed the door, and the click seemed to echo through the suffocating space. Once it was secure, Helen moved to the next door. I wasn't sure if her hand was shaking when she reached for the knob or if it was just my imagination, but I knew mine was trembling. In fact, my whole body was.

The door opened with a hiss and Helen stepped into the lab. I was right behind her.

There were tables along the walls and cabinets and desks, and areas where microscopes and slides were lined up in a neat row. I imagine that it had once been a well-used lab, but the need for it had died twenty years ago when the original virus was released, and I noticed that despite how pristine it had appeared upon first glance, everything was now covered in a layer of dust from disuse. The glass slides were filmy and our feet left footprints in the dust that had gathered on the floor, leaving a trail that made me think of Hänsel and Gretel, and the story of the breadcrumbs they had left behind in the forest.

Helen walked forward, barely glancing at the tables as we went by. She didn't stop until she reached a couple curly, yellow tubes hanging from the ceiling, and I watched as she reached up and grasped one in her gloved hand.

She turned to face me. "Turn around."

I did as I was told. My back was to her, making it impossible to see what she was doing, but I felt her tugging at my suit. Seconds later cool air whooshed in, chasing away some of the moisture that had already collected on my mask. I inhaled deeply, allowing the fresh oxygen to fill my lungs in hopes that the familiar feeling would help chase away my anxiety.

Through my mask I watched as Helen attached the second tube to her own suit. When it was secure, she once again started walking. The tubes were only long enough to get us so far though, and once we'd reached a certain point we had to unhook them and attach new ones to our suits before we could go any further. I did the second one myself, catching on quickly, and Helen gave me a satisfied nod.

"The refrigerators are back here."

I kept a few paces behind her, trying my best not to think about what this room held. The zombie virus was scary enough, but thinking about the other things that could escape this lab terrified me. I doubted very much that Star would lift a finger to stop an Ebola outbreak. He had, after all, wiped out most of the world without batting an eye.

Helen stopped at the far end of the room, right in front of a few stainless steel doors. I could hear my heart thumping, the suit somehow magnifying the sound. It was so loud that it drowned out the sound of the air whooshing into my suit and the hum of the machines that sucked the possibly tainted air out of this room and replaced it with clean, fresh oxygen from the outside world.

Helen passed over the first door, and the second, stopping in front of the third. I watched with my breath held as her fingers wrapped around the handle. She pulled and the door popped open, letting out a burst of light and cold air. It turned to steam when it hit the warmer air in the lab, and then rose up around us like an early morning fog that dissipated only seconds later, leaving the air once again clear.

Inside the refrigerator were a six shelves, each of them lined with dozens upon dozens of vials.

"It's in here." Helen's voice crackled in my ear, making me jump. "I think." She reached up and wiped her hand across the window of her hood, and then shook her head. "I've got steam. Help me read these labels."

I stepped forward and the labels came into view. Ebola Virus. Lassa Virus. Marburg, Crimean-Congo hemorrhagic fever. I wasn't familiar with any of them, but they made my legs shake anyway because I knew that if they were being stored in here, they were bad. No one would be required to put on one of these suits for something small.

There were other vials too, each of them labeled FLU with a year stamped behind the word. I scanned the labels and found four different years represented, including the current one. My hand shook when I reached for the vial at the front. It felt impossibly small beneath my gloved fingers. Like all I had to do was squeeze it and the glass would shatter.

"Is this—" My voice broke before I could get the question out.

"The flu Star released." Helen nodded as her voice pounded against my eardrums. "They created it here in the CDC as a way to control the population."

I let out a deep sigh. "I can't believe it. I can't believe they did this. What's the point? What is Star trying to achieve?"

"Only he can really answer that," Helen said. "He likes power. He wants to control everything, but he's smart enough to know that he has to start small and work from there." She nodded toward the tray in front of us. "Help me find the right vial."

I slipped the vial of death back into its spot on the tray and turned to scan the others tucked away in the fridge. There were so many. So many different names, none of which I recognized or understood.

"What am I looking for?"

Helen shook her head and the plastic of her suit crinkled. "I don't know exactly. Jane never told me what the label would say and Angus didn't seem to know either. It's possible she told him and he forgot, or maybe she didn't even know. Of all the scientists Star has ever had on his team, she was the one he trusted the most, but even she didn't know everything."

It was ironic that Jane had been Star's most trusted scientist considering that she was the one who had ended up betraying him the most.

"Maybe we'll know it when we see it," I said as I scanned the labels.

"Maybe," Helen replied.

There were so many vials lined up on the shelves that after a few minutes of reading labels, I began to feel like my head was spinning. Even worse than the sheer number of vials was the knowledge that so much death and destruction sat on these shelves. And they were man-made too. At least the strains of flu Star had released and the different strains of the zombie virus.

My heart leapt when I spotted a vial labeled *vaccine* on the shelf right below the ones holding the viruses. There was a date on the label, right next to the neatly printed name of that strain. I hadn't even known the strains had names, and the knowledge made my heart beat faster. How would I know which strain Donaghy was infected with? What if I got the wrong vaccine?

My hands were shaking so badly when I pulled out the tray that the vials clinked together. I took a deep breath, hoping to calm myself down. But it didn't work, so I gripped the tray tighter, hoping to keep it still long enough for me to read the labels. The vials seemed to scream up at me. There were so many and this was only one tray out of dozens. I scanned the labels, trying to figure out how they were arranged. The name of each strain meant nothing to me, but the dates printed on the labels did. The vials in my hand all had last year's date on them, and when I looked into the refrigerator I saw that the next tray of vials had an earlier date. They were arranged in ascending order, meaning the strain I needed would be at the back.

I set the tray I was holding back on the shelf and then leaned down so I could get a good look at the vials at the back of the refrigerator. The one furthest back had a number one on it instead of a date, but the tray right in front of that was dated only one year after the outbreak started. This was the vaccine I needed.

I reached back, my arm only an inch above the trays, and the sleeve of my plastic suit skimmed the tops of the vials. The refrigerator was so deep that it seemed like I had to put most of my body inside in order to reach the one I needed, but I did and then my fingers were on it. I could feel the cool glass against my skin even through my thick gloves. I clasped it between my thumb and forefinger, feeling the weight of it as I lifted it from the tray. This vial, this tiny glass bottle of neon green liquid, would save Donaghy's life.

I was pulling the vial from inside the depths of the refrigerator when another label caught my eye. I froze, the glass clutched between my fingers and my eyes trained on the vials lined up in the very last row. There were two words printed on the labels. Two words that were so ambiguous they would mean nothing to most people. But not to me.

*The End.* That was all the label said, but it was enough to tell me that *this* was what we had come here for. I palmed the vial I was holding, tucking it back with the last three fingers on my hand so my thumb and forefinger were free. Then I reached back into the fridge, back behind the rows and rows of vaccines, and grabbed one of the vials in the last row.

I tucked it into my palm, right up against the vial that would be Donaghy's salvation. The glass vials clinked together when I wrapped my fingers around them. The failsafe felt heavy in my hand, like I was holding the future. Which I was. This vial, this tiny little thing, held hope and love and the promise of rebirth. If it worked it would give all of us a new life.

"I found it," I whispered, but the words were loud in my ears.

I turned to face Helen just as she twisted my way. She had to turn her whole body so she could see me, but even through the moisture collected on the window of her hood I could see the hope in her eyes.

"You found it?"

I slipped the vaccine into my other hand, tucking it safely into my palm even as it called out for me to hurry. I could feel my pulse thumping against it; a beat that refused to let me forget that with each passing second, Donaghy was being dragged closer and closer to his own end.

I twisted the other vial around so Helen could see the label and positioned it right in front of her face before repeating, "I found it."

I couldn't believe such a tiny thing could hold the solution to such a huge problem. Maybe we needed more than one. There were several rows of them on the tray, after all. What if the only way to stop the zombies was to release the virus near every settlement?

"You sure this will do it?" I asked Helen as she stood staring at the vial, looking as mesmerized by the contents as I felt.

"According to Jane, yes. She was a lot of things, but she wasn't one to exaggerate. If this virus was created to kill the zombies, it will work."

I slipped the vial into my other hand so it was side by side with the vaccine once again, and then curled my fingers around them before shutting the fridge. "Then let's get the hell out of here and take these damn zombies out once and for all."

# CHAPTER EIGHTEEN

## Donaghy

My heartbeat thumped so hard against my eardrums that I started to wonder if the people around me were still firing.

They weren't, though. The guards who'd shot Parvarti were down, all of them dead now, and our group was taking inventory of the damage. The air in the hall was thick with the scent of blood, and as much as I wanted to deny it, I found myself wanting to reach out and run my fingers through the splatters that decorated the once brilliantly white floors. It was so red. So intoxicatingly red.

"Hang in there," Jada was saying to my right.

I watched, almost transfixed as she probed the injury on Parvarti's shoulder. Red seeped from the wound, coating Jada's fingers. She stood and moved away, but I couldn't take my eyes off the blood. How it glistened under the lights, how it seemed to call out to me.

"Shit."

A hiss of pain to my right made me turn. There, Kelly sat leaning against the wall, her expression a mirror of Parvarti's while a pool of blood collected on the floor beneath her leg.

"It's not that bad," Luke said as he tied a strip of fabric around her thigh.

Kelly hissed out a curse and shook her head. "I'll be okay."

"You better be," he responded.

I couldn't move. I knew that something very bad was happening to me, but all I could do was stare at the blood. It called out to me, the smell of it so powerful that I felt like I could taste it. The sharp, coppery flavor seemed to fill my mouth, and even though I knew I should be repulsed by it, I wasn't.

"Hey." I turned to find Angus at my side, his gray eyes focused on my face. "You alright?"

I shook my head, but before I could speak I had to swallow. "No."

Angus put his hand on the knife at his waist. "You need me to end this?"

"Not yet," I said, but the truth was, I had no idea how much longer I could hold on.

Angus nodded and his hand fell away from his knife. "You tell me."

"I will," I managed to hiss out.

And then I shut my eyes and forced my brain to stop thinking. Forced my body not to picture the blood around me. Forced my brain to repeat the same words over and over again. *It won't be long now. I can hang on. I am going to fight this.*

# CHAPTER NINETEEN
## Meg

The vials were in the palm of my hand when Helen and I stepped out of the lab and into the decontamination room. I wanted to squeeze them, to tighten my grip on them so they didn't accidentally slip away, but I forced my fingers to stay relaxed.

Seconds after the door shut behind us water rained down from the ceiling. The sound of it hitting my plastic hood was deafening. Louder than the sound of Helen's voice booming in my ears had been, louder than the pounding of my heart, which seemed to be beating at an impossibly fast rate.

The shower shut off as suddenly as it had started, surprising me with the sudden silence, and then Helen yanked the door open and moved into the other room with me right on her heels.

It wasn't until I caught a glimpse of the hallway through the window that I remembered the scene we'd left behind. I ripped my hood off and took a deep breath, filling my lungs with fresh oxygen as I hurried to the door. I peered out, expecting to see a bloody battle raging in the hall. It wasn't, though.

"What's going on out there?" Helen asked as she peeled her suit away.

I set the vials gingerly on a bench and began ripping off my own suit, all the while looking out into the hall. There were bodies on the ground, but they were the CDC guards. Our own people were alert and waiting, but seemingly uninjured. Except Parv. She'd been shot before we went in, but I couldn't see her now and I had no clue if she was okay. Donaghy was also out of sight, and no matter how hard I pressed my face against the window, I couldn't spot either one of them.

"They have it under control."

I pulled my suit off and kicked it aside. Underneath I was wearing scrubs, and I started to grab for my clothes, but then I realized it was wasted time. I was already dressed and I doubted Jada had any sentimental attachment to the leather she'd loaned me.

"Is there any reason to assume these clothes are contaminated?" I asked Helen.

She ran her hand through her short, blonde hair almost absentmindedly. "No. Protocol is to change and wash these with bleach, but screw protocol."

"My thoughts exactly," I said.

There was a pocket on my scrub top, and I slipped the vials into it for safekeeping, thankful that it had a small square of Velcro that would help keep it closed. Helen had already scooped up her gun and was heading for the door, and all I had to do was grab my own weapons before heading after her.

The door hissed open and I stumbled out. It probably wasn't any brighter in the hall than it had been inside the lab, but it seemed like it. Although it could have just been that I was having a difficult time taking everything in at once. The guards on the ground, the blood streaked across the white floor, Parv leaning against the wall with her face scrunched up in pain, Donaghy next to her with sweat beaded on his forehead. I wasn't sure where to look first.

"We got them. Both of them," Helen said as she ran out ahead of me.

"Is everyone okay?" I asked.

Jim shook his head. "We're alive, but we have a few injuries."

That's when I saw Luke supporting Kelly. Her leg was bloody above the knee, and a tourniquet had been tied around her thigh to stop the flow. She had to be in pain, but she looked more pissed off than anything. Luke, however, looked ready to get the hell out of here.

My gaze moved to Donaghy. "Are you okay?"

"I'm okay." He dragged himself up off the floor, working hard to stand but obviously determined. "I can work through it."

"What about the fever?" I reached for him, wanting to feel his head, but he jerked away and out of the corner of my eye I saw Angus take a step toward us.

"Keep your distance. I feel..." He swallowed. "I'm hungry, but it's not like anything I've ever felt before."

No. The virus was working harder now, moving faster. He was running out of time.

I turned to Helen. "I need to give him the vaccine. Now."

"No syringes down here," she reminded me. "We'll have to get one on the first floor."

I wanted to protest, but I knew there was no reason. She wasn't withholding it on purpose. If she said there were no syringes on this level, there were none. Which meant we had to move. Now.

"What's the plan?" I asked, looking between Kelly and Parv. It was impossible to imagine that we'd be able to get far with two injured people in tow.

"Luke is going to get Kelly and Parv out of here, and Tony is going with them for backup," Jim said. "They're hurt and they'll slow us down, but they also need medical attention, and soon."

That left eight of us to get through the CDC, get a syringe so we could give Donaghy the vaccine, and then head out into the city to release the bacteria. I didn't know how many guards there were in this building, but I did know that the odds were not in our favor at the moment.

"Help me up," Parv said, holding the hand not pressed to her shoulder out to Jada.

The blonde woman reached down and my aunt clasped her hand around hers, pulling herself up with a great deal of effort. Something had been tied around her wound, but it took a moment for me to realize that they'd ripped up the shirt of one of the dead CDC guards.

"How are you doing?" I asked her.

Parv shook her head. "I feel like shit, but I'm stronger than a damn bullet. I'll be okay."

I believed her.

"Let's get a move on," Angus growled, but he didn't sound angry necessarily, more stressed or anxious to get things done. Or maybe even anxious to get out of this building and know that he wasn't going to get thrown back into a cell.

We had to go up the same stairwell we'd come down, so we all headed up together. Al helped my aunt and Luke helped Kelly. We still moved at a fast pace—as fast as the injured people in our group would allow us—but we worked hard to keep our steps quiet this time.

Donaghy walked at the back of the group like he was afraid to get too close to anyone. His hands were clenched at his sides, his jaw tight. He looked like he was barely hanging onto his control and I couldn't keep my eyes off him as we made our way up. His expression reminded me of how I'd felt when we'd first met, how my life had felt like it was careening out of control and how he had been an anchor for me to hold onto.

I slowed just enough so we were side by side and took his hand, prying his fingers open with a great deal of effort.

"Meg—" he began, his voice as tortured as his expression was. "—it isn't safe."

"Let me help you," I said.

He did, allowing his fingers to slide into mine, and then holding onto me like he was trying to ground himself. I didn't know if it would work, but my theory was that he was still present enough to realize something was changing, so if he could focus on something he cared about he might be able to keep that part of himself closer to the surface for longer.

When we reached the first floor, we stopped at the door so Jim and Jada could look out. Once they had determined that the coast was clear, they turned back to face us.

"Where do we need to go to get a syringe?" Jim asked Helen.

"To the left." She turned to face Luke. "You need to go right to get out of here. Can you find it?"

"I've been studying that map for weeks," he said. "I can get us out safely."

"Can you walk on your own?" Al asked Parv.

She nodded, but before he had a chance to let her go she stood up on the tips of her toes and hugged him. It was something I'd never seen before. Al and Parv had known one another for twenty years, were closer than most real families, but my aunt had always put a wall up around herself, one that had only gotten taller and more secure since Joshua's death.

"Be careful," she whispered in Al's ear.

"You too," my uncle replied.

When they pulled away, Al went to say something to his son while Parv turned to Angus.

"I was right to start callin' you Rambo," he said.

"I was wrong to assume a few zombies could take you out. I should have known there was nothing in the world that could take Angus James down."

He snorted. "Nothin' but my own fool self." He kissed her on the forehead before giving her a quick squeeze with one arm. "When this is all over, I wanna sit on a front porch and smoke a pack of cigarettes."

"It's a date," she said before turning away.

We filed out of the stairwell. Luke, Kelly, Tony, and Parv went right while the rest of us veered off to the left. I kept my hand in Donaghy's, trying to ignore the moisture that collected between our palms and the heat radiating off his skin.

We hadn't gone far when we turned a corner and found a group of guards waiting. Jim and Jada backpedaled, forcing the rest of us to do the same as shots rang through the air around us. A cry broke out and Britt hit the ground, drawing a round of cursing from Jim.

"Everyone, down!" he called as he and Jada dropped.

We did as we were told. Donaghy and I were at the back of the group, but Jim was at the front. He was on his knees and Jada ended up on her stomach, her head just barely around the corner. She fired, as did Jim, and behind them Angus stood doing the same.

Next to me, Donaghy had his body pressed against the wall and his eyes squeezed shut like he was trying to block everything out, only I didn't think that was the best way to handle it. Whatever war was raging inside him, the only way to fight it off was to remember *why* you were trying to win to begin with. To focus on what you had to lose if you gave in.

I pulled my hand out of his and got to my knees in front of him, grabbing his face between my hands. "Donaghy. Open your eyes. Look at me."

He did, and his blue eyes locked on mine. They looked different though, the irises more muted than usual. It sent a shiver through me, but I forced it away and gripped his face tighter, willing him to hang on.

"We're almost there. You *are* going to be okay."

"I don't know if I can hang on, Meg," he said through gritted teeth.

"You can. I know it. You're stronger than this. Stronger than Jackson. You can win."

His Adam's apple bobbed when he swallowed, but he nodded too. He kept his gaze locked on mine while in front of us gunfire burst through the air. I wanted to know what was going on, but I was afraid if I turned my back on Donaghy he would slip away, so I stayed where I was, kneeling in front of him while the battle raged around us.

The gunfire broke off and a second later Jim called out, "Let's move!"

I stood, pulling Donaghy with me, and turned to find the rest of our group on their feet. Britt was the only causality on our side, and even though I hated to think that we'd gotten lucky, especially with his blank eyes staring up at me as I ran by, I couldn't help it. It could have been a lot worse.

We continued down the hall, moving past the bodies of the guards. There were only a handful of them, ten at the most, and I knew the loss wouldn't dwindle their numbers enough to make things even for us. We were still very outnumbered, and all I could hope was that most of the CDC guards had been pulled away to deal with the chaos in the streets and still hadn't made it back here.

We didn't stop until we were in front of a sealed door, and just like all the other important rooms in this building, there was a keypad next to it. Helen had it open in seconds though, and then she was rushing inside. There was no reason for all of us to go in, not when all we needed was a syringe, so we stayed where we were, standing in anxious silence. I pulled the vials out of my pocket and found the right one, and then gingerly slipped the bacteria back into its hiding place.

At my side, Donaghy was leaning against the wall with his eyes squeezed shut.

"We're almost there," I told him. "Just hang on."

He nodded, but didn't open his eyes.

Helen was back in seconds, holding her hand out to me. I was shaking when I dropped the vial into her palm, and once my hands were empty I felt useless. I clutched Donaghy's hand and whispered to him that it was all going to be okay. Everything was going to work out now.

He flinched when the needle slid into his vein. Helen pushed the plunger and the green liquid rushed into his body. I could see it under his skin for just a moment, bright green as it moved through his vein before mixing with his blood and disappearing.

"That's it." Helen dropped the empty vial and syringe, and they clattered against the floor.

"How long?" I asked her.

We had to wait at least an hour to release the bacteria, that much we knew, but I wasn't sure how long it would take for the symptoms of the virus to ease. Donaghy looked like he was in so much pain, and I hated seeing him like this. Hated knowing that every movement hurt him.

"A few hours," Helen said. "It's different for everyone, but the symptoms should start to ease soon and disappear completely within five hours max."

"Fuck," Donaghy muttered under his breath.

"We ready?" Jim called.

I hooked my arm through Donaghy's and helped him move down the hall to join the others. Jada, Jim, Al, and Angus stood like sentries, keeping watch. Only there was no one around. No one to stop us and no guards charging us. It didn't feel right. None of this felt right.

"Where is everyone?" I asked when we'd stopped next to the others. "Why haven't we met more resistance?"

"I don't know," Jim breathed out.

"They're waiting for us somewhere." Jada shoved a few loose dreads out of her face. "Star won't let us just walk out of here."

"Good." Angus pulled the magazine out of his gun and checked his ammo before slapping it back in. "I wanna see that prick. The son too."

177

"I know you probably have a deep, burning desire for revenge," I said, "but I just want to get the hell out of here in one piece."

"No time like the present," Jim muttered.

We continued our trek through the CDC, moving slower this time. None of us said the words out loud, but I knew that like me they were waiting for an ambush. It wouldn't be long now. I could feel it.

We managed to make it all the way to the lobby before it happened.

"This leads to the exit," Helen called, rushing past Jim and Jada.

She was just a few steps ahead of us when she shoved the door open. It swung forward and Helen stepped out, freedom suddenly in her sights. Before I'd even had the chance to get a glimpse of the lobby a gunshot thundered through the air and Helen went down.

# CHAPTER TWENTY
## Donaghy

It seemed to happen in slow motion, but I wasn't sure if it was the virus moving through my veins that made it seem that way or if time had actually slowed. A crack echoed through the building and Helen's head jerked back. I caught a glimpse of a hole no bigger than the tip of my thumb in the center of her forehead and a trickle of blood. Then she dropped.

The thud of her body hitting the floor made my whole body jerk, and I tried to pull Meg back, to turn and go the other way, but guards came out of nowhere. They were behind us, waving guns and forcing us to move forward. We were pushed out into the lobby, stumbling over Helen's now lifeless body, where more guards stood waiting. It took a matter of seconds for them to disarm us, and then we were all shoved to our knees. The yelling was so loud that it seemed to echo in my ears, making my already pounding head hurt even more.

I found it difficult to think. Difficult to focus on what was going on around me, but not on what was happening inside me. My stomach growled with a hunger I'd never felt before. It was overwhelming, threatening to consume me.

When had I eaten last? I couldn't remember, I just knew that I needed to eat *now*. My stomach rumbled nonstop, drowning out the words the guards screamed at us. The pang in my gut was so intense it almost made me double over, but it was different than the usual hunger pains. The need wasn't just concentrated in my stomach; it was also deep in my bones.

I blinked and tried to bring the world into focus, but it was difficult. Between the pain and the hunger and the yelling, I couldn't concentrate, couldn't think. I looked around, barely recognizing my surroundings, but when my gaze landed on the woman at my side, things began to clear. I stared at her, focusing, trying to ground myself. Meg. This was Meg. She was why I was here; she was what I was fighting for.

The realization helped, but the hunger didn't ease. It gnawed at my insides. Begged for relief. But I kept my gaze on Meg, knowing that *she* was the only thing that would bring me out of this.

# CHAPTER TWENTY-ONE
## Meg

The guards were still screaming even though we'd followed their orders and were all on the ground, our hands behind our heads. I flinched every time one came near me even though I knew they'd been ordered to keep us alive. I wasn't dumb. I knew Jackson wouldn't allow us an easy death.

To my left Angus swore, but to my right Donaghy was silent. He looked around like he wasn't sure what was happening, but when his eyes landed on me they seemed to focus a little more. The color was still muted, but just like I'd thought, looking at me seemed to ground him in reality.

"It's going to be okay," I whispered out of the corner of my mouth. "Just focus on me."

As if trying to defy my words, the guards parted and Jackson appeared in front of us.

"Meg." His sick smile seemed to stretch across the entire room, going from wall to wall and threatening to swallow us all. "So glad you made it."

I wanted to cover the vial in my pocket with my hand, but I resisted the urge. We had no clue if Jackson or his father were even aware of our real reasons for coming here. As far as anyone knew, Star was oblivious to the relationship Angus and Jane had shared, so from his point of view, there was no way we knew about the failsafe he'd created. Still, I wasn't willing to put anything past him or his son.

Jackson's gaze moved past us, back to Helen's now lifeless body. His smile faltered just a little when he shook his head. "Helen. I knew that piece of trash was in on this. Dad always did have a soft side."

He shrugged and turned his gaze back to us. I could tell when he recognized Angus, because his body jerked, but he recovered quickly and once again pasted a smile on his face.

"So glad you could rejoin us." He stepped closer to us, and at my side Angus flinched. "Did you miss your old room? Wanted to do the full twenty?"

"Fuck you," my uncle growled.

Jackson rolled his eyes. "I knew not to expect an intelligent conversation from a pin cushion, but I thought you could do better than that."

Angus stiffened.

Jackson let out a chuckle and waved his hand at the guards. "Kill the man with one arm and the zombie slayer—" Jackson's gaze slid from Jim to Jada, and he paused. "Save the blonde. I can use someone who obviously enjoys pain as much as she does."

Jim growled and started to get to his feet, but was knocked down when the butt of a rifle slammed into his head.

"No," Jada gasped and reached for him only to be knocked aside by another guard.

Jackson ignored them both and looked the rest of us over, his gaze stopping on Donaghy. "The virus hasn't turned you yet. I'm surprised." He pressed his lips together for a second before saying, "Put the convict back in his cell. I can use a strong zombie like him." Then his gaze moved to me and I shivered. "The test subject goes back where he came from, but Meg is mine. I'll take care of her right now."

He moved without warning, pushing through the people kneeling around me and grabbing my arm. His grip was so strong when he jerked me to my feet that it felt like my arm was being ripped from its socket. I cried out, and even though I wanted to fight I knew it was useless. I had no choice but to move.

"I was hoping your parents would be here to see this," Jackson said when we had taken the spot he'd just vacated. "But this is better than nothing."

He grabbed my shirt and pulled, ripping it down the front. My hand went to the pocket where the vial was tucked away, trying to get it free before anything else happened. There was no way I could stop this thing he had planned for me from happening, but there had to be a way to save the vial, to make sure the bacteria was still released.

He mistook the gesture for modesty and laughed. "Go ahead and fight. I actually like that."

A shiver ran through me that only got worse when he managed to yank my shirt off completely. He tossed it aside and I dropped to the ground, scrambling for it. My heart was pounding and my head was screaming for me to fight him off, only I knew I couldn't focus on my own safety, not when I needed to protect the vial.

My fingers had just gripped my shirt when Jackson was on me. His hands were on my hips, already pulling at my pants, and I let out an involuntary scream. I kicked back, fighting on instinct even though I knew I had to focus on the vial.

His fingers curled around the waistband of my pants as he leaned forward, pressing his lips against my ear and hissing, "I've been fantasizing about your screams for years."

I squeezed my eyes shut when his warm breath brushed against my face, and it was at that exact moment that the world exploded.

A blast rocked the room and the windowed wall that looked out onto the courtyard shattered in a burst that sent shards of glass raining down on the lobby. All around me cries and yells and gunshots broke out, barely audible over the ringing in my ears. I couldn't figure out what was happening, and Jackson still had a grip on me, still had me pressed against the floor with his full weight. But he was distracted too, doing his best to call out orders to his guards as chaos filled the lobby.

I took the opportunity to pull my shirt closer, my hand digging in the fabric until I was able to locate the vial. It was cold against my skin when I closed my fingers around it, and I pulled it close to my body, doing my best to keep it out of sight. I had to get out. I had to break the vial in the streets where the horde of zombies we'd drawn into the city were no doubt still wreaking havoc on the citizens.

"Get them!" Jackson yelled.

His hold temporarily loosened on me and I took the opportunity to try and crawl away. He let out a growl of frustration and grabbed my hips, his fingers digging into my skin. I screamed and kicked and clawed at the floor, trying to pull myself free, but I was on my stomach and he had the advantage both in size and position.

Donaghy came out of nowhere, pouncing like a wild animal and knocking Jackson off me. They rolled across the floor in a tangle of limbs, and when I flipped onto my back the vial was still clutched against my chest. Donaghy had Jackson on the ground. The asshole was still struggling, but he was at a huge disadvantage with the bigger man on top of him. Then, out of nowhere, Donaghy let out a snarl that didn't sound the least bit human, and I watched in frozen horror as he bared his teeth only seconds before sinking them into Jackson's neck.

The scream that broke out of my former friend was nothing compared to the blood that sprayed from the wound. It splashed across Donaghy's face and neck and chest, and saturated Jackson's shirt in seconds before spreading out beneath them, creating a pool under their still tangled bodies. At first I couldn't move, too transfixed by what was happening to remember that I had a job to do. Donaghy hadn't turned, not completely, but he was like a man possessed as he tore a chunk out of Jackson's throat. Or like a zombie.

"Megan!"

I ripped my gaze from the sight in front of me to find my Uncle Al struggling with a guard, his eyes on me. All around me there was fighting, and dozens of people had flooded the building. They fought with guards as the group I'd come here with did the same, but at first I had no clue where they'd all come from. Then I caught sight of the High Priestess by the door and it dawned on me what had happened. Her followers weren't wearing their usual red robes, but she'd still brought The Church to our rescue.

"Go!" someone shouted, and then Jada was next to me, pulling me to my feet. She paused just long enough to pull off her leather jacket and fling it at me. "Get outside, release the bacteria!"

My heart was pounding as I pulled the jacket on, covering myself before scrambling toward the door with Jada at my side. Once or twice a guard lunged for me, but she took them out every time, her swift movements and exact aim seeming unreal even in the middle of everything else that was happening. The atmosphere surrounding us was loud and out of control, but I focused on the front door as I ran, putting every ounce of energy into it.

Things didn't get any better when I burst out into the dark night. The world was full of moans and growls and screams and cries for help. The music from the festival hadn't faded, and in the distance the sound of chanting had risen up above every other noise, filling the night sky with the same lines that had given me the creeps only two days ago.

"...*you have visited them with destruction and wiped out all remembrance of them...*"

I ran as fast as I could, barely noticing if Jada kept up but knowing that I was running straight toward the zombies we'd released on the city. My legs ached and my lungs threatened to burst, but I kept my eyes on the prize and pumped my legs faster and faster, leaving the CDC behind and charging into the streets, heading toward the chanting.

I didn't slow until I'd made it down the street and turned the corner. The town square came into view, and I was able to see the full measure of what we had done. It was the middle of the night by this point, but the streets were brightly lit thanks to the festival. Lights shone down on the bloody bodies that littered the street, on the zombies feasting on human flesh, on the people still fighting the dead or trapped in precarious positions that would only buy them time, not save them from doom.

I skittered to a halt and gasped for air, knowing that I had reached the right spot. It took a lot of effort to pry my fingers open, but when I did I found the vial resting in my palm. More than ever it looked tiny. Insignificant. Magical.

"Break it!" Jada called out from behind me.

A gunshot cut through the air and I turned to find her firing at a handful of approaching zombies. I lifted the vial above my head, preparing to smash it into the ground. This was for my family, for everything they'd lost, for my uncle who'd spent the last twenty years in a cell, for my sister who'd only been a child when they'd ripped her away from her family, for Parv and Joshua who had lost everything, for Donaghy who —

I lowered my arm, realization slamming into me.

Donaghy.

Not enough time had passed since he'd received the vaccine. The virus was still raging through his body. I knew because I'd watched him rip into Jackson only moments before. If I did this, if I broke this vial now, I would lose him. He would get taken out just like the rest of the zombies.

"What are you doing?" Jada called. "Do it!"

"Donaghy." I spun to face her, my gaze holding hers.

For a moment she looked incredulous, ready to punch me and do it herself, but then something flickered in her eyes and I knew who she was thinking about. Jim. If he were the one infected, if he was the one who would die by breaking this vial, she would hesitate too.

"You have to," she said, but even I could tell it took a great amount of effort for her to get the words out. "You know it."

I did. I knew that even if it took Donaghy out, I had to do this. All around me the world was going insane. Donaghy had taken Jackson down, but Star was still alive somewhere in this city. The Church had managed to subdue the guards in the CDC, but I wasn't foolish enough to think that it would last long. If I didn't take care of this now, we might lose our chance. There were no guarantees that we'd leave these walls alive, and if they caught us, they would destroy the failsafe once and for all.

Jada gave me time to think it through while she continued to take out the dead. Only a few seconds passed, but it felt like years, and when I finally nodded, she exhaled.

I lifted my arm again, holding it over my head dramatically as I took a deep breath. "I'm sorry, Donaghy."

A burst of pain cut through my calf and I cried out as I fell, throwing my hands out in front of me on instinct. My palms slammed into the ground and the vial got smashed between the cement sidewalk and my hand, shattering and sending shards of glass deep into my skin.

I rolled over, struggling to make sense of what had happened while my leg and hand throbbed. Jada was crouched above me, her lips moving as she fired, but no words reached me over the roar of blood and pain pounding in my ears. I squeezed my eyes shut and took a deep breath, trying to hang on, but darkness was closing in and I knew it was no use.

# CHAPTER TWENTY-TWO
## Donaghy

S lowly, like I was crawling out of a deep abyss, I started to register where I was. My body throbbed, my muscles and joints screaming with each move. But I felt better too. I could feel myself coming back from the brink of death. Could feel the vaccine winning out over the virus that had nearly killed me.

I was on my knees, sitting on the floor in the lobby of the CDC. My hands were slick, and I looked down to find them covered with blood. I stared at them as yelling and gunshots rang through the air. The world was chaos and it seemed to swirl around me like a tornado. I was in the middle of it, in the eye of the storm, but for some reason no one seemed to notice me sitting there and I felt invisible. Forgotten.

I blinked, trying to focus and remember what had happened. The blood wasn't just on my hands. It was smeared up my arms and splattered across my legs and chest. There was a trail of it on the floor, starting at me and stopping at the lifeless body of Jackson Star. His eyes were open, staring blankly at me in a way that felt accusatory even though he was no longer capable of that or any other emotion. His throat was ripped open. That was where all the blood had come from. I swallowed, suddenly aware of the coppery taste in my mouth. Of the film that coated my tongue. Of the sticky liquid that covered my face.

Realization slammed into me, and my stomach convulsed.

No. God, no.

I leaned forward, my palms flat against floor. It didn't help, not with Jackson's blood pooled in front of me. I squeeze my eyes shut as bile rose in my throat. Trying to swallow it down did no good, and neither did the deep breath I sucked in. I could smell the blood. It was everywhere. Was I turning? Had we been too late? No. I was better. Things were clearer now. I could think, could focus. I knew what I'd done and it sickened me, but the ache in my body had eased. The hunger was gone. The vaccine was working.

But not fast enough. Not soon enough to stop me from turning into a monster. I didn't remember what I'd done, but the proof was in front of me in the form of Jackson Star's mangled body. I didn't regret that he was dead, he deserved what he'd gotten and a hell of a lot more, but the thought of *how* it had happened, of me becoming animalistic enough to rip a man's throat out with my teeth...

My stomach lurched again, and this time I lost the battle. I heaved and vomited on the floor, my eyes closed so I didn't have to see it. Didn't have to think of what it had once been.

It didn't take long for my stomach to empty itself, and then I turned my back to the mess and Jackson. The fighting had begun to ease, but the number of bodies littering the floor was overwhelming. Too many to count, too many to focus on.

I scanned the people still up and moving around, looking for faces I knew. Angus was kneeling next to Al, helping him bandage what looked like a cut on his arm, and Jim was kicking at bodies like he wanted to be sure they were really dead, but Meg was nowhere in sight and neither was Jada.

I dragged myself up off the floor and pulled my shirt over my head, using it to wipe the blood from my face and hands and arms. It was an impossible task, there was just too much of it, but I managed to get some of it at least. The rest would have to wait.

I tossed the shirt aside when Angus looked up from where he and Al were sitting, and jogged over to join them. My body stiffened as I prepared myself for judgment or disgust in the other men's expressions. They must have seen what I'd done, had to know what the blood that covered my face, and neck, and hands was from.

When I stopped in front of them though, their gazes remained level. "Where's Meg?"

Angus shook his head as he stood, pulling Al up off the ground in the process. "Don't know. Last I saw she was runnin' outside with the vial."

I swallowed, knowing what it would mean for me if she succeeded. It was a moment of conflict, me hoping that she'd managed to break the vial while at the same time praying that she'd held off. Waiting would be stupid, we weren't in the clear yet and the sooner we were able to get that bacteria into the air the better, but I knew it would be the end for me as well. I wasn't ready to say goodbye. Not when the world was about to right itself. Not when Meg was here.

Behind me someone whistled, and the three of us turned toward the front of the CDC. Jim was standing where the door had once been. I didn't remember much of what had happened, but the missing front of the building combined with the glass and charred debris scattered around the lobby told me that there had been an explosion.

Jim waved, motioning for us to come over, and I took off running, unsure if he wanted us to head out or if something had happened. I got my answer when we reached the front and found a man carrying Meg. Her right calf was bloodied, as was the palm of her right hand. Jada walked at her side, somber but unhurt, but I didn't know her well enough to know what the expression on her face meant.

Meg turned her head as they approached, and the second her gaze met mine I knew she'd been successful. The bacteria had been released.

"What happened?" I asked, easing Meg from the other man's arms.

She winced and let out a little gasp of pain, but didn't protest. I was glad. I was about to die, possibly a slow and horrible death, and I wanted to hold her in my arms, to remember what her warm skin felt like against mine as I slipped away.

"Shot," Jada said.

Jim touched her arm and she turned to face him, lifting her eyebrows. They did this thing where they communicated silently for a moment, him asking if she was okay and her telling him she was good.

"Got me in the leg," Meg said.

Her face was so close to mine that I had to stop myself from kissing her. I couldn't, not when I wasn't sure if I was still contagious. I just hoped to God I got the all clear before the bacteria ate away at my brain, because I wanted to say goodbye to Meg properly this time.

"Your hand is bleedin' too," Angus pointed out.

"The vial broke in my hand," Meg whispered, the words trembling with so much emotion it made me want to break down and cry. For her though, not for me. I knew she'd done what she had to, but I also knew that she was going to blame herself forever.

"So it's done?" Al asked.

Jada ripped her gaze from Jim's and focused on Meg. "It's done."

We stood in silence for a moment. The city was still loud, there was still fighting in the distance and screaming, but we seemed to be in the clear. We could leave. All we had to do was make our way back to Dragon's and head out through the tunnel.

"We should go," I said, holding Meg closer to my chest. "Before Star finds us."

She had her arms around my neck like she was holding on for dear life, and at that moment I didn't want her to ever let go.

I had only taken one step before Jada said, "Helen."

I froze, the sudden memory of what had happened to Helen flashing through my mind. We couldn't leave her. Not like she was, lying on the floor in the CDC. Dragon would never forgive us. And then there was Glitter. I barely knew the waitress with the pink hair, but back in Senoia Meg had filled me in on everything I'd missed, and I knew that Helen had been like a mother to that girl. The only real mother she'd ever known.

"We have to take her," Meg said. "After everything she's done, she deserves a proper burial. And her family deserves to say goodbye."

Angus grunted, but nodded too. "Yeah. She saved me, took care of my girl. The least I can do is take her home."

He headed for the CDC, leaving the rest of us standing in the courtyard.

"I'll help," Jim said only a second later, jogging after him.

"I can walk," Meg whispered.

I held her tighter. "No." The word was so ragged that I had to clear my throat. "I'll carry you."

She wasn't heavy, not that it would've mattered. The ache in my body had eased even more and was now barely detectable. Only when I flexed the muscles in my arms was there a hint of pain left. There were still zombies all over the city and people were shouting, but the chaos was dying down. The gunshots ringing through the air were becoming less and less frequent, as were the growls and moans. The dead that had invaded the city were losing the battle, and I could only assume it was because The Church had been ready for them.

From where we stood I could see into the lobby of the CDC. Jackson's body was still lying where I'd left it, as were the guards who had been taken out by the members of The Church. The High Priestess stood just inside, her daughter at her side, both of them staring out into the night as Angus approached. I expected him to pass her by, to be disgusted by the very idea of talking to her. The woman had built a religion that revolved around his death. But he stopped when he reached her. She said something, and even though Angus had his back to me, I could see him nod. The High Priestess's smile stretched wider and it sent a shiver shooting through me.

Jim jogged up to join them, and the woman's smile melted away. Angus stood there for only a second longer before continuing through the lobby and over to where Helen's body lay waiting.

"What are they talking about?" I asked.

Jada had her back to the CDC, her focus on the zombies crowding the city. She looked over her shoulder, her gaze going to the High Priestess. "It's about Star."

"How do you know?" Al asked.

"Because Angus has already said that he won't rest until Star is dead."

It made sense. The asshole had locked him in a cell for twenty years, had tortured his daughter, killed the woman he'd loved, and then dragged his brother there when Angus had finally gotten free himself. I got it. I sure as hell got the need for revenge. But I wasn't sure it was possible. Jackson was dead, but there were still guards. Even with the front window blown out, the CDC was still heavily fortified. After today, Star would do everything he could to make sure the building was locked down tight. It would take an army to penetrate his defenses.

Or a fanatical group of religious zealots.

"He's going to come back," I said, realization dawning on me.

"Of course he is," Meg's uncle, Al, said. "He just went to get Helen's body."

I shook my head, and looked around. My gaze met Jada's and I could tell by the expression in her eyes that she knew what I was talking about.

"I mean, Angus James is going to come back from the dead and lead The Church in tearing down the CDC."

"He—" Whatever Al was going to say died on his lips as the truth sank in. "Holy shit."

"The prophecy the church has been waiting for is about to come true," Meg said.

# CHAPTER TWENTY-THREE

## Meg

It didn't take long for Angus to return with Helen's body, and then we were on our way through the city and heading for freedom.

I couldn't look at my uncle as we ran. Every time I did I found myself hiding my face in Donaghy's chest. I couldn't stand the sight, hated the way Helen's arm hung lifelessly at her side, the way her head drooped to the right. I couldn't imagine how Dragon and Glitter would get through this. It seemed so unfair after everything they'd done for my family, and yet we were all going to make it out of this in one piece.

At least we were for the time being. It was no secret that Angus planned to come back to city. He hadn't even tried to deny it when Al questioned him. All he did was give my uncle a look that screamed *stay the fuck out of this.* It wasn't like any of us could blame him. In fact, if the situation were reversed, I had no doubt in my mind that I would want to come back too. Any of us would. What Star had done to my uncle was unforgivable. He had stolen Angus's life, and it only made sense that he would want revenge. I knew there would be an argument when we got back to Senoia, but I also doubted that anyone, not even Dad, would be able to talk Angus out of this.

The streets of New Atlanta were dark and nearly deserted except for the bodies littering the streets. Donaghy refused to put me down even though I told him I could walk. He hadn't recovered from the virus completely yet and I was worried that carrying me was hurting him. No matter what I said though, he told me he was fine and continued to run, following the others as we made our way to the entertainment district.

I did my best not to look at the bodies we passed, but it was impossible. It brought back memories of the day Margot disappeared. Of Jackson and me, back when I'd thought he was a good person, searching the streets for my missing sister. I'd been so certain after that day that she was gone for good, and yet now she was back. It was a result I had longed for a million times over the past nine years, but one I'd never thought was possible. Now that it was here, I was terrified of what would happen. Of what I would learn when we got back to Senoia and I was finally once again face-to-face with my little sister. She'd been so out of it when we'd liberated her from the CDC, and I tried to tell myself it had been the drugs. Once they were out of her system she'd have to remember us. Wouldn't she? I thought so, but I also worried what nine years in that prison had done to her. How could a person come back from something like that? My uncle had been imprisoned even longer, but he'd been an adult when they'd locked him away. He'd had moments of salvation in his daughter, and her mother. From what we'd seen of Margot's existence, it seemed like she'd been given nothing. No hope, no relief.

But Glitter was okay. Yes, she had nightmares and I was sure there were other side effects of the torture she'd suffered at the hands of Star, but she had managed to adjust and move on. I could only hope that Margot would be able to do the same.

Donaghy shifted my weight as we reached the street that ran through the entertainment district.

"I can walk," I told him for the tenth time.

He shook his head and his arms tightened around me. "I'm fine. There's no sense in hurting yourself when I can carry you. You don't know what walking may do to your leg."

He had a point. The bullet had gotten me in the calf and even though the injury seemed superficial, it still throbbed with each step he took, so I couldn't really imagine what it would be like to walk on it myself. Not that I wouldn't do it if I needed to. I worried that carrying me was putting him at a disadvantage. That he wouldn't be able to defend himself if necessary, or that he would get run down too fast thanks to the virus still left in his system.

"Don't push yourself," I said. "You're still recovering."

Donaghy's grip on me tightened, and his blue eyes focused on mine. "No. I'm not…"

The unsaid words hung between us. He wasn't recovering; he was dying. And it was my fault. I should've held off. I shouldn't have broken the vial when I knew what it would do to him. We could've waited. I could have hidden somewhere in the city and waited an hour or two before breaking the vial. The results would've been the same for the zombies. They still would have died, but it would've given the vaccine time to work its way through Donaghy's system. Now though, it was just a waiting game. Soon the bacteria would spread and begin to destroy the zombies' brains, as well as his.

For a moment I couldn't talk. It felt like someone was squeezing my throat, making it impossible for me to get even a single word out.

We reached the end of the street and stopped outside Dragon's Lair. Donaghy was breathing heavily, and even though I knew it was from the trek through the city, the worry that the bacteria had already invaded his brain was still present.

"How do you feel?"

He swallowed and sucked in a big mouthful of air like he was trying to catch his breath. "I'm okay. I feel better, really."

We both knew it would only be temporary, but neither one of us said it.

THE ADRENALINE FROM OUR ESCAPE MUST HAVE BEEN wearing off, because by the time we got back to Senoia my calf felt like it was on fire. The drive seemed longer than the first time too, and every bump in the road sent a throb pulsing up and down my leg. I sank my teeth into my bottom lip, hoping to bite back the moans of agony that tried to force their way out of me. I wasn't fooling Donaghy, though. It seemed like his eyes were on me the entire trip, like he was memorizing my face, trying to absorb every one of my emotions. I didn't know if he was just checking to see if I was okay or if it had something to do with the fact that he knew he was about to die. Like maybe he was hoping to be able to cling to the image of me even after his brain began to deteriorate.

I wanted to ask him how he was feeling, but I also didn't want to know. We knew very little about the bacteria we'd released. Not how long it would take to start working or how quickly it would eat away at the zombies' brains. Or if Donaghy would suffer.

When we rolled through the gates of Senoia, my focus shifted slightly, but not completely. My mind was at war with itself, part of it thinking of Donaghy and what he would very soon be going through while the other part was focused on my family. On Dad and his injuries, on Margot and the effects of being locked away for so long. Then there was Angus and his vendetta against Star, as well as Dragon and Glitter and how they would react to Helen's death. So much had happened, and it was too much to think about because there was still so much to do, but I couldn't stop thinking about Donaghy and it only made me feel guilty for not devoting a hundred percent of my energy to my family.

The truck rolled to a stop and we all climbed out. Donaghy helped me down, his hands firm on my hips like he never wanted to let me go. It was dark and the town was silent, but I could see Max and Bonnie's house from where we stood. It was lit up, nearly every window glowing with life, and I knew my family was there, together again after all these years. Mom, dad, and Margot. They were waiting for me.

Donaghy supported me as we made our way toward the house. Every step made my leg throb, but I ignored the pain and kept going, my sights on the house that held something I never thought I would have again. A complete family.

We were still a good twenty feet away when the front door opened. Mom stepped out, Aunt Lila at her side, and Dad was right behind her. I craned my neck, trying to look past them, hoping to see Margot there even though I knew it was a long shot. She'd been so drugged up that she was probably sleeping it off, but I couldn't stop hoping. I wanted everything to be normal. Not that I even knew what normal was. Instead of my sister, I saw Dragon and Glitter, and my heart sank.

Angus walked at my side with Helen in his arms. I could tell when Dragon saw her because I recognized the expression on his face. It was the same one Mom had worn after Margot disappeared, after Dad was declared dead. It was heartbreak and devastation. It was a person breaking right in front of my eyes. There was so much hurt and anger and betrayal that it felt like a knife in my chest.

Glitter's hand went to her throat and her mouth opened. As far as I could tell, no sound came out, but it didn't matter. She was as heartbroken as Dragon. He was already moving down the stairs, his hands out and reaching for Helen, but Glitter didn't move an inch. I actually saw it when her legs began to tremble, and then she was going down, dropping to her knees on the porch like she couldn't stand up any longer.

Dragon reached us and took Helen from my uncle. I couldn't look at him, but I could hear his quiet sobs as they forced their way out. My uncle said something I didn't catch, and then he was moving past the sobbing man to the house where his daughter sat in silent shock.

Mom came down the porch to me, but Dad stayed where he was, staring at my uncle like he was looking at a ghost.

"What happened?" Mom asked when she was still five feet away. She reached for me, her hands ready to catch me in case I fell. Her eyes swept over me, moving down to my bloody leg and going wide. "You were shot."

"I'm okay," I said even though I wasn't sure if that was true.

Of course, my uncertainty had nothing to do with the injury. Al had checked it out, and he'd been around long enough to know when a gunshot wound was serious. I'd believed him when he'd said it was minor even though it hurt like hell. But my heart told a different story. The ache in my chest had nothing to do with physical injuries, and everything to do with the things we'd lost and the things we still might lose.

Mom's gaze moved to Donaghy. "Bring her inside."

Donaghy nodded, and before I could protest he swept me up into his arms again. Once I was there I didn't want to argue, because I knew that we had a very limited amount of time left together, and I wanted to be able to remember what it felt like to have his strong arms around me once he was gone.

We followed Mom inside, leaving Dragon behind with Helen's body, passing my uncle who was doing his best to comfort his daughter. When we walked by Dad, he reached out and stroked my head, and the touch was so familiar that it made my eyes fill with tears. I leaned into his hand, squeezing my eyes shut and remembering all the other times he'd done the exact same thing.

The touch was so simple, so small, but it brought back hundreds of memories. Me playing on the floor as a child, how he would walk by me and run his hand over my head without even really knowing he had done it. When I'd had a bad dream and he would sit on the edge of my bed, how he had run his hand over my head, pushing the hair back out of my face. When I was sick, when I was hurt, when I was scared. Those times and so many more. I'd thought that I would never have the chance to feel that gentle touch again, but here he was and here I was. We'd been given a second chance.

Donaghy followed Mom into the house, Dad trailing after us. She led us to the same living room we'd taken Donaghy to just two days earlier when he'd shown up burning with fever. It was the middle of the night, but the house was alive with activity. Charlie sat in a chair next to the couch, staring down at Margot. My sister was resting, covered in a blanket even though the air was thick with humidity. Her face was slack and peaceful, but my cousin's expression was ripe with worry and pain.

"Has she said anything?" I asked, looking to Mom.

"Not yet."

Her voice was level and calm, bringing to mind the woman I'd grown up with. She'd been gone for so long that I'd almost forgotten how strong she could be. Finally, she was back. I could see it in the way she held herself, in the steady way she looked at me, in how she motioned for Donaghy to put me down, her hand not trembling in the least.

"Is she okay?" I asked as Donaghy set me in a chair.

Mom knelt in front of me, her brown eyes holding mine and somehow giving me strength even though at the moment I felt ready to scream. "Right now, we need to worry about you. Margot is resting and she *is* going to be okay."

200

The certainty in my mother's voice helped stave off my worry, but I knew it couldn't last. There was too much to worry about, too much going on to chase the concern away forever.

Mom didn't say anything else but instead focused her attention on my leg. The fabric of the scrubs I wore was glued to my skin thanks to the dried blood. She pulled at the hole, trying to make it bigger so she could examine the wound, but after a moment she sat back and shook her head.

"We're going to need to get these pants off."

Dad crouched down next to her and pulled out a knife. "Just cut the pant leg," he said, and I didn't miss the way his eyes moved toward Donaghy.

Mom must not have either, because she rolled her eyes and almost smiled, something I hadn't seen in weeks. Not since Dad disappeared. If it wasn't for the fact that Donaghy was living on borrowed time, I might've smiled too. Maybe even laughed. I'd thought I would never be able to witness my dad being overprotective again, and it was amazing how something that would have annoyed me in the past now filled me with gratitude and joy.

Despite the eye roll, Mom took the knife and used it to cut the leg of my pants off below the knee. Once the fabric was gone and she was able to get a better look at the wound, some of the worry in her expression faded away.

"It's not bad."

"Al said the same thing," I told her. "I think it just grazed me." I held out my hand then, showing her the cuts on my palm. "This may be more of an issue. I think there may still be some glass in the cuts."

She took my hand so she could examine the injury more closely. "What happened?"

"I fell. The vial broke in my hand." Saying the words was a reminder of what I had done, of how I had sentenced Donaghy to death.

Mom must have realized it, because she froze, my hand still held in hers. "You released the bacteria?"

I swallowed. "I did."

I could see the questions in her eyes, how she was wondering if enough time had passed and what had happened while we were out there. She held my gaze, searching for the answers, and I could tell when she found them because her face fell.

"I'm sorry," she whispered.

"So am I."

Dad looked confused, but I couldn't explain. Not now. Donaghy stood at my side, his hand resting on my shoulder like he couldn't bear the thought of not touching me. I knew he wanted to be alone with me, but I had other things to worry about right now.

I turned my gaze on Dad. "How's your head? Are you okay?"

He nodded and reached out, putting his hand on my knee as Mom went to work trying to get the glass from the cut on my palm.

"I'll be alright."

"Jackson is dead," I said. "I should have listened to you. You tried to tell me who he really was, but I didn't want to hear it."

Dad gave me a crooked smile. "Ain't that how all teenagers are?"

A tear-clogged laugh bubbled up in my throat. "I guess so."

"What 'bout Star?" Dad asked.

"Never saw the bastard." Angus stepped into the room and Dad turned to face his brother. "He's always been the type who gave orders from behind a desk, so it ain't much of a surprise that he didn't have the balls to show up today."

"He can't make it through this," Dad said. "If he does, he'll just figure out 'nother way to take over."

"Then we gotta stop him," my uncle agreed.

Mom sucked in a breath, but I could tell by the expression on her face that she didn't disagree. And sitting here, seeing what Star had done to my family and the people I cared about, I couldn't either.

# CHAPTER TWENTY-FOUR
## Donaghy

I tried to convince myself that I didn't feel any different then I had before Jackson injected me. The effects of the virus had worn off, there was no more pain, no more burning in my veins, no more disorientation, but something else had taken its place, something I couldn't describe even if I'd wanted to, which I didn't. Right now, the only thing I wanted to think about was Star and what we needed to do to take that bastard down. His son was gone, which put him at a disadvantage, but he still had guards and a fortified building that wouldn't be easy to get into. Our biggest advantage was Angus. The Church, those crazy zealots who had been waiting years for him to return, would follow Angus James no matter where he went. Especially if he promised retribution.

"Can we get into the city the way we came out?" Axl asked.

"No," Angus shook his head. "You ain't goin'."

Meg's dad started to argue, but Vivian put her hand on her husband's arm. "You can't. You're hurt."

"If you think I'm gonna sit back and do nothin' after what he did to our daughter—" He choked on the words.

Angus put his hands on his brother's shoulders. "I know you don't wanna give in, but you gotta stay. I know what he's done, and I ain't gonna let him get away with it. You can trust me lil' brother. I'll take care of this, you just gotta take care of yourself and your girl."

Axl's gaze moved to the couch where Margot was still sleeping. Every few minutes she twisted in her sleep, and every sound she let out seemed like a knife in her parents' hearts. I couldn't imagine anyone coming back from this. Her life must have been hell for the last nine years. If nothing else, if he hadn't destroyed the lives of anyone else, Star deserved to die for what he'd done to Meg's sister. But he'd done so much more, so much more than anyone in the history of the world had done. He'd created and released a virus that had destroyed *everyone's* lives, every family had been affected, were still being affected, by what he'd done. Star didn't just deserve to die; he deserved to suffer.

Reluctantly, Meg's dad nodded, but his eyes were still on his daughter. His brother pulled him forward so roughly that it looked like someone had shoved them together, and then Angus wrapped his arms around his younger brother in a tight hug and whispered something in his ear that was too quiet for any of us to catch.

Axl nodded twice and closed his eyes. "You promise me," he said.

"If I hafta die tryin', Star will pay."

Once Axl had accepted the fact that he wouldn't be heading back into New Atlanta, things moved quickly. The usual suspects were going: Parvarti, Jim and Jada, Dragon, Al and his son. I could tell Meg's mom was torn about what to do, but ultimately she chose to stay with her injured daughters and husband. It seemed to hurt her deep inside, but all it took was one look at the determined expression on Angus's face for her to make the decision.

"You'll take care of it?" she asked him.

"You don't hafta worry," he replied.

Vivian nodded once.

"I'm in," I said when there was finally a break in the decision making process.

All eyes went to me, and I knew they were looking for any signs of weakness. I wanted to be angry, but the truth was, they had every right to be worried. I'd ripped out Jackson's throat with my teeth, and even though I could tell the effects of the virus had worn off, no one else knew that for sure. Even more troubling was the fact that a brain-eating bacteria could attack me at any moment. We had no clue how long it would take to work its way through me.

"If something happens," I told them, hoping to ease their concerns, "you can leave me behind. I won't slow you down."

"Fine," Angus said. "But I'm the one who kills Star."

He gave everyone a cold stare, sweeping his gaze across the room in a way that made even me give pause. I would have loved to be the one to draw that asshole's blood, but I knew that if anyone had a right to Star, it was Angus James. He'd probably spent the last twenty years imagining how he would take the life of the man who'd imprisoned him. Those fantasies might have been one of the few things that had kept him sane for all these years. If all went well, by the end of the day he would get to live one of them out, and I couldn't wait to watch.

# CHAPTER TWENTY-FIVE
## Meg

With Helen gone, the settlement's doctor was our only option for medical care. He was a grizzled, old man who I imagined had been close to retirement age when the virus was first released, and who now looked as if he'd been living with one foot in the grave for years.

He gave my leg a cursory glance, declaring that it was going to take time to heal but would be okay, and then graced my hand with four shaky stitches. Parv and Kelly's gunshot wounds were more serious, but nothing that a few stitches couldn't fix. They had both gotten lucky and the bullets had gone all the way through.

When our injuries were done, the doctor checked out Dad, declaring what we all already knew: he had a concussion and needed to take it easy. Then it was Donaghy's turn. Only his diagnosis was less straightforward than all the others had been.

The white-haired doctor was so hunched over that even though he was standing and Donaghy was sitting during the exam, they were practically eye level.

"I can't speak as to what Star's cooked up this time," the old man said, "but it's sure to be a pain in the ass."

The younger man glared at him. "Is that your professional opinion?"

The doctor narrowed his eyes. "I may look like I've lived past my expiration date, young man, but my mind is as sharp as that knife you have strapped to your leg." He slipped his stethoscope around his neck. "And yes, that's my professional opinion." The doctor straightened up as much as he could. "All I can tell you right now is that nothing seems amiss. Your blood pressure and heart rate are okay, and there are no outward signs that anything is going on. But I'm not Superman, and without his x-ray vision, that's the best I can do." His expression softened. "I'm sorry."

Donaghy just nodded in response.

I stayed at his side, my hand resting on his shoulder, as the doctor turned to examine Margot. My sister still hadn't opened her eyes, but she'd mumbled a few unintelligible words in her sleep. Whether that was a good sign or a bad sign we didn't yet know, but I was hoping the doctor could give us some kind of idea about what was going on and what we could expect.

The room was silent as he listened to my sister's heart, took her pulse, and then studied her pupils. He shook his head a few times, but said nothing until he'd pushed himself up — with great effort — and turned to face Mom and Dad.

"She's drugged, that much you know, but I can't tell you with what or how long it's been going on, so I have no clue what the outcome will be." The doctor gave them a sympathetic frown. "After nine years, she's bound to have some symptoms of PTSD. And that's *if* she recovers at all. There are no guarantees, as I'm sure you well know, so I'm not going to sugar coat it. I'm sorry."

Mom pressed her face against Dad's chest and he tightened his arms around her.

"There ain't nothin' we can do?"

"You can talk to her. Remind her about happy times, things that she loved before she was taken." The doctor shrugged. "I'm no shrink, but if she feels safe she may come out of this better. I wish I could tell you more, but there's just no way of knowing what Star did in there."

He turned and shuffled from the room without so much as a goodbye, not that any of us cared. We were all dealing with our own form of heartbreak right now. Mom and Dad had once again taken up their vigil at Margot's side while the rest of my family, my aunts and uncles and cousins, stood helplessly off to the side. Glitter was in the same chair the High Priestess had sat in only a few days ago, her legs pulled up to her chest, her arms wrapped around them like she was trying to comfort herself. It was something she was probably used to, having spent so many years locked up, and now that the only mother she'd ever known was gone, she had resorted to something familiar.

"Where's Dragon?" I whispered to Donaghy.

He shook his head. "Outside, I think. Why?"

"We need to have a funeral for Helen. Let him say his goodbyes."

Donaghy nodded and pushed himself up. "I'll go find him. See if he needs help digging a hole."

I swallowed and nodded, unable to force out any words, and as Donaghy passed, he ran his hand down my arm, leaving goose bumps behind.

Angus was standing at the door, and he said something to Donaghy in a quiet voice before nodding. My uncle's gaze moved to where Mom and Dad where sitting, and then to Glitter. His expression softened, and then he turned and followed Donaghy out.

My leg throbbed when I moved over to where my family sat, but I had already determined that I wasn't going to let it slow me down. I took Margot's hand before taking a seat in the chair at my Dad's side and he slipped his arm around my shoulders.

I leaned my head on him and whispered, "I missed you."

"Missed you, too," he said.

When his lips brushed the top of my head, I closed my eyes. I'd thought that getting them back—Dad, Margot, and Donaghy—would fix everything, but it hadn't. Now we just had a different set of problems, and no solutions. It wasn't as simple as storming the CDC anymore. Now we had to wait and hope. Now there was nothing we could do to fix what Star had done.

"I want to go," I said, my eyes still closed. "I want to go back into the city and finish this."

"Megan—" Mom began.

She was cut off when Dad said, "Go."

I opened my eyes so I could look up into his. "Really?"

"Yes, really?" Mom said, and I turned my gaze her way to find an expression of betrayal on her face. "You're going to let our daughter go back in there? After everything we've been through?"

"It ain't up to me," Dad said. "She's an adult. Twenty. That's how old you was when all this started, and you handled yourself. Megan can too, and if she wants to go in there she'll go whether we tell her she can or not. You of all people should know that."

"But we can try to talk some sense into her," Mom argued.

Dad's lips twitched, the first smile I'd seen on his face since we rescued him. "'Cause that's what you woulda done?"

Mom pressed her lips together, but it only took a second for her to sigh and shake her head. "No. I would have run off even as you were yelling for me to stay."

Dad let out a little chuckle that made my insides ache for everything that had been taken from us. "I know. Trust me, I remember."

"What about her leg?" Mom said, trying a different angle this time. "She was shot!"

"It grazed me," I argued.

"The doc said it's good," Dad pointed out.

Mom exhaled and turned her gaze on me. "You have to promise to be careful. I can't lose you, not when I've finally been given the chance to heal. Understand?"

"I will, Mom." I wanted to roll my eyes—like I planned on being reckless and stupid—but I knew she needed to say it for her own benefit, not for mine.

"Okay, then," she said.

She turned her gaze back to Margot, but not before reaching over Dad so she could slip her hand into my free one.

WE BURIED HELEN IN THE SETTLEMENT'S CEMETERY. IT was under a large live oak tree, the gnarled branches long and the leaves thick enough to shade the area from the oppressive Georgia sun. There weren't a lot of us gathered, just our small group and a handful of people from Senoia, like Jada, Bonnie, and Max. Dragon had dug the grave himself, refusing to let Donaghy and Angus help even though they'd offered, and then he had carried Helen's body out and laid it in the hole.

She was wrapped in a white sheet, which I was thankful for. I hadn't known the woman that long, but now that I knew her history, how she'd saved my uncle and worked so hard to right the wrongs Star had inflicted on this world, I had a deep respect for her and the person she'd been.

Dragon stood with his arms crossed, staring down into the grave as he spoke. "Most people who were alive when the virus was released lost a lot. Husbands and wives, parents and children. I had none of that though, so when the world ended and started over, my life didn't seem that different. Back then I'd worked as a bouncer in a shitty little bar in Atlanta, and that's where I was while the world was dying. There were others there too, people who like me had had nothing to lose and chose to take refuge in a bottle of booze rather than die alone at home. The owner was gone by then, as were most of the employees, and so I took over the job of pouring drinks while I waited for my time to come.

"It didn't though, and I stayed there in that bar long after all the patrons had died off. After the zombies came, and even after the CDC began their reconstruction of Atlanta. Dragon's Lair was the first bar open in the entertainment district, and in the new world that had been created I was a wealthy man. I knew, just like many of us did in those days, that Star was more interested in grabbing power than he was in fixing things, but I didn't care because I was doing well.

"Then I met Amira." He looked up and I followed his gaze to Jim, whose expression looked tortured at the mention of this woman I'd never before heard of. "When she told me what she'd overheard in the CDC, about how Angus James was still alive, I can't say that I believed her all that much. There were all kinds of rumors going around the city in those days. Even when she died I wasn't convinced, despite what Jim said. It wasn't until Helen showed up in my bar that I really began to grasp the reality of what was happening inside the CDC. It wasn't until I met her that I started to care about anything other than myself.

"Helen changed me. She made me a better person, not just because of my efforts to overthrow Star, but because she helped me care about other people for the first time in my entire life. I didn't have a good childhood, didn't have people who loved me and the world that I knew back then was ruthless and selfish, but Helen changed all that. She made my life better." Dragon paused and took a deep breath. "I'll miss her every day for the rest of my life, but I know that she died for something she believed in. She died trying to make up for the part she'd played in all this, trying to make the world better. Because that's who she was."

Angus held Glitter as she sobbed, and my own eyes weren't even a little dry. I leaned against Donaghy, focusing on the steady beat of his heart as Dragon nodded once and then grabbed a shovel. Then he began to fill the hole, dropping shovelful after shovelful of dirt onto Helen's body while the rest of us stood in silence.

When he once again refused help, people slowly began to shuffle away. Donaghy and I did as well, knowing that Dragon wanted to be alone. That he needed to do this himself.

It was early evening already, and I couldn't wrap my brain around where the day had gone. Most of it had been taken up by filling everyone in on what had happened inside New Atlanta, and then on discussions of what was going to happen next. Angus had enlisted the help of The Church, just like we'd suspected, and even though it made all of us a little uneasy, we all knew we were out of options.

I was exhausted by the time we made it back into the house, so I lead Donaghy upstairs, ignoring the look Dad shot my way. He was the one who'd told Mom that I was an adult, so it was time he took that to heart. Plus, at the moment I needed not only to rest, but also to be with Donaghy. We'd been up for over twenty-four hours, and even though adrenaline had kept me going until now, I felt as if I'd suddenly hit a wall.

When we were alone in the bedroom I'd occupied since coming to Senoia, I slipped onto the bed and pulled Donaghy with me. My injured calf and palm throbbed, but I'd been working hard not to let anyone know because I didn't want anyone arguing with me when I volunteered to go back into Atlanta. Which was something I needed to discuss with Donaghy. As tired as I was, I knew this couldn't wait.

"I'm going," I said when he'd settled down next to me.

Donaghy's mouth dropped open and for a moment it seemed like he didn't know what to say. Then he shook his head. "No, you're not."

212

"This isn't just about you. You killed Jackson, but Star is still alive. I know what he's done to the entire world, but do you have any idea what he's done to my family? Do you understand what we've been through over the last twenty years? My uncle, my sister, my dad. Think about what he did to us. Do you really think I can sit back and do nothing?"

His resolve wavered, I could see it in his icy blue eyes, but it only took a moment for him to shake his head again. "You're hurt."

"It's a graze." I waved to my leg, using the hand that had been cut. "I can get through it."

Donaghy clenched his hands into fists like he was trying to maintain control. After a second, he relaxed and scooted closer to me. His hands, which had been tense only a moment ago, now slid up my arms at a feather soft rate. His touch sent a shiver shooting through me, bringing gooseflesh up on every inch of my exposed skin. The way his fingertips grazed over the bumps reminded me of a blind man trying to read a book, how every touch of his hands against the paper was necessary so he could absorb the entire story. Donaghy did that now, sweeping his hands up, his palms flat, his fingers brushing the underside of my arms. It was like he was trying to memorize how I felt at this moment, like he wanted to carry the feeling with him for the rest of his life.

"How are you feeling?" The words nearly stuck in my throat and I had to swallow before I could get anything else out. "Can you feel it? Can you feel anything happening?"

He shook his head, but it was slow and unconvincing. "No." The word was ragged and painful, like it had to rip its way out of him. "A little."

My stomach clenched like the words had somehow wrapped themselves around my insides. "Does it hurt?"

"No."

He didn't elaborate, and I couldn't ask more if I wanted to stay focused on the task in front of us. Which I did. We had a job, we needed to get back into the city and take Star out for good. That was what I needed to focus on once we headed out, not Donaghy. We had time, or at least I had to convince myself of that. I knew no matter what my feelings were right now, setting the world right had to be my number one priority.

"I'm going," I said again.

Donaghy nodded in response, and even though it was hesitant, I could tell by the expression in his eyes that he was done arguing.

His gaze moved to my lips and I realized that he now had other things on his mind, things that we had both been thinking about before but had been unable to partake in thanks to the virus. He had been given the vaccine more than twelve hours ago. It had to have worked its way through him by now.

I knew we should be resting, getting sleep so we were ready and alert when we headed out to storm the CDC, but with Donaghy this close to me, with his body heat seeping inside me, I knew sleep would be impossible.

I moved closer, my sights set on his lips, but he jerked away. "It might not be safe."

"You said yourself that you felt better," I lifted an eyebrow at him. "Was it a lie?"

He shook his head. "No, but I don't want to risk infecting you."

I moved so I was on my knees in front of him and grabbed the hem of my shirt, pulling it up before he had time to stop me. When I'd tossed it aside Donaghy's eyes moved over me hungrily, taking in my bare flesh.

"You won't infect me," I whispered before moving closer, this time hitting the mark and pressing my lips to his.

His mouth was warm against mine, and soft. It felt even better than I remembered, and when his hands moved up my back, so did the feel of his skin against mine. The calluses on his palms were a sign of the hard life he'd had, but they were also one of the things I loved about him. They illustrated his strength, his perseverance.

"Meg—" His voice was ragged, but I silenced him by running my tongue across his bottom lip.

"I'm not going to let you talk me out of it," I said, already reaching for the button on his pants. "Not this time."

His gaze held mine as I undid his jeans, and when I reached inside with my uninjured hand, he let out a low groan. That was all it took for his resolve to shatter, and in seconds I was on my back with him hovering over me, my hand working him over as his lips blazed a fiery trail across my skin. He pulled the strap of my bra aside so he could kiss my shoulder and down my chest, finally moving the cup to reveal my breast. When his lips closed over my nipple, I let out a gasp that was much too loud considering how many people were in this house, but I didn't care. I didn't care who heard or who knew, because I only had a short time left with this man and I was determined to get as much out of it as possible.

We kissed and touched and explored one another as we undressed. My clothes suddenly felt like a prison that I had to break out of, and it wasn't until we were both naked and he was on top of me that I felt any kind of relief. Even that wasn't enough though, because I wanted him closer, needed him inside me.

"I need you," I whispered against his lips, lifting my hips up to meet his.

Donaghy groaned again, his mouth attacking mine as he shifted his weight. He broke the kiss as he slid into me, his gaze holding mine like he needed to see my expression.

Once he was inside, his mouth covered mine again. His movements were torturously slow, as if he wanted to drag this out forever. I pulled him closer, kissed him deeper, wrapped my legs around his waist as the need to have him closer to me grew, not caring that my calf and hand throbbed, not caring because I needed him more than I'd ever needed anyone.

This was only the second time we'd had sex, and the first time had been nothing compared to this. Nothing compared to the slow build of ecstasy, to the special attention Donaghy seemed to give every inch of me, to the way he dragged it out. Even after I'd reached climax, he didn't finish. Not even after I'd come down from the high. Instead, he stopped so he could kiss me, his tongue dancing over mine. When he started to move again the strokes were long and slow, torturous in their unhurried pace. I felt drunk in my ecstasy, high on him, and desperate in my need to keep him with me.

When he finally began to move faster, he held onto me like the same thoughts had entered his mind, like if he just clung to me hard enough this moment would never end. But the end came too quickly, was too sudden and sharp and painful. It brought tears to my eyes, making me feel like a fool, and I found myself pressing

215

my face against his sweaty chest, trying to hide my tears because I had no right to cry when he was the one who was going to die.

"Hey," he whispered, brushing the damp hair off my face. "Stop. It's okay."

I shook my head because I couldn't stop and it wasn't okay, and the tears only came harder.

He tried for a moment to get me to sit up and talk to him, but when I refused he just held me and let me cry. I needed it. Between the lack of sleep and the emotional journey of getting into the CDC to save my family, as well as the losses we'd racked up and the knowledge that it wasn't over, I was due for a good cry.

I WOKE WITH A START, DRENCHED IN SWEAT AND unsure of where I was. Only the heavy breathing of Donaghy brought me back to the present, but even then I wasn't sure if everything had actually happened or if it had been a dream. Had we really saved Dad and Margot? Could Jackson really be dead?

I tried to convince myself that none of it had been a dream, but it was all too unreal and I suddenly felt desperate to see my family with my own eyes. Careful not to wake Donaghy, I rolled out of bed and stumbled in the blackness for my clothes.

The hallway was dark and the wood floor creaked under my feet as I made my way to the stairs. When Donaghy and I had come up, Mom and Dad had still been downstairs with Margot and I had no doubt in my mind that they would still be there. The light that penetrated the darkness when I reached the first floor seemed to confirm it, and when I stepped into the living room the scene I was greeted with wasn't much different than what I'd expected.

Margot was asleep on the couch still, her head resting in Mom's lap, who was also out. Dad, however, was awake and sitting in a chair across from them, his gray eyes focused on his wife and daughter like he couldn't stand the thought of missing even a moment.

When I stepped further into the room, he looked up with a start. "Shit."

"Sorry," I whispered, crossing the room to him. "Did I scare you?"

He held his hand out to me and I went to him, taking it before perching on the arm of the chair. "Don't take much these days."

I glanced toward Margot and my heart constricted. "Has she spoken yet?"

"No." Dad shook his head. "She will. We gotta have faith."

I'd never thought faith was a necessity, but after everything that had happened, I couldn't help clinging to it now. Everything else had worked out, why shouldn't this?

"What about you?" I asked. "How are you feeling?"

"I'm good." He patted my leg absentmindedly.

Dad's gaze was still on the couch, but I was looking him over. His face was so beaten and bruised that he didn't look much like himself at the moment, and even though the swelling on his eye had gone down, it was still dark purple. He had a cut on his lip, right above the scar on his chin, the one he'd had for as long as I could remember.

I reached out and touched it. "Where did you get this scar? You've never told me."

He tore his gray eyes from the couch and focused on me. "It ain't a very nice story."

"There are a lot of stories like that. It doesn't mean I don't deserve to know them."

This time, I was thinking about the things Jim had told me, and the stuff about my biological mother that Angus had alluded to, and somehow Dad seemed to know that I wasn't talking about the scar anymore.

"What do you wanna know?" he asked.

"Why did my mom change her name to Ginny?"

"It was her real name," Mom said, and I turned to find her eyes open and focused on me. "Her real name was Virginia Lucas, Ginny. She changed it to Hadley Lucas when she moved to California to start acting."

"Why did she change it back? Angus told me something happened to her. In Vegas."

I looked between Mom and Dad, giving them a moment to decide what to tell me. I had a right to know, but I also knew that it might not be an easy thing for them to talk about, even after all these years.

After a second, Mom shifted, moving Margot's head so she could slide out from under her. She stretched when she stood, and even though I knew she was probably sore, I also thought she might be buying herself time. Her back cracked and she made a face, but then grabbed a chair and pulled it over so she was sitting in front of Dad and me.

"It isn't an easy thing to talk about," she said when she had taken a seat. "It might be hard to hear, too."

"I'm twenty. I'm not a child."

"Some things are even hard for adults to hear," Mom whispered.

I looked toward Dad, expecting him to be on my side, but his gaze was focused on the floor. The expression of pain on his face gave me pause, but I knew that even if I walked away now, I'd always wonder what had happened.

"I want to know," I said after a few seconds of heavy silence.

Mom nodded. "It happened during the early days of the outbreak. We were at a hospital looking for supplies when your mom and I got separated from Angus and your dad." She nodded to Dad. "This father, not Jon. We didn't know Jon yet, but we met him that day."

A chill ran up my spine at her tone.

"We were in the parking lot when a van drove up. Men jumped out and took Hadley and me. They drove us to the Monte Carlo in Las Vegas where a group of men were living. There were women in the hotel too, but they weren't there by choice. They were currency. The men living in the hotel would go out and gather supplies for the man in charge, and in exchange they were allowed to choose a woman for the night. Back then, everyone knew who Hadley Lucas the movie star was..." Mom's voice dropped off at the last sentence and she had to swallow before going on. "There was nothing I could do to save her. I tried, but I was as powerless as she was."

A sense of dread had pooled in my stomach, and I suddenly found myself wishing I hadn't asked, because I could do math and I had a pretty good feeling I knew what was coming next.

Only, I was wrong.

Mom looked up and captured my gaze with hers. "Your father, Jon, was driving the van that took us."

I shook my head. "No. You said my parents loved each other. You said—"

"They did." Mom grabbed my hand when I started to stand. "They did. It's a long story, so long that I doubt I could remember it all, but know that he only did those things to save his sister. Megan. She was only sixteen and she was in there, a prisoner, and he did what he thought he had to do to free her.

"After he took us to the hotel, he had me sent to his room and told me what was going on. He helped us get out, and even though he was the one who'd brought us there to begin with, once I saw what Megan had been through, I couldn't blame him. And your mom didn't either."

"What happened to her?" I whispered. "What happened to Megan after you got out?"

Mom didn't release my hand, but she did look away. "She was too damaged. She'd been through too much."

"And my dad?" I had to force the words out. "Was he actually *my* dad?"

Her hand tightened on mine. "Yes. Jon Lewis *was* your father."

"How do you know?" I thought of my mom, my biological mother, trapped in a hotel. I didn't have a lot of understanding of celebrities, but I knew enough to know that she had been a big one. It was how I knew what she looked like, because over the years I'd been able to find dozens of magazines with her pictures in them. "I mean— She—" The words stuck on their way out.

"You look just like him," Dad said, speaking up for the first time. "There ain't a doubt in my mind."

I remembered Jim saying the same thing, and I told myself that they weren't lying, but it was a hard thing to wrap my brain around because I had no idea what my father had looked like. Dark hair, yes, but that could have come from anyone, and how many had there been? How many men had gotten the honor of having Hadley Lucas in their bed for the night? Did I want to know?

Mom reached out with her free hand and took Dad's, and when he looked up the expression in his eyes nearly took my breath away. That's when it hit me Mom had been there too, in

219

that hotel, and that Dad hadn't been able to do anything to help her. He must have been going out of his mind with worry, the way we had all these weeks with him missing.

"You were there too," I said, the words coming out before I could stop them. "Did you, I mean... What happened?"

Mom squeezed my hand. "Nothing. I got lucky. Your dads—both of them—kept me safe." She glanced toward the man who had raised me.

"No wonder she started going by Ginny," I muttered.

"She didn't want people to know who she was," Mom said. "She cut her hair and when it started to grow out it was a different color. The world had changed, and somewhere along the way people began to forget about movie stars and sex symbols. She felt safer."

"Did she want me?" I asked, the question impossible to keep inside. "She couldn't have known for sure who my father was. Did that mean she didn't want me?"

"She wanted you enough to travel across a zombie infested country to save you." Mom squeezed my hand. "She loved you. So did your dad."

"So do we," Dad said.

Mom nodded, and I found myself sliding down off the arm of the couch so I was sitting in Dad's lap. I hadn't done that since I was a child and for a brief moment I felt silly, but then his arms were around me and I no longer cared. I needed his support right now. I needed to know that I was loved and wanted and that despite the awful story of how my parents had met, I had somehow managed to end up in a family that loved one another.

# CHAPTER TWENTY-SIX

## Meg

After those life-altering revelations, I knew I'd never be able to sleep, so I told Mom and Dad to get some rest while I stayed with Margot.

I knew that distracting myself from the horrible images of what my biological mother had gone through wouldn't be easy, especially when I thought of my own close calls, but I had a feeling that focusing on my sister just might do the trick. So I sat with her head in my lap the way mom had before, stroking her dirty blonde hair out of her face and whispering to her as the rest of the house slept. I talked to her about games we'd played, about songs we'd sung, even about fights we'd had, hoping that something would bring her out of this stupor.

Then I started talking about what had happened in my life since she was taken from it, focusing on the good things. On the people I'd met, Colton who had been my first love, Dragon and Glitter and Helen. Donaghy. I talked to her about how it felt to realize I was an adult now, how amazing it was to fall in love.

I wept when I told her how much I'd missed her. How alone I'd felt growing up, how I'd wished I could have had her to whisper to at night the way I had before she'd been taken from me. The words seemed to flow out of me in endless streams, but instead of running out of steam, the more I talked the more I thought of that I wanted to share with her. I'd missed my sister more than I'd even realized, and now that she was alive, I was desperate to have her back in my life.

The room was just beginning to fill with the glow of the early morning sun when Margot's eyes opened and she looked up at me. It would have been like looking into Mom's eyes if it weren't for the total innocence that radiated in those brown depths. Instead, it was like once again seeing my sister at the age of nine even though years had passed and she was now a almost an adult.

"Megan?" she whispered.

"It's me." The words were almost drowned out by a sob, so I swallowed before speaking again. "I'm here."

Margot looked around, blinking like she couldn't make sense of what was going on. "Where am I?"

She started to sit up, and I reached out to help her, afraid that she was too weak. Her arm felt impossibly thin in my grasp, and it made everything in me squeeze into a tight ball, but I swallowed the pain, wanting to be strong for my sister now that she was finally waking up. She was going to have so much to adjust to, and she would need all of us to do it.

"Are you okay?" I asked.

Margot nodded, but then shook her head. "I don't— I don't know." Her hand went to her forehead and she closed her eyes. "I have a headache and I don't remember what's happening."

"You don't remember anything?" I held my breath, praying that she wouldn't. Losing years of your life would be a much better alternative to remembering the torture that had been inflicted on you.

"I remember..." Her face scrunched up. "I remember a white room. I remember machines that beeped. I remember..." Margot opened her eyes and looked down at her arms, at the crooks that were covered in scars just like Glitter's and Angus's were. "I remember needles."

I wrapped my arms around her, afraid that if I looked her in the face I'd start to cry. "You're okay now. We're all together again."

"Where are Mommy and Daddy?" she asked, her voice shaking and making her sound like a tiny child.

"They're in bed." I pulled away and quickly wiped at the tears on my cheeks before she could see them. "I can get them."

222

I started to stand, but Margot grabbed my arm and I froze. Her brown eyes swept over my face, getting wider with each passing second. "How old are you?"

"Twenty," I whispered.

"How old am I?"

"Eighteen," I said, even quieter.

Margot's shoulders slumped. "It wasn't a dream. It was real."

"It was real," I said, grabbing her and pulling her in for another hug. "But it's over now. You're safe, and I promise I'm going to make sure you are never hurt again."

The floor creaked and I looked up to find Mom standing in the doorway, her face streaked with tears.

IT WAS A GOOD THING WE'D ALREADY DECIDED MOM and Dad weren't going with us, because after Margot came to they were too distracted to join in on the planning. For me, the break from worrying about my sister and a past I couldn't change was welcome, so when everyone else crowded into the dining room to plan, I went too.

"We can't go back in through Dragon's," was the first thing Jada said.

All around the room people nodded in agreement. Jim was at her side with Luke next to him, but Kelly was out thanks to her injury. She wasn't the only one either, and when I scanned the room I realized how much smaller our group was this time around. Al, Angus, Dragon, Donaghy, and I were all here, but we'd lost the other people from Senoia and Helen. Parv was present too, despite her injury and the fact that everyone was trying to talk her into staying. I knew they wouldn't succeed, just like no one would be able to convince me not to go, so I hadn't even tried to join in that argument.

It wasn't a lot of people, but thanks to Angus, we'd gained The Church as allies.

"What did you and the High Priestess talk about?" I asked, turning my gaze on Angus. "I'm assuming she's still going to help."

"She is, but I gotta reveal myself to her people first. She wants them to know what they're fightin' for."

"Is that something you really want to do?" Parv asked.

"It's somethin' I gotta do. We need the numbers, and hell, I deserve it. They've used me for the past twenty years, I might as well get somethin' outta it."

"He has a point," Al muttered. "If we don't have them on our side, we might as well go to the gate with our arms up and turn ourselves into Star."

"I think we're all in agreement that that isn't an option," Jada said. "So let's focus on the bigger issue. How do we get in?"

"The priestess said they got a way," Angus replied. "I ain't sure what it is, but it's how they got out to come here."

"We're going to meet them then?" Jada asked.

"That's the plan," my uncle said.

"Good." Jada nodded and scanned the group. "That brings us to the next problem. How we get to Star. We're assuming he's going to be inside the CDC, but he might not be. He could be in his house for all we know, which could make things complicated."

"He'll be at the CDC," I said, drawing everyone's attention my way. "I spent a lot of time with Jackson, and if I know anything about his father, it's that he is a workaholic. Plus, the house isn't fortified the way the CDC is. You don't need a code to get in, just a key, and anyone could break the front door down."

"Do we have a code still?" Jada looked toward Dragon.

"I have it." He frowned. "Helen made sure I knew it in case something happened. She wanted to be prepared."

"What about weapons?" Jim asked, speaking up for the first time. "With The Church we'll have the numbers, but what about arming them? We all know their anti-violence stance."

"They got it covered," Angus said.

"The Church has weapons?" Al asked in disbelief.

Angus pressed his lips together and nodded. "I ain't seen 'em with my own eyes, but that's what I was told. The priestess said she's been stocking up."

"For what?" I asked.

"For this," Angus said.

"Then I guess that's it. We can't really make any other plans until we get to the temple and find out what the High Priestess has in mind." Jada shook her head. "I just hope whatever she's thinking helps us, because if we have to fight The Church too we're screwed."

SABINE MET US ON THE SIDE OF THE ROAD ON THE outskirts of old Atlanta. There was a truck parked behind her that — like all vehicles still driving around — had seen better days, and she was flanked by the same large men who had stood at her mother's side in Senoia, all three of them decked out in the same red robes they'd worn before. The plunging neckline of Sabine's revealed a simple black shirt and the bronze pendant she and all the other senior members of The Church wore. It was an eye with a red stone in where the pupil should have been, and it gave me the creeps.

"Priestess," Jada said when we had all climbed out of the truck.

Sabine dipped her head, but as usual her gaze was focused on my uncle. "Angus James."

He grunted in response.

"We've been told you have a way into the city," Jada said.

Sabine tore her gaze from Angus and looked the other woman over, her gaze lingering on the tattoos peaking out of her shirt and moving up her neck.

"Why do you choose to degrade your body in this way?" she asked.

"I don't see it like that." To Jada's credit, she managed to keep her expression even. "And that's not why I'm here."

Sabine frowned, but nodded in agreement a second later. "We have a way in. You may follow us." She waved to the truck at her back. "We will park two streets over and walk from there. It is not a difficult journey."

We climbed back into our own truck and did as we were told. The drive only took four minutes at the most, and then the one carrying the members of The Church pulled into an overgrown driveway much like the one we'd parked in when we'd come into the city before. We were silent as we all climbed out and started walking, following Sabine and her guards, and for once my thoughts weren't on Donaghy and if we'd find Star, but I instead found myself wondering what these people would do if they ran into trouble. The Church claimed they didn't kill the dead, but out here it was either kill or be killed. I doubted any of these three would stand by and allow the zombies to bite them.

It was still light out, and I couldn't help being more than a little nervous when the wall came into view. I had no clue what Star had told the enforcers, but there was no doubt in my mind that whoever was working the wall was on the lookout for us. If we were spotted, all our careful planning would be for nothing.

"Do not worry," Sabine said, almost as if she could read my thoughts. "The guard towers are sparse back here, and men are rarely assigned to them." She waved to the only tower visible and when I squinted up at it, I realized that it was empty. "The wall here is not easy to climb and they keep most of their men at the front."

"She's right," Parv said from behind me. "We've always focused on the gate."

"There is reason for this," Sabine said as she approached the wall, her gaze moving to my aunt. "We have people everywhere."

Parv's back stiffened. "I'm the Judicial Officer. No one told me to make that decision, I just did it."

Sabine lifted her eyebrows in a perfect imitation of her mother. "Didn't they?"

My aunt's steely gaze faltered and she looked away.

Sabine only smiled.

She came to a halt about five feet from an old junker of a car that was right up against the wall, but her guards didn't stop. The weeds around it had grown so tall that you couldn't get a very good view of the car, but the thing didn't look like much more than a rusted heap. That didn't stop the guards from opening the door though, and when they did the hinges didn't even creak.

"This way," Sabine said.

She moved toward the open door, lifting the skirt of her robe as she ducked down. I moved after her, curious, and watched as she climbed into the car. The seats were gone, as was the other door, and what looked to be a tunnel laid beyond that. Sabine was through the car in seconds, and even when she had stepped out she had to stay low, but she kept moving.

I climbed into the car after her, and I was still making my way through when light flooded the darkness. I squinted, trying to get a glimpse of my surroundings through the sudden brightness, and that's when I realized that she'd pushed a door open.

She was all the way through now, standing on the other side and waiting for the rest of us, so I scurried forward, out of the car and through the tunnel that had somehow been burrowed into the wall. When I was through I found myself in an alley that was blocked off on both ends, by what I didn't know, but in front of us stood a building with a door that had been painted a deep shade of red.

We'd reached the Temple.

When everyone was through Sabine opened the door, confirming that I had been right. We followed her in, all of us in a silent line. I'd never set foot inside the Temple before and I wasn't sure what I'd expected, but this wasn't it. It was too simple, too plain for a group of people who were this eccentric.

"This way," Sabine said as she led us through the room.

It was empty for the most part. Large and dimly lit, the starkly white walls and floors contrasted with the doom and gloom this group had always made me feel when they were around. There were no chairs, no tables, and no other objects to speak of except at the very front of the room where a shrine of Angus James sat in the place of honor. It was twice as large as the one in the city square; and four times as big as the one down the street from the apartment I'd grown up in. There were candles around it, their lights flickering in the darkness of the room, and dozens of pieces of paper. I knew what they were without looking, people had done the same thing to the statue on my street for as long as I could remember. Credits, gifts to the messiah, and prayer notes. Desperate pleas from desperate people who were looking for a miracle from the only god anyone bothered to pray to these days: Angus James.

"Where do people sit?" I asked as we approached the statue.

I imagined that this was where the followers gathered to pray, and the statue at the head of the room seemed to confirm it, but the lack of chairs contradicted the picture in my head.

227

Sabine glanced over her shoulder at me. Her eyes were only a shade darker than her mother's and would probably be just as creepy-looking if it weren't for the golden hue of her hair. It helped keep her from looking washed out, and instead made her a strikingly beautiful person, the type who took your breath away when you first met them. At least until she opened her mouth and you realized she was insane.

"We kneel," she said in a tone that implied I was a moron.

"On the hard floor?" Al asked incredulously, and then snorted. "Sorry Angus, we're all happy to see you, but this is the biggest pile of bullshit I've ever heard."

Sabine's gaze moved to Al, focusing on the stump that was his left arm. "You were bitten?" she asked instead of answering his question.

My uncle nodded. "We cut it off."

"You know it does not always work." She tilted her head to his arm like he might have forgotten what she was referring to. "But Angus was with you that day, wasn't he?"

"Yeah," Al said reluctantly.

Sabine turned away from him and continued walking. "Perhaps you should kneel as well and show *Him* your gratitude."

Angus was the one who snorted this time.

We continued at a steady pace until we reached the front and Angus slowed to a stop. Even though Sabine didn't follow suit, the rest of us did, stopping at my uncle's side as he stared down at the statue, an expression on his face that was somewhere between amusement and disgust.

He nudged the paper with the toe of his boot. "This is the money you guys use now, ain't it?"

"Credits," Parv said with a nod.

"So this is what? An offering to me?" He looked up so he could meet my aunt's gaze.

The corner of Parv's lips twitched. "Looks like it."

Angus nodded once before kneeling down. "Alright then."

He sifted through the papers surrounding the statue, separating the credits from the notes people had left behind while the rest of us stood silently at his side. Sabine finally stopped as if she'd just realized we were no longer following, and when she turned to face us, the look of incredulity on her face was almost comical.

"What are you doing?" she asked, taking a step toward us, her hand out like she wanted to stop this from happening but wasn't sure how.

Angus stood, the stack of credits now in his hand. He turned to face her calmly as he shuffled them around, arranging them into a neat pile. "You been collectin' money in my name for nearly twenty years, so the way I see it, I deserve a cut."

"A cut?" Sabine asked, her voice rising.

"I'm back now, and I got nothing to my name. You think Star's gonna hand me a bunch of dough before I slit his throat?" Angus shook his head as he shoved the money into his pocket. "He ain't, and I sure could use the help getting back on my feet."

Sabine's mouth dropped open, but she said nothing in response. She just stood there, staring at my uncle like she couldn't wrap her head around who he was. I wanted to laugh because I knew that this man, as much as he meant to my family, had to be a kick in The Church's collective balls. No one who bothered to create a deity would ever imagine someone like this, a selfish, foul-mouthed, chain smoker who put himself before the needs of his followers. It should have been a major sign to Sabine that her mom was on the wrong track, but I knew these people were too far gone to allow logic to change their minds.

We were still silent when the door behind Sabine opened and her mother walked out. The High Priestess wore the same robes as before, only her hood was already down when she paused to take in the scene.

"Daughter," she said, her voice loud enough that it bounced off the walls of the room. "Why have you not brought them to my chambers?"

Sabine turned to her mom, her head once again down. "I was on the way when Angus James stopped at the statue. He took the credits your—" Her gaze flicked to Angus. "—*his* followers have left behind."

The High Priestess lifted her eyebrows at Angus. "You feel this is something you are owed?"

He met her gaze head on. "Fuck yeah."

She tilted her head, studying him with an expression that made it seem like she still wasn't sure how to take him or if he was in fact Angus James. But it only lasted a moment before she nodded once and then turned her back on him.

"Very well. Follow me to my chambers," she called over her shoulder.

Sabine hurried after her mother without a second glance at us, and we fell in behind her. Angus was chuckling quietly under his breath.

Her chambers were a lot closer to what I'd expected the inside of the Temple to look like. The room was dark, all the walls painted black except for the largest one, which was instead covered in a mural, and the floor was draped in dark rugs. Deep, red curtains that matched the robes they wore covered the single window, blocking out every ounce of light, and candles burned on every surface, their flickering lights making the atmosphere feel both eerie and reverent at the same time.

There were two red couches that sat facing the mural, which took up most of the wall. Whoever had done it was clearly talented, no one could have denied that, but I couldn't say that I enjoyed the subject matter all that much. In the center was a man, clearly meant to be Angus, who stood with his face raised to the sky and his arms held out in front of him. Rays radiated off him, although I wasn't sure if they were supposed to be some kind of magical power or beams of light, and wispy, white clouds floated around him. There were smaller scenes painted in the corners. A man being overtaken by zombies, the same man lying on the ground bleeding but crawling away from a pile of dead zombies, the man lying on a bed surrounded by people, and finally the same people kneeling at a grave. It was so sick that it made my stomach twist, and the faces of the others in my group showed the same disgust. Even the smile on Angus's face was a twisted version of a grin, one that was more loathing than amusement.

Angus turned his back on the mural and looked the High Priestess in the eye. "Why don't we talk 'bout this plan of yours? You told me you had weapons."

The priestess nodded as she headed across the room. "We have been collecting them, preparing for this day."

"I thought The Church didn't believe in violence," Parv said.

"We do not under normal circumstances, but we knew the return of Angus James would require a bloody battle." The High Priestess paused at a closed door and glanced back over her shoulder. "We wanted to be ready."

She pulled the door open and flicked on a light, and even from across the room I could see the rows and rows of guns lined up on the wall. There were dozens upon dozens of them, and stacks of ammo as well. The stash they had here would rival even what the enforcers had in their arsenal.

"Where did you get them all?" Al asked in amazement.

"We have been buying them slowly," Sabine said, speaking for her mother. "From the black market or outside the city walls."

The High Priestess turned to face us, still standing in the open doorway. "It has taken us twenty years to collect this many, but we have the army ready if you are willing to fulfill your duty." She lifted her eyebrows. "Are you willing, Angus James? If you are willing to be the savior we have been waiting for, your disciples will follow you wherever you lead. They will tear the walls of the CDC down with their bare hands if they have to."

Angus nodded even as he pressed his lips together. "The sooner the better."

The priestess's mouth morphed into a grin and she nodded to her daughter. "Call the gathering."

I STOOD IN THE BACK WITH THE OTHER PEOPLE IN MY group, wedged in between Donaghy and Luke. The steady stream of followers had finally died down, and the room was now not only humming with activity, but sticky with humidity as well. The followers knelt just as Sabine said they would, all facing the statue and all wearing the red robes that signified they were bona fide members of The Church. There were hundreds of them, so many that it made my head spin, but I knew this was only the tip of the iceberg. The people here, the ones who were privileged enough to receive a red robe, were just the ones who had been baptized in the blood of Angus James—a ritual I had never seen nor wanted to see—but there were hundreds if not thousands more followers where this came from.

The door to the chambers opened and the bulky guards came out, followed by The Church's trusted priests, and then finally Sabine. A hush fell over the crowd that made the room feel suddenly empty. I'd never known a group of this size to be so silent. It was as if they were all holding their breath, as if they knew what was coming, as if they'd always been expecting this moment.

"Maybe someone let it slip," Donaghy whispered so low that only I could hear him. "That Angus was back, I mean."

"After the explosion at the CDC, they have to suspect," I replied.

Before he could respond the High Priestess herself walked out. Her hood was up and she had her hands tucked behind her back so that not even an inch of skin was showing. She looked like a phantom or an evil spirit, and it sent a shiver shooting through my body.

When she stopped, she was standing in front of the statue of Angus, which still towered over her by nearly a foot. She lifted her head and Sabine stepped forward and lowered her mother's hood, revealing the ghostly face tucked within.

"Welcome, my children," the High Priestess began.

Her voice boomed off the walls and a hum of energy seemed to ripple through the crowd. People shifted and leaned forward, expressions of eagerness on their faces. I didn't know how often they were called to a meeting like this, but I had a feeling it was rare. They had to know what was coming.

"For the past twenty years we have been held hostage by the dead, living behind walls and fearing for our lives. For many there has been no hope, but the faithful, those of us gathered in this room, have known better." The High Priestess's mouth stretched wide, but the smile looked as terrifying as she did. "We have always known that this day would come."

The murmur that moved through the crowd was louder now, and it grew with each passing second until it turned into a chant. The High Priestess seemed to know that this would happen, because she remained quiet and let it happen.

*"...you have visited them with destruction and wiped out all remembrance of them..."*

Like every other time, the words made the hair on my arms stand up. I knew we needed these people to defeat Star. That we needed the weapons they had and the numbers they would bring, but I couldn't help wondering what fulfilling this insane prophecy would bring down on us. It seemed irresponsible to encourage this, to make these people, who were so eager to serve this crazy woman, believe that she had been right all along.

"Shit," Donaghy muttered, almost as if the same thought had gone through his head.

I looked around at my family and friends, and the horror on their faces matched the horror I felt inside. A feeling of dread and foreboding came over me, and I could suddenly glimpse a future without zombies, only it wasn't bright and shiny and promising like I'd thought it would be. It was cloaked in red, just like this woman, and led by zealots.

After a few minutes, the High Priestess lifted her hands and the chant died away. "We have been faithful and God has rewarded us." She turned to face her guards, who in turn pulled the doors to her chambers open again. "Come forward, Angus James."

This time, there was no hum of excitement. Instead, everyone in the room seemed to lean forward in anticipation, myself included. Only seconds passed before Angus stepped out, but it seemed to take much longer, and then he was there, covered in a red robe as thick and long as the one the High Priestess wore, only his hood was down. His chest was bare and the neckline was deep enough to reveal a few of the many bites that I knew decorated his skin. When he walked forward and took his place at the High Priestess's side, there was an expression of pure determination on his face.

"Take off your robe," she called, her colorless eyes trained on him.

He did as he was told, pulling the thick robe over his head. Underneath he wore nothing but a pair of black boxers, allowing everyone to see the scars that dotted his skin. There were even more than I'd realized, because he had them on his legs as well, and in the dim light the candles gave off, they seemed darker than ever against his pale skin.

"Behold," the High Priestess said, turning back to face her followers, "I give you our savior, Angus James. Just as I predicted, he has returned from the dead and will now lead us to the future we have been waiting for. Soon the dead will be wiped out and the CDC will be torn down, and the plague of scientists who have destroyed our world will be brought to justice." The chants began again, and the High Priestess was forced to speak louder so she could be heard over them. "Show them your scars, Angus James!"

My uncle did as he was told, moving through the crowd of people gathered in the room so they could get a closer look at him. As he passed, people reached out to touch him, running the tips of their fingers over the crescent shaped scars on his arms and legs and chest. People wept, people lifted their arms to the sky and called out things I couldn't hear. The noise in the room grew louder and louder the more Angus moved through the crowd until it began to feel like a roar. It pounded against the walls and the ceiling, it felt as if it would shake the building, and it seemed to verify exactly what the High Priestess had said to us earlier. That her followers would be able to rip the CDC apart with their bare hands.

# CHAPTER TWENTY-SEVEN
## Donaghy

I leaned against the wall in the alley, sucking in mouthfuls of air despite the stifling humidity. The throb from the virus was long gone thanks to the vaccine, but the bacteria they'd released had brought another much more terrifying feeling. It wasn't pain exactly, at least not any kind I had ever felt before, and I found it impossible to describe. I just knew it was there. Like a living thing moving through me, slowly taking over. Or destroying me one tiny cell at a time.

My eyes were closed when the door to the Temple was shoved open, and I cracked them just as Angus stumbled out. He didn't seem to notice me because he was too busy sucking in mouthfuls of air, almost like he'd just surfaced after nearly drowning. He hadn't put the ridiculous robe back on, but he also hadn't bothered to do anything other than pull some pants on, and I had a feeling it was because he just couldn't stand being in that damn building for a second longer. Not that I blamed him.

He leaned over and braced his hands on his knees, mumbling, "Fuck me. Fuck me," under his breath. When he lifted his right hand and stared down at it, it was trembling.

After a few minutes he let out a deep breath and stood so he could pull a pack of cigarettes out of his pocket, not looking the least bit surprised to see me standing in front of him.

"Guess it's my turn to be caught with my pants down," he said before sticking the cigarette between his lips.

I snorted as he lit it, remembering the night he'd walked in on Meg and me in the shower. "I guess I should thank you for not kicking my ass since you're Meg's uncle."

Angus sucked in a mouthful of smoke as he looked me over, sizing me up. "I was just lookin' out for her is all, and I knew bein' with you was gonna piss off that little prick somethin' fierce." He blew the smoke out and nodded once. "Least you got revenge on the bastard."

I looked away because the memory of how I'd ripped Jackson's throat out wasn't a good one. "Yeah."

We stood side by side in silence for a few minutes, him smoking while I tried to pull my shit together. I wasn't sure what to say to this man, especially not when all I could think about were the miniscule hours I'd spent locked in that tiny cell and how horrible they'd been. My time had been nothing compared to what he'd gone through, to the days upon days of torture, the weeks of solitude, the years of hopelessness. I couldn't imagine it, couldn't figure out how he was still here and in one piece.

"You going to make him suffer?" I asked after a few minutes.

Angus turned his head toward me, the cigarette stuck between his lips. "Star?" I nodded. "I'm gonna make him squeal like a pig."

"Good," I said before pushing myself off the wall. "I was only locked in that cell for two days. You have to be the strongest son of a bitch to ever walk this earth."

Angus shrugged. "That or the stubbornest."

"Maybe," I muttered, "but I don't think that would get you far when it comes to something like this."

The door behind Angus was shoved open and Jada stuck her head out. "We need to get ready."

Angus snorted, but dropped his cigarette to the ground. "Not sure if I'm lookin' forward to this or dreading it."

Jada held a red robe out to him, along with a pair of shoes. "I think it would be strange if you didn't feel that way."

I followed them inside, back into the stuffy room that was filled to the brim with people in red robes. It took me a few seconds to locate the rest of our group amid the crowd, but only because they were dressed the same way and now blended in.

Meg held a robe out to me when I stopped in front of her. "We won't stand out this way."

I chuckled as I took the thing, marveling over the irony of a red robe on a muggy Georgia day helping us blend in.

"I know." She rolled her eyes and watched as I pulled the thing over my head.

It was tight and the fabric was a hell of a lot heavier than it looked, but as much as I hated the idea of wearing it, I knew we needed to. Some of the people in our group stood out too much. Jada with her tattoos, Jim with his scars and sneer that screamed zombie slayer, Angus who would be recognizable to anyone in Star's inner circle, Meg who had a face most people in the settlement knew. Even Parvarti and Al because they had worked the wall for years and were no doubt now on Star's hit list. But the robes served another purpose as well. They helped hide our weapons.

No one passing us, no matter how out of control things had gotten yesterday, would think a member of The Church was armed. It had been historically non-violent since it was established, and even though the High Priestess and her daughter had made an appearance yesterday at the CDC, no one would have guessed that the other people who had stormed the building were her followers. Not when none of them had been wearing a red robe.

I strapped a gun to my waist, watching Meg as she did the same. She'd told me that she'd gone out with Jada to train before I made it to Senoia, but I still couldn't help thinking about that day outside the walls. I'd barely known her then, but already I'd felt drawn to her. Maybe it was how fast she'd been able to pull herself together after getting attacked, how strong she'd been, or maybe it was something else that I couldn't even name. I didn't know for sure because an attraction like this defied all logic, but I knew that if I weren't going to die in the next few days, she and I would be together forever. I couldn't explain it or justify it, but I knew it in my very core.

I reached out and grabbed her hips, pulling her forward until her body was flush with mine. She looked up at me, lifting her eyebrows as I ran my hands up her back over the thick robe.

"Did something distract you from the mission?" she asked with a small smile on her lips.

We'd promised that we'd put my impending death out of our heads, and I had to give her credit, she was better at holding it together than I was or would be if the situation were reversed.

I leaned down and covered her lips with mine, twisting my hands in her robe as we kissed.

When I pulled back I whispered, "Be careful. Okay?"

"I didn't plan on being anything else."

"Good."

# CHAPTER TWENTY-EIGHT
## Meg

We were in the middle of the group, all of us smashed together and surrounded by other robed figures. Between the thick material covering me from head to toe and the crowd pressed against me, it was nearly impossible to get a mouthful of fresh air. The already humid day had turned into an inferno even though the sun was setting, and I knew it was only going to get worse. Right now we were only walking, but soon we'd be fighting. Soon we'd be running through the CDC in search of Star.

I wanted to be there when he died even if I didn't get to be the one to pull the trigger.

All around me people chanted, their voices and footsteps so in synch that they sounded like they were one person, one voice. The beat of their feet against the ground vibrated through the air, and the echo of their chant bounced off the surrounding buildings as we made our way down the street. I couldn't see much through the crowd, but every now and then I caught a glimpse of the people we passed stopping, either turning to stare or moving forward to join us, the lesser members of The Church getting swept up in the crowd as we moved through the city.

I stood on the tips of my toes as the top of the CDC came into view, trying to get a glimpse of the people at the front of the group. I knew which hooded head was the High Priestess, although I wasn't sure how. Her robe was no different and she wasn't any taller or bigger than anyone else, but somehow she stood out.

I glanced around, catching fleeting glimpses of my friends and family. We were the only ones in the crowd who hadn't joined in the chanting, and even though we were covered in red from head to toe, I felt like we stood out. Like it would only take one look at the crowd for the enforcers and CDC guards to spot us.

I pulled the long skirt of my robe up so I could unhook my gun, my fingers itching to pull it out even as my palm started to sweat.

"You okay?" Jada hissed from my left.

I turned my head and found only her eyes visible in the dark folds of her hood.

"Yes," I lied, and then let out a breath. "I'm fine."

She didn't look convinced, but she didn't ask me again.

We moved closer, our numbers growing with every street we passed. Now there weren't just hooded figures in our group, but people from all over the city as well. Enforcers who had most certainly worked side by side with my dad, parents with their children, people from the construction and maintenance crews, and even men and women who looked like they had been on their way to the entertainment district for a night of fun. So many people that we took up not just the street, but the sidewalk on both sides as well, the crowd swelling and growing the way a wave did when a storm rolled in.

We didn't stop until we'd reached the courtyard of the CDC, and it was the High Priestess who signaled for the break. It was our cue to move forward, and Angus went first, but the crowd had thickened so much that it wasn't easy to push our way through. He had to force his way between the followers surrounding us to get them to part, but once they did it was like Moses parting the red sea as robed men and women stepped aside and made way for him.

They bowed their heads when he passed and we followed, sticking close to one another as if we expected the sea of red to slam in on us once Angus had been led by. Jim and Jada were right behind him, with Donaghy next and me close on his heels. He had a gun in one hand, concealed by his robe, and with the other he reached back and grabbed my hand. His palm was moist and I tried to tell myself it wasn't from a fever or the bacteria moving through his system, but it was a hard thing to believe when I knew his time on this earth was slipping away with each passing second.

The High Priestess was turned toward us, waiting for Angus to join her at the front. When he reached her side the expression on her face once again sent a feeling of doom surging through me. I wasn't sure that *this* was the right way to destroy the CDC and Star, not if it opened the floodgates for this group of fanatics, but I also knew that Angus had been right: we didn't have another choice.

Guards were already outside the CDC when we came up, but even more streamed out as we stood there. There were dozens of them, each of them armed with several guns and even a few grenades. The sheer number of weapons in front of us was daunting, but when I looked back over the crowd and saw how many more of us there were, I knew the guards didn't stand a chance.

"Are you ready?" the High Priestess asked when Angus had stopped at her side.

He nodded and then he climbed up on the ledge of a flowerbed. Up there he was nearly a foot taller and was able to look out over the crowd of followers. A hush fell over the area, and with the sudden silence the guards at Angus's back shifted uncomfortably, as if the calm was even more unsettling than the chanting had been.

Angus once again wore no shirt under his robe, and already people had begun to whisper about the bite marks that were visible on his chest. Then he pulled it up and over his head, tossing it aside, and the voices grew louder. The people who hadn't been in the temple for the revealing craned their necks as if trying to figure out who he was.

They didn't have to live in suspense for long.

"I am Angus James," my uncle said, his voice floating out over the crowd.

A guard at his back rushed forward, his gun raised. "Get down. Get your hands up!"

The High Priestess pulled out a gun and shot the man in the head, and before his body had even hit the ground every single robed figure at the front of the group had their guns out as well.

241

"Do not move," the High Priestess called.

The guards shifted and looked back and forth at each other. Some lowered the weapons while others raised theirs higher. Some took a step back while others shuffled forward. None of them knew what to do. None of them had expected this.

"We just want the man," one of the guards called.

"You will not take Angus James again," the priestess replied.

It happened quickly after that. One minute Angus was towering over us while the guards tried to decide what to do, and a second later the High Priestess had given her signal and the crowd was surging forward. Angus dropped down as the chants rose up, once again joining us in the sea of red. The bodies swelled around us, pushing us forward as they moved toward the CDC. Some of the men guarding the doors yelled for us to stop while others backed up, unsure of what to do in the face of such a large group. I moved with everyone else, tethered to Donaghy's side by the hand he had wrapped around mine. I felt like I was holding my breath as I waited for the inevitable gunshots. There was no way this would go down peacefully, and I knew it was only a matter of time before someone pulled the trigger.

Even though I'd been waiting for it, my body still jerked when it rang through the air. The chant that swelled around us was broken as some people gasped and others cried out. Still, there were other church members who weren't at all fazed by the burst of violence. They continued to chant, seeming to call out louder so they could make up for those who had faltered.

The first gunshot was followed by a second, and then another, and within seconds the sound of gunfire popped through the air like fireworks. Screams joined the sounds, both from the people around me who were surprised by the violence and those who had been hurt. There were others too, shouts from far off, probably from citizens who weren't members of The Church but had gathered to see what was going on.

"Come on!" Jada yelled from in front of us as she shoved past men and women wearing red robes.

Donaghy pulled me after her, and to my right I caught sight of Luke pulling his robe over his head as he hurried alongside. I fumbled with my own robe, but with my gun in one hand and the other one trapped in Donaghy's grip, it was impossible. It would have to stay for now.

As far as I could tell, my group made it into the lobby without having to fire a single shot. Once inside the red robes thinned out, but the chaos didn't. Some of the guards had run inside, either retreating to the safety of the locked halls or rushing to Star's aide. A few fired from the back of the lobby where they were fighting to get through the only open door, but we were well out of range thanks to a huge pillar.

"What's our next move?" Jada asked as she slid the blade of her knife down the wide neckline of her red robe, cutting it away.

I pried my hand from Donaghy's so I could do the same, anxious to free myself from the stifling fabric. When he saw what I was doing, he copied me while Jim did the same and Dragon pulled his own robe over his head. Al had already gotten his off, as had Parv, and in seconds we were all back to our normal clothes. Even though I was grateful to be out of the robe, I felt suddenly vulnerable. We would be totally recognizable now. There was nowhere to hide.

"We go where they're goin'," Angus growled, his gaze focused on the door the guards had just fled through.

He was shirtless still, thanks to The Church's twisted desire to see the scars that covered his skin, and in the bright lights of the CDC lobby, they looked more jagged than ever.

"He'll be in his office for sure?" Jim asked.

"That bastard will be wherever he's safest," Angus replied. "That's either in his office or in the hall."

His gaze flickered our way and I could tell which one he thought it would be. The hall. It made sense, Star wanting to be with the zombies he had worked so hard to create. If the guards weren't enough to keep him safe, he'd have an extra layer of protection in the dead.

"Then that's where we head," Jada said.

Outside the fighting continued, but the gunshots were getting fewer and fewer. With the number of guards who had fled into the building, we knew we'd need the backup, and thankfully all it took was one whistle from Angus and a group of robed figures rushed toward us. Sabine was among them.

"My mother wants me to make sure you succeed," she said when she stopped in front of us. She nodded to the men at her back and I recognized them as the same men who had escorted us into the city. "She's sent her most trusted warriors."

I never thought of The Church as having warriors before, but I was learning that there was a lot more to them than I'd ever expected.

"No time to waste," Angus muttered, and then took off across the lobby.

With Star's code in our possession, getting through the CDC was a snap. I wasn't sure if he had no way of knowing how we'd gotten around the last time we were here or if he'd intentionally kept the code working in hopes of luring Angus back into the building, but I was hoping it was the first one and he was in for a major surprise when we finally found him.

Just like the day before, the halls of the CDC felt like a maze, but Angus and Jada seemed to maneuver them with very little effort. They must have memorized the layout of the building, because we reached the now familiar locked door that led into the observation hall without taking a single wrong turn. It wasn't until we were standing in front of it that we stopped to take a break, but even then it was only so everyone could double check their weapons. We were all breathing heavily, but it was as much from adrenaline as it was from the trek through the building, and that wasn't likely to get better until we took Star out.

"Be ready," Dragon said as he punched the numbers into the keypad that was mounted on the wall.

The beeps seemed twice as loud as before, and with each one my heart pounded faster. I inhaled slowly, my fingers tightening around my gun as I waited for the door to open. I had no doubt in my mind that there would be a surprise waiting for us, and I was relieved not to be at the front of the pack. Let the bulky guards from The Church go in first. After all, they were the ones who had been waiting twenty years for this day.

The door clicked, signaling it was open, and the scent of death that wafted from the hall caused the hair on the back of my neck to stand up.

# CHAPTER TWENTY-NINE
## Donaghy

As I waited for Dragon to get the door open, my heart raced the way it had before stepping into the ring. I had no clue how many cells were in this hall, but I had no doubt that Star had spent the last twenty-four hours making even more of his deadly pets. It might also account for why there had been so few guards outside the building. The asshole would do anything to make sure he came out of this victorious, even if it meant turning his own guards into these creatures.

A growl reached us before the door was even open, and my pulse raced faster as my body prepared for the fight. This would be easier than the others, or at least that's what I told myself, because this time I had a weapon and people who had my back, while all the times I'd gone up against the zombies before I'd been alone and unarmed.

"Let me up there," Angus pushed past Meg and me, moving to the front of the group.

"What are you doing?" Jada asked.

He shot her a look that said she was an idiot. "They get a bite outta me and I'll be fine. Can you say the same?"

That shut her up, and it suddenly occurred to me that I should be up there too. I wasn't immune like Angus, but I was already dying. Everyone else here had a chance, and it wasn't fair for me stand back and let them go first. Not even the crazy robed guys the High Priestess had sent with us.

"I'm coming with you," I said.

I didn't look at Meg before pushing past the people in front of me because I was pretty sure it would change my mind.

"Donaghy, don't." Her protest made my steps falter, but I forced myself to move.

Angus's gaze met mine and I said, "I'm dead anyway."

"There ain't nothin' in this life that's a sure thing, you know that don't you?"

"I know that the people behind me aren't going to drop dead tomorrow if they make it out of here," I replied.

Angus nodded. "Fair 'nough."

Meg said my name again, but it was barely audible over the growls from the hall. Now that I was right outside the cracked door, the smell made my eyes water. I adjusted my grip on my gun, wishing that my palms weren't so moist, but there was nothing I could do about it because at that exact moment Angus ripped the door open.

The hall looked nothing like it had the last time we were here, because now it was crowded with the dead. It took one look around to see that the doors to the cells had been thrown open to let them out, but just like I'd thought, there were more zombies than there were rooms. Dozens more, and many of them were still wearing their uniforms.

I lifted my gun as the dead moved our way and nodded past them to the end of the hall. "He's got to be in the last cell."

It didn't take a genius to figure out that Star had locked himself in the room furthest from us. That's why he'd allowed the dead to leave their cells. He'd created a gauntlet of zombies that anyone looking for him would be forced to run.

"Let's move," Angus growled just before he squeezed the trigger.

The crack of gunfire made my ears ring, but the head of the nearest zombie exploding made it worthwhile. I took aim and fired too, and yet another body dropped to the ground. Angus and I moved forward side by side as the dead advanced. Most were newer strains that changed the person faster, which meant they were also quick and more calculating than the zombies who'd been infected by the older strains of the virus. It blew my mind how quickly these creatures were able to change their tactics. How they zigzagged through the hall like they were trying to make it more difficult for us to take aim, how they moved lower like they were trying to avoid the bullets, and how insanely fast they were.

More people stepped into the hall behind us, but I was too focused on firing to see who it was. Bursts of gunfire joined ours, and the dead fell, but more came. They seemed to pour out of the open cells at the back of the hall, one after the other after the other in a never-ending procession. Either Star had pulled people from the city yesterday and injected them, or he'd had his guards collect the injured and zombies from the streets before he'd infected them as well. Whatever had happened, there had to be nearly fifty zombies in front of us.

"Too many," Jim said from my right.

I fired faster as I stepped forward, trying to make room for the rest of our group even though every nerve in my body begged me to shut the door so Meg couldn't step in. Somehow, even without looking, I could sense it when she'd walked in behind me, and it made my pulse race faster, made me fire more rapidly, made beads of sweat break out across my body.

The zombies dropped steadily, none of them getting close enough to make it within five feet of us. The growing number of motionless bodies littering the floor helped slow them as well, but even that obstacle wasn't enough to stop one of them. I caught a flash of him as he dodged behind others, using his less intelligent brethren as shields so he could weave his way through the hall to us. I stepped forward and knelt and shifted, trying to get better aim, knowing that he was a hybrid just like the one I'd fought in the ring. Knowing how strong and agile and intelligent he was.

No matter how I angled my body, I couldn't get a good shot, and then he was there, swooping around the handful of zombies separating us and charging right for me. The shriek he let out seemed louder than the gunfire, and even when a bullet hit him in the arm, he didn't slow.

I only had a moment to register that it was Meg's crewmember, Matt, before he slammed into me. My gun went flying, skittering across the floor, and I crashed to the ground. My already injured ribs throbbed, but I'd been here before. Head to head with a creature that had no business living, hurt and unarmed, desperate to fight so I could live to see another day.

He was on top of me, snapping his teeth as he fought to get closer. I let out a sound that was halfway between a growl and a shout as I held him off, putting every ounce of energy into it and throwing him back. The zombie hit the wall, but he was up in a second and headed back my way. Only I was ready, and before he could take me down I rammed my shoulder into his stomach and slammed him back against the wall a second time.

The hybrid shrieked again and fought, but I pressed him back, using all my strength to hold him in place as I grabbled for the knife at my waist.

He was too strong though, and I found my grip slipping, found that my ribs were throbbing more than they had been before, found that the tingle I'd been feeling all day now made my legs shaky and my arms feel weak and nearly useless.

One more shove and he had me on my back, and I knew even as I tried to shove him off that I wouldn't be able to succeed this time. That the injuries I'd sustained at Jackson's hands were too much and the bacteria that was in the process of eating my brain had taken too much out of me. This creature was going to win.

A shot rang out and the zombie's head jerked back as blood sprayed across the wall behind him. He dropped to the floor and I twisted around so I could see who had taken the shot. Meg stood over me, her gun still pointed at the creature even as her gaze scanned me for injuries.

"Are you okay?" she asked, kneeling at my side.

I swallowed so I could find my voice and then said, "I'm okay."

I tried to get up, but I found that my legs were wobbly and weak. Meg frowned as she tucked her gun away and moved to help me, and I hated that I needed it, but I did.

The shots had died down, and when I was back on my feet I saw that only three zombies were left standing. Jim and Jada fired almost simultaneously and two more went down, leaving only one. Angus was already moving toward the thing, already putting his gun away as he did. He pulled a knife when he was still two feet away and the thing growled. It was an older zombie, decayed and slow, and it took almost no effort on Angus's part to sink his blade into the thing's brain.

The air in the room was thick with the smell of death and gunpowder, and the floor was littered with bodies, but we'd succeeded. I looked around, surveying the people who had come with our group, and found the daughter of the High Priestess on the floor with one of her men. The sleeve of his robe was ripped open and blood pooled on his skin, as dark as the fabric draped over his body.

Dragon knelt at his side. "If we move now, there still may be time to get you the vaccine."

The man shook his head and pushed himself to his feet, forcing Dragon to stand too. The priestess's daughter did as well, her gaze moving over the room to Angus.

"If he is meant to live, Angus will save him," she said.

"You were given the vaccine when you were bitten," Meg pointed out. "Why deny someone else?"

The woman's gaze moved to Meg. "That was before the resurrection. Now that our savior is back, we must not be dependent on the drugs of man. If he has enough faith, God will heal him."

Angus, who had been in the middle of picking his way down the hall, paused so he could look over his shoulder. But I didn't get a chance to see his expression, because all of the sudden my legs wobbled and my heart sped up, and before I knew it I was going down.

# CHAPTER THIRTY
## Meg

D onaghy went down so suddenly that it took me a second to register it. I dropped to my knees at his side, reaching for him as if I would be able to change his fate even though there was nothing I could do for him. There was nothing anyone could do for him, not anymore.

"What is it?" I gasped.

He shook his head as if to tell me there was nothing wrong, but the beads of sweat on his forehead told a different story. "Just my ribs. They were bad after Jackson got ahold of me and I think that bastard made them worse."

Donaghy nodded to the hairless zombie I had just shot, the one that had at one time been Matt, but the way he avoided my gaze told me he was lying. Or at least not telling the whole truth. It was the bacteria.

Behind me, the others were moving down the hall, following my uncle who was already past the piles of bodies and had stopped in front of the last cell. I looked from him to Donaghy, feeling torn about what to do. He was hurt, but I wanted to be there when Star died, I wanted to see it with my own eyes so I could sleep at night and never have to wonder whether or not he'd really taken his last breath.

"Go," Donaghy said. "I'll be okay."

I slipped my hand into his for a moment, ignoring how clammy it was, and gave it a gentle squeeze. "I'll be back. Hang in there."

"I'm not going anywhere," he grunted out.

I ignored the twist in my gut that reminded me that wasn't true and got to my feet. The beep of the keypad told me that Angus was already typing in the code and I wanted to run so I could be there, so I could see Star, but the bodies littering the floor made it impossible to move too quickly. It was like an obstacle course, and I had to hop over them or take wide steps so I didn't trip.

By the time I'd reached the others, Angus had the door open and was already inside. No one else had moved, and I pushed past Jim and Jada so I could see what was happening. Al and Parv stood closest to the glass, but Dragon was there as well and I could tell that he was itching to get his hands on Star too. Not that he would steal this moment from Angus. We all knew my uncle deserved to be the one to take Star out.

I looked into the room to find Star standing in the middle of the floor, a gun in his shaky hand. It was pointed at Angus, but that didn't stop my uncle from stepping closer. I almost called out, almost told him to stop, but I knew it was no use because nothing could stop him now. Plus, I also knew—just as well as my uncle did—that Star would hesitate before killing his favorite test subject.

"Stop," Star yelled, his voice so shaky that it didn't sound the least bit like him.

"You ain't gonna shoot me," Angus said, his calm tone contrasting with the terror that dripped from the other man's. "You and I both know that, so why pretend?"

Star shifted his aim so the barrel was pointed past my uncle, but he must not have been able to see any of us through the barely cracked door, because it was only seconds before he was once again aiming at Angus.

"Why not?" he said, "I'm dead anyway."

Angus took a step closer to him. "You're right 'bout that."

Star squeezed the trigger without warning and the crack of the gunshot was so loud that it made my body jerk. His aim was wide though, and the bullet hit Angus in the arm, ripping across the tattoo on his bicep in a burst of red. He grunted in pain even as he lunged at Star, and the smaller man barely had time to look surprised before my uncle had slammed into him and he was on the ground. He ripped the gun from Star's hand and threw it aside. It clattered across the floor, sliding under a chair and out of sight.

Angus James sat on top of the once confident scientist, staring down at the man who had destroyed not only our family and the entire world, but who had held him prisoner for twenty years, who had tortured him, tortured his daughter, and killed the woman he loved. Until now I'd never thought of myself as a twisted person, but standing there at that moment, watching through the glass, I felt an overwhelming need to know that Angus was going to make Star suffer. To witness it, to hear his screams, to listen to him beg for mercy, to see his blood pool on the floor as the life drained out of him.

"I been dreamin' 'bout this moment for twenty years," Angus said, his gaze trained on Star. "Thinkin' 'bout what I'd do if I got my hands on you. Not just you, but your son too." He paused and the corner of his mouth turned up. "I didn't get the pleasure of rippin' his throat out, but I gotta tell ya, seein' his blood on the floor felt damn good." He leaned closer and lowered his voice. "But not as good as hearin' his screams did."

Star squirmed and his face grew red, but he pressed his lips together as if trying to stop the words from coming out of him.

Angus lifted his eyebrows. "I know what you're thinkin' right now. You're thinkin' you ain't gonna give me the satisfaction of listenin' to you beg for your life. I know because I know you. I been watchin' you come and go for twenty years, seen what you've done to people. How you've tortured 'em, killed 'em, used 'em. You think that just 'cause I was locked in a cell I wasn't really a part of it, but I was. More than you know." Angus paused and held Star's gaze. "See, I'm the reason your most trusted scientist turned against you. Jane wasn't just tryin' to save our daughter that day. She was tryin' to save me too. She loved me—" My uncle's voice broke and he had to swallow before he could go on, but once he did his words came out steady and clear. "Which is why she told me all 'bout the failsafe, why she betrayed you, and why she made it look like our daughter was dead even though she ain't."

Star's eyes went wide. "She's alive?"

Angus gave the man a little grin as he nodded. "She is, and I'm gonna make sure she stays that way."

His smile faded as he slid his hands around the other man's neck. Star bucked and scratched at the fingers trying to squeeze the life out of him, but Angus's grip was too tight, too strong. There was no way he could get free. I moved closer to the glass, my gaze focused on Star's panicked face. It grew red and his eyes doubled in size as terror set in, and then the color slowly morphed until his skin had a slightly blue tint to it. His mouth opened and closed, his nails dug into Angus's flesh until they drew blood. His feet skittered against the floor like he was trying to flee, but my uncle never eased up, never blinked, and never took his eyes off Star's face.

When Star finally stopped moving and his hands went slack, it felt like everyone around me let out a collective sigh of relief. Angus's grip loosened, and he slid off the body of the man who'd tortured him for twenty years, but he didn't look away or make a move to leave. No one else did either, and even though there was a definite feeling of relief inside me, there was something else as well. Confusion and disappointment, and a sense that we had all been robbed. This wasn't how I'd thought it would end. I had anticipated blood, pain, screams, but not this. Not this quiet death. Star had deserved more than this for all the sins he'd committed, all the people he'd killed and plotted to kill, he had deserved to suffer.

Parv was the first to move, and when she walked into the room and knelt at my uncle's side, I expected her to yell at him or hit him, to tell him that he'd robbed us all of our chance for revenge. Only that wasn't what happened. Instead, she hugged him.

"It's over," I heard her say. Her words were so soft that I could have convinced myself I'd been mistaken if it wasn't for the next thing out of her mouth. "We did it."

How? Of all the people, of all the pain, my aunt had been the one to hold onto her hatred harder than even Angus. She'd had a family stolen from her, a baby and the chance to ever have another one, and then her husband as well. How could she think *this* was justice?

I moved before I could think better of it, pushing past Al and stumbling into the room, suddenly so blinded by my own rage that I felt like the whole place had been dipped in red.

"Why didn't you make him suffer more?" I asked, surprised by the way the words shook when they came out of me but unable to stop. "You made it too easy. After everything he's done, how could you let it end like this?"

My aunt pulled away from Angus, but her hand was still resting on his shoulder when they turned to look at me. The emotion in their eyes nearly took my breath away, because it wasn't just pain anymore. It was a sense of deep relief that I couldn't understand because I *couldn't* feel the same way. Not after this.

"I ain't like him," Angus said. "He deserved to die and I wanted to be the one to do it, but I ain't a monster." He pushed himself up so he was standing, pulling Parvarti up as well. "The good Lord knows Star tried to turn me into one. Twenty years he was at it, but he didn't succeed. This here, what happened today, it proves it."

I turned my gaze on my aunt. "What about you? Don't you think Star deserved to suffer just a little?"

"He has an eternity of suffering ahead of him," Parv said, "in hell."

The air left my lungs and I found myself leaning against the wall. Maybe they had a point; maybe it was better to be the bigger and better person, to hold onto your humanity. My uncle was right after all, we'd all spent the last twenty years trying not to become one of the monsters Star had created, and the thought that even in the end we'd been able to defy him gave me a sense of satisfaction.

My uncle walked away from Star's body without a second glance at it, stopping when he was standing in front of me. "You sure do remind me of your mama when you get angry like that. She was a spitfire, just like you."

"I've heard that a lot lately," I said, my gaze still on Star.

"I know you talked to your folks 'bout what happened in Vegas." My gaze flicked to him. "Hadley was angry after that. Real angry. And I didn't think she was gonna be able to move on, not that I woulda blamed her. We got separated for a bit, not sure if you heard that part. She and your dad was off on their own, and it was months before we caught up with 'em. She was like another person then, like her old self almost, 'cause she let go of her anger. 'Cause she figured out how to move on."

"How?" I whispered.

"Your dad, you. She found somethin' to make life better and focused on that, and that's what I'm gonna do. What you gotta do."

Angus patted my shoulder as he moved past, and Parv did the same. I stayed where I was for a few seconds longer, staring at Star's body and thinking about all the chaos and pain he'd left in his wake. My uncle was right. Focusing on what I had would help me move on. The problem with that was obvious, though. I wasn't done losing. Not yet.

I left the cell and headed back down the hall. Donaghy was still on the floor, and by the time I reached him he was sweating so much that his shirt was clinging to his chest. I knelt at his side and felt his forehead, but he wasn't hot like he'd been before.

"Can you walk?" I whispered.

He nodded, but when he pulled himself up his steps were wobbly. I grabbed him before he fell, and between my support and the wall he was able to stay on his feet.

"It's not just my ribs," Donaghy said even though we both knew I'd never thought it was. "I don't think I have much time."

I swallowed before whispering, "I'm not ready to say goodbye."

"I don't think you have a choice."

Tears balled in my throat, trying to force their way out. Somehow, I managed to keep them down, but it wasn't without a lot of effort. In fact, it took more strength than I knew I had.

"We should say goodbye now, before it's too late," he whispered.

He pulled me close, and when his mouth covered mine his lips were trembling. He wrapped his arms around my waist, but his embrace felt different. It was weak and stiff, not at all like the man I'd met in Dragon's Lair.

"I'm not sorry," he whispered against my mouth.

I lost my battle to keep the tears at bay. They streamed down my face when I squeezed my eyes shut, and I pressed my face against his neck as a sob broke out of me. I didn't want to let him

256

go, didn't want to pull away from him, but the rest of our group was ready to leave and I knew staying here wasn't an option. We had to get back, had to make Donaghy comfortable. It was the only thing left to do.

Dragon had to help him walk as we headed out, that's how bad it was. The maze that was the CDC felt endless on our way out, and it seemed that with each passing moment Donaghy found it more and more difficult to put one foot in front of the other. Not just that, but a strange sense of déjà vu came over me. This same thing had happened the last time we were here, Donaghy struggling to make it out as a killer raged in his body. Only this time there would be no miracle vaccine. No way to stop the thing that was slowly killing him.

We'd left Star's body where it was when we'd fled the hall, and Sabine had left the guard who wasn't bitten to watch over it. I had no clue what The Church had planned, but I knew that the High Priestess would want to make a spectacle of Star, and the sick feeling in my stomach told me that my uncle had been right. It was better not to embrace the monster inside.

When we finally made it to the lobby, she was waiting for us. Her hood was down and a smile curled up her lips the second she laid eyes on us, but her gaze was focused mainly on Angus until her daughter stopped in front of her.

"It is done?" the priestess asked.

Sabine nodded. "He is dead."

Her mother's gaze moved to the guard who had been bitten, but her smile didn't fade and she didn't even blink before saying, "Take him to the Temple. We will see how strong his faith is."

Sabine nodded once before leading the man, who was looking a little shaky on his legs, toward the hole that had formerly been the front of the CDC.

Once they'd walked away, the High Priestess turned her pale eyes back on Angus. "You have fulfilled your part."

"If you mean killin' Star, yeah, I have."

Her smile grew. "The zombies. My sources tell me that they have begun to die."

"Sources?" Parv asked.

The priestess didn't look at her. "I told you, I have people everywhere."

I believed her.

"Come." She turned and began to walk, and even though I had no desire to follow her, I did because we were headed in the same direction anyway.

The rest of my group did as well, and the closer we got to the street, the more people turned to look at us. At first I thought they were staring at the High Priestess, but then we walked outside and I heard my uncle's name being murmured over and over again. That's when I noticed that all eyes were on him.

He was still without a shirt, and the scars from the many bites he'd received marked him as the man they'd been waiting for. Angus James, savior of the world and destroyer of zombies. He'd returned just like The Church had promised, had ripped open the walls of the CDC and killed Star, and apparently was in the process of taking the zombies out as well.

"What will you do now, Angus James?" the High Priestess asked as we moved out into the crowd.

"Live my life. Be with my family."

She nodded, the smile still on her lips. "You have earned it."

The crowd parted as we moved, allowing us to make our way through the courtyard to the street. I scanned the faces of the people we passed, took in the fanatical look in their eyes, the way they knelt when my uncle walked by or bowed their heads. Every single person here was looking at him in awe. Before today most of the population had already bought into the crazy teachings of The Church, but now that Angus was here, now that he'd confirmed what the High Priestess had been saying for years, it was going to get so much worse. Would anyone in the city be able to deny anything she said after this? Probably not. She could make up any crazy prophecy she wanted and they would all believe it. They would be like sheep following her to the slaughter if that's what she wanted them to do, and the thought caused a sick feeling to form in the pit of my stomach.

# CHAPTER THIRTY-ONE

## Meg

The High Priestess was right. All we had to do was drive through the streets of old Atlanta to see it. At first glimpse the motionless bodies that dotted the ground were nothing unusual. Dead zombies weren't uncommon, especially this close to the wall. But the further we drove, the more we saw. The older ones seemed to be going first, their brains either weaker or that strain of the virus more susceptible, but even some of the less decayed zombies we passed were acting irregularly. Stumbling when there was nothing in their way, bumping into trees. Something was definitely happening.

Of course, I didn't really need to see the zombies to know the failsafe was doing its job. Donaghy's deteriorating condition was enough proof for me. Before we'd even made it out of the city limits he was writhing in agony, so much so that when he finally slipped into unconsciousness, it was a relief. As much as I didn't want him to die, I couldn't stand to see him in pain.

He didn't regain consciousness. Not during the drive, not when we reached Senoia, not when Angus and Dragon carried him into the house. They laid him out on the couch Margot had been on before and I sat at his side, ignoring everyone else, too focused on him because I knew we only had a few precious hours left. My sister was up and moving around, and deep down I knew I should check on how she was doing, but I couldn't make myself leave Donaghy's side.

His face twitched in his sleep, giving off the impression that he was still in pain even though he wasn't conscious. I hoped not. I hoped he had slipped into an abyss of darkness that held onto him until his heart stopped beating.

"Megan." I turned at the sound of Mom's voice and found her holding a steaming mug out to me. "Soup."

I shook my head. "I'm not hungry."

"You need to eat," she said, trying to force it on me.

"Would you?" I asked, giving her a pointed look. "If Dad were lying here, would you eat? Oh wait, no you wouldn't. I know because I watched you refuse to do anything for weeks when he disappeared."

She jerked back at my words, but sat down next to me anyway. "That's why I'm doing this," she said. "Because I want you to be stronger. I *know* how much you hurt, believe me, but I won't let you lose yourself. Understand?"

Tears filled my eyes, and even though I tried to blink them away, they refused to listen. They rolled down my cheeks and I had to wipe at them with the back of my free hand, the other one wrapped around Donaghy's motionless one.

"It's not fair. Things were going to get better. We were going to have a chance."

Mom set the mug on the floor so she could pull me in for a hug, and even though I needed it, I still refused to release Donaghy's hand.

"I'm sorry, I really am. If there was something I could do for you, you know I'd do it."

"I know," I said.

She sat with me for a while, but we didn't talk. Other people came and went, and I caught glimpses of my sister who looked clean and more alert, whose hair was pulled into a neat ponytail, and who was wearing clothes that didn't look wrinkled from lying on the couch. Once I even saw her smile, and the sight of it would have been enough to break my heart if it wasn't already shattered.

It was late, and slowly the house quieted as people went to bed. Mom tried to stay, and even though the gesture touched me, I refused. I didn't want to have someone staring at me, watching me for cracks in my already shaky exterior. I didn't want to have to look strong when I knew I wasn't.

Before long it was just me in the living room, and I pulled my chair up to the couch as close as I could get it and rested my head on Donaghy's chest. His heart thumped against my ear and I squeezed my eyes closed, trying to memorize the sound. Trying to let it comfort me. It didn't because I knew the beats were numbered, but I clung to the sound anyway.

"MEG."

I knew the voice that woke me couldn't be real, and even though there was a part of me that wanted to allow myself to drift back into that dream world where Donaghy could still whisper my name, I opened my eyes. Maybe it was better to accept reality than to cling to something that could never be.

I was still in the same chair I'd been holding vigil in for the last few hours and my head was still on Donaghy's chest, but my face was turned toward his feet. His heart was still beating, I could feel it against my cheek as well as the steady rise and fall of his chest. He was still alive.

I didn't know how much time had gone by since I'd fallen asleep, but the kink in my neck told me it had been a couple hours. How much longer could he hold on like this? How much more could his brain take before he finally slipped away?

"Meg."

I froze. It couldn't be real. There was no way he'd just whispered my name. At least that's what I tried to tell myself, but the fact that I'd felt the word vibrate through his chest defied all logic, and when a hand brushed against the top of my head, it completely swept away my ability to be rational.

I didn't sit up, but instead twisted my head so I was looking at Donaghy's face. His eyes were open, just as I'd hoped they would be, and he was staring at me with an expression of pure wonder.

I swallowed. "You're alive."

"I'm alive." He shook his head and sat up, pulling me with him. His hands were on either side of my face and somehow I

261

ended up on his lap, so close that I could feel it when he exhaled. "I don't know how, the last thing I remember feeling was weakness and pain, but it's gone. It's all gone."

A sob broke out of me, but it disappeared the second Donaghy closed his lips over mine. Whatever had happened had to have been a miracle, but I didn't care. I didn't care how he'd survived because he was here and I was with him.

We kissed like we hadn't seen each other in years, and every brush of his tongue against mine made my heart beat faster. I moved closer, twisting my body so I was straddling him. His hands moved from my face to my back, his fingers flexing against my body like they were itching to rip my clothes off. I wanted him to. I wanted him to undress me so I could undress him, I wanted him to explore every inch of my body in a world where both the Stars were dead and the zombies were dying off. I wanted us to celebrate this moment and this miracle that I hadn't even dared to hope for.

Something clattered to the floor behind me and I pulled away to see my mom standing in the doorway, a coffee cup lying at her feet. "You're okay."

"I'm okay," Donaghy said.

"How?" she whispered.

He only shrugged in response.

"Maybe the vaccine had time to work." I was still on his lap, still straddling him, but I didn't care. "Or maybe it was Angus's blood."

Mom's eyebrows shot up, and then she let out a laugh. It was loud and light, and seemed to come from the past, from a different person and a different time, back before Margot and Dad were taken and everything had started to spiral out of control.

"I'm not sure I'll ever get used to Angus being the hero," she said.

I laughed too, and then laid my head on Donaghy's chest when tears came to my eyes with the laughter. Before I could stop them, sobs were shaking my body, and even though I wanted to savor this moment, the emotions I'd been holding back for the past few days bubbled over and burst out of me like a fountain. I couldn't hold it in.

"Shhh," Donaghy whispered, his lips brushing my cheeks even as the tears fell. "It's okay. We're all going to be okay."

That only made me cry harder though, because for the first time in years he was right. We were *all* going to be okay. Margot and Dad were back, Angus was alive, the Stars were dead and the zombies were on their way to joining them. But it was too much to take in, too many miraculous things had happened for me to wrap my brain around them all, and now that Donaghy was okay too, I felt like I had been sucked into a dream and if I wasn't careful I'd wake up and find myself in some twisted world where none of this was real.

"Megan," Mom said from behind me, her voice full of worry.

I pushed away from Donaghy and wiped my face with my arms. "I'm okay. It's just so overwhelming. I can't believe it. It's like a miracle." Then I laughed. "Maybe The Church is right. Maybe Angus is the savior of the world."

Mom shook her head while Donaghy kissed my cheek.

"I know I'm a believer," he said.

I laughed, but a part of me wondered if there wasn't something to it. Angus's immunity had seemed like a miracle to everyone back in the beginning, but now it seemed like so much more. It had taken my family on a journey that had led them all the way across the country and spanned twenty years, one that had been full of heartache and loss, but one that had ended up leading them to a solution to the zombie problem. If Angus hadn't been held in the CDC he never would have had Glitter or fallen in love with Jane, and if those things hadn't happened none of us would have ever learned about the failsafe. As twisted as it sounded, it felt like fate. Like Angus had been destined to do all those things.

Maybe I was a believer too.

# CHAPTER THIRTY-TWO

## Meg

The sight of the red robed men standing in the guard towers was jarring even from a distance. More so than the bodies scattered across old Atlanta, or the sight of the occasional person walking down the street like it was nothing, because those robes reminded me of the foreboding feeling that had come over me the day we'd stormed the CDC here. How uncomfortable I'd felt as we'd followed Angus through the crowd of believers. Yes, we'd all suspected this would happen, but that didn't make seeing it any less disturbing.

Dad slowed the car to a stop outside the gate and we sat in total silence as we waited for it to open. Mom was in the passenger seat while Uncle Angus rode in the back next to me. I'd insisted on coming even though I wasn't really a James—of course, neither was Mom when you looked at it that way—because I'd needed to know what was happening inside the walls, needed to know what The Church was up to. But right now, I was starting to wonder if ignorance wasn't better.

The gates opened with a creak that could have been mistaken for thunder, revealing even more guards in red robes, and dad threw the car into gear.

"Let's get this over with," he mumbled.

He drove through, but he didn't make it far. A robed man with an automatic weapon stepped in front of us, forcing dad to slow to a stop just inside the gate.

"Looks like The Church has changed their mind about violence," Mom said under her breath.

"You surprised?" Dad muttered as he rolled the window down.

"State your business," the man with the gun barked.

"Axl and Angus James," Dad said. "Here to see the priestess."

The man hunched over so he could get a look inside, his gaze sweeping across the four of us so fast that I doubted he'd be able to describe us even if a gun was held to his head. Then he said, "Weapons?"

"Always," Dad replied firmly.

The man's gaze held his for a moment. "We do not allow guns in the Temple. You will leave those in your vehicle. Do you understand?" When Dad nodded once the man stepped back. "You may proceed."

Dad rolled up the window and did as he was told.

None of us spoke as we drove through the city. I'd only been back once since the night Star was killed, two days later so I could go into the Biosafety Level four lab again, this time with Dragon. The Church had been in a hurry to demolish the building, but we'd known that we needed to get every vial of bacteria out of there before they did it. It was the only way to ensure that the zombies were wiped off the face of the earth in a timely manner.

After I'd broken that first vial, the zombies in the area had started dying off quickly, more of them dropping every day. But logic told us that if we waited for this thing to spread on its own it could take years to reach the rest of the country. The original virus had spread fast because people traveled a lot back then, but these days it was rare, meaning we were going to have to take matters into our own hands.

So Dragon and I had put on suits and gone back into the lab of death. My family hadn't been thrilled with the idea of me going in a second time, but with Helen gone, I had been the only one who'd had any knowledge of how to maneuver the lab. So I'd gone, and together Dragon and I had gotten every vial of the failsafe out of there safely.

266

We'd done it just in time too. We'd heard reports that The Church, led by the High Priestess, had blown up the CDC only two days later, and now that we were in the city I could see the proof of it with my own eyes. There was nothing but rubble where the building had once stood. Chunks of concrete, twisted metal, and glass were all that remained of the building where Star had plotted to destroy the world, but nothing about the sight was satisfying. Not when I knew the rubble symbolized something much bigger than the death of Star. The Church had destroyed it for a reason. That pile of rubble symbolized the death of science in New Atlanta. Faith now reigned here. Faith in what, I wasn't sure. The Church had held my uncle in high esteem for nearly two decades, but now that they were no longer waiting for his return, I had no clue if they were still worshiping him or if they'd moved on to something else. I just knew that things inside these walls had changed drastically in the seven weeks since Star's death.

I was used to seeing the red robes of The Church, but this was a whole new level of crazy. Every single person over the age of eighteen now wore one, and those who were still considered children all wore red as well. Red dresses, red shirts, or red pants. It didn't matter as long as they were sporting the color in some way. The sidewalks of New Atlanta were now a sea of crimson, and it was so disturbingly unreal that I felt like I'd been sucked into another world.

"Did they force out the people who didn't want to join The Church?" Mom asked as we passed a group of kids who were kicking a ball across a small patch of grass.

"They must have," I muttered.

The truth was, we were pretty clueless about what had been happening. We'd moved to Senoia and started over there, and for the past seven weeks all of our time had been devoted to healing and learning to be a family again. The Church and New Atlanta had been in the backs of all our minds, but we hadn't returned. Hadn't checked on what was happening. Hadn't planned to. Not until the High Priestess had summoned Dad and Angus here.

We knew it had something to do with the James blood, which was why we'd intentionally left Margot and Glitter back in Senoia. The Church had no idea that Glitter existed, and as far as they knew Margot had died nine years ago. That was how everyone wanted it to stay. With Angus now alive and The Church in the middle of reinventing itself, I had no trouble imagining them grasping onto my innocent younger sister as the new object of their obsessive insanity.

Dad pulled up in front of the Temple and put the car in park, but for a second none of us moved. The same statue that had always been out front was there, which I took to mean that they still revered Angus to some degree, but that hunk of cement wasn't what drew my gaze and I doubted it was what anyone else was looking at either. No. I was focused on the bodies hanging on either side of the door. They were rotten now and even more grotesque than the zombies that had formerly ruled our world, but I knew who they were the second I saw them. Jackson and his father.

"That who I think it is?" Angus asked, his voice making me jump in the silence that had settled over us.

"Gotta be," Dad muttered.

Mom turned her face away. "It's sick."

"All this is sick," Dad said as he shoved the door open. "Let's get this over with so we can get the hell outta here."

We climbed out and headed to the front door together. I did my best not to look at the bodies, but it was impossible to avoid the smell. I thought I'd been around the stench of death enough in my life to at least be over gagging from it, but as we neared the bodies and the stink hit me, I discovered I'd been wrong. My stomach convulsed and without my permission my eyes flipped up, focusing on the way the corpse's throat had been ripped open. The knowledge that this was Jackson, a man I'd been close friends with for years, only made the twisting inside me more intense. He'd deserved to die, just like his father had, but displaying their bodies like this was beyond twisted.

Thankfully, I managed to make it inside without losing my lunch, and once the doors were shut the smell faded away enough that I was able to regain control of my body.

The room was no different than it had been the last time we were here. It was still empty of furniture and the statue of Angus still stood front and center, and it still looked nothing like my uncle — not that anyone affiliated with this freak show seemed to care.

There were no robed figures in the room to greet us, so Angus and I led the way across the room to the priestess's chambers. We found her alone, sitting on one of the red couches. For the first time she wasn't wearing a red robe, but instead had on a pair of simple black pants and a black sleeveless shirt. Against the dark fabric of her clothes, her skin looked even more ghostly pale than ever before, and without the flowing robe covering her body I was able to see just how thin and frail she was. She had spots from the sun and age dotting her arms, which were so bony that they gave off the impression she might be ill with some debilitating or terminal disease. She didn't look as imposing, didn't look nearly as capable of taking over as she had within the protective folds of her crimson robe.

That impression didn't last long, though. She stood when she saw us walk in, and even her frail frame couldn't hide the wild expression in her impossibly pale eyes. They focused on the two men in our group, taking in Angus first before sweeping over Dad and then returning to my uncle. Mom and I were invisible, or at the very least too useless to be acknowledged.

"You came," the priestess said, and then she swept her arm across the room toward the second couch, motioning for us to take a seat.

We didn't move.

"We only came 'cause we wanted you to know that this is it for us," Angus said. "We done our part. We took out Star and I took out the dead like you wanted. That's it. I ain't a part of this no more. I'm done lettin' people use me."

"We have no wish to use you, Angus James." The priestess shook her head in a way that reminded me of a mother reprimanding her child, but the smile on her lips was slightly mocking at the same time. "We want to offer you sanctuary in our city. You and your brother—" Her pale eyes flitted past my dad and uncle long enough to acknowledge that there were other people with them. "—and the rest of your family. We have safety and serenity inside these walls. Here you can live out the rest of your days in peace."

My uncle's mouth scrunched up and I held my breath, waiting to see if he was going to spit or throw words in her face that might have her calling for her guards. When he said nothing, I let the breath out, but the tension in my body didn't ease with it.

"We're good where we are," Dad said after a few seconds of heavy silence.

The priestess nodded, and despite the disappointment in her eyes, I could tell she wasn't surprised. "Very well."

She turned her back on us and I braced myself for a fight. By the way Dad's hand moved to his side, he did as well. We'd been told no weapons inside the Temple, and I'd done as I was told, but based on the bulge at my dad's side, he hadn't been nearly as obedient.

The priestess didn't go for a weapon or call for backup, though. Instead she swept her robe off the hook where it hung and pulled it over her head.

Without turning to face us she said, "Know that your refusal means you will no longer be welcome inside the walls of our city. We have sent members out and have taken over the production of oil, as well as electricity and water." She turned then, still adjusting her robe. "As a gesture of goodwill, we will continue to provide your settlement with these items, but there will be no trading of goods. We wish to remain separate from the outside world and have no desire to mix with the *sullied*."

"Sullied?" I said, unable to keep quiet, not with the way she wrinkled her nose at us.

"Times are changing," she replied. "We have new laws. From here on out our people will treat their bodies like the temples they are meant to be. There will be no more tattoos. No more piercings. No alcohol or tobacco. We will remain a healthy people, and as long as we are left alone, peaceful as well."

"What about people who already have those things?" Mom asked. "Do you allow them to join your church?"

"Every member of The Church must be baptized in the blood of Angus." The High Priestess lifted the hood of her robe as walked past us, headed for the door. "Come. You will see."

I hesitated, unsure of whether the rest of my family would follow or if I wanted to witness the ritual I'd heard so much about. It was something people had whispered about in the streets for as long as I could remember, but something no one outside the highest members of The Church had actually seen. Before now, only the elite had been baptized in the blood of Angus, but it seemed that like almost everything else I'd become accustomed to, that had changed.

Angus was the first to move, and even though I could tell by the tightness in his jaw that he wasn't excited by the prospect, he must have been as curious about the ritual as I was. Dad followed, and then Mom, who reached out and took my hand as she passed me. Whether it was for me or for her, I wasn't sure, but I wrapped my hand around her bony fingers anyway because it helped me feel more secure about what we were walking into.

We'd arrived at the Temple no more than ten minutes ago, but when we stepped back into the main room it was a different world than it had been before. It was packed with people in red robes, all of them on their knees and facing the statue of my uncle. My family stopped dead in our tracks just outside the High Priestess's chambers, but The Church's leader continued forward until she was standing in front of her people.

Not a word was uttered. Not even when the door at the other end of the room opened and the bulky guards that usually flanked the High Priestess walked through. They were carrying a pig that had been hog tied and was now secured to a metal pole. It wiggled and squealed with each step they took, but the men didn't slow or seem to care in the least as they moved through the crowd and headed for the front.

While they did this, four people materialized from the sea of red figures. They weren't wearing robes, but instead wore white one piece outfits that looked like something an infant would wear. They consisted of shorts that ended several inches above the knees and a top that was sleeveless, and the material was so thin that nearly every inch of them was visible.

There were three men and one woman in the group. The oldest man, who was probably in his fifties, had a scraggily beard that was dotted in gray and arms that were covered in tattoos, while the other three appeared to be free of marks or piercings. The youngest man and the girl were both just teenagers, probably barely over the age of eighteen, and the boy trembled so much as the men carrying the pig neared the front of the room that I started to wonder if he was going to faint.

When the men with the squealing pig stopped in front of the High Priestess, she stepped forward and lifted her arms. She held a knife in her right hand, and the blade glinted in the flickering light of the candles.

"Welcome, my children," she said, her voice booming enough to erase the frail impression I'd had of her when we'd first arrived in her chambers. "We have come today to baptize four new followers. For twenty years we had nothing but faith, but the return of Angus James has brought us to a new era."

As the High Priestess spoke, Sabine seemed to materialize from the shadows at her mother's back. In her hands she held a large golden chalice, which she placed under the pig's head. In the blink of an eye, the High Priestess had sliced the blade of her knife across the animal's throat. It let out one final squeal as blood poured from the cut, filling the cup and dripping onto the floor and Sabine's hands and arms. It was as dark red as the robes these people wore, so dark it almost looked black in the shadows that the High Priestess and her guards cast across the dying pig.

When the cup was full, the priestess took it from her daughter who once again stepped back. Her head was down, her eyes cast to the ground just like they always seemed to be in her mother's presence.

Cup in hand, the High Priestess approached the four initiates kneeling at the front of the church. She stopped in front of the first, the older man with sleeves made of tattoos.

"Do you renounce the ways of the old world and embrace the saving blood of Angus James?" she asked loud and clear.

"I do," the man replied, his voice not nearly as loud despite the firmness of the words.

The priestess nodded, and then she poured some of the blood over the man's bent head. It ran down the sides of his skull and over his forehead before trickling into his eyes. My stomach lurched as I watched the red make a line down his face to his chin where it pooled for just a moment before dripping onto the floor.

She moved to the next man and repeated the process, and then to the girl who was just as sure and confident as the two before her had been. The fourth and final person, the teenage boy, watched all of this from the corner of his eye, which was barely visible with his head bowed. He seemed to tremble more and more with each passing second, and when the priestess finally stopped in front of him, I didn't miss the way his throat bobbed when he swallowed.

"Do you renounce the ways of the old world and embrace the saving blood of Angus James?" the priestess asked again.

The boy lifted his head long enough to look her in the eye, and then quickly lowered it. "I do," he mumbled, his words as shaky as he was.

The High Priestess didn't notice or didn't care, because she tipped the goblet over and poured the remainder of the pig's blood onto the boy's head. He squeezed his hands into fists as it ran over his hair and down his body. Just like all the others, it made streaks of blood down his face before dropping to the floor, but unlike the recruits before him, this boy didn't relax even after the priestess had turned back to face her people. He stayed tense, his hands clenched at his sides, and I couldn't help wondering why he'd decided to take this step if he was so obviously conflicted by it.

"Behold," the High Priestess said, holding her arms up with the chalice still clutched in her hands. "The saving blood of Angus James."

A chant started then, and it was the same one as before. The same one I still heard in my sleep.

"...you have visited them with destruction and wiped out all remembrance of them."

When the chant had faded away, the family or friends of those who had been baptized came forward to present the new members of the church with their robes, no doubt congratulating them on their wise choice. Two people who I could only assume were his parents joined the boy, and the smiles of delight on their faces said it all. They were the reason he'd done this.

"He didn't want to do it," I mumbled to my mom.

She nodded and gave my hand a squeeze, which was still clutched in hers. "Maybe he didn't have a choice."

It wasn't long before the crowd gathered in the room began to disperse, and when that happened the priestess turned back to face us.

"We accept everyone who is willing to renounce their old ways," she said as behind her the room emptied.

"Do you force people to join?" I asked, the uncertainty on the boy's face fresh in my mind.

"At the age of eighteen, our citizens must make a choice. Be baptized into The Church or leave the city. Everyone is free to choose their own path," she replied. "But if they leave, they are not to return. Ever."

I didn't point out that being forced from the only home you've ever known and leaving your family behind wasn't much of a choice for most people. Like that boy, who'd most likely been born inside these walls and not only had no clue how to take care of himself in the outside world, but probably didn't know a soul out there.

The High Priestess focused her gaze on my uncle when she said, "You have made up your mind? You do not wish to join The Church?"

Angus pressed his lips together and glanced across the room, over to where the statue that was supposed to represent him stood. "You still prayin' to me?"

I knew he wasn't considering a lifestyle change, but his words seemed to give the priestess hope that he might be, because she smiled. "You were the vessel that led to the salvation of the world and we will always hold you in high esteem," she replied calmly, her tone making her words sound almost sane. Almost. "But your reign has come to an end and we have now entered a period of paradise. We will always thank Angus James for the part he played in freeing us, so we will continue to pray to you."

"But I ain't your god no more?" my uncle asked.

"You were never a god to us, Angus James," the High Priestess replied. "You were merely the vessel God chose. As I said, we have entered a state of paradise, much like the one Adam and Eve lived in. It may fall, just as that one did, but when it does God will send us someone new who will once again overthrow his oppressors. Until then, we will live as we are. Peacefully."

"So New Atlanta is like the new Garden of Eden?" Mom asked. "What about the other settlements around the world? Are those gardens too?"

"We will deal with them as the zombies die off," the High Priestess said in a noncommittal way. I wasn't sure if she didn't know yet or just wasn't willing to share, and before I could ask she said, "I have already dispatched my men to the prison colony of

DC, and they have wiped the vermin living there off the face of the earth."

"What do you mean wiped them out?" I asked.

Something about her tone told me exactly what she meant, but I didn't want to accept it. Yes, bad people had been sent to DC. Murders and rapists. But there were other people there too. People who had done nothing other than get in the way of Star or someone else with power. People like Donaghy.

The High Priestess focused her colorless eyes on me. "Before we destroyed the CDC, we took a few vials from one of the labs and released their contents on the colony. Those who have not died already will very soon."

"Shit," Angus muttered, but I found it impossible to speak.

Mom took a step away from the priestess. "I'm ready to leave."

"You gonna stand by your word?" my uncle asked, his words nearly coming out as a growl. "You gonna let us keep our electricity and water even if we don't move back here? You gonna leave us be?"

"I will," the priestess replied calmly. "I had hoped you would join now that you've seen proof of my divine connection to God, but I cannot make you. Either way, you are free to live your life Angus James. You have earned it."

"Alright then," Angus said. "I don't think we got anything else to talk 'bout."

"Very well," the priestess said. She nodded to the door behind us, the one we'd first come through. "You know your way out of the city. Remember what I have said. Once you leave, you will not be welcome back."

"There ain't nothin' you can do to make me come back here," Angus said as he turned and stomped away from the priestess.

THE RELIEF I FELT AT DRIVING THROUGH THE GATES OF Senoia was mirrored on the faces of my family. Dad's hands finally loosened their death grip on the steering wheel and Mom let out a deep sigh. Even Angus, who hadn't spoken since leaving the city, seemed to relax. Being away from The Church and the walled city that now felt more like a prison than ever before was only part of it, though. The rest was just being back here. Back in Senoia with our family and friends and knowing that life had started over again. The walls were still up and probably would be for a while just as a precaution, but no one had seen a zombie in more than three weeks. Soon we'd begin the process of gathering the bodies so we could burn them, of cleaning up the city beyond our walls, and maybe even repairing what was left. For now though, we were just trying to cling to the knowledge that hope had finally arrived.

Dad pulled into the driveway of our new home and put the car in park. Glitter was sitting on the front porch, and she waved when I opened my door. From where I stood I could see into the backyard, and I stood frozen for just a second, watching as my sister played with one of the neighbor's kids. She laughed as she ran from him, and it felt like the sound seeped inside me and twisted around my heart, squeezing it. She still had her moments, dreams and signs of PTSD just like the doctor had predicted she would, but she was better than I could have ever imagined.

She spun, turning the tables on the little boy who had been chasing her, and then scooped him up into her arms. Just as she swung him around she spotted us and waved, and then she was running across the yard, carrying the child as she called out to me.

"Meggy!"

Emotionally, she didn't seem her age most of the time. The nine-year-old Margot we'd lost seemed to be trapped inside the body of this eighteen-year-old almost woman, but she was happy and healthy and free, so we were counting our blessing instead of trying to fix what very well could have been unfixable. She might never mature or get married and have kids, but she was here and that was what was important to all of us.

"You're back," she said when she stopped in front of me. She was out of breath and her cheeks were pink from exertion, but her brown eyes sparkled. "We're playing tag. Come play with us."

The little boy squirmed in her arms, and when she set him down he darted off, back to the yard they'd just vacated.

"In a little bit," I said, patting my sister on the shoulder. "I want to check on Donaghy first."

She wrinkled her nose. "All he does is work."

I laughed. "He's trying to fix our house, Margot."

My sister shrugged once before turning away. She called out greetings to our parents as she ran past, and like me they watched her run off with a combination of awe and amusement in their expressions. Despite her bad moments, Margot seemed to be determined to enjoy every second of her new life and I loved her for it more than I ever had before.

Angus was already on the porch when I walked up, sitting next to his daughter while he smoked. She was asking him about New Atlanta, but since I wasn't interested in hearing a recap of what we'd just seen, I headed inside.

The downstairs had been transformed since the first time I'd visited this house. Since it had never been finished, no one had ever lived in it, and for the past twenty years it had been mostly used for storing supplies, as well as the zombies in the basement. They were gone now, and thanks to the combined efforts of our group, the walls were now up and the kitchen had cabinets. There was a man in the settlement who had once been a plumber, and he'd been more than willing to help Dad get the sinks, bathtubs, and toilets up and working. The place was really starting to look like a home, which was what all the work had been about. Making a home for my newly reunited family.

I could hear the scrape of feet against the floor upstairs, and I followed the sound. The four bedrooms were already packed with furniture even though the floors were nothing but plywood, but none of us cared. Mom and Dad had one, Angus another, and Glitter and Margot shared the master. The fourth was all mine, though. Well, not *all* mine. I shared it with Donaghy.

That was where I found him now, standing in our room with a can of paint on the floor at his feet. It was blue and in my opinion totally pointless—I didn't care what color the walls were as long as we were together—but he'd insisted, saying that he wanted the room to look as much like a home as it could. I got it in a way. How he wanted to feel not just like we were moving forward, but like some of the old world was coming back. Like with the destruction of the zombies and the CDC, we were able to go back in time. It was impossible, but a nice idea all the same.

"Looks good," I said when I stopped in the doorway.

He stumbled back, barely missing the can of paint, and let out a low curse before turning to face me. "You scared the shit out of me."

"Sorry," I said with a laugh. "I thought you heard me."

He laughed too, and then shook his head as he set the paintbrush down. When we stepped back and surveyed his work, he nodded. "I like it."

"I do too," I said, crossing the room to him. "You were right."

He smiled and grabbed my hand so he could pull me against him. "I'm glad you like it, but you know this arrangement isn't always going to work. One day our little family will expand and we're going to need our own house."

"Are you trying to tell me you're pregnant?" I asked, lifting my eyebrows.

"No," he said, laughing. "Although, with all the miracles going around lately, nothing would surprise me."

He leaned down and kissed me, and the second his mouth was on mine everything that had happened inside the walls of New Atlanta vanished. With it gone, there was nothing scary or twisted in the world. There was just Donaghy and me. Together. As a family.

I stood up on the tips of my toes and grasped his face between my hands so I could kiss him back. My fingers threaded through his hair, which had grown so much over the last seven weeks that I'd almost forgotten how short it had been when we'd met. How he'd had to shave when he was inside DC, how he had at one time been a prisoner there.

Since I didn't want to spoil the mood, I pushed the thoughts aside and focused on the moment. On sliding my tongue over his. On pressing my body against his chest.

He broke the kiss so he could whisper, "You know what happened the last time we decided to have sex in the middle of the day."

I laughed when I remembered my mom walking in on us in the bathroom. "She should have knocked."

"Or we should have taken that as our cue to find our own place."

He was half-joking, but I also knew there was some seriousness there. We'd had this discussion more than once, and

278

even though I got where he was coming from and there had definitely been more than a few awkward moments over the last several weeks, I wasn't ready to leave home yet. Not when I finally had my family back, and for now I wanted to enjoy it.

"We will. After they take down the wall. I promise."

Donaghy smiled and gave me a small peck before turning back to the can of paint. "I'm almost done here. Give me an hour tops."

"You don't want help?"

He shook his head and said over his shoulder, "I'm good."

I headed back down the stairs, thinking about DC and knowing I'd have to tell him about it. It was hard to say how he'd react. The prison colony had been a hole from everything I'd heard, and his time there hadn't been fun. He'd only gotten out by winning fights, which was how he'd ended up here to begin with. But the people in there had still been *people*, and if he hadn't been out on the prison release program when everything went down in New Atlanta, he would have been inside DC when The Church released that virus. Meaning he would be dead now too. It was bound to shake a person up.

I scanned the now nearly finished downstairs as I passed through. The living room had several dingy couches shoved into it that were a hell of a lot more comfortable than they looked, but what was supposed to be the dining room had been enclosed so Parvarti could have a room in our house as well. The dining room table we'd found in an abandoned house outside the walls of Senoia looked cramped in the corner of the room, but when all of us were gathered around the thing it was more homey than suffocating. These days, it felt like a totally different life than the one I'd been living only a few months ago.

I went out the back door and found Margot no longer playing tag but instead being pushed on the swing by Glitter. Charlie sat on the grass at their side, watching the two with an expression on her face that was almost serene. Dad had put the swing up only last week, and since then my sister had spent hours upon hours on it, sometimes refusing to come into the house until long after the sun had set.

A few of my other family members were gathered in the backyard as well. Dad was arranging logs in the fire pit while mom and Lila shucked corn. She, Al, and Charlie had taken a small apartment above what used to be a coffee shop, but they still spent most of their waking hours here. Since zombie slayers were a thing of the past, Luke had taken up permanent residence with Kelly, much to his mother's delight. I had a feeling she was counting down the days until she found out that she was going to be a grandmother, although I doubted that starting a family was on Luke or Kelly's mind at the moment.

"Where's your boy?" Angus asked when I stopped next to him. He was watching dad build the fire, smoking as usual but missing his normal partner, Parv.

"Finishing up painting the bedroom," I said. "Where's Parv?"

My uncle got an amused expression on his face. "Just got back from huntin'."

"Bet you wish you could have gone with her," I said.

He snorted. "Anything woulda been better than what we did today."

He wasn't exaggerating about that.

It wasn't long before Al and Luke showed up with my aunt in tow, as well as a big chunk of meat. Courtesy of Parv. She must have gotten it a few hours ago since it had already been butchered and divided up between the families in the settlement. It was the normal way things were handled for now, any food that was found or hunted was passed out to as many people as it would feed, but there always seemed to be more than enough for us. At least for the time being.

Dad already had the fire going, so he focused on the meat while Parv took her usual place at Angus's side. He had a cigarette ready for her, which she took from him wordlessly. This had become a common sight, the two of them side by side, and even though no one had mentioned it yet, I knew I wasn't the only one watching to see what would happen. They'd both been burned in love, more than once from what I'd heard, but since my uncle's return it seemed like he felt more comfortable in Parv's presence than in anyone else's, even Dad's, and I felt like it was only a matter of time before something developed between them.

Kelly showed up for dinner shortly before the meat was done, and she had a couple surprise guests with her. Jim and Jada.

Unlike Luke, Jim hadn't settled into post-zombie life easily. After two weeks of being stuck in Senoia, he'd volunteered to join a group heading out of state to release the bacteria near another settlement. Jada had taken it all in stride, and even though I'd expected her to volunteer for the trip as well, she hadn't. I hadn't really understood it at first, but now that Jim was back and I saw them together, I got it. She hadn't wanted to chase him away, which was what she would have been doing if she'd followed him uninvited. So she'd let him go and had waited here, hoping he'd return on his own. And he had. Even more, his entire attitude toward her seemed to have changed. He stood closer than he had before, reached out and touched her when they talked. And he smiled, which was something I'd never seen before, and as a result she seemed happier too.

When Donaghy finally came out of the house to join us, I couldn't help laughing. "You have paint on your nose," I said, reaching up to flick the blue speck away.

He grinned down at me. "Did you get it?"

"I got it."

"Good," he said, and then gave me a quick kiss.

Dragon was the only one missing from our group, but we all knew we'd see him later. He'd liberated every salvageable thing from his bar inside the walls of New Atlanta so he could open one here in Senoia. It had taken him some time to get it going since he'd had to brew the ale and make the moonshine, but he'd finally had enough stocked up to open the week before and business had been booming. Of course, with The Church taking over New Atlanta and the old government gone, currency was questionable at the moment. He was still taking credits when people had them, as were most businesses, but he was also taking trade. We all knew that soon we would have to figure out a new currency system, but at the moment we'd decided to let it go. There was still more than enough to scavenge and with the zombies gone it was going to be easier than ever.

Of course, after our visit to New Atlanta today, Mom, Dad, Angus, and I knew that scavenging would soon be the only way for us to get supplies. Something everyone else was about to learn.

Even though I knew the others had to be dying to find out what was happening inside the walls of the city, they didn't ask and Dad waited until we'd all finished eating to bring it up. Once we were settled around the fire, he told everyone what we'd seen. The red robes on everyone, the bodies outside the temple, the baptism. Then he told them what the High Priestess had said.

"No trading at all?" Lila looked around at everyone else. "So we're totally on our own?"

"Better than bein' in there," Angus muttered.

"I'm not arguing that point," my aunt countered. "I'm just thinking about some of the things we got inside that are going to be impossible to find out here. Flour for one, sugar for another. We can grow food and hunt, but I don't know the first things about grinding wheat to make bread."

"She's right," Mom said. "This is going to be a much more drastic change than we realize."

"There are other ways of getting things," Jim said.

"How's that?" Dad asked.

"Raiding the supply trucks. People living outside the city have been doing it since the beginning of Star's reign, and there's no reason to stop now."

He had his hand on Jada's knee, which I didn't even think he realized. She did though, despite the tension in the air, she had a look of contentment on her face that made her look like a different person.

"That's all well and good," Dad said. "Except that if she finds out, she could decide to cut our power off."

"I don't want to go back to not having power," Lila said with a groan. "Remember how awful that was?"

"We need to put solar panels up." Al leaned back so he could gaze up at the roof of the house. "Someone here has to know how to do it."

"That'd help, assuming we could find some," Dad muttered.

The discussion went on and on, people pointing out issues we were going to face, as well as what we could do. It felt too familiar, too much like the first couple days here when all we did was plan and talk about what obstacles we were going to have to overcome. I hated it. Hated knowing that our idyllic life had once again taken a wrong turn.

"I think it's strange that no one has brought up the most obvious question," Jada said, speaking up for the first time since we started discussing the whole thing. "What are we going to do about it? I mean, we are going to try to put a stop to this. Aren't we? We just risked everything to get rid of one dictator. We can't just sit back let another one take control."

Silence settled over the group.

It was something we hadn't discussed after leaving New Atlanta, and something I had never even considered. Was Jada right? Could we do something about what was happening inside the city? Should we?

"I'm tired." Angus was the first to break the silence, and his words were followed by a deep sigh. "If everybody else wants to go to war again, I'll do it, but I ain't gonna lie. I'm beat."

He looked around, and the exhaustion he'd just spoken of seemed to etch lines into his face right before my very eyes. It wasn't just him either. I could see it in Mom and Dad's expressions too, in Parv's. The weariness, the emotional scars left behind by all the wars they'd fought in the past. I'd heard about them all, more recently than ever before, and I knew it wasn't like my family to walk away from something like this. But I also knew they were getting older. Not old, I couldn't see my parents as old, especially when they suddenly had so much more life to live, but older. Tired like Angus had said.

"I just can't do it again," Mom said. "I don't think I have it in me." She reached out and took Dad's hand even as her gaze moved across the yard to where Margot sat. "As selfish as it sounds, I can't risk losing what I just got back."

"Me neither," Parv whispered, her gaze on the ground. "We've given up too much already. Let someone else take this battle."

Jada frowned and looked around at the people gathered in our backyard. Al and Lila were nodding, as was Dad. Even Jim seemed to silently agree with Mom and Parv.

"So you're saying we do nothing?" Jada asked, turning her gaze on Jim.

He grabbed her hand. "I'm saying we need to think of ourselves for once."

I had to agree with him. It wasn't fair that my family, who had already been put through so much, should have to take responsibility for the world yet again. We'd fought and clawed our way here, and for once we were together and whole. I wasn't ready to sacrifice that. Not so soon after getting it. And we'd be risking so much more this time, because we were still hiding the existence of both Glitter and Margot from The Church. Starting a war with them would put all of that at risk, and with as twisted as their teachings were, I couldn't even begin to imagine what they would do if they found out about my sister and cousin.

"We can't," I said, drawing Jada's gaze my way. "If the High Priestess finds a reason to come here she could find out about Margot and Glitter. What do you think will happen then?"

Glitter, who was sitting at my uncle's side, scooted closer to her father.

"No," he growled, as he pulled her against him. "That ain't gonna happen. We gotta stay out of it this time. It's for the best."

"They said they planned to be peaceful," Mom pointed out. "That all they wanted to do was live in their new paradise. Who are we to stop that?"

Jada's determination wavered, but she still shook her head like she had a hard time wrapping her brain around it.

The discussion went back and forth, but the original sentiment Angus had expressed seemed to be echoed in the words of everyone around me. They were tired. This was one fight they couldn't take responsibility for no matter how guilty it made them feel. They had no steam left.

No longer interested in a debate that was totally devoid of a satisfactory solution, I eventually got up and went over to the swing where Margot still sat. She was staring at the dirt, pushing herself back and forth with a shove of her toes against the ground, but she lifted her head when I walked up and smiled.

"Meggy." Hearing my name on her lips still gave me goose bumps, but I was getting more and more used to it every day.

"You want me to push you?" I asked.

She shook her head. "No. I was just thinking."

"What about?"

When I knelt at her side, she was forced to look down at me. Her face scrunched up the way it did when she was thinking something through, which always reminded me of how Dad pressed his lips together when he was thinking, and then she shook her head.

"You can tell me," I said gently.

"Are you and Donaghy going to move out?"

I smiled and reached up to take my sister's hand. "Not right now, but one day. One day we'll need our own house because we'll want to have a family. You know, kids. You'd like that wouldn't you? Being an aunt?"

Margot pressed her lips together. "I guess."

"I think you'd be a great aunt."

My sister shrugged and pulled her hand from mine so she could once again start swinging. It was slow and lazy though, and her gaze was fixed on Donaghy as she did it.

"Do you love him?" she asked finally.

I followed her gaze to find him watching us, his blue eyes taking in the scene like he knew what she had asked me and he was waiting to hear my response. We still hadn't said the words out loud to one another, not just because it still felt too soon, but also because things had begun to feel less urgent. I'd started to tell myself that we had time. That life was going to be simpler from here on out. After today, I now knew that wasn't true.

"I do," I told Margot, my eyes still on Donaghy. "I love him very much."

He smiled, but I could tell by the way he tilted his head that he had no idea what I'd said, which was fine with me. When I told him, I wanted to be standing right in front of him so we could kiss.

After dinner we all walked over to Dragon's new bar to get a drink. I'd only been inside a couple times, but I'd passed by the building on a daily basis because it was on the main street. It was nice, a lot cleaner and cozier than his place in Atlanta had been, with polished wood floors, a saloon type bar that reminded me of the old west, and glass chandeliers that sparkled from above. It was the name that really got to me, though. A new life meant a new name for his bar, and Dragon had chosen the most obvious and touching one possible. *Helen's*. The tribute brought tears to my eyes every time I saw it.

Dragon waved distractedly when we walked in, too swamped to do much more, and I found myself turning to Glitter. "Looks like he's going to need some help behind the bar soon."

She smiled, paused long enough to pull her hair—which now had brown roots that were nearly two inches long—out of her face,

285

and then practically skipped over to the bar. When she ducked behind it and took her place at Dragon's side, he grinned, revealing the gap where his two front teeth used to be.

"What about you?" Donaghy asked, nodding to the bar. "You want a job?"

I laughed and shook my head. "I don't know what I want to do with my life, but I know waitressing isn't it."

The sudden change in our lives had made careers uncertain for all of us. Dad, Al, and Parv had worked the wall for as long as I could remember, something we really didn't need anymore, while Luke, Jada, and Jim had been thrust into unemployment thanks to the death of every zombie around. Mom alone had job security because of her training as a midwife, but the rest of us were still floundering. And with the uncertainty about how we would even get paid, we weren't rushing to find anything either.

Donaghy got our drinks and we settled around a table with the rest of my family, talking about more pleasant subjects than what was going on with The Church. Margot was at Mom's side, looking out of place in the bar but smiling like she was having the time of her life, while Dad looked back and forth between all of us with an expression of contentment on his face. Like me, he seemed to be trying to soak it all in rather than focus on the bad things.

People started wandering off as it got later and later, and I didn't miss it when Angus and Parv left together. Based on the look Mom and Lila shared, I wasn't the only one who'd noticed how much time those two were spending together.

It was late by the time Donaghy and I found ourselves walking home. The settlement had mostly turned in for the night and most of the houses we passed were so dark they looked abandoned, but despite the hour we moved at a leisurely pace, holding hands and enjoying the cool evening that told me fall was on the way.

When we reached the old gazebo at the end of the street, I pulled him into it. He didn't protest, but instead allowed me to lead him to the bench. My heart was pounding, but it wasn't nerves. It was anticipation. Excitement, even.

I twisted my body so I was facing him and smiled.

"What?" he asked.

"I have something I wanted to say." He nodded and I swallowed. "It's something I've been thinking for a while now. I held back for so many reasons, but after today all those reasons seem stupid and I realize I can't keep it in anymore. Donaghy, I—"

"I love you," he said. My mouth dropped open and he laughed. "I wanted to say it first."

I laughed too, and then I was up on my knees on the bench, kissing him, whispering the words against his lips, "I love you. I love you so much, and I'm so glad we get to start this life together. No matter what happens, I just want to be with you."

He wrapped his arms around me and kissed me back, and the hope I'd felt before going to New Atlanta today returned. Things would never be easy, I'd been fooling myself to think they would, but we could handle it. Donaghy and me, along with my family, which was now achingly whole. No matter what happened, we could handle it together.

# CHAPTER THIRTY-THREE
## Donaghy

The team was in place. Now all we had to do was wait.

From my spot behind a group of bushes I could see the barrel of Meg's rifle. It peeked over the roof where she was perched, only the tip of it showing. I doubted anyone passing through would notice it, but they weren't looking for her. Not the way I was.

Only a couple feet away from her a second rifle was visible, which I knew belonged to Max. He'd been a sniper in Afghanistan before his legs were blown off, and Meg had spent nearly a year training with him. She was getting pretty good, and enjoying it too. She liked the job because it gave her purpose, but I liked it because it kept her out of harm's way. I wasn't the only one either. It made her dad happy too.

When the sound of a whistle broke through my thoughts, I pulled my gaze back to the street. There was a bend in the road about thirty feet from where I sat crouched, which made it impossible to see much. Angus was up that way though, and I knew that he was the one who'd whistled. It was a warning to be ready, and one I wouldn't take lightly.

Only a few seconds passed before the sound of an engine reached me. Our trap was already set, and when the truck rounded the bend the driver slammed on the breaks, skidding to a stop less than three feet from the roadblock we'd put up. He reacted the way they all did, throwing the truck into reverse, but by then Jim had already pulled our truck onto the road behind him, completely blocking his escape.

All around the truck our people poured out of the woods. Angus and Axl had their guns trained on the driver while Parv, Al, and Luke focused on the passenger. I kept down, staying out of sight for the moment, while across the road from where I crouched Jada did the same.

Jim hopped out of our truck, gun already drawn, and headed over to join the others.

"Climb on out," Axl called.

No one in the truck moved, and a second later the driver yelled back, "You might as well shoot us. The priestess is out of patience. If we lose another shipment, she'll do it anyway."

"We ain't gonna kill nobody if we don't gotta," Angus said.

There was still no movement in the truck, and I felt my body tense up. I raised my gun, pointing it at the windshield, and poised my finger over the trigger. The glare from the sun made it impossible to see inside, but I knew that Meg and Max would have a good view from where they sat. A good shot too.

Finally, after a tense couple of minutes, the passenger door flew open and a man hopped out. "I'm not dying for her," he muttered. He had on the same red robe that everyone in the city wore these days, and he ripped it over his head and tossed it aside the second he was down. "Never believed all this bullshit anyway," he said, spitting in the dirt as he shook his head. "Only went along with it so I'd have food on the table, but this is too much."

We'd been hearing the same sentiment a lot lately, but that didn't mean The Church still didn't have a hold on the majority of the population. They did, and it was stronger than ever.

"Come on out with your friend," Axl called to the driver.

"He's not my friend," came the sneer.

I saw Axl stiffen and I moved closer, waiting for the moment I was needed. It never came though, because only a split second later a gunshot broke through the air and a hole appeared in the truck's windshield, cracks spreading out from it like a spider web. The passenger hit the dirt, swearing up a storm, but Axl and Angus lowered their guns.

290

"You got him!" Axl called.

"Stay alert," Jim said as he headed to the back of the truck.

Jada came out from her hiding place and so did I, and together we walked toward the truck. I glanced up when we were halfway there and caught sight of Meg, still lying on her stomach with her rifled aimed at the truck.

"Anyone in the back?" Al was asking the passenger.

"Just the two of us." He glanced toward the driver. "Dumb son of a bitch."

I heard the truck's back door groan open and a second later Jim called, "Clear."

"Why isn't she sending backup?" Jada asked me as we walked.

"Stupid. Arrogant. Who knows? We've been hitting her trucks for months, and we can't be the only ones," I replied.

These runs had become a normal routine for us, and a matter of survival. With The Church cutting us off, things had gotten sticky. We needed the supplies, especially in the winter months. We had food growing and we hunted and stored things, but we had new people coming in every day, leaving the city or finding us after wandering the now empty countryside. The population of Senoia had doubled since the zombies disappeared, and there was no sign of it stopping any time soon. We'd set up a rationing system similar to the one that had been in place when the walls in New Atlanta were first put up, but there were times when we barely squeaked by. Without the food we stole on these runs, we wouldn't be making it.

Luke slung his rifle over his shoulder. "Let's wrap this up."

"Anxious to get back?" his dad asked, slapping his son on the back.

Luke rolled his eyes in response.

Footsteps scraped against the ground at my back and I turned to find Max crossing the street and headed our way. Meg was at his side. Even though this run had gone smoothly, I found myself looking her over to make sure she was in one piece.

"Stop," she said when she caught me doing it.

"I'm just worried about you."

"You don't need to be. I can fire a gun just fine."

"Better than fine," Max said. "You see that shot?"

I didn't look at him when I said, "I saw it."

"Let's load up!" Jim called from behind me.

Max headed over but Meg didn't move. She was waiting for me to do it, I knew she was, and just to be difficult I held back and instead grabbed her hand and pulled her toward the others.

"Let's get home."

She napped on the way home, her head resting in my lap as the truck bounced down the street. The other people riding in the back of the truck with us were sprawled out too, Al, Max, Luke, and Axl. Jim and Jada drove, while Angus and Parv had taken responsibility for the truck we'd just hijacked. We'd headed out early so we could snag this run, and everyone was as exhausted and ready to get home as I was.

Meg's dark hair slid across her face and I brushed it away. She shifted at the touch, but didn't wake. She'd been exhausted lately, but despite my best efforts at trying to convince her to stay behind today, she'd insisted on coming. Eventually she was going to have to slow down, but I knew it was going to take some real convincing to get her to admit it.

It took us about an hour to get back, and Meg didn't stir until we'd rolled to a stop in the center of town. Everyone else did as well, standing and stretching their arms above their heads in hopes of getting the kinks out. Meg moved, yawning, and I took the opportunity to twist my back, cringing when it popped.

"Luke!"

I was familiar enough with everyone by now to recognize Lila's voice, as well as her panicked tone. Luke did too, and he didn't even bother grabbing his stuff before jumping out of the truck. Al was right behind his son.

"You think it's time?" I asked Meg.

She dragged herself to her feet. "It would be early, but it's possible."

We climbed out, me first before turning to help Meg down. Luke and Al were already halfway across the common space in the middle of town, running at Lila's side toward the house.

"What's happening?" Jada called from behind us.

"Probably the baby," Meg said, and then she looked up at me with her eyebrows raised, waiting.

I held back again. It was harder than the first time and she smiled like she knew it, like she knew I was dying to do it, and I realized she was teasing me. Laughing at me. It made me more determined than ever not to give in.

We left the supply truck to be sorted by the people in charge of inventory and headed across the town after Luke. He and Kelly had moved into a new house two streets over, but we knew she'd be at Axl and Vivian's. The first floor bedroom Parv had originally taken up residence in had been converted to a delivery room months ago, making it easier for Meg's mom. As the only midwife in the settlement, she was busier than ever. Thankfully, she'd found a good apprentice in Charlie.

Meg slipped her hand into mine. "You're really not going to do it?"

"Do what?" I asked, knowing that she didn't buy my ignorance for even a second.

She snorted. "You're a bad liar."

I gave her hand a squeeze, but mostly so I wouldn't give in.

We reached the house to find Al and Lila on the porch, holding hands and anxiously awaiting the birth of their first grandchild. They didn't look old enough to be grandparents. Not with the way Al's eyes twinkled when he smiled or the flawless skin on Lila's face that seemed determined to defy the years that had passed, but it was happening just the same.

"How long has she been in labor?" Meg asked when she stopped next to her aunt.

"It started about five hours ago." Lila's smile stretched so wide that it looked painful. "You guys got back just in time, I think. I was afraid Luke would miss it."

Axl climbed the steps behind us, stopping beside Al so he could slap the other man on the back. "Congrats, grandpa."

"Grandpa." Al laughed as he waved his stump in front of us, covered by a prosthetic sword at the moment. "I remember a time when I thought I'd never see another day, and here I am, twenty years later."

"Can't believe it's gone by so fast," Axl said.

Angus charged up the stairs, grinning from ear to ear with Parv right behind him.

"I got somethin' hold on," he said, and then ran into the house.

"Never seen him move that fast," Axl said, chuckling.

Parv stopped at his side, her usual calm demeanor contrasting with the joyful atmosphere.

"Where's he going?" Meg asked.

"He has something," her aunt replied, but she was smiling too.

Angus was back in less than five minutes with a brown bag in his hand. He unrolled it and the paper crinkled loud enough to draw everyone's attention his way, so not a single person missed it when he pulled a handful of cigars out of the bag.

"Nice," Al said, grinning. "Where did you find those?"

"Some new guy traded 'em to Dragon for a keg." Angus's eyes sparkled. "Glitter swiped 'em for me."

Axl laughed. "You sure got your hooks in her fast."

"Apple didn't fall far from the tree," Angus said in agreement. "We'll pass 'em out once the proud poppa is here. I just didn't wanna forget 'em."

Meg had been around enough births to know that it could take some time, even if five hours had already passed, so we settled into a chair on the front porch to wait. It wasn't long before Angus had produced a bottle of whiskey. He took a swig and then passed it to Parv, who took a drink before passing it on, and I watched as she said something to him that made him smile. He patted her leg and she actually blushed. The expression made her look softer than I'd ever seen her before. Almost happy.

About an hour went by before the door to the house finally burst open and Luke came out, grinning from ear to ear. "It's a boy."

Lila burst into tears as everyone cheered, and Al threw his arm around his son. Through her sobs the new grandma begged to see the baby; and seconds later both grandparents were being escorted inside by their son. It was a moment that seemed to wash all the bad things in the world away and give me hope more than anything else had lately. Well, almost anything.

I reached over and put my hand on Meg's stomach and she smiled.

"I knew you wouldn't be able to hold off forever," she said.

"You know me too well."

Two weeks had passed since she'd told me that she was pregnant, and I'd found myself reaching out to touch her stomach at least five times a day since then. I couldn't help it. Couldn't get over the awe of knowing that life was going on despite how hard Star had tried to squash it.

Meg covered my hand with hers. "I think today is a good day to tell everyone."

"You know they're going to be furious that you went out today, right?"

She rolled her eyes. "I can still shoot a gun when I'm pregnant."

Since I knew I wouldn't win the argument, I didn't try, but instead leaned down and kissed her.

It wasn't long before we were all crowded inside. Kelly sat in bed, beaming up at Luke and their new baby as we all gathered around. He had a sprinkle of dark hair on his head and brown eyes, just like his father, and a huge family who couldn't wait to spoil him.

"What's his name?" Charlie asked, beaming down at her new nephew.

Luke glanced toward Kelly, and then at Parv. "I want to name him Trey."

Parv's mouth fell open and it took a few seconds of shocked silence before she managed to get out, "Why?"

"Dad told me that Trey was his next door neighbor growing up, and that the two of you went to his house looking for his family. They were all dead by then, but because of that trip Dad survived. He was just a teenager and he was alone, and if you and Trey hadn't taken him back with you, he might not have lived." Luke's gaze moved to Lila. "And he wouldn't have met mom."

Tears filled Parvarti's eyes when she looked up at Al. "He would have loved knowing that you remembered him even after all these years."

"Trey was always nice to me," Al said. "He was the cool jock and I was the nerdy computer geek, but he always took the time to stop and talk to me. I appreciated him for that, even before you two saved my ass."

Parv crossed the room so she could hug Al, then turned and did the same with Luke. When he handed the baby to her, she looked like she might break down. I didn't know the whole story of who this Trey had been to Meg's aunt, but I didn't need to. The look on her face said it all.

Trey got passed around for the next hour or so, but eventually started to cry and had to be returned to his mother. It was getting late by then, but we still hadn't announced our news. I was probably dying to do it more than Meg was, and not just because I wanted someone to back me up when I tried to tell her to take it easy.

I cleared my throat and called out, "We have some news."

Meg's eyebrows jumped up at my sudden declaration, but by then all eyes were on her. Color flooded her cheeks and she reached up to twist a strand of hair around her finger.

"Megan?" Vivian's expression told me that she already knew what we were going to say, and I doubted she was the only one.

Meg held her mother's gaze when she said, "I'm pregnant."

The cheer that rose up was loud enough to shake the walls, and so many congratulations were thrown our way that I couldn't figure out who was saying them, but I was happy. Happier than I'd ever been. Vivian hugged Meg and cried, and Axl shook my hand while Margot looked on with starry eyes that said she was having one of those days where she wasn't quite connected with reality. It happened from time to time and probably always would, but for the most part she was adjusting well.

By the time we dragged ourselves upstairs to bed, Meg looked beat. Angus and Parv were right behind us, and when we reached the top of the stairs we paused so they could give us yet another round of congratulations.

"You're gonna need to get your own place," Angus said, slapping me on the arm.

"I'm working on it," I replied, earning me a look from Meg.

Her uncle nodded in approval as Parv pulled Meg in for a hug.

"Congratulations," she said. "I'm so happy for you two."

When she stepped back there were tears in her eyes, but she didn't bother swiping them away. Angus stood waiting, and when she reached out to him, he took her hand and together they walked into the room they now shared.

In our own bedroom, Meg sprawled out on the bed and let out a sigh. "I'm exhausted." But she was only down for a second before sitting back up. "What were you saying about a house?"

"I started looking the day you told me you were pregnant," I said, taking a seat next to her. "The old town's filling up but there are still a lot of options available, assuming you're willing to put in the work."

"So you found something?"

I grinned. "I did. It's two stories, three bedrooms. It has a nice backyard that has almost been taken over by azalea bushes, and a swing already hanging from a live oak tree. It just needs some upkeep."

"When can we go look at it?" she asked, smiling up at me.

"First thing in the morning."

She kissed me and I found myself doing it again, covering her stomach with my hand. She wasn't very far along, eight weeks maybe, but already I was counting down the days until we would meet our child. The knowledge that we had created a life together, that it was inside her now, took my breath away. Back in DC when I'd been a prisoner, I'd thought my life was over, and then in a twist of fate everything had changed. I'd managed to win a few fights, and then I'd joined the prisoner release program where I'd been sent to New Atlanta, and where I'd met Meg. None of it should have happened, but it had and I now found myself part of a big, mismatched, happy family. After years of struggling and zombies and death, it was almost too good to be true.

# THE END

# ACKNOWLEDGEMENTS

It makes my head spin to think about how far I've taken this cast of characters. I've enjoyed writing about them so much, and the continued messages that I get from readers raving about the world I've created never gets old. Really. I love that everyone is so enthusiastic about this series, and I love that I've been able to take a group of misfit survivors and mold them into a family, and I want to extend a huge thank you to all of my readers for loving them as much as I have.

Yes, I had hoped to get this book out to you much earlier than I did, but once again life got in the way when I dislocated my shoulder this past June. To say the injury has been eye opening is an understatement. Three months after it happened and I am still recovering. Thankfully, it only put my writing behind by a month or so since I was planning to get TWISTED FATE out by mid-September at the latest, and for that I am thankful. For your amazing patience, yet again, I am also grateful. I'm not a person who enjoys doing nothing, and the month following my injury it was extremely very difficult for me to take it easy, but it has paid off because I am doing much better despite the fact that I am not yet 100%.

A very big thanks goes to Jan Strohecker for once again doing a great critique on my first draft. This series now spans ten books and twenty years, which makes for a lot of backstory and characters to keep track of, and I really appreciate having someone who pays so much attention to detail on my side. I *scrambled* to get the first draft done before my vacation (seriously, I had one night where I got up at three o'clock in the morning and didn't go to bed until ten the next night) and Jan was wonderful enough to read through it twice while I was out of town so I could dive right back in when I got home. It makes a very complicated conclusion to a very long series so much easier.

I'd also like to thank Jennifer Foor, Mary Jones, and Karen Atkinson for taking the time to search for typos. It's always helpful to have multiple sets of eyes, and you have no idea how much I appreciate the time you put in!

I also need to acknowledge the chant I used in the novel whenever The Church was around. It's a verse from the *Bible*, Isaiah 26:14 ESV: "They are dead, they will not live; they are shades, they will not arise; to that end you have visited them with destruction and wiped out all remembrance of them." It seemed to fit perfectly and taken totally out of context, added a nice creepy tone to the people who worshipped Angus.

I know what you're thinking: *Is this really the end?!*

I've said it before and changed my mind, but at this moment in my life I don't want to commit to writing another book in this series. I love this series and the characters, don't get me wrong, but like Angus, I'm tired. Each book I add becomes more and more complicated because there are so many details to keep track of. When I finished the first draft of this book, I had a whole page of questions I needed to answer, little details from the previous books that I had to go back and search for so I was sure to get it all right. It's been fun, but part of the joy I get from writing is creating new characters and new worlds, and at this point I'm just adding on to what I've already made, which not only takes more time and work, but isn't as enjoyable. I want to start something new. What? I'm not sure, but I hope readers will give it a chance the same way they did with *Broken World*.

So, for now, this is goodbye to Axl, Angus, and Vivian, as well as all the characters who has joined them along the way. Hopefully, it's a satisfying end for everyone.

~

# ABOUT THE AUTHOR

Kate L. Mary is an award-winning author of new adult and young adult fiction, ranging from post-apocalyptic tales of the undead, to speculative fiction and contemporary romance. Her young adult book, *When We Were Human*, was a 2015 Children's Moonbeam Book Awards Silver Medal winner for Young Adult Fantasy/Sci-Fi Fiction, and a 2016 Readers' Favorite Gold Medal winner for Young Adult Science Fiction.

For more information about Kate, check out her website: www.KateLMary.com

CPSIA information can be obtained
at www.ICGtesting.com
Printed in the USA
LVOW07s1455181017
552888LV00010B/775/P